Black Harry

Glossopdale's Elizabethan Folk Hero

Mark P. Henderson

Stairwell Books //

Published by Stairwell Books
161 Lowther Street
York, YO31 7LZ

www.stairwellbooks.co.uk
@stairwellbooks

Layout Alan Gillott
Cover design Dawn Treacher

ISBN: 978-1-913432-68-3

Also by Mark Henderson

Novels and novellas
National Cake Day in Ruritania
The Engklimastat
The Definitive Biography of St Arborius of Glossopdale and his
Thin Dog (e-book only)
The Cat of Doom
Perilaus II
Con

Performance Pieces
Cruel and Unusual PunNishments

For children
Fenella and the Magic Mirror (e-book only)

Short stories
Rope Trick: Thirteen Strange Tales

Plays
Forget it, it's History

Non-Fiction
Murders in the Winnats Pass
Folktales of the Peak District

To the memory of my parents, Walter and Alice,
who would have enjoyed this story.

Some village-Hampden, that with dauntless breast
The little tyrant of his fields withstood,
Some mute inglorious Milton here may rest,
Some Cromwell, guiltless of his country's blood.

Thomas Gray: *Elegy Written in a Country Churchyard.*

The 'historic' novel is, for me, condemned... to a fatal **cheapness.** *You may multiply the little facts that can be got from pictures and documents, relics and prints, as much as you like – the real thing is almost impossible to do, and in its essence the whole effect is as naught: I mean the intention, the representation of the old* **consciousness,** *the soul, the sense, the horizon, the vision of individuals in whose minds half the things that make our, that make the modern world were non-existent... You have to simplify back by an amazing* **tour de force** *– and even then it's all humbug.*

Henry James criticizes *The Tory Lover*
Ferman Bishop, *American Literature* **27(2),** pp. 262-264.

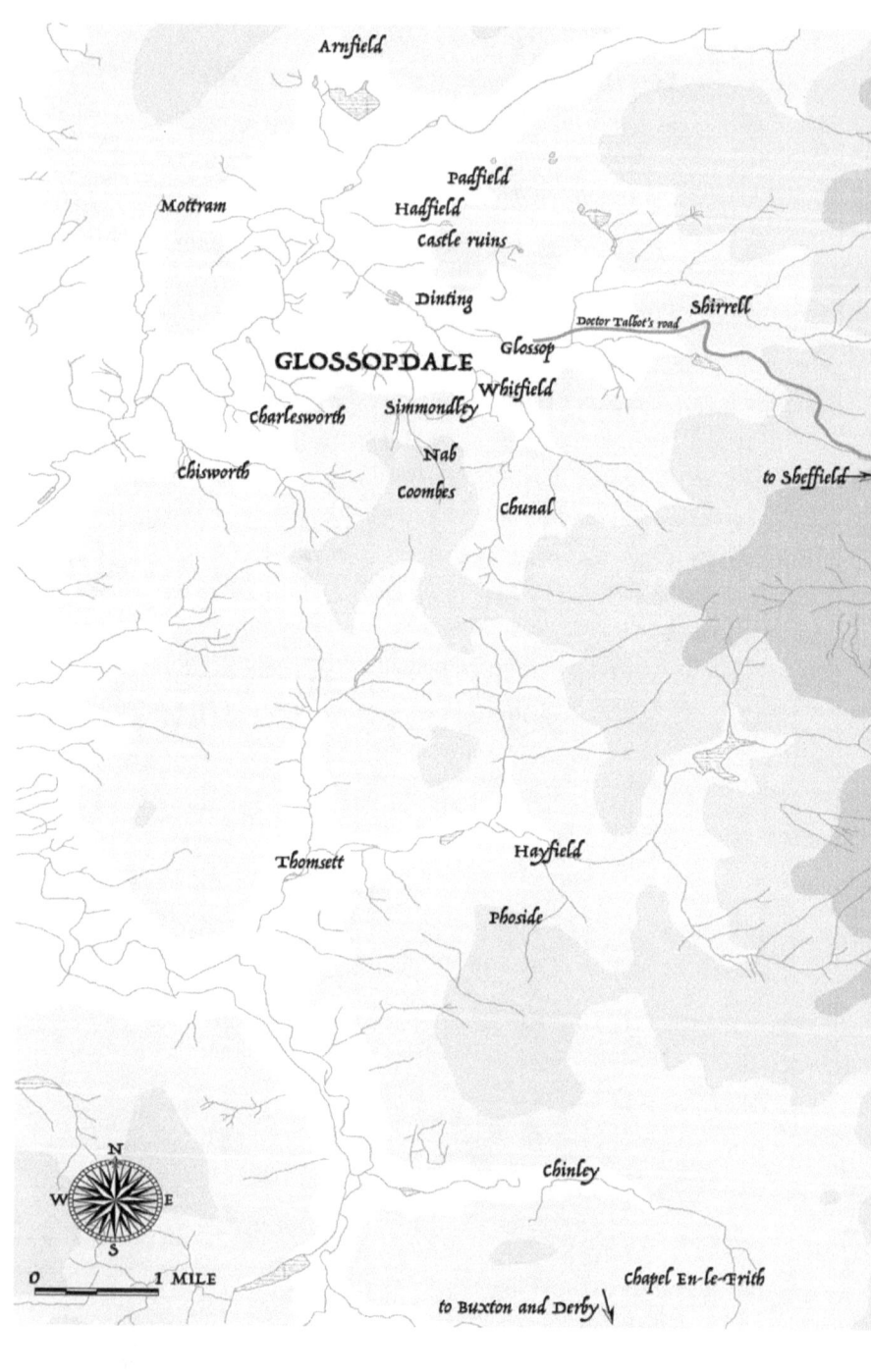

Foreword

Henry James's dubiety notwithstanding, some historical novels (not least Hilary Mantel's) are great literature. I don't imagine I could emulate them. However, I've long wanted to tell the story of Glossopdale's sixteenth century folk hero, "Black Harry" Botham, and doing so might help to mitigate James's critique.

Even the most diligent historians can unearth only tiny scraps of information about Harry Botham, and I'm not a historian. This book is fiction. I've tried to make it historically plausible by exploiting expert advice and background reading (details in the Afterword), but authorities on late sixteenth century England, and on the Peak District during that time, are sure to question my interpretations and conjectures.

Many novels are set in the Tudor era. This one is distinctive in focussing on the lives of commoners and people of middle rank, not royalty or aristocrats (who are present nevertheless; their authority over their inferiors was all-pervading). Every second chapter is written from the imagined viewpoint of William Dickenson, who was Bailiff of Hallamshire and the earl of Shrewsbury's man of business during the late 1500s. For the other chapters I've invented the voice of Thomas Booth, who is recorded as one of the tenant farmers who journeyed to London with Harry Botham to confront Elizabeth's Privy Council, and was subsequently one of the four who were evicted for their effrontery. Thomas presumably lived in the Glossopdale hamlet of Simmondley, as Harry did, but history is silent about him.

Black Harry is an attempt to reconstruct the life and times of a remarkable but uncelebrated man. He deserves to be better known.

Mark P. Henderson, 2023.

Glossopdale, April 1570

He come over brow of Nab on St Alfege's Day an hour after sun were up, bossing skyline like a moorland rock with ravens on it. Old Tom Jackson and me wondered at first who he were and what he were doing, stood there. Other men as were with us were asking and all. Happen he were watching birds: larks sprinkling valley with song, swallows come out of their winter sleep under water to dance in morning air, curlews sorrowing over their customary lands. Then he come striding downhill and I knew him: black tangle of hair and beard, wrestler's shoulders, bowed legs, ash staff an ell long, pack on his shoulder, purse heavy on his belt. Old Tom frowned.

'Not Harry Botham's lad, is it?'

'Aye,' I said.

There were three youths from Chunal and Whitfield with us, shouting and scrapping and throwing one another, and they stared at Black Harry marching down hill and reckoned they could throw him and all. Made me laugh.

Simmondley man like me, Black Harry, only a fortnight older. He were born on a Thursday, me on a Friday. Hadn't seen him in nigh on eight year. When he were a furlong away I limped up to meet him. Speedwell and dog violets smiled and yellow archangel shone. Yesterday's rain were cutting its own gutter down middle of track. Lads behind me were still going on about how they could take him. Men were muttering: *Favours his mother. Gypsy whore.*

Folk had talked same road about Harry's mother as long as I could remember: *Ticed Old Harry into jumping broom so she could get her hands on*

Storth. Five kids, Black Harry and two girls and two what died. Then she were gone. Back to her gypsy folk. Old Harry's never took another wife. I were sick of hearing it. Black Harry's mother weren't no gypsy and I reckoned they'd best not bad-mouth her when Harry could hear. If he hadn't gone soft in eight year he'd been away in service he'd break their heads or rip their tongues out. His Dad would've done same, only he's old now.

I clasped his arms and shouted, 'Ayup, Harry lad!'

He nodded. 'Tom Booth! Spiderlegs Tom! All right, Tom?'

His mouth did that sideways shift it used to do when we were nippers. Him smiling, that shift. Looked like he'd kept all his teeth. And that scar over his left eye. I blinked and run my wrist over my nose.

'Aye,' I said. 'How were Ashford?'

He shook his head.

'Met folk from Ashford but I weren't a servant there. I were in Castleton, then Peak Forest. Different soil nor here, better corn. Then I were off south and east. That were different again.'

I were sure he'd said eight year back he'd be in service in Ashford. Mind, I don't always remember right. None of us does.

'Easier work?' I asked.

'In flat country down south it were. Still got yon old open field system, a lot of them. Rest of Peak were hard as here. Folk in Castleton spend half their time digging lead. Old ones get bellanded. Folk are same everywhere, though; they all smell of shit and onions.'

I laughed, though I were a bit choked.

'Still using old field system in Chunal and all. What's stock like in Castleton and Peak Forest?'

'Same sheep and beasts, Spiderlegs. Same landlord and all.' He stared past me. 'I see Tom Jackson's still above ground. Who's yon lad he's propping up?'

It were all right Harry calling me Spiderlegs, same as he always had, though I didn't like other folk doing it.

'Malachi Lomas. Remember his dad, Charlie, as were nobbut elevenpence in shilling? Died while we were in service. Malachi's got leasehold for Herod now. Needs help, mind.'

3

I'd been back nobbut three week but I knew Malachi couldn't do a lot. Talked to his sheep. Talked to rocks and all, and his sister, and folk as weren't there, and none of them couldn't answer. Fairies had his wits most of time. Sister turned into a hare a-nights and her lips stayed same come daylight. Coney, they called her. She were magic at curing sick sheep and beasts, Coney were, and her bees lived on heather and made best honey in Glossopdale; best for sweetening food, best for covering wounds. Way them bees thrived, you knew there weren't no blasphemy or sacrilege up at Herod. Anyroad, there couldn't be: Coney couldn't talk and Malachi couldn't much neither.

Harry looked up at yon wastes where we'd seen headless women and boggarts when we were nippers. Nowt much grew up there because it were Devil's ground; land were dead. Happen innocent blood had been shed on it, time out of memory of man. But Lord Shrewsbury were enclosing chunks of it, charcoal streaks of stone wall across them withered heights of bracken and heather, golden plovers and peat. *Same landlord.* Old folk said he'd done good, his lordship; we'd three sheep for every one there'd been in Abbey times. Mind, sheep didn't make same money these days. There were still snow up yonder, white as old Maggie Dawson's hair. It weren't going to shift while turned St Mark's Eve, after Maggie had spent her night in church porch seeing who'd die in Glossop parish over twelvemonth coming. Same every year: while God were blessing land with new life, promising eternity to come after Resurrection, cunning-men and wise-women were seeing them as Death were bound to come for.

Harry asked, 'Where were you in service, Spiderlegs?'

'Yorkshire to start with, other side Settle. Ma's cousin. Then Hull way, and then back this road, near Barnsley. Been home again since Lady Day. Seen bad things this past year, Harry.'

'Heard tales. Troubles didn't get down here. Not them sort, anyroad.'

He sounded sorry he'd missed them. We set off down hill, splashing through wet and crushing flowers, and he slowed his steps for me. Flowers would pick themselves up again when we'd gone. I told him about them Catholic earls running off to Scotland when Lord Sussex's army chased them out of Yorkshire. It were like tales as old Tom and

Harry's Dad telled of that do thirty-odd year back, afore I were born, when they had to go fighting with rebels up north as had wanted a different king on throne and Bishop of Rome back.

'Queen won't let folk worship how they want no more, not after that do. Ordered one man hanged in every village. Seven hundred, they reckon, and none what'd followed them Papist earls. Swung 'til they rotted and crows had them. I saw one or two.' I shook my head. 'Never rains but it pours.'

Harry snorted.

'Seven hundred? My arse there were that many. And does Queen think a few hangings will stop fools wanting Bishop of Rome back?'

'They reckon Pope – Bishop of Rome, like – he's said anybody as kills Queen will have his blessing.'

Old Tom Jackson and other men were stood watching us. Harry nodded. Them three lads as reckoned they could throw him started forwards, only Harry grinned and lifted his staff and they backed off, all three of them, and quick about it.

'Who's vicar now?' he asked. 'Still Ralph Bower?'

We said, 'Aye', and he laughed and spat.

'That one will never hang, anyroad. Strong for reformed faith when I were a boy and Edward were king. First time folk saw a priest wedded. Then Mary were Queen so he turned Papist and hid his wife. And when Mary married yon poxy Spaniard and give birth to a viper, and Devil took her soul, and her sister were crowned, he went reformed faith again and brought his wife back. What's he now, a Puritan?'

We laughed, but old Tom said Harry shouldn't talk that road about vicar, and Puritans weren't allowed to be vicars anyroad. Harry took no notice. We walked towards Storth and left old Tom and rest of them muttering. Some didn't like Bothams.

*

At dip over Horse Clough, Harry stopped. It were like his eyes were clemmed with thirst and fields of his home were a jug of Jacob Morton's dagger ale. Brown as a wet peat grough on Glossop Low, his eyes, and they shone like a mill pond. They took a long slow drink of them fields.

5

Happen he were minding their names: White Lies, Pitt Dole, Haugh, Coisfall Meadow, Bready Butts, Knockle Close, Pillat Close, Cowsich Dole; and right beside Storth, Overtwhart. He were reckoning up: Easter two week behind us; *a fine Easter, a fine harvest*; spring oats planted at new moon – half a quarter to an acre, and happen you'd get four or five quarter back; lambs out to pasture now ewes had ate roots on ploughed lands; sheep sold at fair, new wethers bought at six pound to a score. Linnets and chaffinches sang welcome. Bluebells shone under yon brushwood as give Storth its name. Elder and hazel wore fresh green. Oaks were budding.

Harry turned and scanned valley, slow like a bull sizing up heifers. Smoke other side Glossop, where John Rowland burned charcoal. Clang of iron and rasp of whetstone from Randolph Swann's forge, Randolph singing *Blow away yon morning dew*, his wife cursing him. Simmondley noises: daft Hugh Platt shouting at summat, happen a tree; dogs barking; Alice shrieking at Willie and getting a slap. There were sweet-briar in our garden at Cloud, but Willie could still give Alice a slap when she needed one. Then sky went dark over Coombes and a crow come and sat on wall so rain started again, and Harry's eyes turned back to me.

'How's your Ma? And your young brother?'

'Willie got given leasehold for Cloud afore God took Dad.' I pointed at my bad hip. 'Better nor me at plough, Willie is. Bailiff and his lordship's agent said same. We paid fine and heriot. I do my bit.'

Thatching were summat I could manage better nor most. It helped being tall. There were plenty of reeds up Horse Clough. *A rood of reeds will thatch a house if there's good turf on good timbers.* That were what Dad said. Mind, heather can give as good a kick as reeds if you lay it right, or oat straw if it's bottled proper and not too dry.

'Your Ma?'

'Aye. Alice and Ma ... Alice Oliver as was. Come to Cloud as servant and Willie married her.'

They reckon folk had only married lasses from their own tithings at one time, but there's nowt of that sort these days. Alice were a Dinting girl. Sang like a moorland clough over pebbles. Proper Monday's child: eyes colour of bluebells, hair like ripe oats. I thought she might have wed me, bad leg or not, but family and most of tithing said it wouldn't suit. Parish would have said same: she were best hitched to Willie seeing as he'd got leasehold. Anyroad, same as I've always said, what woman wants a man with weak body and bad hip? God's will be done.

'Your sister?' asked Harry.

Joanna and Harry had been handfast since she were sixteen and him eighteen. It hadn't been no bother for neither my Dad, God rest his soul, nor Harry's. Old Harry said he'd flit up Bank to yon little place as had been Jack Harrop's afore he died, after Black Harry had been in service and come back with enough money to wed; then him and Joanna could have Storth. Parish stuck their noses in, saying Black Harry's mother were a gypsy vagrant and not proper married to his Dad anyroad so he weren't a fit match for no Glossopdale girl. Old Harry and my Dad shut their mouths for them. Megan were Welsh, not a gypsy, Old Harry said, and no vagrant neither. Churchwarden reckoned he knew better so he got a black eye and a broken nose and lost three teeth, and then our Dads dropped money in poor box so they wouldn't get had up in front of Manor Court and fined or put in stocks. Joanna had been in service with William Newton and his wife at Heath, and then with Shuttleworths in Whitfield, and she weren't long back at Cloud.

'Aye,' I said. 'Best get banns called, Harry. Time Joanna were seeded. They reckon women get greensick when they're turned twenty if they're not tupped. Elena's wed already. Married Olly Hall. Living in Glossop.'

'Greensick. Aye. Anybody else tried tupping Joanna?'

Them as had tried it while she were in service at Heath hadn't got nowhere, and I didn't want to say nowt about Richard Shuttleworth. Joanna hadn't lifted her skirts for him or nobody else neither while she were a servant. I reckoned Willie and me would have known if she had; and if Shuttleworth had tupped her daughter, Ma would have run him out of Glossopdale. He'd reckoned to have Joanna two or three year running when we were a-Maying but she hadn't let him. Then he asked her to live with him for eleven day after Lammas to see if they got on, like yon old custom; but she'd said no, she'd wait for Black Harry. Other lads had tried their luck. Couldn't blame them; strong good-looking lass,

Joanna. But it were Shuttleworth as kept at it. Willie had warned him off but he'd tried again behind our backs.

'She told them to clear off,' I said.

'Did they?'

'Oh, aye. Here, got your bagpipe, Harry? We'll want it come May Day.'

He pointed his thumb at his pack and said, 'Cleared off? All of them?'

He knew there were summat I weren't saying. Must have seen it in my face or heard it in my voice. I had to tell him at finish.

*

It weren't long afore Harry had been to Manor Court in front of bailiff, paid entry fine, got his leasehold granted and agreed heriot: he'd plant ten oak and give bailiff a fowl at Whitsun. Agent agreed; a young lad, not Scargill. So Harry were in Storth. His Dad flitted up Bank like he'd promised. Banns were called, and Joanna were smiling like I hadn't seen her smile since we were knee-high to a grasshopper. Harry were round at Cloud every day but he weren't for tupping Joanna afore they were wed. Ma and Harry both had spirits bigger nor their bodies, and they liked one another, but anybody as tupped her unwed daughter would have got on wrong side of Ma. And you didn't want to be on wrong side of Ma, not even if you were Black Harry.

I asked Ma why some folk had took against Bothams. She said it were because Old Harry's wife Morag had caused bother, and after Morag had gone Old Harry had caused a lot more. She wouldn't tell me nowt else. It were summat I couldn't shift out of my head, though.

At market in Glossop a week after, I went to see my sister Elena and her husband Olly. They'd lost a babby and Elena were sick. Maggie Dawson and her lame daughter Agnes were tending to her, same as they always did when folks were poorly. We got talking. I asked Maggie if she knew why Morag Botham had left her family.

'I don't, Tom,' she said, 'but there were never nowt bad about Morag. Thing is, it were what they call a clandestine marriage. Bothams were householders of credit: good neighbours; honest; did one good turn for another. Trouble were...' She put another poultice on Elena's belly.

'Trouble were, folk whispered about yon marriage, and Morag were foreign. She could talk English but it were hard work. And they said there were summat bad about her brother, though nobody in Glossopdale ever met him. So Bothams started getting cut out of tithing, for all everybody were scared of Old Harry. I reckon Morag knew it'd never be right for them while she were there. Happen that's why she left. Must have been hard for her. Nippers missed her when she'd gone. That's why young Harry likes being with your Ma, and me.'

I were on my road back to Simmondley when bailiff stopped me. His Dad were my granddad's cousin so he were like an uncle. Nicholas Booth: short, fat, not a lot of hair under his hat, eyes screwed up with too much writing, ink on his fingers. He said, 'Tom, a word of warning: you've been friends with Black Harry Botham since you were lads, but keep your distance. He caused trouble while he was in service, and he'll cause trouble here now he's back.' I told him Harry had never caused no bother to me or mine and we were bound to be brothers-in-law and neighbours and all, so no, I weren't keeping no distance; and why were some folk down on Bothams? Bailiff said: after his wife had gone, Old Harry had been to court about enclosing farms and having different leases in different parts of manor, and young Black Harry had gone with him, shooting his mouth off. And then he'd gone and caused bother in Castleton and Peak Forest while he were in service, arguing about rents and tithes and knocking enclosures down, and he'd do same now he were back in Simmondley. 'And I don't want you caught up in it, Tom.' I said being crippled might mean I weren't much of a man, but I were still enough of a man to stand up for friends and family; and if Black Harry were that bad, why had agent let him have leasehold for Storth? Bailiff said it were because young Mr Roberts didn't know him and hadn't listened to no advice. 'Mr Scargill wouldn't have granted leasehold to a known troublemaker,' he said.

I reckoned that said more about Scargill, and happen my uncle and all, nor it did about Black Harry.

*

A few day after that, Malachi Lomas come down to Cloud. Fairies had Malachi's wits most of time, same as I said, but sometimes he talked sense. He asked whether Willie or me had heard owt about Richard Shuttleworth.

'Ayup, Malachi. No, not seen Richard for a while. Why, what's up?'

Malachi looked round like he didn't know where he were. Jaw slack, fairy folk wanting his brains for playthings again.

'Oh, Tom Spiderlegs, he needs help. Needs help he does, Tom Spiderlegs. Both arms broke, Richard has. Both arms. Can't do nowt in neither house nor field, not with both arms broke, Richard can't. Nowt at all. And he's lambs to get out to pasture same as rest of us.'

Both arms broke? You could never tell whether owt Malachi said were right, but it turned out this were. Richard Shuttleworth were dead a fortnight after. One of his arms hadn't mended proper. I'd seen it afore, folk dying after they've broke summat. My uncle went a few day after ox stood on his leg and broke it. My aunt were poorly at time and all. Never rains but it pours.

So God had took Richard Shuttleworth to his bosom, and I couldn't help but wonder if Black Harry had sent him there. I prayed for his soul.

There weren't no bother about it, mind. Happen Richard's family blamed Harry, but none of them said owt only Richard's brother-in-law, Henry Waterhouse, and Harry soon shut Henry's mouth for him and broke his nose while he were about it. Harry went and touched Richard's body and all and it didn't bleed. Ma said it were by-our-lady daft, reckoning you could tell a murderer that road, but there's a lot believes it. Shuttleworths do, for a start.

I still couldn't help but wonder. It didn't bother me, mind. I were happy: back in Glossopdale where I belonged; and Black Harry were here again. I'd missed them both.

Sheffield, May 1570

William Dickenson's mare plodded through mud and drizzle towards Sheffield. The rich chamber in the countess's beloved Chatsworth still glowed behind the rider's eyelids: Lord Shrewbury caressing his white satin peascod waistcoat, beard silky and groomed, face tired and lined, her ladyship devouring him with feldspar eyes. Her hair was red like the Queen's, her lips narrow. People whispered that since the earl and countess were both middle-aged, both wealthy and both blessed with heirs and spares, they must have married for love. Dickenson sneered. Noblemen loved their mistresses, he'd told Katherine, not their wives. There were reasons enough for the Shrewsburys' wedding and for the unions among their heirs. Marriage to Elizabeth St Loe had brought more estates than ever under Lord Shrewsbury's control, to say nothing of Derbyshire's lead field, barmasters included; much-needed compensation for the decline of the broadcloth trade. In return, marriage to the realm's premier earl – Knight of the Garter, Lord Lieutenant of three counties, her majesty's lord chamberlain, and now Privy Councillor – had raised her ladyship to a status above any woman in the realm save her majesty.

Now, riding home after long hours attending the earl and countess, Dickenson was content in spite of his drenched hose and limp ruff. His honour had appointed him Receiver for his estates in three counties, Thomas Sutton's soul having been called to Heaven. Also, because of James Turner's illness, he was Bailiff of Hallamshire in all but name. Like his late father, Dickenson was a brewer, proprietor of an inn, provider of sacramental wine to St Peter's; but his diligence and aptitude

11

for figures had earned him positions of trust, and he was not yet thirty. Katherine would be proud.

His mood soured as he rode through the castle gates: there was no servant to stable his horse. Why not? He was a person of consequence now, mean birth notwithstanding. He dismounted, secured the horse and strode into the hall. It was empty. He scanned the unadorned walls and glowered. The tapestries and furnishings wouldn't return uninjured from Tutbury. What would restoration cost? Or replacement? He must investigate. Expenses were rising and Mr Turner's accounting had grown slipshod. His head ached.

Noises from within and without the castle scuttled around the naked walls: sheep crying to their lambs in the Castle Folds, servants scurrying and gossiping, voices from an upper floor demanding sweetmeats, prayers and fresh laundry. Nathaniel Eyre's harangue thundered above them all. Headache and weariness notwithstanding, Dickenson grinned; builders at the manor house had provoked the steward's wrath. Was Nathaniel more hard-pressed than he? Surely not, but for how much longer would he be condemned to tolerate this bare space?

At last a servant appeared. He took a glass of wine from her, placed his grey hat on the exact centre of the window-seat, flicked a thread from his violet doublet and turned his back on the denuded chamber. Evening light reached through the window to cast a blessing on his tall figure, burnishing his hair. He gazed out over the burgeoning town, clustered houses and shops, outbuildings, gardens, crofts and yards, the tower of St Peter's pointing them all to Heaven. How many residents? Around two thousand, he supposed. It irked him not to know the exact number. Many of them couldn't survive without the charity of neighbours; their cottages had tiny gardens. Yet the apron-men, the cutlers, prospered; which spelled work for him. More work. He thanked God that weaving and the manufacture of horn spoons lay outside his jurisdiction.

Aromas from the kitchens – fresh bread, roasting mutton, thyme and rosemary – mingled with the rotting stench from the moat. The wine was sour.

Eyre marched into the hall, a head shorter than Dickenson but broad of shoulder, black-clad as a Calvinist or a mourning mercer, white ruff freshly starched. Anger coarsened his features. He nodded.

'William.'

'God save you, Nathaniel.'

'Aye, God save me. God save me from builders, carpenters, plasterers, Papist rebels, Puritan servants, the pox, the Spaniards, the plague, the French, and all other agents of the Devil. The Queen of Scots above all.' Eyre gulped wine and spat. 'Why have you've ridden here, not straight home to your wife?'

'To delight in your company, Master Steward.'

'Pfah!' A smile flicked like a passing candle-flame across Eyre's face. 'You saw the Scottish Queen? What news from their honours?'

'Tidings to calm your troubled breast, Nathaniel. You and Sir Godfrey Foljambe no longer need to raise men.'

'How so?'

'You recall Sir Thomas Gargrave's complaint about soldiers lingering in York?'

'Her ladyship said Sir Thomas feared for his purse. Doubtless true. What of it, William?'

Dickenson was conscious of the gulf in status that strained their friendship. Nathaniel Eyre had been a justice of the peace since Dickenson was a boy. His family had been Derbyshire gentry since before the Black Death. In times past, Eyres, like other rich Derbyshire families, had been Master Foresters. Now his honour the earl held that post, which had become more ceremonial than judicial.

'The difficulty has vanished, Nathaniel. Sir Robert Constable sent to his honour from Berwick on St Dunstan's Day: Radcliffe of Sussex has pursued the recusant earls over the Border. Hume Castle has surrendered. His honour will apprise Sir William Cecil; and, I suppose, the rest of the Council.'

A tight smile forced its way on to Eyre's face. This time it lingered.

'If his honour writes in his own hand it'll be one letter less for you or me to compose. My quills have worn themselves to stubs since you and James Turner persuaded him to dismiss Thomas Morgan.' Eyre refilled

13

his wine cup. 'You were right, of course. His honour's interests could never have been served by employing a Welshman as secretary.'

Dickenson studied his pewter mug. His voice softened.

'I recall that her majesty's grandfather was Welsh.'

Eyre swigged more wine.

'I think Morgan was dismissed around the time you caused your brother John to be made keeper of his honour's wardrobe.' He wiped his mouth. 'I'll inform Sir Godfrey of Sir Robert's news. Now: tell me of Chatsworth and the Scottish Queen.'

Dickenson stared through the window again. So many responsibilities.

'Mary's apartments overlook the new terraces on the south of the house. I glimpsed her twice. The rumours are true. A beauty: tall, raven hair, grey eyes. Thomas Morgan won't be the only man to dance attendance on her.'

'Will *you* dance attendance on her, William?'

Such are the times, thought Dickenson: *two friends united in service to my lord Shrewsbury hoarding suspicions about each other.*

'I dance attendance on only one woman, Nathaniel, and thanks be to God she's married to me.' He swallowed his wine and grimaced. 'Her majesty trusts the earl and countess to serve as Mary's custodians.' Dickenson didn't add that her majesty's trust was provisional, or that privileges could be withdrawn, or fortune prove fickle and costly. 'But not all his honour's servants merit trust. Morgan wasn't alone. Henry Hall is spreading sedition around Derbyshire. He should hang.' His mouth twisted.

'Did you talk further with his honour about the lead trade?'

'Not in the countess's hearing. But we'll make the lead workings provide more for his honour's purse than all the fines and rents and tithes and heriots from his estates, or even his confiscation of outlaw goods. Humfrey's smelting furnace and German sieve will yield ten times the returns from the Queen's Field than bole smelters and footblasts ever did. A smelter like that at Beauchief is to be built at Chatsworth. Did you know that, Nathaniel? With water-powered bellows. And we'll control the trade to Hull and beyond.'

But will all that, Dickenson wondered, *generate enough income to pay for custody of the Scottish Queen, and for the countess's extravagance? And the repair of those Sheffield tapestries that are rotting in Tutbury?*

'Then all the more will go into his honour's coffers. And the taxes on our cutlers will add to it. Will he need any further income? I see you've revised Mr Sutton's accounts, William. They tell me the Talbot estates in seven counties together yielded ten thousand pounds last year –'

'Ten thousand one hundred and fifty-three pounds, fifteen shillings and fourpence. Yes, Nathaniel. Further income will be needed.'

Dickenson knew the steward had studied his account books, page after meticulous page of detail, room in the right margin beside each entry to record "Paid", spaces for his honour's signature. Annotations in the left margin testified to thoroughness and precision. Without thoroughness there could be no satisfaction. In precision lay beauty.

Eyre gestured impatience and pointed towards the Great Park.

'Aye. There'll be costs aplenty if yonder manor house is to be made fit for Mary and all her damned household before Advent, as his honour commands.' He shook his head. 'He plans a great new gatehouse. It will fall upon you to negotiate the contracts and payments, William. I think he has no trust in Chatsworth's security.'

Dickenson needed more wine, sour or not.

'Her majesty seems disposed to allow her cousin greater freedom. Mary's removal from Tutbury to Wingfield and then Chatsworth received royal approval. She may now ride abroad within two miles of the House provided she's watched. They say she's a fine horsewoman; revels in the hunt.' He sighed. 'If only she could be restored to the throne of Scotland –'

'The Scots distrust her, William. More to the purpose, so does her majesty.'

Dickenson's turn to gesture impatience.

'England should be rid of her. Papists are drawn to her like flies to a laystall. She has a spymaster's wit and a viper's tongue.' He stretched. His back ached. 'She's started rumours, Nathaniel. She whispers that the *countess* smuggles letters in cypher to her supporters, that the *countess* spreads gossip about her majesty's dealings with Robert Dudley and other men; and if she's ever removed from his honour's care, the *countess* will help her escape to her Catholic friends. If Mary brings ruin upon her ladyship with those slanders she'll bring his honour down as well, and us with him.' He contrived a smile. 'Her beauty makes her more dangerous. Best to be blind to it.'

As Dickenson recovered his hat and prepared to leave, Eyre grinned.

'Moderate your attire, William. His honour is a stickler for sumptuary laws.'

*

Dickenson strode over the drawbridge pier and pinched his nostrils; the moat exhaled its customary miasma. Turning his back on the River Sheaf, the cries of wrestling children and shrill wives, the clank and hammer of industry, he passed the Castle Laiths at ninety steps per minute, each step one yard. His shoes skirted the ubiquitous filth. He turned left along Bull Stake, but before he could enter Dixon Lane an altercation snared his attention.

'What is this?'

The embattled cutlers turned, cudgels raised, but found themselves facing a capital burgess, the man they'd begun to recognise as bailiff: tall grey hat, trimmed beard and moustache, cutwork-edged collar with matching cuffs, violet doublet, velvet hose, flat black shoes with rounded toes, all burnished by the westering sun. Dickenson's eyebrows were raised, his fists on his hips. *Sumptuary laws be damned; I shall dress to signify my authority.* The cutlers bobbed their heads and touched their woollen caps.

'Mijnheer Dickenzon, zor, zis fullow –'

Like many Dutch iron-workers, the speaker had fled to England to escape the duke of Alva's cruelties, but he struggled with the language. In Sheffield, his name had become "Jervis". He couldn't pronounce it.

'Well?' snapped Dickenson.

"Jervis", famed for making penknives with stamped brass handles, accused Oliver Ferris of stealing the tortoiseshell with which he decorated them.

'Bought yon tortoiseshell in London!' shouted Ferris. 'It's not right, Mr Dickenson. These foreigners come to England, sneak into Sheffield, steal our jobs, take houses from decent Englishmen, swyve our women, accuse –'

'Are you aware, Master Ferris, that *her majesty* invited the Dutch iron-workers to England, along with other fugitives from Papistry? And *Lord Shrewsbury* persuaded her to settle them in Sheffield? You've criticised the Queen. Do you know the penalty? And do you question Lord Shrewsbury's orders?'

'Well, no, sir, I didn't mean – I mean –'

Dickenson turned to the Dutchman.

'Master Jervis, if you've disobeyed the Ninth Commandment you'll be whipped. The burgesses will erect a pillory where Market Place and High Street meet. Within a year, deceivers will be made sport for the people there. Why do you accuse Master Ferris of stealing your tortoiseshell?'

'Mijnheer Dickunson, zor, I hove only tortoizezhell in Zheffield, zeller on London zell only to me, he hove zell not to ony oder, not to zis *Ferris*!'

Dickenson stilled Ferris's protest with a gesture.

'Bring the bill of sale from London to my house before nine tomorrow morning, Master Ferris, or you'll go before the Justice and be hanged for theft, unless you pay Master Jervis for the tortoiseshell. Now go, both of you, and never disturb the Queen's peace again.'

He was proud to discharge his duties. The cutlers must be regulated; their taxes must go to the earl. The cutlers' juries were answerable to the Manor Court and therefore to Eyre, but Dickenson was obliged to oversee the registration of cutlers' marks, the control of apprenticeships and working practices, fair trading in the mills that drove the grinding machinery, the resolution of disputes, the import of steel from Sweden. Sheffield now manufactured more knives, scissors, shears, sickles, scythes and arrows than anywhere except London. More work for him. More responsibility.

Dickenson watched Jervis and Ferris go their separate ways, then walked the few remaining steps homeward to the company of the only woman he trusted: obedient, honest, thrifty, hard-working, resolute keeper of the inn, good mother to his sons. He proceeded at ninety steps per minute, one yard per step, evading the filth.

*

Katherine Dickenson left her spinning, brought water for her husband to wash his hands and face, gave him ale and ordered the servant to fetch food. Her bodice and skirt were of fine wool but the colours were sober. The laces securing her sleeves were neat. When she walked in the town she wore fine silk stockings and farthingale, but while she was indoors or supervising the inn she eschewed ornament. Dickenson approved the balance between elegance and modesty. He divulged some of his news.

'Does the countess's beauty rival that of the Queen of Scots?' she asked. Her spinning-wheel began to hum again. She played it with a lutenist's skill.

Dickenson snorted. 'The countess is twenty years older than Mary. Those two great ladies spend their days together, talking in French, occupying themselves with needlework. Mary's tapestries are beautiful. Maybe she is, too.'

'Ah. The countess keeps her company, so the earl is relieved of that part of his duty as custodian. It's kind of her. And she and the Scottish Queen will find much to talk about.'

'How so, Kath? I can't guess what topics might sustain two great ladies through long hours of embroidery.'

'Come, William. The countess has enjoyed three marriages and embarked on a fourth. The Queen of Scots has suffered three marriages and perhaps hopes now for a fourth. From what I hear, neither of their first marriages was consummated. There's much there for great ladies and not so great ladies to slide their needles into. And French, I think, is the ideal language for the purpose.'

Katherine's expression was bland. Only her eyes laughed.

'What else do you hear, Kath, about those whom God has placed above our station?'

'A little here, a little there. For instance, the St Loe family accuse the countess of taking more than her due from the late Sir William's estate.'

'Say no more of that. You know better than to heed tattling tongues.'

The countess will take all she can from the Talbot coffers, too, thought Dickenson, *to give to her Cavendish sons. And I fear her intimacy with the Queen of Scots ... If God should call her majesty's soul to His keeping, which we most earnestly pray He will not, Mary must become* our *queen ...*

'You're troubled, William.'

'Tired, Kath. I must rest.'

He ate a platter of pork and onions and retired to the screened-off parlour to lie down. Katherine went out to the kitchen to cover the remaining food. The boys returned from their prescribed labours at the inn and she hushed them: 'Your father is resting'.

An hour later, Dickenson awoke to find a pockmarked face and angry eyes glaring down at him. George Scargill had entered, discreet as a lusting bull.

'What's so urgent, George?'

'Glossopdale, William. Young Botham's back. Given leasehold. Married. Damned piece of shit. Pray God the woman he's spliced can't breed.'

Glossopdale? thought Dickenson. *Ah yes, a poor valley beyond the wastes west of Hallamshire. Trouble there when his honour succeeded to the earldom. Enclosures, perhaps. Mr Sutton once told me that a tenant called Botham and his son were the greatest annoyance in all his honour's estates.*

'Why does this young man concern you, George?'

'The Bothams will concern us all before long. Ditch-born pedlar's breed. The father kept the peace while the son was in service, but the young bastard stirred trouble in Castleton, too, *and* in Peak Forest, *and* in –'

It's unlike George to be so hostile to a mere tenant. He blusters and curses but he's usually generous.

'What trouble did he stir, George? And if he's so eristic, why did you grant him leasehold in his honour's name?'

Scargill snorted. 'His lordship had enclosed a piece of common in Peak Forest. Botham stirred up the rabble of tenants and they tore down

19

his walls. My cousin Edward tried to protect them and Botham beat him. Then the villain complained of inequalities in rents. Got more Peakland villages seething with discontent. As for granting him leasehold, Richard Rogers acted in my stead. Young fool. Less brain than a pox-ridden gnat. I was with tenants in Walkley so I sent Richard to Glossopdale, not knowing the knave Botham had returned. Richard and the Glossopdale bailiff signed –'

'Have you told Mr Eyre of young Botham's return?'

Scargill shook his head. *So Nathaniel wasn't privy to this news when we spoke earlier*, thought Dickenson.

'No, William, but his honour must be told. Before there's more trouble. Will you –?'

'I will not. His honour has more serious concerns than a young man's return to Glossopdale, notwithstanding his assault on an enclosure in Peak Forest and on your cousin, and his complaints about rent inequalities. Go home, George. Let me sleep.'

Scargill mumbled an oath and lurched away into the Sheffield evening. But Dickenson couldn't sleep again. After a while he rose to lead his family in evening prayers.

Glossopdale, June 1572

Two year had gone by since Black Harry had took Storth, and it were like all Glossopdale were holding its breath, watching and listening, though I didn't know what for. Folk weren't doing nowt different nor usual. Happen it were nobbut me as noticed because of what bailiff had telled me about Harry. It were just a feeling, anyroad.

St Barnabas's Day were hot and dry. Swallows and martins, birds as mourn for Our Lord, chattered under thatches; lucky sign, they reckon. We heard cuckoo again; she'd be back under fairy hill soon, sleeping while next spring. Had me remembering two year back, when Joanna and Harry were married in face of church. Cuckoo sang then and all. A fortnight after, Joanna asked if I'd ever seen yon Devil's-head birthmark on Harry's left shoulder. What if I had? Like I telled her, birthmarks don't mean nowt.

Noise out of Storth after they were wedded made me feel like I were choking. Worse nor Willie swyving Alice. Harry said he reckoned nowt to yon Puritan stuff about not swyving on feast days, fast days, Saints' days, Sundays, when woman's unclean, and all rest, or you'd end up doing it nobbut one night a week and that weren't healthy. Mind, after little Edmund were born, he kept off Joanna all forty day while she were churched, and he wouldn't let her go visiting neither, so vicar were happy, and Harry didn't bring no bad luck on his wife; no black beetle crawled on floor at Storth. And like any man, he were in Jacob's alehouse while babby were coming: house darkened; Maggie and Agnes Dawson there, same as they always were when they were needed. Women's work, babbies getting born, all yon blood and noise and mess, worse nor

21

lambing. And if folk don't call Maggie and Agnes to childbed, fairy midwife will happen come in her red cloak and hood, and then babby gets took and an ugly little hob left in its place. Harry had carved a charm on a bit of cheese for Joanna to hold while pain were on her and she were praying to God and St Margaret, but when it were done it were God and Maggie she needed to thank. And Agnes.

Ma says a twisted body hides a twisted soul and happen she's mostly right, but there's nowt twisted about Agnes Dawson only her withered leg.

I put a silver penny in little Edmund's hand first time I saw him, like you do with a new babby. Never seen Harry's eyes go soft like they did when he first held his son.

Anyroad, morning of St Barnabas's Day: boys scaring rooks off young crops, fighting one another with sticks and stones. Some were old enough to get shown manor and parish bounds and Gospel Oak, and edges of commons, but road they were carrying on they still wanted their arses kicking. Randolph had forged and whetted our scythes so we could get first cut of hay. Women were helping with sheep-dipping, singing along with grasshoppers:

By a bank as I lay
Myself alone did muse,
Hey ho!
A bird's sweet voice did me rejoice
She sang before the day.
Methought full well I wot her lay,
She said, The Winter's past,
Hey ho!
Down, derry down,
Down derry, down derry,
Down, derry down, derry down,
Derry down, down!

We needed to get hay in fast, day after it were cut, but sheep needed doing and all; so while we were mowing we kept us eyes on women, making sure they washed sheep proper. Ewes blarted, splashing up clough to get back to their lambs. Everybody says three washers can dip thirty dozen sheep, only women can't do that many. We'd good ewes among us: white even teeth, thick necks with plenty of wool, deep wide bellies, round bodies, broad arse ends, long bushy tails. We always dodded them; they lamb better with no horns. Road they were looking this year, six fleeces would make a stone of wool if weather stayed good, then vicar could take his pick for tithe. *A man as is bound to clip his sheep/ Prays for three fair days and one fair week.* I'd need Randolph to sharpen my shears.

Me and Josh Warhurst of Crow Car and daft Hugh Platt of Primdale were mowing down side of White Pot. Josh's brother Henry were mending a wall. Never had no luck, Henry and Josh. Ma said it were because they were lazy pouses, but I reckon they worked hard. Weren't no use, mind; crops failed, stock died, hay rotted. Folk reckoned they hadn't bowed to new moon, or they'd stood on a stone when first cuckoo sang, or done summat daft like burning yew or carrying mayblossom into house instead of hanging it outside. More likely it were Josh's wife giving silver penny to yon old woman in red cloak and hood as had come a-begging. Some folk haven't sense to stop fairies and witches putting evil on them. She whistled and all, Martha Warhurst did; and like they say, *A whistling wife and a crowing hen/ Are good for neither God nor men.* Old Maggie had give mugwort to Martha for her women's troubles but it hadn't give her no better sense, and Henry and Josh still had no better luck. Crow Car had got most of bad land from open fields when closed farms were leased.

Henry said yon agent, Scargill, were good with them when it come to paying rent or heriot or tithe. That were hard to believe. I reckoned Scargill had deep pockets and weren't nobody's friend. Henry said William Newton, him as had took Joanna in service, were good with poor folk and all; helped them out with money when they were short. But like I told him, Newton had enclosed eight acre of common at Heath years back so he could graze more sheep, and that weren't good for poor folk or nobody else neither. Mind, Joanna had done all right in service there. Newton had treated her proper: paid her what were due, give her good food, stopped two or three other servants trying to tup her.

23

We talked about Newtons while we were mowing. William's cousin had just enclosed common land at Dinting. Been well off for generations, Newtons had; like Phil Woolley said, them as sells themselves to Devil always has plenty. You do right to look after your family, but making money for its own sake, that's what vicar called avarice. Newtons only listened to vicar when it suited them.

'It's all right enclosing wastes,' said Josh. 'Enclosing commons what families with no land need for their beasts is summat else.'

'Aye,' I said. 'Not Christian, enclosing commons. Poor folk starve or end up vagabonds, and there's laws as says vagabonds are to get whipped and burned through an ear to stop them being idle.'

'New law says they can be taken for servants instead, Spiderlegs,' said Josh.

'Enemies of commonwealth, folk as enclose commons,' said Hugh.

He'd learned them words off somebody, Hugh had, and he'd said them more times nor I could count. I reckon he didn't know what "commonwealth" were. He'd nobbut two little fingers on his left hand and that weren't all as were up with him. His face looked like somebody had been chopping wood on it. Harry reckoned Hugh only had half a brain and half of that didn't work right. Good with his sheep, mind. Could handle a scythe and all.

'There's poor folk doing spinning and selling it back in Chapel and suchlike,' said Josh. 'Merchants don't pay what they do in town, but it's a few welcome shilling. Martha's earning a bit that road.'

*

When mowing were done I set off home. Women had dipped a fair few sheep; now they were gossiping next to well. When you get anywhere near gossiping women they shut up 'til you're gone. You'd hear a bit, like one of them showing her bruises and black eye and saying, 'Look what he give me for nowt', and Ma telling her, 'Pay yon by-our-lady bastard back twice'. When Ma said summat of that sort, she meant it. Not even Dad would have dared slap Ma around. Men beat their women and curse their farms, but they'd never leave neither.

Seeing yon women gossiping after I'd been talking to Josh and Hugh about Newtons and their enclosures, I remembered hearing them a while back moaning about Lizzie Newton. 'Showing off with her pewter pots.' 'Aye, and her red-dyed skirts.' And Alice had said, 'Thinks she *is* somebody, sewing buttons on her sleeves like a lady, and she isn't no better nor nobody else.' I'd never heard no more about Lizzie Newton. Same as I said, women shut up when they see you.

Down by Storth, Harry and his Dad were looking over our tup. Me and Willie said we'd lend yon ram out round tithing come St Luke's Day, but folk would want to be sure of him.

'What do you reckon, Dad?'

Old Harry had white hair and wrinkles now, and he weren't neither as tall nor as angry as he'd been at one time. I'd been proper scared of him when I were a nipper. He were still best judge of a ram in Glossopdale, mind. He run his hands over tup and nodded. 'He'll do, son. Horns dobbed, high forehead, decent staple, longish tail, good stones in cod.' Then he saw me limping down road. 'Ayup, Tom. How many shears?'

'Three.'

'Reckon he'll service thirty ewe a season 'til he's had five shear,' Old Harry said, 'then you'll want a change.'

He reckoned tups were like ewes in yon rhyme we learned when we were nippers:

> *A four shear ewe is in her prime*
> *A five shear ewe in lambing time*
> *As good; six past, she will decline*
> *Ere seven come, away with thine.*
> *Yet many men for profit keep*
> *In warm low grounds and pasture sweet*
> *An eight, a nine, or ten shear sheep.*

Joanna were back from alehouse with her oatcakes cooked and she were digging onions, little Edmund in her arms. Harry give her that sideways shift of his mouth. She'd got mallow and mugwort and parsley and borage growing next to house in a patch five yard by ten. Ma had same at Cloud, only her herb patch were bigger, nigh on a perch. Joanna

25

had bought linen an ell wide at St Matthew's Day fair, made an apron out of it and dyed it blue, and she were wearing it over yon rough brown wool dress she'd made after babby come. Black Harry were pointing at his meadow.

'Good hay crop. Ottie reckons it won't rain while John Baptist Day because moon won't change on a Sunday afore then. God's good to us.'

Ottewell Wood could smell weather a month ahead, let alone a fortnight. Said his cat showed him: if its eyes widened or it sat with its back to fire it were bound to rain. It'd rain if black snails crossed his path and all, or scarlet or yellow pimpernel closed her petals afore noon. Ottie were wedded to Harry's sister Mary. Like Dad used to say, there were a time years back when neighbours married neighbours like they shared their fleas and lice, but fleas and lice get shared further and wider these days.

'Aye, son, prayers sometimes get answered,' said Old Harry. 'You did right to get ewes on your meadow at Candlemas, and round yon apple trees and all. Nowt like sheep shit for growing hay. Good crop now, same as you said.'

I reckoned soil smelled good where Joanna were digging.

Harry said, 'I need a pot of ale.' He tossed his buff jerkin to Joanna and told her to take it indoors. We went up to Jacob's.

*

Jacob were chasing two lads as had started playing nine men's morris in corner where it were dark. 'I'll have constable on you, breaking law and making me break it! Think it's Christmas?' Lads grabbed board and counters and ran off to play at home. Weren't no good arguing with Jacob; nigh on as good a wrestler and weight-thrower as Harry. Wouldn't have folk with crooked dice in his alehouse, neither, reckoning to cheat decent folk. And ale-conner never had nowt bad to say about Jacob's drink, only it were strong enough to make grown men fall over.

Old Harry had come up with us. Bob Wolstenhome of Hargate Hill were having a drink and all, and one-eyed Phil Woolley of Dodge Croft, and Reggie Harrop of Knockle Croft. I could tell one from another with my eyes shut even when they said nowt: they all smelled different. You could tell them apart over them smells of ale and baking bread and oatcake as you get in a good alehouse; it weren't just shit and onions like Harry said. Then Malachi Lomas come down from Herod smelling of heather and wet peat. He sat and mumbled at wall. Phil and Reggie started having a laugh at him.

'Going to be constable when Dewsnap's done, Malachi? Lock loose beasts up in pinfold? Put vagabonds in stocks for three day and whip them out of parish? Catch rats? Deal with poachers and drunks, wall-damagers and church-avoiders, whores, fathers of bastards?'

Malachi made a noise same as a clogged-up mill wheel. Reggie made same noise and laughed again but Phil give himself a talking-to: 'Don't mock and despise a poor simple and innocent person; thank God for blessing you with better wits.' Sounded like fire in a thatch, Phil's voice. Chest had been bad since he were a babby. Maggie had give him agrimony but it hadn't done no good. He drunk his ale and shut up. Reggie went on, though.

'Getting your sister wedded, Malachi? Who's lucky man?'

'Leave him be, Reggie,' said Black Harry.

'Nobbut a bit of fun, Harry. Anyroad, what's it to do with you?'

Harry banged his ale mug on trestle and stood up. Fists size of penny loaves.

'I'll show you what if you don't shut your gob, you dog's arse!'

Reggie took a couple of step back. Old Harry nodded. His lad were doing what he'd taught him: *speak truth boldly to all men and let your words be your deeds*. Looked more like his mother nor his Dad, mind, did Black Harry.

'It isn't no fun for Malachi, Reggie,' said Bob. 'And you go up Herod like rest of us when you've a beast sick or want good honey.'

Bob bought Malachi a mug of ale. Reggie reckoned to grab it and Malachi thrashed and yelled like a trapped fox. Harry stood and bunched his fists again. Jacob stepped forwards.

'Yon Newton's enclosed land at Dinting,' I said. 'Heard about new vagabond law? More homeless folk'll get put in service for punishment when enclosures starve them. If their ears don't get burned through, like.'

27

'Poor folk won't get treated that road no more, Spiderlegs,' said Bob. Smart lad, Bob, but soft-like. 'Justices are keeping names of what they call "old, decayed and impotent poor". Paying a Collector to see how they get looked after.'

Phil reckoned it meant we'd all have to pay poor relief or else constables would put us in stocks. 'May God in his infinite mercy forgive them overseers,' he said. Then Bob said poor had been looked after proper in Abbey times, with neither overseers nor poor relief. 'Better world in them days.'

Jacob were pouring more dagger ale for us but he weren't having none of that. 'Watch your mouth, Bob Wolstenholme. I'm not having no Papist talk in here.'

Jacob were right; folk gossiped, and constables had to look like they were doing summat. Black Harry said nowt, but road he stared at Bob, it felt like toads crawling down my back. Happen I shouldn't have told Harry about Bob's family lifting pictures out of St Mary Magdalene Chapel in Charlesworth, what were left of it. Will Garlick and John Beeley had took some and all. Even Ma had two of them hung up at Cloud. A lot of folk were Papists on quiet, but they went to church of a Sunday like law said, so they didn't do no harm and they didn't come to none.

'Abbey took its tithes, Bob,' said Reggie. 'That were poor relief with a different name.'

'You reckon, Reggie?' Bob weren't buying it. 'When Abbey fixed us fines and rents, tenancies were ours and our children's as long as we feared God and obeyed church and forest law. We're more like tenants-at-will with Lord Shrewsbury now we've got closed farms. And we still pay tithes to vicar and his lordship's agent, and rents to bailiff.'

Jacob's face could have soured his best ale. We weren't tenants-at-will, we'd leasehold, but Bob weren't far wrong; his lordship's agent, Scargill, were sniffing round again, grumbling about subtenancies and underwoods. Bailiff always turned a blind eye to doings of that sort. I didn't reckon much to Scargill, working tithes out wrong so he could take more nor he should. He'd had a run-in with Bob over it, and Old Tom Jackson had thrown him in a ditch. Mind, there's two sides to everybody. Bailiff told me Scargill wouldn't let Malachi pay more nor a few shilling rent at Herod or give more nor half tithe. And while we were mowing that morning, Henry had told me he were kind to him and Josh. So happen he weren't as bad as he seemed. Not to some folk, anyroad.

'There's more folk living longer these days, Bob,' said Old Harry. 'That's difference. Look at me and Tom Jackson! At one time, landlords begged for tenants. Now men with no lands are begging landlords for farmholds. There's too many folk to have a severalty each. And that's why them as can afford it are enclosing commons.'

You could hear everybody thinking while they supped their ale: 'Aye, Old Harry's right; fifty-two households in Glossopdale, half of them nigh on landless, all getting poorer.' Black Harry kept watching Bob. He weren't smiling.

'I don't know where it'll end.' Old Harry stared at his ale. 'Too many folk in England; not enough land for them all, not enough food. Where will everybody live? At finish there'll be nobbut a score of rich men with farms. Rest will be landless and starving. I'm glad I'm not a young fellow no more.'

Phil said, 'May our heirs and their heirs live dutifully as fits their place, and God bless them and grant them long life and health according to His goodness and mercy.'

We all said, 'Amen'. Could have been a preacher, Phil, only for his voice. Mind, happen folk wouldn't reckon much to a preacher with nobbut one eye. Or a preacher as tormented Malachi.

Roger Wragge come in, kicked Malachi off his stool for a laugh, took a pot of ale and looked round at me.

'Ayup, Spiderlegs. Thatch needs doing.'

'Ayup, Roger. House or mill?'

'Both. Give you a bushel of rye flour for it.'

Get plenty of brown bread out of a bushel of good flour and a peck of pease. Happen he'd got rye off them Newtons, or else Chapel market. Alice and Ma could make dough out of rye flour and bake it alehouse, and we'd give Jacob a loaf for payment.

'Aye, all right,' I said, 'if Willie doesn't need me tomorrow I'll have a look. I can happen do it for a bushel of good flour if you've proper turfs and two or three women who'll bottle your oat straw and give me mud for fixing. If you're short of straw I can find reeds.'

I'd need to see what his turfs and straw were like. Same as I telled folk: no use laying good reeds or straw or even heather on rotten turfs, or turfs as aren't a yard long and cut with a proper swallowtail, no more nor putting good turfs on rotten timbers. If you do, roof falls on your head.

Black Harry said, 'Tom and Willie have enough work with ewes and hay crop, Roger Wragge. Do your own damned thatching.'

I started to say it were all right, I'd do Roger's thatch, but Harry were leaning forward with his jaw thrusting like a bull-baiting dog. Roger took one look at him and were out of yon alehouse quicker nor a rabbit dodging a weasel. Reggie drunk his ale for him.

*

I still had that feeling like all Glossopdale were holding its breath. Were it in other folks' heads and all? I wanted to ask, but Ma and Alice would have said I were daft, and Willie would have said it were nobbut work as needed doing with hay and ewes, and Harry would have said, 'Nay, Spiderlegs, wind sometimes blows and sometimes it doesn't, but valley doesn't breathe or hold its breath'. Bailiff Booth once told me winds happen because sun draws warm air up off earth, and then heavens send it back to us sideways as they turn above us. I wondered about going and telling *him* about Glossopdale holding its breath, but I didn't. He'd have been too busy to bother.

I reckon it weren't such a daft thought, though. A man's made of arms and legs and head, hands and eyes and mouth, and inside him there's veins where blood runs, a heart as heats it, lungs and brains as cools it, and bowels as keeps on making it while they're turning food into shit. Valley's made of fields and roads, houses and walls, woods and commons, rivers where water runs, rocks for bones, crops and beasts as live and grow, die and rot. It's a living creature, our valley, same as a man is. God puts souls into men and I reckon He put a soul into Glossopdale.

Land everywhere has a soul unless Devil's took it, like up on wastes. So if a man can hold his breath waiting for summat, Glossopdale can hold its breath and all.

From what I'd seen and heard at Jacob's, happen Glossopdale were holding its breath for shadows of Papistry to shift; shadows of them as said Queen's mother were nobbut a whore as hadn't been proper married to King Henry, so her majesty were a bastard and yon Scottish Queen should be ruling England. I'd heard Bob say summat of that sort when he were drunk. Mind, Bob said Old Harry hadn't been proper married neither.

Road he'd stared at Bob, happen Black Harry wanted to shift them shadows of Papistry with his own strong hands, and shift Bob Wolstenholme with them.

Sheffield Castle, September 1572

William Dickenson prayed for the thousands murdered on St Bartholomew's Day in France. The Spanish King had applauded the atrocity. The Bishop of Rome had struck a medal to celebrate. French Queen, Spanish King, Bishop of Rome: three emissaries of the Devil.

His honour had been compelled to oversee the trial and execution of Thomas Howard, duke of Norfolk. The countess's latest letter to her husband oozed empathy, for Howard had been his honour's friend; but her protestations were juxtaposed with matters of business. Dickenson's lips curled. Howard's death had made Lord Shrewsbury earl martial of England. Her ladyship's joy at her husband's elevation glittered between the sorrowing lines.

'Her majesty let Howard of Norfolk out of the Tower, so he must have been innocent of treason.' George Scargill thumped the table. 'So why chop his head off? Was he prettier without it? They say his honour wept when he had to pronounce judgement.'

Dickenson and Eyre told him the tale of Norfolk's conspiracy with the Florentine banker Ridolfi: Spain's support, the Bishop of Rome's interference, troops to be sent from Holland, her majesty assassinated, the Scottish Queen on England's throne, Norfolk married to her.

'Thanks be to God the plot failed. Her majesty ordered the Scottish Queen to be close-confined, since she'd colluded.' Dickenson chuckled. 'Whereupon Mary fell into a decline. Food wouldn't stay in her stomach. Mr Eyre begged their honours to return from London lest she die during their absence and poisoning be suspected; at which she recovered. If she were a man she might join a troupe of actors and earn her bed and board thereby.'

Eyre nodded. The earl, he observed, had found three letters in cypher under a stone outside Sheffield Castle and sent them to London. William Cecil had interpreted them; they proved Mary's foreknowledge of the Ridolfi plot.

'That damned woman can't be confined more closely than she already is until she's in her coffin; at which we'll all rejoice.' Scargill gnawed venison from a thigh bone, swallowed spiced wine and belched.

'Eighteen months ago, William. Remember?' Eyre ground his teeth. 'When his honour brought Mary here with all her confessors and chaplains and astrologers, her lutenists and physicians, apothecaries and laundresses, ladies of the bedchamber, ladies of the wardrobe, scullions, butlers –'

'Pause for breath, Nathaniel.'

'– How he imposed rules? Ordered the gawking mob of townspeople back to their hovels?'

'I wrote down those rules,' said Dickenson. 'None of her household would be permitted to carry weapons.'

'Not even the ladies of the bedchamber?' Scargill guffawed.

'All must retire to their lodgings by nine at night. They must remain there on pain of death. They must not ride out during the day without permission –'

'Yet three attempts have been made to free her.'

'Each as ill-conceived as Ridolfi's plot. The scheme at Chatsworth was risible. Then she tried to climb from her chamber here on a rope, to be spirited away by Sir Henry Percy. She was led back to her chamber. Percy's in the Tower.'

All at his honour's expense, thought Dickenson. *His income must be increased. How? I owe fourpence for the tavern steps, which I'll pay at Michaelmas. But such payments are trifles.*

Dickenson had studied his honour's correspondence while setting it in order. There was a request to approve Humphrey Gilbert's expedition to support the Dutch against the Spanish; Sir Thomas Gargrave's inquiry about laws and customs pertaining to the enclosure of

33

woodlands on his honour's Yorkshire estates; an apology from Robert Dudley, now made earl of Leicester, for encouraging his honour's heir Lord Francis Talbot to repair to Court; the Queen's demand for names of commissioners to collect subsidy from the West Riding; a further inquiry from Sir William Cecil, now Lord Burghley, concerning security around the Scottish Queen. His honour had drafted a reply to Burghley: Mary was fully secured; and for all her anger, for all her deadly hatred against the Queen's majesty, she wouldn't be allowed outside the castle grounds. He'd added to her guard: thirty armed soldiers watched under her window day and night. Unless she could transform herself into a flea or a mouse, it was impossible she could escape. All this was in obedience to her majesty's commands; but it had made Mary stormy and hostile towards him.

Lord Shrewsbury had written to his friend Robert Dudley of Leicester, too, seeking to delegate some of his duties as earl martial. Lord Leicester's reply had been diplomatic.

The correspondence also included an unsettling message from his honour's second son, Gilbert, who loitered around Court: the Queen was at Windsor and her smallpox had recurred. Dickenson felt his face whiten. If her majesty died then Mary would succeed her, plots or no plots, and the Papists would be resurgent. Perhaps no Englishman, not even a Catholic, would countenance Mary as Queen: thrice-married, suspected of complicity in her second husband's murder. Nevertheless her majesty had reason to fear her cousin. Therefore, Mary must remain close-confined, yet treated with the courtesy due to a queen; which compelled the earl and countess to be at once custodians and courtiers, spying on Mary's correspondence while they prepared themselves to be numbered among her future retinue.

Useless to dwell upon what might be. Our concern is what is and what must be done. For the rest we must pray. Her majesty's life is in God's hands, as are all our lives.

*

'You say the countess outwitted the earl regarding his deed of gift, William.' It had become customary for Katherine Dickenson to sit at the spinning-wheel when her husband was present. He delighted in the skill of her fingers, her composure of face and voice. 'How so?'

She fell silent, awaiting his reply, eyes on her spinning.

'His honour has gifted lands to the countess's younger sons; lands she'd brought to the marriage. She'll retain life interest in them.'

'Valuable estates?'

'I have no exact figures, which is annoying; but I estimate a thousand pounds a year in rents.'

'Then his lordship seems generous. But was the gift agreed between the earl and countess before they married? And will he also benefit?'

'The deed pays off debts the countess has incurred on his behalf, and also the money he must transfer to her sons when they come of age. Indeed, the young Cavendish men paid *him* for that part of the settlement.'

'In that case, William, the earl has gained as much as the countess; so in what way was he outwitted?'

'His honour's gains are short term. Hers are lifelong.'

Katherine smiled.

'You dislike her but you admire her acumen.'

'It is not for people of our station to like or dislike those whom God has placed over us, Kath. Our duty is to respect and obey them.'

The settlement mitigates the cost of housing the Scottish Queen, he thought, *but only partly, and only temporarily; and neither the lead trade nor the cutlers' taxes will make up the deficit. I must speak to his honour. When he has time.*

'You're worried about the earl, William.'

'He's unwell, Kath. Evil whispers have reached the Queen and Privy Council.'

'What whispers, and what ill wind bore them south? The renegade servant, Henry Hall?'

'Hall's been captured and hanged but rumours continue: the countess is too intimate with the Scottish Queen; security at Sheffield Castle is lax despite his honour's claims...' Dickenson shook his head. 'The strain undermines his health. He's asked Lord Burghley to have Mary transferred to a custodian more robust in mind and body. There's been no reply.'

'Who spawned the whispers, William? And how can they be silenced?'

'Recusants want the Scottish Queen to be removed from his honour's custody to less secure care so she may escape to Spain, or France, or her English supporters.' Dickenson rose and paced the room. Katherine's eyes lingered on her spinning. 'Who?' he continued. 'Persons whom the foolish mass of mankind will believe. Persons familiar enough with his honour's household to give substance to their lies. In other words, Papist clergy with livings on the Shrewsbury estates.'

He stalked to the corner of the room, unlocked his chest and counted the money. In another two years he'd have saved enough to build a fine new dwelling at the location he'd chosen, the junction of High Street and Change Alley. Then Katherine and the boys would be richly and securely housed in the centre of Sheffield; and when God called him, his sons would inherit property.

*

Michaelmas approached. In the small room set aside for him in the castle, Dickenson bent over his accounts. The parsonage at Ecclesfield must pay its rent of ten pounds six shillings and eightpence to add to the sixteen pounds paid before Whit Sunday. He'd travel to Ecclesfield on the twenty-ninth to collect the money. While he was there he'd attend to the execution of the will of a tenant named Laurence Fox, written and witnessed on the fourth of April 1571; the task was overdue. He could also visit his own small estate close to Ecclesfield.

The earl entered, shoulders sagging under his velvet gown. The countess had returned to Chatsworth again.

'Here, Dickenson,' he said, 'is a tract that Dr John Jones has composed and dedicated to me: *The benefit of the ancient baths of Buxton, which cures most grievous sicknesses, never before published.* Dr Jones treats infirmities of both bodies and souls. I must try whether the Buxton waters will relieve my hands of the gout. When the present danger is past I shall beg her majesty's permission to take our royal guest there so her ills too might be relieved.'

The bailiff scanned the tract.

'It seems a learned work, your honour. If it persuades the Queen's majesty of the virtue of Buxton's waters, she might graciously grant your honour's request.' Dickenson licked his lips. 'Your honour, it seems to me your tenant farmers pay too little rent —'

'My poor tenants in Attercliffe have begged me to be a good lord to them and not to impose high rents, or such entry fines as other lords demand,' said the earl. 'Would God prefer me to listen to your representations, Dickenson, or to heed the pleadings of the poor?'

He walked away, clasping Dr Jones's tract, not hearing his servant's whispered riposte: 'The Devil's tongue might be in such pleadings, your honour'.

Glossopdale, 1573

There's nowt like a May Day Ale for making your soul dance. Mind, men need to watch their sisters and daughters, and happen their wives; rain or shine, lasses sup ale and lads are off with them. Then there's weddings at Lammas and babbies five month after. Same with Midsummer Ales: weddings while apples are picking, childbed near Lady Day. Sprites and hobs make mischief in woods on May Eve and a week or two after, but lads do worse, even if they haven't slept after their Mischief Night games. You need to hang a shovel or a besom outside your house on last day of April if you don't want Mischief Night lads visiting. But your soul can still dance on May Day.

There's red deer browsing in sunny glades in yon woods and all, oak and pine standing guard. Too many to count, but foresters can still have you in court for killing them. They reckon wild boars sharpened their tusks round here at one time, and wolves howled. Nobbut stories to frighten nippers now. But deer are still with us.

Like every May Day we wore us Sunday best and hung birch in house for luck, and when we'd said our prayers and ate our bread and cheese and onion and chucked scraps and a few beans to pig and fowl, we walked over to Glossop. Blackbirds and finches sang us through Whitfield and across brook, and even yon grey mist as covered whole valley from Coombes to Arnfield couldn't stop forget-me-nots smiling. Road from Whitfield leads to market ground at Glossop. From there, Doctor Talbot's road goes east over wastes, and road to Dinting goes west. Hadfield road comes down other side church so ways don't meet at a four-lane-ends; nobody wants ghosts and witches and black dogs at market.

Funny place, Glossop, most of it down bottom of hill where it gets flooded when brook runs full. Old folk said it were built there so carts could get to market without having to climb; it's a steep hill up to bailiff's house and church fields. They reckon village used to be higher up afore there were a market, well above brook; but if that were true, it were time out of memory of man.

Maypole were a birch trunk, set up next to market cross like always. Folk started drinking and singing afore they'd done picking greenery. Tom Blood sung loudest. His voice come from underground. They reckoned it could split rocks.

> Go no more a rushing, maids in May;
> Go no more a rushing, maids, I pray;
> Go no more a rushing, or you'll fall a blushing,
> Bundle up your rushes and haste away.
> You promised me a cherry without any stone,
> You promised me a chicken without any bone,
> You promised me ring that has no rim at all,
> And you promised me a bird without a gall.

Black Harry played his bagpipe. Randolph Swann had his fife; it were a lot smaller nor his hands but he could get a good tune out of it. Henry Warhurst played fiddle his granddad had brought back from Italy. Young John Booth banged his tabor. Far-off cousin of mine, young John. Next news we were all singing *There chanced to be a pedlar bold* and *As I were going to Banbury*. Lasses danced round maypole and everybody only Ted Shaw from Chunal laughed and were happy. Ted reckoned he were a better piper nor Harry, only he weren't. I hoped he wouldn't say nowt; we didn't want Harry wasting time beating shit out of Ted Shaw instead of playing. Anyroad, Ted kept his gob shut so Harry played, and Randolph and Henry and young John with him. Lasses young and old showed their legs while they danced, all their eyes on Black Harry. I couldn't take my eyes off him neither.

When everybody had supped enough ale they wanted to get cripples dancing. Black Harry and Henry Warhurst played tunes in no sort of

39

time and made notes come out wrong so everyone had a good laugh at me and Agnes Dawson. Only Agnes's brother Will didn't think it were funny. Face like a sore arse. Mostly up for a laugh, Will – could copy any voice so you wouldn't know whether it were him or them talking – but he didn't like his sister getting made to dance. I told him cripples always had to dance on May Day but he took no heed, happen because Maggie didn't like it neither. Maggie were like unmoving Earth, and Agnes and Will were moon and sun sailing round her.

Getting dogs drunk were another laugh, and a few fights started so there were bleeding mouths and bruised fists. Folk played quoits and bowls outside their own gardens and our constable Tom Dewsnap tried to stop them, but he were soon told where to shove his "forcement of law", and games went on. It were all part of May Day.

Yon pedlar they call Scotsman had come back and Edmund Bower yelled at him: 'Here, you, you plague sore! See yon aprons you selled my missus last year? Fell to bits in three week! Give my money back or I'll cut your balls off and roll them in pig-shit!'

'Get lost, you ditch-born whore's son! Those aprons were fair trade. Should have taken proper care.'

'I'll fair trade you, you poisonous toad!'

'Back to your trough, you rooting hog, or I'll rip your guts out!'

There'd have been a proper set-to only both constables come and stopped it. Crowd moaned; everybody likes watching a fight. Edmund still wanted to kill yon pedlar, constables or no constables, 'til he got some dragon's milk down his throat, and then he started singing. Pedlar didn't know how lucky he were. Sold more of his rubbish afore he left valley, mind. I reckoned he'd be back next year, and then happen we'd see a good fight as long as we could keep constables out of road.

Then Morris men started up with Henry W's fiddle and Reggie Harrop's shawm, and his sister shaking a pig's bladder full of dried seeds. Give Harry's pipes a rest so he'd time for a drink. Folk gathered round to watch Morris men dancing them dances as had been learned off fairy folk time out of memory of man, and everybody sang and clapped. Better nor good ale, it were; better still *with* good ale.

40

Agnes limped up to me, smiling. Plump lass, long fair hair under her bonnet. She'd a few teeth missing but her face were still a spring morning.

'That ear trouble shifted, Tom?'

'Aye, yon roasted onion trick cured it. And Phil Woolley says he's better of his kidney stone since you give him yon boiled horsetail.'

'Ma taught me all them cures.'

It were right; she'd learned them all off Maggie. I'd seen Maggie cure a babby of a cough as might have killed it by cutting a lock of hair off its head and burying it in garden, and she could make sore eyes better with morning dew off celandine leaves or a brew of hawkeed. When my Ma had ague, Agnes took a lock of her hair and pinned it to a poplar tree and told Ma she mustn't say nowt to nobody afore sunset because Maggie had said she mustn't. That were hard for Ma because she's more jaw nor a sheep's head, but she managed, and she never had ague again. Today, Maggie were watching Morris dancers and selling tansy leaves to cure folk of worm. Agnes told me tansy were good in spring, but after midsummer it did more harm nor good. They give folk all sorts of cures, Maggie and Agnes: nettle brew for gout, witch hazel for gnat bites, cowslip for ague. They could rid you of warts by knotting oat straw and burying it; warts went when straw rotted. Ma reckoned you should touch wart with your knife and then cut a notch in an elder stick, but Maggie said you couldn't shift warts that road, it were just an old tale. I reckon God give us cures for all pains and troubles as Devil made, and Maggie and Agnes knew them. Sometimes, as God willed, pain won, for all Agnes and Maggie did. Pain's there to test a Christian's faith. But I reckon there can't be no harm in making it quiet if you can.

*

Bailiff Nicholas Booth were talking to yon Newton from Dinting. I weren't listening, but a few words floated past me like thistledown in September – *stirs folk up, wants kicking out, pillory* – and summat about Scargill. I didn't like road they were staring at Black Harry. Planted tares in folks' ears, yon Newton, same as his cousin did. Ale started turning inside me like curds in a churn.

41

Mind, I'd held back on ale so I didn't fall over while I were dancing with Agnes. Anyroad, I wanted to win at shooting. I weren't bad with a bow, mark set as far as fifty rod, as long as I weren't drunk. God hadn't made me so I could wrestle or throw stone or bar like Harry or Jacob or Will Garlick's dad Reggie, or run like Olly Smith as had married Harry's sister Kathy, or fight like Edmund Bower; but to make up for my bad hip He'd give me a steady hand, a strong enough arm and a good eye. I thanked Him every day for His merciful goodness.

Next news, Edmund and Nick Mellor were talking to me. Seemingly they'd heard what Newton and bailiff had been on about, and they wanted to know if Black Harry and me were still pals. I said Harry were my brother-in-law. Edmund said aye, but we were close when we were nippers, so were we still? I reminded them about tup knocking Harry over when were seven, which were how he'd got yon scar over his eye, and my hip getting hurt when I ticed ram off him. Same as I said, you're pals for life after summat of that sort. Nick and Edmund looked as though it were first time they'd heard that tale. 'Thought everybody knew it,' I said.

'Never mind no ram, Spiderlegs,' said Edmund, 'we'll be pulling Scargill and bailiff off Black Harry afore we're much older.'

My inside were a churn again. I reckoned it were a churn as were making half a dozen two-pound cake of butter.

Nick spat. 'Newton's cousin William, him at Heath! Engrossed his holding to a virgate. Pox on him. Made Tom Smith landless. Newton's took him and his household for servants. Tom says it were either that or wandering and begging. It's Lord Bloody Shrewsbury puts Newton and his like up to it, him and that thieving dog Scargill. Satan take both their bastard souls, and Newton's and bailiff's and all!'

'Here, Nick,' I said, 'you can't talk yon road about Lord Shrewsbury. God in His wisdom made him our liege lord.'

'Liege lord and God's wisdom my arse, Spiderlegs! At Second Coming, do you reckon Lord Bloody Shrewsbury gets judged different nor us?' Nick's blood were hot enough for him to father nowt but sons. Then he stopped shouting and said, 'There's nobbut Black Harry will stand up against Lord Bloody Shrewsbury and his dog when it comes to

42

it, or against them Newtons. If you're still pals, Spiderlegs, take care of him and try and keep him out of trouble. We'll need him.'

Harry could take care of himself better nor most, I telled Nick, and then I left him and Edmund to do whatever they'd a mind. I'd always watch Black Harry's back. Folk ought to know that.

*

Same as I said, there'd been mist that morning, hovering over valley like a big grey hawk, nowt floating above it only bald tops of Shirrell and yon hill where they reckon castle had stood, time out of memory of man. Mist hadn't lifted while noon, when goatsbeard telled us it were time for eating. Then it had risen without a whisper, like soul leaving a dying man's body. Afternoon were warm now; blue sky, white clouds like doves, like Holy Spirit floating above us, and sun were shining like a bride's eyes while we went up through top of town to Church Fields, past where John Rowland burned his charcoal. We took our jerkins off; we were sweating, and anyroad you can't draw a string proper with owt tight round your shoulders. Can't nock an arrow right with sweaty hands, neither. Agnes come to watch us. She held my jerkin.

There were a dozen of us with bows. John Stedman nodded to me and shook his hair out of his eyes. Hair like dry grass.

'Ayup, John. All right?'

'Ayup, Spiderlegs. Aye, not bad.'

John's wife had died giving birth a couple of month back, for all Maggie and Agnes had tried. Like they said, John's apple tree had bloomed out of season, and owl had shrieked at night, so there were bound to be death. God took babby at same time as Tilly so their souls could stay together. Well, some folk reckoned they *couldn't* stay together, but I were sure our merciful Lord wouldn't stop Tilly holding her nipper in her arms just because its spirit had been took afore John could get it christened. Anyroad, John had buried it afore sunrise.

John's farm weren't in our tithing, but when Black Harry heard about Tilly and her babby dying, he got ox as soon as Phil Woolley were done with it and ploughed John's lands as well as his own. Stirred me up, seeing Harry forcing plough blade into soil. Soil could yield or it could

43

resist; made no difference to Harry. If he said it were getting ploughed, it were getting ploughed. Then he marked John's lambs for him and got Coney down from Herod to help his beast while she were calving, and then he took calf out to grass tail first like you should. 'Spiderlegs,' he'd said, 'come and mend John's thatch while I patch his wall.' We did it and all, mended his house and thatch for all March sleet fought us and east wind tried to break my turfs and drive my reeds to Mottram. Makes a man feel good to do his Christian duty, for all vicar warns about sin of pride. It were good for John and all: he'd get a gallon of milk a day off his beast come Whitsun, happen while Michaelmas. I didn't know if he'd keep her over winter, mind. Takes three load of straw to keep a beast over winter, and he wouldn't get that much straw off his oats. None of us would. Anyroad, John were working again, getting his sheep up to tops and cutting willow and drying it in shade ready for folding, like rest of us: good stakes, bars seven foot long, to cover lands where we planted corn.

Him and me were best shots among dozen on yon hill above Glossop that May Day. He were shorter nor me but he'd big shoulders and chest. My arrows were good, though: I'd boiled bluebell bulbs to make glue to fasten goose feathers. When other ten had missed mark twice at twenty rod, they shifted it to thirty so John and me could fight it out between us. Folk were betting halfpennies or even pennies, some on me, some on John. We hit yon mark three time apiece, so then it were up to forty rod, and they'd have shifted it up to fifty only my third shot missed and John's didn't. Coins changed hands and folk called me names.

'Yon arrow were going straight 'til wind caught it,' I said.

'Aye, Spiderlegs, they all say that.'

'Beat you next time, John!'

From up Church Fields you could see all round: from Dr Talbot's road over wastes, past Shirrell, past Whitfield and Chunal, over to Simmondley and Charlesworth, round to Dinting and hill as hid Hadfield, yon hill where castle had been. All Glossopdale: wood and marsh, brook and mill, farm and alehouse; a bowl with brown hills for rim and brawn setting in it. We were brawn, us as were born here. It give me that feeling again: valley were a living thing as were holding its breath. I loosened my bow and got my jerkin back off Agnes.

'Come on, John, let's have a drink,' I said.

We went down to Glossop alehouse, just above market ground, and I bought him a groat's worth of ale. It weren't like Jacob's but it were right enough. While we supped it we had a laugh about folk as couldn't shoot straight. When I left he were casting eyes at young Rose Miller, who'd drunk more nor a lass ought. I reckoned Rose would get tupped afore night were over; John were missing Tilly. Same as I said, it were May Day.

Nobody were working. There were no smoke from John Rowland's charcoal, no noise from Randolph's smithy. A few men were betting over a cockfight, some drunk enough to bet a noble. Daft beggars. They'd none of them that much for betting. End up in stocks for drunkenness, they would, or wearing a hollowed-out barrel; bailiff's house were only a few yard off, just up from church, and Tom Dewsnap were close by, watching them like a weasel watching rabbits. Black Harry were at cockfight but he weren't betting and he weren't as drunk as some. Bagpipe were in his pack again and Ted Shaw had started playing, only nobody weren't listening or dancing. I reckoned Harry would take some of them drunken lads home from cockfight and play them at nine men's morris for a shilling a game. Dab hand at nine men's morris, Harry.

Agnes come up again and said I were better at butts nor John Stedman for all he'd won. Then she looked at me like she were going to start skriking and asked if my heart still hurt because Alice had wed my brother. I said I'd better things to do nor sit around in a wet sack moaning about a woman as had married somebody else. She said she could cure my heart if it *were* hurting, and then she limped off fast as she could and buried her face in Maggie's bodice. Happen she'd drunk too much, like young Rose, only there weren't nobody trying to tup her. We'd always got on, Agnes and me; but she were a woman, and I couldn't make no more sense of women nor I could of ways of God.

*

45

I went home for a game of fox and geese with Willie while Alice and Ma made us a stew of barley with a bit of kale and a couple of strips of bacon in it. Alice wouldn't let me stir yon stew in case I stirred it wrong road round instead of following sun. She'd been looking sour at me for months. No idea why. I drew geese, Willie got fox. He sat on stool, me on bench, and we put board on table. I'd made a good job of yon trestle table; mature oak, dark as midwinter, solid as church tower. It stood four-square because Willie had beat floor level and hardened it with lime afore Alice spread rushes. I'd made frames for beds and all; mine were in far corner. Ma had stuffed mattress with thistledown, blaspheming when it got up her nose. I slept all right on it, even in May when twilight come late and dawn early, and chickens back of house and swallows and martins under thatch wanted to wake us afore sun were up. We all slept a fair few hours unless we were poorly. Same as folk said, a good night's sleep is wages for a good day's work.

'Tom,' said Willie, while I were getting his fox trapped, 'I were only an hour in Glossop this morning, what with needing to cut willow for folding. Were folk saying owt about rents?'

'Not as I heard, Willie.' I moved another goose. 'What about rents?'

He tried to get his fox shifted but he were running out of space and I hadn't left a goose he could take.

'Didn't Harry tell you? There's two lots of twenty-one year leases in Glossopdale. One lot run out back in '63; rest needs renewing in '78, like ours. First lot never got renewed in '63.'

'How did that come about? No, Harry's never said nowt to me about it.'

'Old folk reckon Lord Shrewsbury wanted to make it simple; leave all fifty-two tenancies 'til '78 so all entry fines and new rents get paid at same time. His lordship's father had only been dead three year in '63, Dad said, so his lordship had enough on his plate without bothering with folk of our sort. And it were when they were starting to shift us from old open fields to closed farms like we have now. Still, it weren't a good idea. Half Glossopdale's living on tenancies as haven't been renewed in ten year. Owt could happen.'

I remembered Old Harry going to Manor Court in front of steward when I were a lad, arguing with his lordship's agent and bailiff about rents and tenancies coming due at different times, and how some folk would get a bad deal with closed farms instead of getting different strips in this field and that, changing year on year. Happen him and Black Harry had gone to Duchy Court and all. I'd heard nowt about it since. I weren't leaseholder so it weren't my business, and we were all right with closed farm at Cloud. Still, you'd had thought I'd have heard summat.

I shifted a goose. Willie's fox were getting throttled for space.

'It's another five year to '78,' I said. 'Why would folk talk about it today?'

'Folk talk more at an Ale, and they say Black Harry's stirring it again. His Dad's tried to shut him up. I reckoned you'd have heard summat.'

Were that what Newton and bailiff had been on about, and Nick and Edmund and all? Why hadn't Harry said owt to me? I asked Willie again: why were it getting talked about now?

'Seems Black Harry went on fighting about it while he were away in service, stirring folk up around Castleton and Peak Forest. Happen Ashford and all. Said it weren't fair dealing, different folk paying different rents, and closed farms weren't fair because some folk ended up with all bad lands, like Josh and Henry did at Crow Car and Lomases at Herod. Now he's been back in Storth three year and settled with our Jo and nipper, he's started riling folk up here again. Thought he'd have telled you. You've been closest to him ever since yon ram –'

'Happen he thought I knew.'

I could never reckon up whether I'd saved Harry from ram as had scarred his forehead or saved ram from Harry. Had his eating knife in his fist while he were getting up after it had knocked him flying; looked set to slit its throat. Blood were running in his eye from yon gash. All I did were kick tup in cod so it turned on me instead of him. Anyroad, none of three of us died, me nor Harry nor tup, so everything were all right only my hip. None of us talked about it. Folk knew, though. Some folk, anyroad.

'Rent's nowt to do with me, Willie,' I said. 'It's your leasehold.'

'Ours. You're my brother.'

47

I'd stopped caring about fox and geese.

'Give you that game.'

'What for? You've nigh beat me.'

I walked outside past where pig were wallowing. We'd ringed its nose in case it wandered and we got fined in Manor Court for it grubbing up common or somebody's fields. Alice were coming back from well with a couple of bucket of water. I'd made yon buckets like she'd wanted but I'd never got a word of thanks out of her. She stopped and looked at me like I were a thistle in an oat crop, and then she come out with yon nagging line again.

'Nowt but a bushel of rye flour for thatching Roger Wragge's house and mill! What were up with you, Tom? Could have got two bushel if you'd stood up for yourself, happen half a quarter.'

'Half a quarter of flour for a bit of thatching?' It weren't funny but I laughed. 'And it were a year back! Don't talk daft, woman. If Willie hears you he'll thrash you.'

I limped up road grinding my teeth. Willie only thrashes Alice when she talks out of turn, like Harry does with Jo. Some men like Reggie beat their wives two or three time a week to keep them in their place as God willed, whether they've talked out of turn or not. Others don't. Bob Wolstenholme never beats his Martha unless he's drunk, whether she talks out of turn or not.

Gnats bit me round eyes and made them run. I could have done with some of Agnes's witch hazel but I hadn't got none, so I went up hill and sat where there were more breeze. Sun were getting ready for bed and sky were growing colours like a meadow full of wildflowers. Blackbird were still singing, loud and clear as church bell. Valley were breathing out mist again. Bats were swirling like autumn leaves. Lasses used to chant to them when we were nippers:

> *Airy mouse, airy mouse, fly over my head,*
> *And you shall have a crust of bread,*
> *And when I brew and when I bake*
> *You shall have a piece of my wedding cake.*

Owl started calling. It were a whoo owl not a screech owl so it weren't unlucky.

When sun goes down, trees turn to night afore owt else. Hills and fields are still full of light but trees go black as coal, black as Harry's hair, black as pit in your soul when them you love spites you. Rest of world takes longer.

I sat there drinking it in, and then breeze whispered: *Alice's miserable because she's been married four or five year and God hasn't sent them a babby; and she takes it out on you, Tom, because she daren't talk that road to Willie. Harry will tell you what he's got a-mind when he's sorted it out for himself.*

'Aye, happen,' I said.

It were getting cold, and I were tired, so I went back down to Cloud. It were nigh time for evening prayers. Stars were coming out, whispering to one another. Happen they were saying their prayers, too. I remembered another rhyme we said when we were nippers:

> *Star light, star bright,*
> *The first star I've seen tonight,*
> *Would it were that I might have*
> *The wish I wish tonight.*

Some folk reckon stars make music when they whisper, only nobody can't hear it.

Sheffield Castle, August 1573

'Strong clergy. Secure in the reformed faith.' Nathaniel Eyre snatched a mug of wine from Anne Dacres and dismissed her with a flick of his hand. 'That's what we need. These boys from Hugh Price's college at Oxford are wet behind the ears. Nothing like the strength to drive recusants out.'

Dickenson took off his hat and sank on to the window seat. He'd ridden from Medhope; tenure of two oxgangs transferred from John Greves de Hallfeld to George Street and John Hattersley, seisin witnessed by John Bright and others. As always, he'd recorded every detail, in order.

'God will give them strength, Nathaniel.'

'Strength to rid us of seditious chaplains like the two you exposed?'

'Let's pray that Corker and Haworth are so punished that those who share their persuasion will be taught to abjure slander.'

'His honour might deem two chaplains with minor livings unworthy of his notice. Punish them lightly. If at all.'

Dickenson handed the steward a letter from the earl's London agent.

'Thomas Baldwin assures us otherwise. His honour has already acted by proxy: Lord Leicester has committed Corker to confinement in Dr Wilson's house and he's sent to apprehend Haworth.' Dickenson set down his wine cup. 'I must speak to the builders at the manor gatehouse.'

The earl had planned to inspect the new gatehouse in person, but pain in his joints had precluded the adventure. He'd been ill again. So had the Scottish Queen. Some said she hadn't recovered from Norfolk's execution, and the restrictions imposed after her bungled escape attempts had aggravated her condition.

'His honour asked the Queen's permission to carry Mary to Buxton, Nathaniel, so she could take the waters and he could do likewise. Her majesty said she couldn't deny the request provided Mary spoke to no other resident.'

'I'm aware of that, William. They've been in Buxton much of the summer while you've ridden hither and yon administering land transfers and inheritances and all the rest. He planned the trip a year ago, before the French troubles, before there were further plots to liberate Mary. He caused a great chamber to be built around the healing spring in anticipation of his sojourn. Have you seen it?'

'My travels hither and yon haven't taken me to Buxton. The longer his honour remains there, the less likely he'll be to inspect the gatehouse this year. I, however, must examine it forthwith.'

Eyre set down his wine cup and yawned. The countess was keeping company with her husband in Buxton, he observed. Lord Burghley and his servants had joined them; he too suffered pain in his hands. There was plenty of space for him and his retinue. The earl's Buxton house could accommodate five times the number of guests: four storeys, thirty rooms.

'I'm told they all seemed comfortable together,' said Dickenson, 'until the Queen heard Lord Burghley was consorting with Mary. Tom Baldwin says her tantrum was worthy of her father. Lord Burghley galloped back to Greenwich as though the Devil were at his heels.'

'So her majesty terrified her chief minister from a distance of a hundred and fifty miles.' Eyre guffawed.

Dickenson paced the room. *Would his honour accept Lord Leicester's invitation to London after he returned from Buxton,* he wondered, *and would the countess go with him? She was said to be popular at Court, the Queen well disposed towards her. But surely the Scottish Queen's custody would preclude such a journey, at least for the earl.*

'Her majesty's rages might consume all who cross her, but God be thanked she's recovered again from the smallpox. She wrote to tell his honour so.'

'Indeed. Personal letter. His honour continues to enjoy her favour. As you say, God be thanked.'

'Nevertheless, the Queen's favour pays no bills.' Dickenson paused. 'There are profits from lead, profits from cutlers' taxes, income from the Shrewsbury estates, but his purse still can't meet the demands on it. Do you deem the tenants' rents too low, Nathaniel?'

'Do you?'

'Some haven't changed in forty years, since the tenancies were wrested from the monasteries.' *Even those "poor tenants of Attercliffe" should pay more. His honour is too susceptible to the pleadings of those who should remain silent. They take advantage of his Godliness. They forget their place.*

'Other landlords balance their cash flows with high entry fines,' said Eyre.

Dickenson shook his head.

'Entry fines bring immediate money once in a generation; his honour needs regular income. Rents should rise. George Scargill says tithes and heriot should be heavier too. He asserts this with Scargillian force.'

Eyre summoned Anne Dacre to bring more wine.

'Her majesty should dispatch George to the French court as a diplomat. High time England was at war with France again.'

Both men laughed.

Now Nathaniel will speak to his honour about rent increases and declare the proposal his, thought Dickenson. *Then he, not I, will be rebuked. But what matters a rebuke if his honour will consent to raise the rents on his farmholds?*

Dickenson put on his hat and went to examine the gatehouse.

*

Raising rents seemed a simple strategy, but was it? On the fifteenth of May, following the death of William Wainwright at Barnsley, the inquisition jury had failed to agree about two fields of arable and an acre of meadow in Over Midhope and the assart land meadow and wood in Nether Midhope. Dickenson had imposed his will to settle the argument, incurring the jury's wrath. He cared little for that; tenants could never alter the determinations of Authority; and better by far that the powerless direct their rage towards him than towards the earl.

Nevertheless, the Barnsley inquisition had demonstrated how stubborn tenants could become when their supposed customary rights were threatened. Might rent increases therefore unleash discord?

If rents were raised and there were discord, and if force were needed to suppress the discord, force would be deployed.

Glossopdale and Chinley, April 1574

Black Harry had started going missing two or three week at a time and there weren't nobody knew where he went, not even Joanna. He didn't tell none of us. When he were home he worked his farm same as he always had, and he always found time to help folk in need, so when he went away it were like air round Simmondley had a hole in it. Me and Willie and rest of tithing did a bit to help Joanna with lands and his stock, and John Stedman or Olly or Ottie come over to Storth and lent a hand, but it were always better when Harry were back.

I'd been keeping my ears open since last May Day, when Willie had told me Harry were stirring Glossopdale up about rents. Folk were saying different things about him. Some like Nick Mellor said Harry were right and he'd stand up for whole parish, but a few reckoned he should think about his own household and leave everybody else alone. And Newton and his cousin said he were nowt but a bother-causer.

Summat as happened day after second Sunday of Easter showed me there were truth on all sides. Black Harry had been away another fortnight, and he'd only been back in Storth a day or two when two brothers come from Chinley looking for him. Kyrk they were called, Reynold and Edward. Young Bob Stone were with them. Bob had got tenancy when God took his father. Folk said he were wild but I reckoned he weren't a bad lad; did well with his sheep. I weren't sure about them Kyrks, mind.

'What do you want with Harry?' I said.

'His uncle sent us.' That were Edward Kyrk. I'd a job telling him and Reynold apart. 'George Bradshaw's enclosing herbage. Needs stopping.'

Uncle? Black Harry's Dad didn't have no brothers living. And I'd never heard of no George Bradshaw. But enclosures were bad news, only on wastes. I took all three of them to Storth so Joanna could give them ale while I fetched Harry. He come striding down hill with a frown black as his hair, gleaming with sweat of labour, and barged into house like a mad tup.

'What are you three after? Who's this uncle?'

Edward answered. He'd more jaw nor Reynold. More nor Bob, even.

'Master John Birtles. Your mother's brother, Master Botham. Reynold read summat as Master Birtles had wrote and went Chester way to fetch him to Chinley. Master Birtles says stars telled him Bradshaw's enclosures can't stand. William Bearde and Ralph Bradley says he's right, so Master Bearde's give us money to fight Bradshaw. We've all put a bit in and we're getting ready, arming ourselves. Anyroad, Master Birtles wants to see you, you being his nephew, like.'

Harry quaffed his ale and stared at oiled cloth over window like he didn't know what it were. Edward had trotted out names I didn't know and I reckoned Harry didn't neither. But I'd heard of John Birtles while I were in Yorkshire and I didn't want to hear no more about him. Wanted hanging, John Birtles, and his books of prophecy burning. If conjurers like Birtles stirred riots, even against enclosures, it were treason. And if Edward Kirk were telling truth, Birtles were three hours' walk away, spouting prophecies in Chinley. And he were Harry's uncle? I remembered old Maggie saying there were summat bad about Morag Botham's brother. Well, if Morag's brother were John Birtles, Maggie were right. It were a warm day, linnets singing, lambs blarting, but I felt cold.

Harry said, 'Spiderlegs, go up Bank and fetch my Dad.'

It weren't above a furlong there and back. Bluebells were smiling and other birds were singing beside yon linnets, but I heard nowt of them because I were too busy wishing them Kyrks and young Bob hadn't come to Simmondley. Old Harry took his time pulling his cap and boots on afore he come down to Storth. He said Megan had never talked a lot about her brother and he weren't going to say nowt about him neither. But enclosures were another matter. Making closed farms out of open fields because old strip fields couldn't grow enough corn to feed folk, that were bad enough. Some did all right out of it, like Harry, and some didn't, like Josh and Henry. But enclosing common land, that were wickedness.

'There's miles of waste above Mainstonfield can be enclosed for sheep, like his lordship's done up yonder.' I pointed up at moors. 'Approvement as doesn't hurt nobody. How come they're scrapping in Chinley over a few hundred acre of herbage?'

'Aye well, Tom, his lordship doesn't have as much use for sheep these days. And yon few hundred acre of assart in Chinley is more crop land nor vaccary, so it's got highest rents of any herbage in Duchy. From what I've heard, there's been arguments for a while about lease in reversion and whether yon Bradshaw's any right to it. I've met Bradshaw. His father were nobody to start with, but he did well for himself when they pulled monasteries down and sold land; then he were somebody, or reckoned he were. Got money, Bradshaw has. Doesn't bother about nobody else. Gentry listens to him.'

Back in Storth, Old Harry said it were one thing fighting enclosures, but he didn't want none of us meddling with John Birtles. But Black Harry said if Birtles were his uncle, he were going to Chinley to meet him. 'Aye, happen, Harry,' I thought, 'but it's thought of fighting as draws you, same as a rushlight draws a moth. And I'd best go with you for Jo's sake.'

Joanna weren't happy. 'We've work enough, Harry, without you going off again when –'

'Hold your tongue, woman!' Harry smacked her against wall. Then he stared them three from Chinley in eyes, one after other. 'Right. What wants doing?'

Little Edmund started skriking. Didn't like his Ma getting smacked. Last time I'd seen Harry bruise Joanna were when milk turned sour and she told him hobs from wood had turned it. She were happen right; hobs spoil crops and make ewes give birth to dead lambs unless you leave them dish of porridge and pot of ale. It wouldn't have been first time they'd soured milk or stopped butter churning. But Harry reckoned nowt to tales of that sort.

Bob Stone said lads from Peak Forest and Castleton had telled him Black Harry were always up for scrapping with them as needed scrapping with, so after he'd met his uncle, happen he'd help with fighting Bradshaw. Harry liked hearing words of that sort. Happen Bob hadn't talked to men in Peak Forest and Castleton as reckoned Harry had swyved their sisters or daughters as well as their servants; but right enough, there were plenty of others spoke well of him. Chinley men were ready with bows, pitchforks, clubs, staves, swords and daggers, Bob said, but they could still do with any help they could raise. Reckoned they'd set fire to Bradshaw's quickset willows and stockages, and do mischief to Bradshaw himself if he got in road. It were all music to Harry's ears. Afore long, him and Bob were like a two-hound pack hungry for kill, and Kyrk brothers were set to follow them.

'Yon Bradshaw,' said Edward Kyrk, 'he'll make Chinley like Greenfairfield, other side Chapel. Enclosures. Driving poor folk to starvation and beggary. Only a few living in Greenfairfield now. Half of sheep belong to one man —'

Then Reynold Kyrk spoke. First time we'd heard him.

'Nay, Ted, there weren't no prophecy for Greenfairfield. Thing is, Master Botham, Bradshaw reckons he bought right to herbage six year back off a London man called Richard Celey, who'd bought it off Master Lawrence Myntner. But Queen can't grant lease in reversion to Master Myntner while 1579 because King Edward had granted it for thirty-one year to George Grimsdyke in '48. So it's another five year afore Master Myntner gets it, or can sell it to Master Celey, or him sublease it to Bradshaw. So Bradshaw's no claim in law.'

Black Harry asked what George Grimsdyke were doing about it since it seemed like he were getting robbed, but they couldn't none of them tell him. His Dad said Queen could do whatever she'd a mind with a lease in reversion so George Grimsdyke didn't matter. Happen he were dead anyroad.

Bob thumped table. '*All* tenants in Glossop and Chapel parishes should have herbage and pasturing of Chinley, according to ancient customs and rights agreed time out of memory of man.'

We all shouted, 'Aye', even Joanna. *Custom, time out of memory of man*: words as made blood rise and fists clench. Anybody as reckoned they could trample on custom would face knives and staves, cudgels and billhooks, arrows and daggers. Then Joanna started talking again. She'd been sat on floor since Harry smacked her but she weren't for being quiet. Some women won't do what they're telled. It's hard shutting them up. Took after Ma, Joanna did.

'Haven't you took this Bradshaw to Manor Court for ignoring custom? Duchy Court, come to that? Instead of letting him rile you up like a nestful of wasps as lads have poked?'

'Bradshaw's got friends in them courts, Mistress Botham,' Edward Kyrk said. 'We'd get no hearing.'

'Enemies and all, mind,' Bob said. 'Like Master Manners. Duke of Rutland's son. Had Bradshaw up in Duchy Court two year back, but Bradshaw's friends made sure he got off and they'd do same again. To Hell with courts. Yon common purse as Master Bearde raised has give us men and weapons enough to clip Bradshaw's wings. Don't need no courts.'

'Thus shall them prophecies in yon book of Master Birtles be fulfilled,' said Reynold.

Reynold talked like Phil Woolley, only his voice sounded better. And Phil wouldn't have said owt good about a damned conjurer.

I asked, 'What does Master Bearde want for this common purse he's raised?'

'We'll give him land,' said Edward, 'and tell vicar he's to be buried in parish church. After he's dead, like.'

'Aye, right enough,' I thought. 'More land while he's alive, six foot of it under church after God's took him.' But I said nowt.

Then Old Harry spoke again. 'Duchy and Queen's Bench Courts will order you to keep peace, young fellow. If you've read owt as Master Birtles wrote' (he looked at Reynold), 'Bradshaw can claim it's treason, like they did up in Yorkshire five year back. And you know what courts will say, what with yon Scottish Queen not so far off. Best mind what you're doing. You get hanged for arson; you get worse nor hanging for treason.'

58

Talked sense, Harry's Dad, and Joanna said same, but Black Harry and them Chinley lads weren't listening. Afore day were much older we were off. I went to Cloud and got my bow and a few arrows, and when Willie and Alice and Ma asked where I were going I telled them nowt. Ma shouted summat about watching what I were by-our-lady doing, but I'd gone.

*

There were men from all over Peak gathered in Chinley: Peak Forest and Castleton, like Bob had said, but other villages and all. Some looked all right but others were neither use nor ornament. Ottewell Higginbottom from Marple for a start. Sooner shoot his mouth off in an alehouse nor shear a sheep, Higginbottom would. Followed Harry about like a motherless duckling.

'Hold off 'til tomorrow,' Harry said. 'May Day. And then we'll gather greenery from Bradshaw's hedges. Might wreck his enclosures; but it's May Day, so he'll understand.'

Chinley lads laughed and said aye, that's what they'd do. Then Higginbottom said same as Harry, like he'd thought of it first. We ate our noontide food and then gathered our weapons and went to listen to William Bearde. Talked smart, did Master Bearde, stood on a rock like a wandering preacher, Ralph Bradley beside him.

'Remember what happened here in '69, while courts were busy with happenings up north? George Bradshaw said he'd bought the lease, so he divided the herbage into forty neighbourhoods of eight acres and rented them out, five shillings and a groat each. That seemed a fair rent; herbage was ten pounds and a mark a year. All six hundred acres were agisted at sixteen beasts to the neighbourhood. Bradshaw said anybody who leased a neighbourhood could sublet it in halves or quarters, and they could build cottages. Even a quarter-neighbourhood would be enough for crops to feed a household if God sent good weather. But would God always send good weather? To Chinley? And what about our sheep? Before long, we couldn't get to our sheep because of Bradshaw's hedges!'

Folk were muttering: 'Aye'; 'Pox on Bradshaw'; 'Damn his soul'. Sounded like murder. Master Bearde give us a minute to rile ourselves up and then he went on.

'We were making our own enclosures and building cottages for years before Bradshaw started his neighbourhood divisions. Then Duchy Court ordered us to take our enclosures and cottages down and stop cutting wood, as though forest law applied in a herbage! *That* was Bradshaw's doing, persuading Duchy Court to issue the order. Then he planted willows and stockades so folk couldn't get to their crops, let alone pasture for their sheep. And then he enclosed more than his share. Did he care if folk starved? Did Duchy Court order *him* to stop what he was doing? Of course not!'

Anger started billowing like a winter storm around crowd of us. We could feel it, smell it, taste it. It lifted us up and carried us. Harry and Bob Stone went and stood next to Master Bearde and shouted about rooting out willows, breaking stockades and burning them. Mind, there were elder among them willows; we wouldn't burn elder, what with Our Lord having been crucified on it. But after Harry had spoke, Bradshaw's willows were done for. There's nobody like Harry for stirring folk to action. He had everybody yelling that loud they'd have drowned church bells if they'd rung, and they were waving pitchforks and staves and knives above their heads and nigh on dancing with one another. A few sneaked away but we reckoned nowt to them. Following day, we found out they'd sneaked off to tell Bradshaw what were happening and then gone to fetch bailiff, my uncle.

Chinley folk let some of us sleep in their houses that night, only lads as had set out for mischief like they do on May Eve. Rest slept in church or alehouse out of rain with besoms hung over doors for protection. We were up at dawn gathering greenery, mostly off Bradshaw's hedges like Harry had said, knocking stockades down while we were at it. Then nobody cared how much it rained because there were maypole and singing and drinking and wrestling, and Morris men come out dripping wet, and it got wilder and wilder same as May Day always does.

Then, while everybody were making merry, Bradshaw come with bailiff and two constables and few big lads carrying staves and knives, reckoning they'd arrest Bob Stone and Kyrk brothers so they could *quell this rioting*. Merriment stopped dead. For half a minute it went that quiet you could hear raindrops falling on folks' heads. Then women started, waving knives, telling Bradshaw they'd cut him as small as herbs to pot. There weren't nowt bailiff and constables could do about that because women's husbands hadn't known what their wives were doing, so they were above law. But them big lads as had come with constables went for women anyroad with their sticks, and then there were a proper set-to. Curses flew, fists flew, weapons clashed, blood flowed, heads were broke on both sides. One big lad tried to knife Black Harry so he got one of my arrows in his arse. Rest of them grabbed Bob and Kyrk brothers and started dragging them to lockup, but in we went with staves, clubs and daggers, and I shot two more arrows and hit one bastard in leg; and afore you'd time to chant two verses of a psalm, Bob and Reynold and Edward were cut loose, constables were spitting out teeth, and bailiff were running for his life and Harry were chasing him with bill-hook in one hand and knife in other. He could run, could Nicholas Booth, for all he were little and fat. He needed to. Bradshaw had run off even faster; he'd shit himself. Women took Master Bearde and Ralph Bradley out of road so they wouldn't get caught.

Harry come back laughing, slapped me and Bob and Kyrk brothers on our backs, and said that were Bradshaw sorted out, and bailiff wouldn't be back in no hurry neither. Everybody only constables were cheering, even them with broken heads, unless they were knocked senseless or dead. Women were patching up wounds and letting dogs lick them like they'd done to Lazarus.

Then up come Master Birtles. Everybody only Harry went quiet and backed off. You could tell they were kin: black hair and beard, broad face, big hands; only Master Birtles had white in his hair, and his face were that lined with wrinkles it looked same as a winter field a drunkard had ploughed.

They talked a bit, him and Harry. I went a few paces back so I didn't hear much. Master Birtles muttered summat about stars saying Harry would save innocent lives and cause deaths of friends, and Harry give a laugh as weren't a laugh and asked where his mother were. I didn't hear no more; only Harry stopped laughing, even that laugh as weren't one.

What stars said? Heavens are a wonder, and all what God made has its purpose, but did He want men to read His stars? What does it cost their souls when they do? Does God or Devil teach them? Happen John Birtles knew. All I know is, stars come out while sun sleeps. They dance around pole star like maids round maypole, only slower; they whisper; they happen make music; and God put pole star in sky so sailors can find their way at night. Some stars come out in winter and some in summer so folk know when to plough and sow and reap, but most are there all year round. It's bad luck to point at them, or at moon; but if you see one of them shoot across sky you can make a wish and happen it'll come true. I don't know nowt else about stars, or about what they say, if they say owt at all.

It were a while afore Master Birtles stopped talking to Harry and went off with Reynold Kyrk. Then Harry come up and muttered, 'Let's go home, Spiderlegs'. Looked like he'd never laugh again. We set off and Ottewell Higginbottom come running up behind us saying if Harry ever needed fighting men at his back he'd have them. Hadn't seen a lot of Higginbottom while we'd been scrapping. He'd kept out of road. Harry said nowt, so Higginbottom shut his gob and cleared off home to Marple.

Harry said nowt to me neither, not a word all road home, and I knew better nor ask. Every furlong we walked he looked up at wastes; what for, I don't know. Sometimes you'd see wild cat prowling up there, stalking grouse and hare through heather. Eagles would darken yon barren heights with their shrieks. Otters would sink in stagnant pools, sullen, scaring ducks. Golden plovers would cry 'Glory' in praise of God and warn sheep as were straying. But I saw nowt up yonder that afternoon only seven magpies in a field, and three ravens on a rock.

When we passed Hayfield and Thornsett, folk come out of their houses and stood in rain cheering, chanting Harry's name and cursing them as enclose commons. Harry strode straight on, ash staff in his fist, looking neither right nor left. I'd a job keeping up with him, but when I stepped in his footprints they felt warm. Watching him marching ahead of me calmed pain in my hip and drew me forwards. I could feel slap of his hand on my back again, hear his bagpipe playing a dance.

Road into Glossopdale east side of Coombes and Nab keeps shifting. There's that many folk fetching goods to market in Glossop and going home again, highest stretch of road gets worn out, and then they can't walk on it after it's rained; up to their knees in mud. So they walk at side of it instead and make a new road. Harry and me walked on a new piece of that sort coming back from Chinley that day. I minded how he'd wandered off road four year back, when he'd come over brow of Nab on St Alphege's Day on his way home.

We crossed yon track as went to ruin of St Mary Magdalene's Chapel over Charlesworth. Bill Goddard told tales about monks walking that track in Abbey times. Good tales, but happen not true. Monks had made road we all used out of Charlesworth through Simmondley and Whitfield down to Glossop; that were true enough; all old folk said it. But yon track under Coombes, I reckon they hadn't made that. Why would they? It weren't no use to nobody.

When we started walking down from top, sun come out and there were a rainbow right across Glossopdale, a bright arch stretching from over Mottram to out past Shirrell. They reckon rainbows have all colours of Joseph's coat. I wonder how old Jacob dyed yon coat for his favourite lad so it come out looking like a rainbow. Happen one of his four women did it for him, Leah or Rachel, Bilhah or Zilpah. Women are better nor us at jobs of that sort.

Sheffield Castle, Christmas Eve 1574

Dickenson had penned in his diary: 'In my beginning, God be my speed in grace and virtue.' Either that prayer or his wife's had been answered: his long illness had been lifted from him; and now that James Turner's soul had been called to Heaven, his appointment as Bailiff of Hallamshire had been made official. *Not before time.*

'Kath, help me check the gifts his honour commanded on the twentieth.'

Katherine squinted at the page. Her husband's writing was compact. Her fingers were numb. Outside, snow swirled on a famished easterly. The cold forced its way into the house and stabbed through the warmest raiment.

'Isabell Parker; Lawrence Bower; Old Butternodes; Old Smith's wife; Uxor Littlewood; the old woman at the park gate… Has the old woman at the park gate no name, William? Or Old Smith's wife either? Or Mistress Littlewood?'

'There's no need for names if the identity is clear. Thank you, Kath. I've already checked the gifts in Rotherham and Chesterfield, Winfield, Pomfrett…'

'They're small gifts.'

'Many received a pot of ale on the sixth of the month, and some a loaf of bread to ameliorate the privations of December. I trust they're all on their knees thanking God for granting them so kind a lord. Now: the Castle servants and their quarter's wages.'

Katherine squinted again. The entries formed pleasing shapes on the page, like ice crystals.

'Twenty shillings to William Harris; ten shillings to John Wise; eight shillings and fourpence to Richard Wilson, keeper of the Little Park; six shillings and eightpence to George Morris...'

Dickenson sighed. Would his honour's income over the past twelvemonth cover at least some of this annual extravagance, obligatory on all noble landlords? Katherine read on:

'The Sheffield households have paid thirteen pence for each swine admitted into the park to devour beech mast between the tenth of October and Martinmas. George Scargill has delivered a tithe of fifty-eight capons from Glossopdale. That seems like a lot of meat from a poor parish, William. Thirty of them have gone to Hawsworth, twenty to Milne, eight retained in Sheffield.'

'George has also paid the fifteen shillings and tuppence rent for his house in Crooks. Whatever we might say of George, he's honest.'

'In his dealings with you and his lordship, perhaps. Is he honest with the poor?'

'He's generous to the poor but keeps his generosity secret for fear of trouble. Common people can be trusted no more than foxes. Unlearned they might be, but they're proficient in evading duties. Above all, they're skilled at avoiding tithes and rents. If they learned that George takes more in tithe and rent from those who can afford it so he can take less from those who cannot, they'd riot. Let us go back to January.'

Katherine turned the pages again. 'Uxor Collins purchased more than three thousand lathnails from Parker, the first batch at twenty pence the hundred, the next at ten pence; the seventh batch at tuppence the hundred... I suppose Mistress Collins is a widow with money enough to build a new dwelling.'

Dickenson smiled. 'So it seems. But her new dwelling will be nothing like as grand as the house you shall have, Kath.'

During the summer, Dickenson had written: "The pain laid upon the inhabitants of the lordship of Balderstone touching the grinding at the lord's mill; these I duly looked into so that if the same by any of them happen to be forfeited, it may be levied and gathered; otherwise it may be a precedent unto them for their purpose to absent themselves hereafter and to be at their liberty, as they would be".

'I'll allow those miscreants until Lady Day to make good their debts,' he said. 'If they don't, then with his honour's consent I'll seize their assets, evict them from their holdings and put trusted tenants in their place. No good comes of leniency to commoners.'

'Some might deem your firmness harsh, William. Mr Scargill seems more flexible.'

'If they choose to complain when they're evicted, Nathaniel will hear their case in Manor Court. Let us continue with the year's income, Kath.'

'Oxen sold at Rotherham on the twentieth of November for fifty-seven shillings,' Katherine read, 'yielding tithes of five shillings and eightpence halfpenny per head... Twenty-seven stones of wool from Chapel parish, forty-two from Hope, thirty-four from Hartington, thirty-seven from Glossopdale; in total, fourteen stones in tithes to his lordship and *pro rata* for the vicars... I see you've persuaded his lordship to increase rents on some tenancies.'

'A small step forward.'

'Robert Priest now pays two shillings a year instead of twenty pence for his portion of Bell Hey. Thomas Smith and John Leyland pay twenty-six shillings instead of eleven shillings and eightpence per year – those are big rises, William.'

'They are not yet sufficient.'

*

The room in the castle assigned to Dickenson now boasted a chimney lined with good brick. It breathed in much of the smoke, exhaling it over the rooftops, and heat flowed from the fire like a benediction. His honour had been reluctant; several lords of the Privy Council had told him tales of poor bricks exploding in the heat and of unswept chimneys catching fire and burning houses to the ground. But having taken guidance from her ladyship's master mason, Robert Smythson, Nathaniel Eyre had persuaded him that the construction could and would be made safe. Grateful to both Eyre and Smythson, Dickenson set down his quill and rubbed his hands in front of the blazing logs.

The manor house in the Great Park would soon be ready to accommodate the Scottish Queen and her immoderate court. The unwashed masses believed Mary would live in the three-storey Turret House in the outer court, though anyone but a fool could see it was too small for her retinue and could never be made secure. The Turret House would be a gatehouse and would serve as his honour's hunting lodge. It had been costly to build, but thanks to Hallamshire's best masons the work had been done well; well enough for Dickenson to decide that he too would engage the Rhodes brothers for building his town house. And he'd insist they install a chimney.

'*Her majesty's orders concerning Mary's custody are being obeyed,*' he mused, '*but the Crown still provides too little. Far too little.*'

He left the fire and returned to his records. In four woods at Totley there were nine hundred and sixty-eight oaks fit for harvesting, and one ash. Richard Ladd had paid forty-five shillings and sixpence for nineteen and a half stones of tallow at two shillings and threepence per stone delivered on the twenty-first of October. There were sales of steel from the Sheffield store-room. The Attercliffe mills owed money for iron to the furnaces of Kimberworth and Wadsley. His own small holding beyond Attercliffe had six mature oaks, also ripe for harvesting.

Eyre entered and strode to the fire.

'Cold as a witch's quim! Ho, my hands welcome this warmth, William! You've read Lord Leicester's letter to his honour?'

'The one reassuring him about her majesty's health and suggesting that her relationship with her cousin had been somewhat restored; or the more recent one about the Queen's proposed marriage to the duke of Alençon?'

Eyre chuckled.

'Trust you to be abreast of correspondence. Relationship with Mary restored? Pah! Where's the trust? Who'd trust this Catholic Queen of Scots, least of all her majesty, whose skill in mental alchemy amalgamates perception with suspicion? No, I meant the Alençon proposal. Lord Leicester's right: unpopular union. Valois of Alençon was up to his neck in the Bartholomew Day atrocity.'

'You believe Alençon's unpopularity is Lord Leicester's only objection to the proposed royal marriage?'

Both men laughed.

'We mustn't ask, William. But it would be one more matter to preoccupy his honour as earl martial: he'd have to arrange the wedding. I hear that ambassadors have come to Court from both King Henri and Alençon. Uncomfortable timing: the Prince of Orange has sent an ambassador offering the Queen sovereignty over the Low Countries.'

Lord Leicester had also assured Lord Shrewsbury that his investment in the Muscovy Company adventure would yield a satisfactory return. Dickenson would never doubt a nobleman's word, but he'd believe in profit from a maritime adventure when he saw it.

'Silver lining in the clouds,' said Eyre. 'Thanks to these several distractions, his honour has yielded to your persuasion. Rents on some tenancies have been increased. Tenants in Peak Forest are complaining about it.'

Dickenson knew about those complaints. Lord Shrewsbury had not only raised the rents in Peak Forest, he'd also imposed manorial pre-emption on lead ore sales at less than the free market price established at Wirksworth Wappentake. Moreover, he'd forced enclosures around the village. The tenants had protested to the Duchy Court about the rent rises and pre-emption, obtained no satisfaction, and carried their complaint to the Court of Chancery. The Peak Forest bailiff and barmasters declared that the tenants had grown so rebellious they could no longer impose the earl's will. Enclosures had been attacked and even torn down.

'Those commoners will achieve nothing at Chancery except to waste court time. But they'd never have taken the matter so far if someone hadn't provoked them. One wonders who might have done so.'

'Litigation's become a pastime for all.' Eyre shook his head. 'At any moment, one man in five in England is entangled with the law. The common rabble is a many-headed monster, always apt to rebel. Only the law can regulate it. Our monarch is the wellspring of the law and her authority comes from God.'

'Perhaps, Nathaniel, but in the case of Peak Forest —'

'Also, there are more people living in England than in our fathers' time. Goods are scarce, prices rise, people demand credit, more interests in land are sold. People eschew verbal agreements about finance, property, sales; they go to court instead. They sue when deals go wrong. Church Courts hear more defamation cases. There are more common law slander actions. Neighbours sue each other for verbal slights; particularly women. All trivial matters. Continual irritations. Even you, William, demand further regulations on our cutlers.'

'Those regulations are needed, Nathaniel.'

As Eyre summoned wine, George Scargill lurched into the room. Snow cascaded from his rabbit-fur garb.

'God save you, George. William wonders who might have provoked the Peak Forest tenants.'

Scargill eyed the wine cups. None had been offered to him.

'I can only guess, Mr Eyre.'

Dickenson felt his mind forge a connection.

'Three or four years ago, George, you entered my house with tidings of a newly-granted leasehold in Glossopdale.'

Scargill's feet shifted, seeking either to stir or to inter a recollection.

'What's that to do with Peak Forest?' demanded Eyre.

'A cup of wine might lubricate George's memory, Nathaniel.'

Scargill drank like a man dying of thirst.

'You mean Botham.' He made to spit but thought better of it. 'I've eyes and ears on the bastard. Give him rope, William. He'll hang himself.'

'Botham!' Eyre grinned. 'Don't let his honour hear that miscreant name! What has Botham to do with Peak Forest?'

'This is old Botham's son, Mr Eyre. In service at Castleton and Peak Forest during the '60s. Led a mob that tore down his lordship's enclosure in Peak Forest and injured my cousin, who was trying to defend it. Complained about security of tenancy, fines, subletting, tithes, pushing tenants into central farms... Same in Ashford, I'm told. Everyone in those villages knows the villain. Alas, some of them trust him.'

'Is there evidence he's a recusant or favours recusancy?' asked Dickenson.

'Or speaks ill of the Queen?' added Eyre. 'Or of his honour?

'No.' Scargill's voice grudged the constraint of honesty. 'He talks and acts like a man loyal to church, Crown and liege lord. Yet he could teach the Devil how to brew trouble. Complains about fines, subletting, breaches of custom…'

'Has he committed an offence that should be brought before a court?' asked Eyre.

'Or threatened such offence?' added Dickenson.

'Some say he caused the death of one Richard Shuttleworth in '70 or '71, but the testimonies prove he was provoked into fighting. And Shuttleworth died two weeks after, not at the time.'

'That's nothing.' Eyre shook his head. 'This young knave might complain and stir discontent, but he can't be the demon his father was. How's he offended you, George? By wrecking enclosures and injuring your cousin?'

Scargill stuttered and spilled wine.

'It offends me that Botham has leasehold. He offends me by living. By breathing.'

'That doesn't make a case in law, George,' said Dickenson. 'However… Nathaniel, did you hear what befell in Chinley this past April or May? A mob beat down enclosures and assaulted the constables. The bailiff fled for his life. I'm told the Chinley tenants made up scarcely a quarter of that mob. The rest came from other villages: Castleton, Peak Forest… perhaps Glossopdale. Might we see a pattern?'

'Patterns aren't evidence.' Eyre scowled. 'But enclosures bring trouble. The so-called Pilgrimage of Grace back in '36 was as much about enclosures as fools hankering after the Bishop of Rome. Although —'

'Although it was almost enough to unseat the king and put a Plantagenate Papist back on the throne, so my father told me,' said Dickenson. 'It happened before I was born, of course. I believe his lordship's father led an army that helped suppress the rebellion, and that Sheffield remained quiet thanks to his leadership; and so did Derbyshire.'

'Same leadership kept Derbyshire quiet in '49, too.' Eyre frowned again. 'The rebellion in '36 was driven by nobles and gentry. The "commotion time" troubles that afflicted most of the country in '49 were led by commoners, no higher than yeoman class. We've had few if any commoner-led riots since then, save some feeble stirrings in '51; but I wonder whether these events in Peak Forest and Ashbourne could herald a new "commotion time". That is a disturbing prospect.'

'Surely,' said Dickenson, 'unless they're led by nobles or gentlemen, commoners only protest when they suppose their livelihood or prosperity to be at risk.'

'Hmm. Some events in '49 were driven mostly by the slow advance of the reformed faith and bad local government. Kett's rebellion in Kent, for instance. In other places the rebels wanted a return to Papism. That was what happened in Yorkshire despite the memories of '36. But enclosures were a source of many complaints. All the riots that arose from it were commoner-led, and many of them demanded a voice for the common people in local government. William Cavendish had enclosed a hundred and twenty acres of common in Northaw by '44 and he was still enclosing. No consideration for his tenants. Small wonder they rebelled in '48 and '49. The troubles spread from there over most of England.'

Scargill glanced from one of his companions to the other, biting his lip.

'One wonders, Nathaniel, whether the late Sir William's family might stir up trouble again.' Dickenson smirked. 'Master Booth the bailiff believes it was Botham who chased him out of Chinley with a knife. He isn't certain; but he *is* sure that the conjurer John Birtles was in the village. There's a villain whose dealings with the Devil should hang him. If Botham were linked to Birtles –'

'Can he be?' asked Eyre.

'I've heard no evidence.'

'Evidence enough for me!' roared Scargill. 'Botham should be evicted from his holding! And if he's had dealings with Birtles he should hang beside him!' He grinned. 'I'll tie the noose. Or roast him alive, and castrate him, and rip his guts out –'

'Not all at once, George, and not without due process.' Dickenson finished his wine and rose from his seat. 'When are Glossopdale's leases due for renewal?'

Scargill shifted his feet again.

'Some of them three years hence, Michaelmas '78. The others... date isn't clear.'

Eyre's eyes widened.

'Date not clear? How can that be? William, can such a thing –?'

'I can't answer you without studying past years' accounts, Nathaniel. They were Mr Sutton's accounts so I'd need his honour's consent. But Michelmas 1578… If Botham seeks to stir trouble in Glossopdale it will be then. Plan how best to act, George. Within the law. We might yet need to apprise his honour of our disquiet.'

Servants were bringing greenery into the Castle to celebrate the end of Advent, the continuation of life beyond winter. On the morrow, after the Christmas Eve fast, twelve days of feasting and merrymaking would begin. Dickenson would encourage feasting in his own household, but no merrymaking would intrude on his responsibilities. Duty to God and Lord Shrewsbury would always take precedence over revelry.

Glossopdale, Christmas Eve – 6th January 1574/5

Daylight were finishing when we come out of church. Twilight air were lying in wait, bitter and starving. It pounced on us, weasel teeth biting noses and throats. Pain in my hip had me gnawing my finger so I didn't moan. I couldn't feel my hands or feet. And I were proper hungry, same as we all were with fasting every Friday and Saturday through Advent like Godfearing Christians should. I said nowt. Like Ma told us: if you're that hungry, you can go and live on window and chew daylight. Skins off sheep we'd slaughtered kept us a bit warmer a-nights, them as we hadn't took to market and selled for tenpence each, but they didn't stop hunger even when you chewed them; and you could still lie abed and watch snowflakes grow in your rafters and fall on you. Women got short of milk and their babbies died. Old folk died. Even younger ones as couldn't manage two day fasting every week. Never rains but it pours.

Sunset dyed everything red and purple – snow, icicles, branches – colours of noblemen's cloaks and doublets. I thought, 'Aye, God's made a lovely world when you've done and said all, no matter what evil Devil puts in it.' Happen that were why He chose to have His only son born of woman in middle of winter, when world's at its darkest, after corn's been planted at new moon, and old sheep and beasts have been slaughtered for scraps of salt meat, and folk mend walls and ditches if stones and laths aren't frozen to ground. It's Our Lord's birth lets us see how grand a world he's give us, for all there's pain and suffering in it.

'What do you reckon to him?' said Reggie Harrop.

'Who?' Hugh Platt drooled.

73

'New vicar, you addlepate,' said Reggie. 'Master George Yeaverley.'

'Not a lot, Reggie.' That were Bob Wolstenholme. 'Puritan, only he won't admit it. Says he doesn't want your shawm or Henry's fiddle played in church. Wants psalms chanted instead of hymns sung. Happen he'll be happy with this new Archbishop as is coming in next year. They reckon he's easier on Puritans nor Lord Parker's been.'

I thought vicar's sermon had been right enough. 'Use measure in all things,' he'd said. 'Don't be a niggard and don't be too liberal. Give to the needy but only according to your ability. Live within your own compass and seal up secrets in your heart, so you don't say what could hurt somebody. Don't take friends for enemies or enemies for friends. Let your mind rule your tongue.' Good sense, I reckoned.

Road were all ice, crackling underfoot like dry bones. You had to mind you didn't fall and happen break a limb. Nippers jumped on it and laughed. They were carrying rag dolls and suchlike, learning how they'd take care of their own nippers when they had them.

'Happen you're right, Bob,' I said. 'He told old Maggie there weren't going to be no more St Mark's Eve vigil because it's Papist. I couldn't make no sense of that. What's Papist about knowing who's going to die in next twelvemonth? And how'll we know if Maggie doesn't keep vigil and tell us?'

Everybody muttered, 'Aye, that's right'; and then we all went quiet for a minute, remembering. Rose Birtlebank were drowned washing linen a few month back. Old Maggie floated a loaf with quicksilver down brook, and it stopped and spun where Rose's body were, so we found her and got her buried. She'd have come to surface after nine days, same as drowned folk always do, but it were best to get her out sooner. Rose's brother were drowned a fortnight after; he were shitting in a ditch and fell in. Roger Bishop drowned taking oats to mill; clothes got soaked crossing ford. Tom Goddard, storyteller Bill's dad, cut his arm on his scythe and it went bad; so *he* died. Margery Hill went with a fever. Maggie had Seen them all last St Mark's Eve: Rose and her brother, and Roger, and Tom, and Margery. Master Yeaverley reckoned she shouldn't have Seen none of them.

He'd telled her and Agnes other daft-like stuff and all, like how curing folks's ills were Devil's work: plucking tansy at end of Lent to cure worms, and giving willow bark for pains, and comfrey for breaks and bruises, and all rest of what they do. I suppose vicar knows better nor me, but Our Lord give comfort to sick folk when He were here on Earth, so it were God's work then; and if were God's work then, why is it Devil's work now? Anyroad, I don't like nobody calling Agnes bad, not even a vicar.

Then Black Harry spoke.

'If Master Yeaverley were Puritan, Bob, he'd be threatening hellfire on Mistress Elizabeth Bower for killing her husband.'

'We don't know she did owt of sort, Harry,' said Reggie. 'Reverend Bower fell down his well. Nobody saw him pushed.'

It were getting dark; only sky over Mottram way were still red. There were a holly tree with bright berries where we were walking, but berries had turned black with sun going down, and leaves and all. Same as I've said, night falls in trees afore anywhere else. There were a crow sat on a dead oak next to holly. I were shivering and my hip felt like a dog were worrying it.

'Happen not,' said Harry, 'but there's plenty heard them yelling death and damnation at one another afore he died. Mistress Elizabeth wouldn't forget how he'd set her aside while Bloody Mary were Queen, and wouldn't take her back 'til he knew Elizabeth were reformed faith. So any damned Puritan would reckon she'd killed him, Reggie. And a Puritan wouldn't keep his gob shut about it neither. So no, Bob, I don't reckon Master Yeaverley's Puritan.'

A few folk laughed. Harry could make you believe black were white if he'd a mind to it, but happen Bob were right about Master Yeaverley. Then Phil Woolley said we should rejoice and praise God for sending us a good new vicar as weren't tainted with stink of Papism, and Harry wanted to mind what he said about him.

'I said I don't reckon he's Puritan, Phil. What's bad about that?'

'You said he didn't threaten Mistress Bower with fires of Hell like he should have,' said Phil. 'I reckon he wants us to forgive one another's trespasses and hope Our Lord will forgive ours. If vicar starts blaming

75

us for sins folk reckon we've committed when we haven't, what's he bound to say about them as we *have* committed? Like what will he say to you, Harry, for stirring up enclosure riots in Chinley and rent riots in Peak Forest? And what will God say to you about them doings on Judgement Day?'

I thought Harry were bound to break Phil's head, but God be thanked he didn't so much as raise his voice.

'Them riots were stirred up anyroad, Phil,' he said. 'All I did were point Chinley lads and Peak Forest lads to right road for getting what they wanted.'

Harry had done a lot more in Chinley nor point right road, but nobody said nowt, not even Phil. But I reckon they were all wondering about him sending his Peak Forest friends to Duchy Court. I knew more about that nor they did. When I'd finally asked Harry about rents in Glossopdale and whether what Willie had told me were right, he'd said: 'Aye, there'll be trouble here, Spiderlegs. His lordship's put rents up in Peak Forest and folk are struggling to pay. He'll do it here, happen worse if that bastard Scargill gets his road. Bailiff will do what Scargill tells him.'

'Happen rents *will* go up, Harry; but Lord Shrewsbury's landlord. There's nowt we can do only pay what bailiff tells us. That's road God made this world.'

His mouth did a sideways shift, only he weren't smiling.

'Let's see what Duchy Court says about Peak Forest. I've telled them lads if Duchy Court doesn't do them no good, they should get to London, to Chancery Court; and if that doesn't do no good neither, they should go and tell Queen's chief minister and get *him* to do summat.'

I'd have thought he were joking, or happen dreaming, but Harry were never a dreamer, not even when we were kids. Unless them ghosts we saw up on wastes were dreams.

'Queen's chief minister?'

'Aye, Spiderlegs. Lord Burghley, he's called. Think about it. Lord Shrewsbury's earl martial of England. That means nobody's above him only her majesty, and there's nobody above her only God. So there's only Queen or God can do owt about complaints against Lord Shrewsbury and his agent, and you can only complain to Queen through

76

her chief minister. Happen rest of Privy Council will hear about it and all, but mostly it's Lord Burghley.'

'Privy Council? I've heard of that, Harry. What is it?'

Harry slapped my back. 'Top nobles and gentry, makes sure other lordships and us folk lower down does what Queen says. Anyroad, Spiderlegs, we'll see how them Peak Forest lads get on. Then happen we'll know what to do when *our* rents get raised.'

'When tenancies are up for renewal, like, in '78?'

'Happen afore.'

I thought about it.

'Aye, Harry,' I said, 'you'll want everybody in Glossopdale on your side if rents change. I reckon that's why you didn't beat shit out of Phil for what he said when we left church. You don't want no enemies in Glossopdale,'specially not in Simmondley.'

Harry did have enemies in Glossopdale, though he'd more friends. Seemed he were well liked in Peak Forest and all. And Castleton. And Chinley. And happen Hayfield, and other places beside.

He give a bit of a laugh.

'Like vicar said, Spiderlegs: don't take friends for enemies. And happen we should make friends of them as *wants* to be enemies.' Even in dark I could see him grin and wink. 'We'll have best Christmas feast ever at Storth this year. Can't have our Mary and Ottie over, or our Kathy and Olly; they're keeping Christmas together in Glossop. But Reggie and Martha will be with us, and we'll have William and Lizzie Newton from Heath and all. They're bringing as much good food and drink and fruit and spices with them as I reckon Lord and Lady Shrewsbury will have.'

It were a minute afore I could say owt.

'Newton? William Newton? You and him can't stand sight of one another! And Alice and Ma reckon nowt to his wife. What –?'

'Joanne got on with William and Lizzie while she were in service, so I asked them for her, and they said Aye. His cousin won't come, mind.' Harry's mouth did its sideways shift again. 'Doing like vicar says, Spiderlegs; and we'll have best Christmas feast in Glossopdale because of it.'

I couldn't say nowt else. This were last fasting day, then Advent would be done, and when sun woke in morning it would be Christmas. Then we'd have twelve day of rest and being less hungry. But whether we'd get through Christmas Day without bloodshed, what with Harry beside yon Newton, and Ma and Alice beside his wife, that were another matter.

*

We'd all fetched greenery to Storth. I'd woven birch and hazel crown; Harry and Willie and Reggie threaded holly and ivy through it. Like yon Newton said, it were only time of year you could cut holly without bringing bad luck. Nippers ran around, chasing one another and laughing.

'More holly nor ivy in Storth, right enough,' said Reggie to his wife, thinking I couldn't hear him. 'Be other road round at Cloud.'

Martha give him a nudge to shut him up, and I shouted, 'If you think Alice's boss of Willie, Reggie Harrop, you can think again!' Reggie said it were nobbut a joke. Joanna stood with her fists on her hips staring at him like a bear-baiting dog, but she give me a nod and went back to work. I didn't say nowt else because we were making merry, like.

We'd killed pig between us afore last full moon so meat would swell in pot; made brushes of its bristles, greased ploughs and scythes with its fat. Now women were getting its head ready for feast. Ma's fingers were stiff, for all Maggie and Agnes brewed herbs for her, so she told Joanna and Alice and Martha how to get skull out, stuff skin with chopped meat to get it back in shape, and sew it up and pickle it in vinegar with bay and mustard seed. They did it right; folk do what Ma says or they get an earful. Lizzie Newton were standing watching, doing nowt, so Ma looked her up and down and told her to go and look after nippers. She went.

'Mistress Newton's good at heart, Ma,' said Joanna. 'It's her as give us raisins. Harry wouldn't let me buy none. Cost too much.'

Alice snorted. 'Aye, and you said nowt back to him. What do we want for fire under stone, Ma, oak or beech?'

I couldn't reckon up why Alice talked nasty to Joanna, but Harry said Jo had another babby in her belly so Alice were jealous. Happen Willie needed some of Old Maggie's cow parsnip wine.

'Beech'll do,' said Ma. 'Ash, come to that. Need to keep pig's head boiling between noon and sunset but you don't need slow cooking. Have you got pudding done?'

It were only frummity, yon pudding, but with a bit of ginger put in while milk and wheat were boiling, and some nutmeg and cinnamon as yon Newton had fetched with him, and bits of dried apples and plum and all, your mouth watered. Ale posset were last thing we drunk on Christmas Eve, frummity first thing we'd eat on Christmas Morning. Joanna had made shred pies with what she reckoned were eight sorts of fruit, four different spices and a few scraps of mutton. Ma had taught her pastry-making when she were a girl, but she'd never had that much fruit and spices afore for making shred pies. None of us had. Harry were right; Newton had spent a lot for Christmas feasting.

Anyroad: Christmas Morning, we put candle out as had burned all night to welcome Our Lord, then over to church for mass three hour after bell. Then it were all eating and drinking, only everybody in Simmondley wanted Harry to come into their house first because of his black hair. He promised Newton he'd be first through door at Heath and all. Women went out to kitchen and it weren't long afore stone were hot enough to take fire out so they could set pies to cook, while Harry and Willie and Reggie and me and yon Newton went and played nine men's morris in Jacob's alehouse. Harry won three groat off me. It were a lot more of a surprise when Newton won two shilling off Harry. I'd never seen nobody beat Harry afore, and Newton didn't look like he were that clever at nine men's morris.

It were bitter cold but Jacob's ale warmed us, and when we come down to Storth again, pig's head were decorated and on table, and we all got us pottage, and then pork and ham, and then pies and fruit. Them pies were best I'd ever ate. Then Harry brought cheese out and bread with it. It were always a good do at Christmas, unless harvest were bad and we hadn't enough fruit and flowers to put in church to thank God for His blessings, but we'd never had a Christmas feast this grand afore.

When platters were cleared and logs blazing in middle of floor, Bill Goddard told some of his stories of giants and fairy folk, like that one about Joe Sheldon finding a magic fife inside yon stone circle. Then Harry got his pipes out, and Reggie fetched his shawm; and Tom Blood come down to Storth, and him and Alice sang, one an echoing cave and one a mountain clough, and we all joined in.

> *Robin Hood, he dressed him in shepherd's attire,*
> *Derry, derry, down!*
> *And six of his men also,*
> *And, when the Bishop he did come by,*
> *They around the fire did go.*
> *Derry down! Hey! Derry, derry, down!*
>
> *'We are but poor shepherds' quoth bold Robin Hood,*
> *Derry, derry, down!*
> *'And keep sheep all the year,*
> *But we've resolved to taste to-day*
> *Of the best of our King's deer.'*
> *Derry down! Hey! Derry, derry, down!*

Even Alice and Joanna were all right with one another, and Ma talked to Lizzie Newton without slapping her. Harry and yon Newton sat with their heads together, muttering: Newton asked questions, and Harry said summat about only wanting fair rents for everybody; Newton asked summat else, and Harry said if rents were doubled it would be right enough as long as everybody got treated same; and then he asked whether Newton had heard owt. I tried listening to more of their talk but I couldn't make nowt of it. Alice held little Edmund in her arms and played with older nippers and kept them happy, and I reckoned it were right what breeze had told me: she needed a nipper of her own. Then it were dark, and churchwarden's bell sounded; and Harry said it were time to cover fire, because you can't take ashes out while seventh day of Christmas. Rest of us tumbled home under a moon like blazing frost, and we slept.

There's not a lot gets done over twelve days of Christmas. Beasts and sheep as haven't been killed need feeding, but that's about all. We made merry: St Stephen's Day, St John's Day, Childermas, St Thomas Becket's Day, and all rest. We could play games in public on seventh day but it were mostly archery. We set butts up topside Charlesworth and this time I beat John Stedman, and he didn't have no excuse for his last shot because there weren't no wind. I telled him he'd lost his touch since he'd married Rose and put a babby in her belly, and we punched one another and had a laugh and went for a drink.

I always reckoned it were funny welcoming New Year on first day of January, not waiting 'til Lady Day, but that's road it were. Women made wassail cakes with first egg a young goose had laid, like they always do on seventh day. They reckon sheep and beasts kneel and pray on sixth night but I've never heard them.

Twelfth Night were best fun. Old Tom Jackson got pea in his piece of twelfth night cake so we put paper crown as Reggie's Martha had made on his head, and we played egg-catching, and old Tom took us wassailing from house to house round Glossopdale. Got around fine, old Tom, for all his long years. Tom Blood and our Alice led us singing Coventry Carol, and In Dulce Jubilo, and Ding Dong Merrily, and we wished everybody *May you live as long as you want to, and want to as long as you live, by God's good grace and mercy.* We got food and drink for our singing from them as could spare it; plenty of it off Newton and his cousin. Happen Newton weren't as bad as some of us had reckoned.

Then twelve days were done. After next Sabbath it were Plough Monday; back to work for us all, only for youth race other side Buxton as were good fun every year.

I thought about Mr Yeaverley. We hadn't seen nowt of him while we were merrymaking, so I reckoned Harry were wrong and Bob were right: he were a Puritan. And then he proved it. All them pictures on church walls as had been there time out of memory of man – Eve and serpent, Moses crossing Red Sea, Our Lord getting baptised and then crucified and then sitting in judgement on Last Day – they'd gone. All of them. Vicar had made churchwarden whitewash over top of them.

Made me sad, that did. Made most of Glossopdale sad. Them pictures had spoke to us and to our fathers and grandfathers, and to their fathers and all, and now they couldn't speak no more.

Sheffield Castle, October 1575

Dickenson summarised the accounts. Eyre cursed.

'So his honour was obliged to spend three hundred pounds on French wine, damask, fine linen, live quails, writing paper and sweets for the Scottish Queen? While his own second son received only the poorest furnishings and hangings for his castle, and the cheapest of linen cloth?'

'Men of our station can be prudent, Nathaniel. Noblemen can't. And I thank God for blessing me with a thrifty wife.' *Will Nathaniel suppose I'm criticising the countess again?* 'However, Lady Shrewsbury mitigated his honour's parsimony. She provided Master Gilbert and Mistress Mary with bed, hangings and tapestries from Chatsworth. In any case, Master Gilbert worried more about his father's illnesses than the furnishings of Goodrich Castle.'

And not only his illnesses; Dickenson believed Gilbert Talbot to be no less concerned about the earl's workload, his cash crisis and his unprecedented truculence. His honour had become irascible, acknowledging no opinion but his own. The countess also seemed worried, though her husband's correspondence (such as Dickenson had seen) voiced unwavering affection. According to one servant, when she asked the earl what was amiss with him, he said he'd eaten too many herrings.

The clamorous people of Peak Forest had angered Lord Shrewsbury by daring to protest in Duchy Court and then in Chancery against his "great extortions". Two poor fellows from the village had gone so far as to complain to Lord Burghley's clerk. Master Gilbert had sent them home and reported their impertinence to Derbyshire's Justices of the

Peace. *If the instigator if those protests were identified*, mused Dickenson, *this canker could be severed from the flesh of the Peak manors*. Yet he insisted they remain patient until the Glossopdale leases fell due for renewal. To ensure the best outcome, his honour should be informed little by little, with careful timing.

Dickenson had seen letters in which the earl advocated marriage between Lord Burghley's daughter Elizabeth and Lord Edward Talbot. Burghley had thanked Lord Shrewsbury for the honour but could not consent: Elizabeth was still a child, and a proposed marriage with the earl's family might aggravate her majesty's suspicions about his friendship with the Scottish Queen. *Those letters*, thought Dickenson, *reveal Lord Burghley to be a diplomat, but they cast doubt on his honour's judgement.* He voiced his anxiety to Eyre.

'Sudden impairment eight months ago, William; twenty-sixth of February; day of the earthquake.' Eyre grinned. 'Earth shook, buildings shook; Scottish Queen feared the Devil was visiting. Perhaps his honour feared the same, though had the Devil appeared it would surely have been to bear Mary's soul to Hell, to the benefit of all England, and perhaps Scotland also. Yet a month later he supervised his grandson's birth and christened the child himself. His judgement's altered, but it isn't lost.'

The times confuse everyone, especially great nobles, Dickenson reflected. *Her majesty appoints a new Archbishop of Canterbury who favours the Puritans, yet she dislikes the Puritan cause and grants a monopoly of music publishing to two confessed Papists.*

'Full replenishment of his honour's purse could answer our prayers for full restoration of his wits, Nathaniel.'

*

Dickenson recorded receipt of a waif, a small grey horse, from Nicholas Clarke of Chesterfield. He put it into the Little Park. He returned home to his wife and sons and lodgers; then he walked to the site of his new house, next to Mistress Braye's residence below the market cross. His diary recorded every detail of the construction: thirty-five shillings to John Rondsley for slate stone; twenty shillings to his honour for use of said stone, and four pounds for eight trees; five pounds to John and Christopher Rhodes for masonry work; sixteen shillings to Master West for seven trees "given to my wife"; eight shillings to Duke the glazier; four shillings and eightpence to Thomas Leyton and his brother for seven days' work, and ten shillings for their meat; two shillings and fourpence board wages for the workmen posting the timbers for the house; eight shillings to Robert Hill for four thousand lathnails; thirty-seven shillings and fourpence for fifty-six loads of stone, two persons for every load at fourpence each for meat; fourpence per day for the wallers; fourpence per day for the plasterers, and the same again for meat; sevenpence per day for daubers, and the same again for meat; orders for bolt and bar, window with glass two yards broad and four feet high, doors for the parlour and the privy off the parlour; and "fifty-one shillings paid to my wife for the board wages of the work folks". He was convinced that progress would cease unless he came every day to supervise the work.

'Our new house shall be all you wish,' he told Katherine. 'You will be far enough from castle and rivers to be troubled by neither, but close to wells and market. I shall be as near the cutlers' shops as the castle. There will be stabling for my horses so I can ride without delay when my duties take me from town.'

'William, why do your duties so often take you far from home? Of course you must collect rents in Hallamshire and you must regulate the cutlers, but his lordship's other manors have their own bailiffs.'

'Since Thomas Morgan was sent away I've been the earl's secretary, Kath, and he's accorded me the honour of overseeing the accounts of manors from Rotherham and Barnsley to the High Peak holdings as far south as Ashford, which is her ladyship's. There are rents, fines and tithes to collect, but also wills to witness and revenues from lead to record.' Dickenson kissed his wife. 'I'm well paid for those labours, despite the condition of his honour's purse, and every penny goes to our home and family.' He patted the locked chest. 'You'll have the finest house in Sheffield outside his honour's own estate.'

Glossopdale, October-November 1575

Ma said when earth shook a few month back, and dogs howled and buckets fell over, it were a sign trouble were coming. Vicar said same. And right enough, trouble come.

Harry had been off again more nor a fortnight, and still none of us knew where. He weren't even back home for tharf-cake joining. Joanna said he never telled her nowt unless he wanted to. 'Aye,' I said, 'me and all.' She'd had new babby back in June, but it were nobbut a girl and it died three day after it were christened. I can't mind what name they'd give it. Joanna skriked, like women do when God takes their babbies, but she were right again in a week. And then there were Malachi and Coney Lomas. Like I said, trouble. Never rains but it pours.

Harry come back to Simmondley on St Luke's Day, north-west wind flinging sleet in his face. As soon as he were home he called everybody in tithing to Jacob's alehouse. We were all busy, same as we always are: mixing tallow, pitch and tar to keep filth and scab off ewes, arguing about who could put their ewes to which tup, Joanna wanting first use of our ram for Storth sheep. Alice were moaning about tripe-wives in Chapel wanting fivepence a pound for tallow. But Black Harry had summat to tell us so we all stopped what we were doing and went to Jacob's to hear what it were.

'First off,' he said, 'Lads from Peak Forest got nowt out of Duchy Court or Chancery Court, so I telled them to go and see Queen's chief minister. They got their complaint wrote down and give it chief minister's clerk. Then his lordship's son, what's his name, Master Gilbert, telled them to go home. And they just went, daft beggars.

Whether they'll get owt off chief minister I don't know. Pray God they do.'

I didn't know nobody in Peak Forest. Bill told us there's a farm there where two sisters lived. They wanted same man, so younger one killed older one, and older one's bones wouldn't rest in her grave, so they put them in a cheese vat next to window. Them bones protect house and farm. Nobody dares to bury them because farm gets a lot of bother if they do. I reckon Peak Forest sounds a funny sort of place.

'None of that's nowt to do with us, Harry,' Phil Woolley said. Sometimes you can't hardly hear what Phil's saying, his chest's that bad. 'Peak Forest business isn't Glossopdale business. We'll pray for them as went to London, but –'

'Shake your brains up, Phil. Same landlord. Rents go up in one manor, they go up in another. Peak Forest's fight is our fight.'

'Same as Chinley's fight, Harry?' Reggie grinned like he'd got one up on Black Harry.

'No, Reggie. Different.' Harry sunk his ale and held his pot out for more. 'In Chinley it were all about enclosures making poor folk poorer. Needed fighting or we'd get more of it. Peak Forest is more about rents. Anyroad, second thing…'

'Owt worth making us stop greasing our ewes for?' said Bob Wolstenholme.

'You'll happen think so, Bob. Justices of peace have wrote summat to his lordship about his *clamorous and uncivil tenants*. They don't only mean Peak Forest tenants; they mean us and all. I reckon his lordship will use yon justices' letter to wind Scargill up.'

'Scargill doesn't need no winding up,' said Old Harry. 'But you're right, lad, owt justices write about us will make him worse.'

'Aye, Dad. Third thing…' Black Harry swigged his next pot of ale and grinned. 'His lordship's got enemies. Sir John de Zouche: castle at Codnor, down near Heanor. He were High Sheriff of Derbyshire four year back. He were asked to help his lordship with jailing that Papist Queen of Scots bitch in '69 or '70 when his lordship were poorly. He did summat his lordship didn't like; I don't know what it were, but seemingly they'd a right set-to. His lordship says Sir John's a bother-causer as steals public funds –'

'What's it matter to us, gentry fighting gentry?' said Bob.

Old Tom Jackson spoke. He'd never liked Bothams, but what Harry had done in Chinley had happen altered his mind.

'Never heard folk say, "My enemy's enemy is my friend", Bob? If we're arguing with his lordship and Scargill, and happen Mr Booth and all for being bailiff, this Sir John might be *our* friend. Pray God such a man will help us in our need. Seen owt of him yourself, Harry?'

'Talked to his man of business. You're right, Tom. He might do good for us one of these days.'

Harry were pleased with himself, but we'd news for him and all.

'Heard owt about Malachi and Coney, Harry?'

'I've been out of Glossopdale nigh on three week, Spiderlegs. What's up with them?'

Everybody started telling him, making stuff up as weren't right, 'til Jacob yelled at them to shut up and told it like it were.

'Coney's expecting. Malachi says it's rabbits, and she's bore rabbits afore.'

'That's a turn-up, Jacob,' said Harry. 'Who's father? I mean, who'd want to tup Coney? *Were* it a rabbit?'

'Happen only one answer, Harry,' said Jacob.

*

All Simmondley and a lot from other tithings were at Manor Court that Michelmas whether they'd suit due or not. We reckoned Simmondley frankpledge included Herod, and it weren't no use Reggie saying nobody had took no notice of frankpledge since his granddad's time. Right enough, folk didn't take no notice, like they took no notice of Forest Law. But Forest Master and Surveyor-General could still have you up in Exchequer Court for this or that if they'd a mind, like not cutting your dog's claws off; and you could still be had up at Manor or Duchy Court for not keeping frankpledge to uphold law in your tithing, or for not throwing crows' nests down at start of breeding time. Didn't happen much, but it could.

Anyroad, jury of twelve leaseholders gathered, and Mr Yeaveley led us in prayer afore steward started to hear from constables and other folk as had a beef about summat. Usual stuff, mostly: John and Rose Stedman were fined a groat for turning a common way past their holding; Nick Mellor got his usual shilling fine for outcry against law; Ted Shaw were done for making a laystall on highway and ordered, 'Clear that shit off road afore next Sabbath'; a woman from Padfield got fined tuppence for eavesdropping and carrying tales; keeper of Glossop alehouse were ordered to half a day in stocks for letting folk play ninepins (stupid, that, living a few yard from bailiff's house); Edmund Bower denied what Tom Dewsnap and new constable, Humphrey Andrew, had said about him stealing pigeons at night and failing to clear a ditch at side of his holding, or killing leverets in snow with dog or bitch. Jury didn't have no argument with most of it. We all knew Ted Shaw were a beggar for dumping shit on road, and Edmund were forever getting pigeons at night. But then they got to Coney.

'The constables say you're with child, Mistress Lomas,' said steward. He could look like a lord, could Mr Eyre, dressed in fine clothes with fur trims and big white ruff. I were a bit scared of him. 'Is this so?'

Coney made noise like she usually did; might have meant owt. Mr Eyre rolled his eyes.

'Who'll speak for this woman?'

Malachi jumped up and waved his arms; not as Malachi would ever be on a Manor Court jury. Humphrey Andrew whispered to steward.

'The constable says you're the woman's brother, Master Lomas. You live with her at... Herod Farm. Is that correct?'

'Aye, Master, aye, Herod Farm, aye.' Malachi nodded. Looked like his head were bound to fly across field same as a stone off a sling.

'And your sister, who's unmarried, is with child?'

'Rabbits, sir. It's rabbits. She's bore rabbits afore, Master. Having more rabbits, she is.'

Jury were laughing. Steward weren't, as far as I could tell.

'Rabbits. I see. And who is the father of these *rabbits*, Master Lomas?'

'Rabbits, Master.' Malachi looked wise, and that weren't summat you saw every day. 'It's rabbits as father rabbits, sir.'

'So I'm told.' Steward looked around jury. 'Can anyone throw light on this matter?'

Up stood William Newton. He were full of himself for being made churchwarden. Mind, he did job right, giving poor folk money out of box and making sure church roof and walls were sound.

'Mr Eyre, if this female's with child by a rabbit, the rabbit must be found and hanged for miscegenation and she must be whipped for consenting. But if the father be a man, both must be tried before Church Court and ordered to marry; unless their kinship forbids the sacrament of marriage, and then a Quarter Session Court might judge both shall hang, as God in his mercy commands.'

He were saying what we all knew: there were nobbut Malachi could have tupped Coney. But it weren't right, saying folk should hang or get whipped when fairies had their brains so they didn't know what they were doing. Mr Eyre started saying he didn't need nobody telling him what Church or Quarter Session Court might decide, but then Harry stood up.

'Master Steward,' he said, 'Master Newton would be right if Coney were like other women, only she isn't. As you see, sir, she can't talk, so she can't tell you who father is, man or rabbit; so nobody can't be made to wed her, or get hanged neither if he's a rabbit or too close kin, because there's no proof, like. On top of that she's an innocent, and how can an innocent be guilty of owt, or a court punish her? And Coney makes poorly sheep and beasts better by touching and singing to them, God bless and keep her, and she makes best honey in Glossopdale, so we thank God we have her and she's in all our prayers. I reckon if she bears rabbits, sir, like Malachi says, them rabbits'll get proper well looked after.'

There were a commotion, and constables had to stop a set-to between Harry and Newton. Mr Eyre banged table and ordered silence.

'Maybe so, fellow, but I deem her more likely to bear a child than a rabbit. The parish will care for the child from the poor box. Then none need be punished.' He glared at Malachi. 'You, Master Lomas, will see that your sister consorts with no more *rabbits*, on pain of *severe* punishment. Is that understood?'

Malachi did his head-nodding again, and I reckoned steward were good and merciful to heed Black Harry more nor William Newton. Happen he could tell Harry were smarter nor Newton and most of jury were with him. But Mr Yeaverley had summat to say.

'Let there be no doubt in this court that sin has been committed, and God demands that those who sin against His law shall be punished.' He pointed at Coney. She tipped her head sideways-like and made a noise like she were laughing. 'Has that woman previously borne a good character for virtue, sobriety and honesty? If Master Andrew the constable speaks truth, as he is sworn to do, she has not. Therefore we cannot construe her to have been forced by either man or rabbit. And what of these rabbits her brother says she has borne? Hosea chapter two, verse five: *For their mother has played the whore; she who conceived them has acted shamefully.* And St Paul warns us in First Corinthians chapter six, verse eighteen: *Every other sin a person commits is outside the body, but the sexually immoral person sins against his own body.* Or *her* own body. And if this female has lain with a kinsman, as my churchwarden seems to suppose, I ask you to recall the eighteenth chapter of Leviticus: *You must never have sexual relations with a close relative, for I am the Lord... Do not have sexual relations with your sister or half sister.* Some might declare her innocent, yet she has sinned in the sight of God, so the matter is for Church Court. As for curing sick beasts by touching them, that, Master Steward, is witchcraft, if it be true; and remember God's command in Exodus chapter 22, verse eighteen: *You shall not allow a witch to live.* And all men know that witches commit the foul sin of incest.'

If there'd been a row after Harry spoke there were a bigger one after vicar were done, everybody shouting, punches thrown. Constables got stuck in, but it were a while afore steward could make us all shut up again. Then jury decided vicar must be right because he were vicar, so Mr Eyre didn't have no choice: Coney had to go to Church Court, and Malachi with her, and happen she'd face assize for witchcraft. Harry shouted again, and steward asked who it were as were shouting, and when Humphrey Andrew told him Harry's name his face went colour of a bad plum and he shouted back, 'Go, Botham, you miscreant, before

91

I commit you to the stocks!' Mr Yeaverley didn't make no friends that day, and Harry's face were brandishing daggers when we set off home.

'I said yon vicar were a damned Puritan, and folk didn't believe me.' He slowed down a bit and his mouth did its sideways shift. I didn't tell him he'd said Mr Yeaverley *weren't* a Puritan. It were Bob as had said he were. Folk don't always remember right, not even Harry. He went on: 'Church Courts can't do nowt these days, mind, only excommunicate folk and take tithes.'

'Can send cases to Quarter Sessions,' said Tom Blood. 'Wants stopping, this does.'

'It will be,' said Harry.

*

Church Court were in Derby. Like Harry said, that were far enough to walk, but at least it weren't Lichfield. Archdeacon of Derby would stand in for Bishop Bentham, but Bailiff Booth told me it would be Archdeacon's top lawyer, John Hacker, as would decide about Coney. There were a few of us went fifty-two mile to Derby with Coney and Malachi: Harry and me, Bob Rowbottom and Mr Yeaverley. Stopped a night in alehouse in Bakewell, off south again following morning. There weren't supposed to be no women in Church Court, only them as were accused of summat, but Harry took Joanna with us to hearing because Coney needed a woman as could speak for her.

At midnight a few week afore yon Court, Coney had give birth; babby were a girl, not a rabbit. Malachi tried to get it christened but Mr Yeaverley weren't having none seeing as how it were a bastard. Malachi were still going on about father being a rabbit. Made no difference to Mr Yeaverley: babby were a bastard, rabbit or not.

'It isn't babby as is a bastard,' Harry muttered, 'it's yon damned vicar.'

Archdeacon started off Church Court with a prayer, and then him and his lawyers tried all sorts to find out who'd fathered Coney's little girl. But Harry stood up and said there were no way of knowing, and he told them Manor Court had ordered parish poor box to pay for babby's care. Archdeacon said Coney were to get whipped for fornicating, but Harry said no because we could give *compurgation*. No idea where he'd learned a word like that, but he'd got Bob Rowbottom, as knew his letters, to write summat. Then twelve of us as were Malachi's neighbours had put us marks under it, and Joanna had made one for Coney after ours. Lawyers read out what Bob had wrote and Archdeacon's face went red as a wrestler's.

'Very well.' Weren't happy, Archdeacon weren't. 'If Mistress Lomas is not to be whipped because twelve neighbours of her rank have sworn her innocence before this Court, she must do public penance, because there is no doubt she has fornicated.'

Then yon lawyer, Hacker, as Bailiff had told me about, stood up and said Coney were hereby ordered to stand at cross wearing a white sheet on market day, three times over, for her penance. Mr Yeaverley said he'd make sure she did it. He weren't happy because Archdeacon hadn't said nowt about Coney going to Quarter Session to be tried for witchcraft, or her and Malachi being hanged, and now she weren't even getting whipped because of Harry's *compurgation*. But he still smirked because 'an example was being made of her'.

That were that. We walked back home.

Coney only stood with yon white sheet on one market day, not three, and it were a proper laugh. Joanna and Alice and Martha helped Coney down to market ground and they all three wore white sheets, and so did every man from Simmondley, and a few from Glossop beside. There were twenty or more folk in white sheets around market cross that day, and when farmers and tanners and weavers and rest as had come to market from manors east and west and south of Glossopdale asked what were happening, Bill Goddard told them. Way Bill tells stories, he made Mr Yeaverley sound a right fool; and Agnes's brother Will Dawson joined in, making stuff up as he pretended were in Bible and giving chapter and verse in a voice as sounded like vicar's; and Tom Blood made a song about it with farting noises in chorus:

> We're all fornicators and we'll wear a white sheet,
>   And laugh at one another at next court leet;
>   Vicar's daft preaching sounds like sheep a-bleat,
>   And if he doesn't shut his gob he'll get shit to eat,

and everybody sang and laughed and cheered, even them from outside manor.

'It were Harry yonder as got as all doing it,' Will said, when farmers and tanners and weavers asked him. 'Best bit of fun we've had since last May Day.'

'I don't reckon as Coney will have to do her other two penances,' said Bill Goddard, 'but if she does we'll have same fun again.'

'That'll teach vicar to be a Puritan!' Bob Wolstenholme laughed 'til tears ran.

Mr Yeaverley went and hid in house as had been Reverend Mr Bower's afore he died falling down his well. Didn't show his face again 'til church next Sunday, and even then folk were laughing while he preached. He were still vicar after that, but nobody took much notice of him no more. But he found out Harry had been behind yon market day mummery, and there weren't much Christian forgiveness about him when he did.

'You've made an enemy of yon vicar, Harry,' I said.

'Aye, Spiderlegs, happen I have. But he's made an enemy of me and all, so I reckon he's made a bigger mistake nor what I have.'

Sheffield, August 1576

Katherine Dickenson was inured to her husband's worries about Lord Shrewsbury: health, family, finances. Finances above all. But pride in her new house in the heart of Sheffield triumphed over all anxieties. She delighted in watching the common townspeople gaze in awe at the height and girth of the building, its distinguished white walls, its glazed windows. Dickenson celebrated its completion by spending forty-eight shillings and eightpence on ale and inviting his brother John and his wife, Katherine's sister Jane, Nathaniel Eyre and his wife, the master joiner and plasterer, two master cutlers, and a handful of servants to share it with him.

Nevertheless, his concerns were not allayed. The earl had been ill again and Francis, Lord Talbot, had been indisposed since March. His honour had been unable to complete the payment of knights' fees to Thomas Bullock of Tickhill Castle or the release for the manor of Worksop, notwithstanding demands from the chancellor of the duchy of Lancaster and from Judge Bromley. Lord Shrewsbury's cash problem was worsening.

Dickenson shared his musings with Nathaniel Eyre. Eyre had his own worries.

'Her majesty has allowed his honour to carry the Scottish Queen to Buxton again –'

'He too might take the waters, Nathaniel. I pray they'll relieve the gout in his hands and thereby grant us respite from writing so many letters for him.'

'Yes, yes, we pray every day for his honour, we pray for his health, of course we pray.' Eyre ground his teeth. 'But he's persuaded her majesty that Mary should return here to Sheffield after she's taken from Buxton. Why?'

'To enjoy the splendour of the manor house, surely.'

'Pfah! I'll have to find food for all those confessors and chaplains and astrologers, lutenists, physicians, apothecaries, laundresses, ladies of the bedchamber –'

'The list is familiar, Nathaniel.'

'– and enforce the restrictions on which his honour insists.'

'On which her majesty insists. No doubt we should consider it a privilege, as their honours do. I understand that Tutbury remains unfit for a queen, despite sweetening.'

Eyre expectorated his opinion of privilege. The Scottish Queen wouldn't thank him for his hospitality, he observed, if she spoke to him at all; but his honour would listen to her complaints and then take him to task for a thousand imagined shortcomings.

'I share your troubles, Nathaniel. I must find money for her hospitality – from somewhere.'

His own cash flow, unlike the earl's, could be regulated. His new house had depleted the locked chest but not emptied it; he never allowed his family's expenditure to exceed income, and never permitted his savings to become altogether exhausted. He examined his personal accounts under the evening light, balancing income and savings against foreseeable needs: oats for winter storage to sustain the horses and enable Katherine to make oatcakes, which his son Gilbert loved; enough coal for the cold months. Prices would rise between now and October.

Naming his elder son after his honour's second hadn't wrought the magic he'd sought.

'See, Gilbert, this is why you must learn your letters and your sums.' He seated the boy before the account book. 'This is the money your father brings to the house. This is the money I spend to keep us fed and clothed and warm. This is what I have saved during the past month. Hold the quill as I showed you – no, boy, like this – and copy this page into the book I gave you…'

A Chatsworth servant arrived the following morning and stared in wonder at the new house. Dickenson gave him ale. *Impressed by my abode, though he's from Chatsworth?*

'Lady Shrewsbury ordered me to summon you, Mr Dickenson. She wishes to see you today.'

'At Chatsworth?'

'Yes sir.'

The road remained treacherous despite the dry weather, so Dickenson devoted two hours to the fifteen mile ride. Chatsworth's five storeys exuded elegance; even in the dull morning light the white walls smote his eyes. He was admitted immediately but offered no sustenance. The house still smelled of spices and freshly-cut oak, flowers and herbs from the terraces, Lenten fare from the new fishponds. Hardly a spoonful of sand had trickled through the hourglass before he was led to the chamber where six years earlier the earl had bestowed the Receivership on him. Here, the scent of roses cloyed the atmosphere. Otherwise, little had changed: he remembered the dark panels, tapestries depicting hunting scenes and sea voyages, the portrait of his honour, the heraldic shield, gleaming trestle table, padlocked chest. He bowed to Lady Shrewsbury. *Is she seated,* he wondered, *or enthroned? That chair is upholstered, perhaps in velvet.*

'I understand you are concerned for the health of Lord Shrewsbury's purse, Dickenson. You believe it can be restored by imposing higher rents on tenants.'

Katherine would expect him to describe her ladyship's clothes as soon as he returned home. There was velvet and fine holland in her attire, lace and gold. Her ruff gleamed white as refined flour. Her folded fingers bore a fortune in jewelled rings. Her heavy overdress was slashed and a petticoat bright with images of birds and flowers shone through.

'Yes, my lady.'

'However, some tenants might prove troublesome. Particularly, I'm told, in Glossopdale.'

'That seems likely, ma'am.'

Her earrings were pearls. The pendant on her necklace was a ruby. Strands of red hair snaked from under a linen coif with blackwork embroidery and lace trimming.

'There are many demands on his lordship's time and energy, inimical to the health of his body and soul as well as his purse.'

'Of course, ma'am.'

Her eyes left his face and drilled into an imagined scene behind his left shoulder. He let his shoulders relax and breathed more easily.

'The agent who collects fines, rents and tithes in the Peak manors … What is his name?'

'George Scargill, ma'am.'

'Scargill. Yes. I'm told the tenants have little love for Scargill.'

Her voice had the flavour of bitter aloes. A smile curled the corners of her mouth. It softened her eyes not one whit.

'No tenant loves a landlord's agent, ma'am.'

'But Scargill is loved less than others, is he not?'

How to answer? Despite his boorishness, his bullying, the cuts from landlord's tithes that he pocketed, George was diligent; and poor men in Sheffield, and the poorest tenant farmers, and even landless wanderers, were grateful for his kindness and generosity.

'By some in Glossopdale and other Peak manors, my lady. Elsewhere –'

'Which also concerns you. Does it not, Dickenson?'

'It does, ma'am, but if tenants make trouble when their rents are raised we can bring them to heel. If force were needed –'

'Force would cost time and money and the need for it would distress Lord Shrewsbury. There is a better way.'

What is she planning? And how am I to be implicated? Dickenson's eyebrows rose in courteous inquiry.

'One of my sons will collect Glossopdale's rents next year at Michelmas. It is too late for the present year. Every household will be surveyed. Scargill will not be involved. Lord Shrewsbury will know nothing of the matter until the rents are paid. You will apprise the Glossopdale bailiff of this arrangement. There is ample time for you to do so.'

Dismissed from the chamber, Dickenson availed himself of bread, cheese and ale from the Chatsworth store and rode back to Sheffield. New anxieties buzzed around him with the humblebees. Her ladyship planned to relieve his honour of one of his innumerable concerns; but no matter her intentions, he might not deem the action truly uxorial.

Glossopdale, August 1576

Feast of Assumption, there were always a fair at Chapel where we got salt and tallow and plough blades afore winter set in. Lammas being past, we'd gathered second hay crop and looked over stock as we'd happen slaughter at back end. Keep two dozen sheep over winter and they need half a load of straw and half of hay among them, and you don't want to keep none with foot rot or scrapie or louping ill or owt of that sort. Women were reaping oats with their threepenny sickles and we'd started picking fruit, throwing first pick over our heads while we asked God to send us luck. Ploughing would start afore long, and them as reckoned they could grow winter crops would plant them at next new moon. Peas and vetches looked all right but they needed another month afore they were reaped and pulled. Job for a misty drizzly autumn day, gathering peas and vetches.

I borrowed Olly's old nag and Joanna and me set off with skins, scraps of salt meat and some apples and plums. Horse and us were carrying goods for most of tithing. Folk in towns buy fruit, and everybody needs skins as have been cleaned and don't have no holes in them. Black Harry were busy helping Reggie and Josh and Bob with gathering rest of hay, keeping an eye on his lad while he were about it. Little Edmund were picking blackberries and moaning about getting scratched. Harry give him a good answer: 'Don't moan about blackberry bushes bearing brambles, boy. Praise God that bramble bushes bear blackberries.' Aye, I thought, and don't pick no blackberries after end of September, lad, because Devil's pissed on them by then. Nobbut five year old, Edmund, but quick on his feet. There one minute, gone next,

100

and you'd have to look for him. Mind, you'd soon find him because you'd hear him laughing. Harry and Joanna were bringing him up right. He helped with herding sheep and beasts, did a bit of reaping, gleaning and binding oats, and he were good at children's jobs: fetching water, weeding, tending pig and hens, picking fruit, bird-scaring, helping his Dad set up for ploughing. Joanna had taught him a bit of cleaning and mending and all.

'I'm frightened yon hob will take my Edmund one of these days and leave a changeling,' Joanna said.

I told her not to be daft; he'd grown too big for fairy folk to steal. Mind, somebody in tithing still needed to leave ale and porridge on threshold for yon hob. I'd told Henry and Josh to do it. Might change their luck.

Old horse were slow going round Nab, slower still up Phoside past Hayfield, and it weren't a lot quicker downhill. But there were plenty on road to Chapel and none of them no faster nor us: folk on foot driving lambs and beasts with dogs and curses, women with baskets of cheese and butter and eggs, cages of fowl. There were vagabonds next to road begging coins or bread. Some lads driving sheep pushed a couple of beggars into ditch for a laugh. Same every year.

We left horse in meadow at Chapel same as everybody did. I put pack on my back and we took all our stuff for selling into market square. Mob were that dense, talking and shouting and haggling, you couldn't hardly breathe. Lammas Fair were always that road. Somebody were playing a fiddle and one or two were trying to dance. We got ten pound of tallow for a groat a pound – they wanted sixpence but nobody were bound to pay that – and two stone of salt for fivepence a stone, and we looked at knives and plough blades them cutlers from Sheffield were selling. We got good ones in exchange for a couple of cured sheepskins and shoved them in my pack with salt and tallow. Constables had nabbed a pickpocket and put him in stocks afore he'd time to pinch enough to get hanged. They were watching for folk buying more nor two bushel of grain and all, or buying so they could sell it again for more money; law said sellers had to let poor folk buy grain cheaper. And they'd caught a smart lad trying to sell ale in short measure, so he were in pillory. Joanna's face lit up like sun coming out of a cloud.

'Here, Tom, get them rotten onions, and them old cabbages…'

She were a crack shot with stinking vegetables, my sister. Yon swindler in pillory weren't going to smell good when they let him out. He got a bad onion in his mouth and afore long his hair and face were green and slimy. Crowd laughed and Joanna got cheered. Her face went red and she grinned.

There were bull-baiting next to lane as goes up Eccles Pike. I went to watch while Joanna bought oatcake and ale and stopped to stare at a group of lads wrestling. There were more women nor men around them lads, shouting and betting a halfpenny one road or other. Out Whaley Bridge way, two or three men were counting sheep for selling, *Yan tan tethera fethera fimp, sethera lethera…* and arguing prices. I weren't buying. We'd more ewes nor we could keep over winter already. I looked around market a bit more, but we'd sold or bartered everything we'd brought and bought all we wanted, so I were for getting home. I pulled Joanna away from them lads she were betting on and dragged her back to horse.

'Enjoyed yon wrestlers?'

'Nowt wrong with looking.'

'Reckon that's what vicar would say?'

'To hell with vicar.'

'You've drunk too much ale, Jo. Reckon that's what Harry would say?'

'What? To hell with vicar, or nowt wrong with looking? Or I've drunk too much ale?'

'I know what he'd say about vicar, I've heard him. But I don't know what he'd say about you watching young wrestlers as are covered with spots and rashes. Wanted some of yon bittersweet remedy as Maggie and Agnes makes to shift spots, them lads did. Or oil of lavender.'

Horse took his time. When his back legs moved, plough blades rattled. Tallow stunk in my pack. Joanna went quiet a bit, and then said: 'Where does Harry keep wandering off to, Tom?'

'Hasn't told me nowt.'

'Telled me nowt, neither. But he wouldn't. I reckon you can guess.'

'Aye.'

She turned her head and stared at Eccles Pike.

'Woman. Or women.'

'Eh? No, not road you're thinking, Jo.' She'd started asking what that were supposed to mean when I saw summat as shouldn't have been happening. 'Ayup, what are yon lot doing? Trying to enclose common land?'

Joanna looked, and then turned off track and walked up to four men as were getting stuck in with spades. I limped after her. Horse stood where it were and ate a bit of grass at roadside.

'Ayup,' she said, 'what're you lot doing, digging common up?'

One of them leaned on his spade, looked at her and spat.

'Dog's gone down yon hole after a fox. What makes it your business?'

'Dog or bitch?' asked Joanna.

'Dog. Why?'

'Any of you know where there's a bitch in season?'

'Aye.' Another of them dropped his spade and rubbed his hands. 'I've got one.'

'Go and fetch her,' Joanna said. 'Dog smells her, he'll be straight out. You can stop digging.'

All four of yon men stared at her. Then him as said he'd a bitch in season went to fetch it. Joanna walked back to track and I followed. Horse were still eating grass and weren't for walking again until I gave him a whack with my stick.

'Harry teach you that trick?' I said.

'I don't need Harry nor nobody else to teach me how nature works.' She didn't even look pleased with herself. Just like Ma. 'What did you mean, Tom, "Not road you're thinking"?'

It took a few breaths afore I got what she meant. How do women remember what you were chattering about afore summat important happened? I knew Harry had tumbled lasses in Castleton and Peak Forest, mostly them as were in service with him, because he'd told me; but I were sure he hadn't swyved nobody only Joanna since they were wedded.

'I reckon he's looking for his mother.' Happen he were off stirring folk up about rents and enclosures and all, but I needed to shift Joanna out of road she were thinking. 'When we were in Chinley a couple of year back –'

'His mother? Nay, he'd have telled me. And why would he look for her? She left her home. What sort of woman goes off and leaves her children?'

'We don't know what happened, Jo. We were only nippers when she went, you and Willie and me. Folk have always bad-mouthed Morag Botham. Old Harry were never same after she'd gone, but if he heard anybody talk foul about her he shut them up fast and no mistake; and your husband did same, though he were nobbut a lad.'

Joanna looked across valley towards Mainstonfield. Chinley. Wind had got up, westerly. I reckoned it would rain later. Rooks were gathering where lands had been reaped. There were tits and finches. Poppies and cornflowers watched from between fields, warming my eyes. Then Joanna started again.

'You haven't noticed what my Harry's been like this past twelve month. That's trouble with you, Tom, you never notice nowt. You could have had Alice Oliver if you'd wanted her instead of letting Willie take her. She'd have let you. Never notice nowt, you don't.'

How had me and Alice got owt to do with Harry and his wandering, or with Morag?

'All folk in tithing said it weren't right, me having Alice. Anyroad, she's all right with Willie. Just wants a babby and God hasn't sent them one, for all Alice went and drank from Dewrie Well at Bretton and we pray –'

'See? You're not saying you *did* want her. You said she were pretty and you loved her singing, but that were all. Harry wouldn't have took no heed of what other folk said, not if *he'd* wanted her. I'm glad he didn't, mind. And she's a right scold to Willie. To you and all. Must have wedded on a Friday. You've never noticed how Agnes Dawson wants you, neither.'

'Agnes? Don't be daft, Jo.'

'Tom, she'd have you in two flaps of a sparrow's wings if you asked her. There's only you can't see it. And if you reckon anybody in parish could stop *that* match because you're both lame, you don't know Dawsons.'

Happen Joanna were remembering them daft games girls play, trying to find out who they'd marry: counting seven stars in sky for seven night in a row and then waiting for next man to say Ayup to you; putting salt into yolk of a hard-boiled egg, eating it fasting and going to bed backwards without saying owt... I can't mind them all. When man she wants takes no notice of her, girl sticks a knife in a lamb's shoulder-bone and chants some soft rhyme, and then he suffers that much pain he needs to go and talk to her. Boys don't bother with stuff like that; only some play dare-Devil, going to bed with a mouldy ha'pence and a bit of mouldy cheese and saying Lord's Prayer backwards. Young Ben Bradley did it, and his door rattled and knocked 'til he shit himself and prayed for mercy and never played dare-Devil again. I shook my head.

'She's a grand lass, is Agnes. Does a lot of folk good. But I'm no use to no woman, Jo. Look at me. Can't go up and down lands all day, not with this hip. Can't plough a straight furrow...'

Same as I said, Harry had lifted a few lasses' skirts while he were off in service, but I never had. They wouldn't want likes of me swyving them. Joanna looked at me road sisters and mothers do when they want to pick you up and shake you. I rubbed my wrist across my nose.

'You think that's all as matters? You're kind, Tom, you're a good friend, you're quiet, you don't drink much ale, you're best thatcher in five parishes, and folk trust you. And for heavy work, Agnes's brother can –'

'Give it a rest, Jo. It wouldn't suit. And stop mithering yourself about Harry. What would he want another woman for when he's got you?'

'That's a daft question if ever I heard one.' Next news she started skriking. I never know what to do with women when they skrike. When nippers skrike you can pick them up and hug them and talk soft, but women aren't nippers. At least Joanna were quiet, just tears running. Her voice were choked, mind. 'He weren't happy when my little Ellie... he wanted another boy. It were like I weren't a proper wife no more.'

I remember what my Dad said about taking a wife. *Get one that's wise, decent and orderly, and make sure she's quiet, faithful, sober and chaste. Go and see what her mother's like because women grow up like their mothers. Choose right one and she'll look after you and your household like you want and bring your children up so's you're proud of them.* Funny, what Joanna had said. Agnes were everything as Dad reckoned you wanted in a wife. Only it were no use me thinking that road.

'Now who's being daft?' I give Joanna a hug. 'Babbies die, Jo, when God wills. It isn't nobody's fault. And you've one fine boy, and you'll have more afore you're done. Reckon Harry doesn't know that?'

She shook her head.

'I don't know, Tom. Happen… I don't know.'

She shut up and there weren't no more I could say. We went through Hayfield, slow as a funeral. Weren't nobody standing outside their houses cheering like they'd done when we come back from chasing Bradshaw out of Chinley. Harry weren't with us this time.

It started raining, same as I'd said. I were getting as good as Ottie Wood for seeing weather coming. See, Jo? Summat as I'd noticed.

Sheffield, 1577

Katherine had lain ten days with a fever. Dickenson's duties compelled him to entrust most of her care to servants, but he was her companion whenever the numerous demands on his time and attention allowed; bringing food, comforting his sons. Yet even at her bedside his thoughts strayed: *Thomas Barnbie of Barnbiehall must pay two capons at Whitsun; witnesses William Gillot, Robert Shane, Hugh Gillot and John Wainwright.* And later: *his honour believes Sir John de Zouche persuaded the clamorous tenants of Peak Forest to exclaim against him. I suspect villains far inferior to Sir John of encouraging those tenants to complain to Lord Burghley's clerk.*

Glossopdale, he sensed, was a problem in waiting, a new Peak Forest; perhaps worse than Peak Forest. Her ladyship's plan had been implemented: her son Henry Cavendish had visited and surveyed the manor. According to the Glossopdale bailiff, Mr Cavendish's visit had disquieted the leaseholders. Dickenson counselled him to withhold action: Mr Cavendish seemed to have little enthusiasm for his allotted task, so Lady Shrewsbury might yet change her mind; and to preclude anger and conflict, his honour should not be alerted unless the intrusion was sustained.

Katherine's voice was faint but the beloved smile graced her lips.

'William, your mind wanders over your troubles even while your body kneels beside me.'

'My troubles are nothing compared to my love for you.'

'Nevertheless, tell me about them. Love lives most in sharing, and your voice relieves the pain in my head.'

Dickenson's eyes prickled. He cleared his throat.

'I thank God for blessing me with you, Kath. I wish the union between his honour and her ladyship were as robust.'

The earl, he explained, had asked permission to move the Scottish Queen to Chatsworth, where Lady Shrewsbury spent most of her time and money, while the Sheffield manor house was spring-cleaned. But before the Privy Council could respond, her ladyship had written that Chatsworth had no suitable provision for the royal prisoner; also, the earl seemed unwilling to go there himself. And he had sent no money to her.

Katherine closed her eyes. 'So the countess *is* jealous of his lordship's dealings with the Scottish Queen.'

'Her ladyship's letter expressed undiminished affection for him, Kath.' *Such affection as there ever was.* 'They say rumours were circulating at Court while the countess was there; you've heard their echoes.' Dickenson rose to his feet and massaged his legs and back. 'I pray matters will yet be resolved without hurt to either party.'

'I shall pray also.' Katherine steadied her breathing. 'If Mary must be removed from Sheffield but can't be housed at Chatsworth, where will she go?'

'Buxton again, for part of the summer. Lord Leicester wishes to join his honour there. I believe his real desire is to meet Mary so he can carry news of her to her majesty.'

'Especially news of his lordship's attendance upon her.'

Dickenson smiled. 'You're jealous on Lady Shrewsbury's behalf, Kath. I suspect her ladyship will invite Lord Leicester to Chatsworth when he leaves Buxton. She'll want him to reconcile the Queen to her daughter Elizabeth's marriage. And, no doubt, to promote her infant granddaughter as her majesty's successor. If there's to be no royal marriage, that is.'

'I'm sure you're right, William. The countess knows Lord Leicester can influence the Queen.'

'Indeed, he's said to have her majesty's ear.'

'And other parts, if rumour be true.'

'Such rumours are best not whispered, Kath.'

'Many people say it.'

108

'Many people also say his honour has shared the Scottish Queen's bed; another wicked slander that should never be repeated.'

'Though perhaps her ladyship gives it credence.'

*

'I know what it's about, William. So do you.'

'The cost, Nathaniel. Again, the cost.'

'For you and me, yes. For his honour, no. He frets and complains about his cash crisis but expects us to solve it while he goes on spending. As a great lord must.'

Dickenson considered Lord Shrewsbury's ill humour. What was the cause? The suspension of Archbishop Grindal for allowing too much freedom to Puritans? Unlikely: his honour had blocked Ralph Sacheverell's appointment as Sheriff of Derbyshire *because* of his Puritanism. The pain, the gout, that compelled him to delegate ever more secretarial work? But he had suffered so for years.

'Why now, Nathaniel? Surely he owns enough great houses besides his castle here and at Tutbury.'

'Enough? Who can say what is "enough" for a great lord? He holds Pontefract Castle; manor houses at Handsworth, Wingfield, Rufford Abbey; hunting lodges at Tutbury, Sheffield, Worksop; the house in Buxton...'

'Yet he must build another mansion to stand beside the Worksop hunting lodge, *and* must engage Robert Smythson to design it! Smythson, of all people!'

Eyre grinned. 'Certainly. His honour desires that his new house in Worksop will rival Chatsworth.'

'It will anger her ladyship.'

'Oh, I'm sure he wouldn't wish that, William.'

*

The quarrel between Lord and Lady Shrewsbury during July had nothing to do with the new house at Worksop, or with Glossopdale, or with Peak Forest; or even with the Scottish Queen. It emanated from a trivial misunderstanding. Dickenson blamed the source on his brother John, keeper of Lord Shrewsbury's wardrobe.

'I'd no choice, William.' John perspired. 'Security –'

'The men who accompanied her ladyship were a security threat to neither castle nor manor house. The countess is joint custodian of the Scottish Queen. Those she employs are loyal.'

'You've said yourself that not all servants are to be trusted.'

'Those to whom you denied hospitality were not servants. They were embroiderers, tapestry repairers and hangers, upholsterers, brought by Lady Shrewsbury to prepare the manor house for the Scottish Queen's return. All they asked was a night's lodging in the castle. Security risk? Did it surprise you, John, when they chose to complain to her ladyship's groom, since *none* of her other servants were present?'

'You know his honour insists on security. Especially in his absence. He'd gone to Bolsover; estate business. He said I'd done rightly.'

'Her ladyship said you'd done wrongly.'

'I'm his honour's servant, not hers. As are you, William.'

'To sow or foster dissent between the earl and countess is in neither of our interests. Adapt, John. Obey his honour's orders in spirit but not necessarily in letter. Then peace might reign.'

Dickenson sighed. It was a squall, not a storm; kinder weather should return. Meanwhile, he must revise his opinion of his honour's second son. Master Gilbert had long appeared to him a spendthrift, hovering on the fringes of Court without furthering his family's fortunes, but his attempt to heal this breach between father and stepmother showed judgement and skill. Lady Shrewsbury had infuriated the earl by returning to Chatsworth while he was away in Bolsover. He'd attributed her departure from Sheffield to malice. Master Gilbert had explained her need to transact business with Sir Thomas Stanhope, and had represented her to his father as 'grieved in her mind at your lordship's shows of anger and evil will towards her' and 'unable to doubt that your lordship's love and affection is clean turned to the contrary'. Gilbert had been diplomatic concerning her ladyship's remark about finding peace and happiness at Chatsworth but only restrictions at Sheffield.

Katherine's fever was abating and Dickenson shared happier thoughts with her. It would do much to reconcile his honour to the countess, he said, if she helped Sir Thomas Stanhope win his case against Sir John de Zouche. Her ladyship would seek to accomplish this feat unaided; if the matter went to Star Chamber, or to the Privy Council, her intervention would avail little or nothing. She was inclined to favour Sir Thomas's suit because Sir John had so far forgotten his family's friendship with her as to spread rumours around Court when her daughter married Charles Stuart without royal consent. Perhaps it was true that Sir Thomas had attached Sir John's followers at Derby, but Lady Shrewsbury had chosen to focus on the clear evidence that Sir John had embezzled funds.

'I believe you told me the Privy Council had pressed his lordship to resolve the Stanhope-Zouche quarrel,' said Katherine. 'So if her ladyship can settle it on his behalf, his lordship must be grateful.'

'Indeed; but the Stanhope-Zouche quarrel is a small matter among many greater ones. His honour also worries about the Scottish Queen's plans, the administration of his estates, his pains, his duties as earl martial, his duties as lord lieutenant... Notwithstanding all we do to lighten his burdens, or what her ladyship does, he will find many reasons to worry.'

Glossopdale, 1577

There were a lot of talk about custom again. Custom were only friend of poor folk, they said, except for Our Saviour. Old men like Harry's Dad and Tom Jackson reckoned things had got slack in Glossopdale: some households weren't paying tithes or heriot like custom said, and there were subletting and tree felling and overstocking. We were none of us supposed to do them things without his lordship's say-so. Black Harry shook his head. They'd been going on that many years they'd *become* customary, he said, so there were nowt wrong with them now; and nobody wouldn't bother about them anyroad if it weren't for yon Scargill, as were only trying to line his own pockets and happen bailiff's. A lot in Glossopdale thought Harry were right, only his Dad told him to stay quiet and said there were bound to be bother. He were right and all, Old Harry were, only bother come about in a road neither he nor nobody else had expected.

It started back in April, twenty-fifth day of Lent. Just as night were gathering, darkness swallowed moon. Edmund Bower said same had happened at end of January. Edmund reckoned he'd been spreading dung and black ash on his meadow after dark and giving his sheep summat to eat that January night, though it were more likely he'd been out stealing pigeons or tracking leverets again. He'd been up in Manor Court a time or two for them tricks. Anyroad, everybody knew signs in sky, like darkness swallowing moon, meant summat bad would happen; even when moon come back after an hour, like it did.

Twenty-fifth day of Lent: swallows were out from under water again, birds building nests, Coney's bees busy, lesser celandines and archangel and forget-me-not flowering, butterflies all colours kissing them, birch and hawthorn coming into leaf, last of snow up on wastes hanging on by its fingertips. Hugh Platt reckoned he'd heard cuckoo so it were time for getting scythes sharpened. But like Black Harry said, Hugh couldn't tell a cuckoo from his own arse; it were most likely a wood pigeon. Then, while we were welcoming April, cuckoo or no cuckoo, a gentleman rode into Glossop down Doctor Talbot's road. He'd six or seven with him, blades in their belts. You could tell he were a gentleman: road he were dressed, fine-looking horse, and them six or seven calling him 'Sir' and doffing their hats. From Padfield to Chunal, Glossop to Charlesworth, folk were staring and asking, 'Who's yon?' Nobody knew. Not to begin with.

Afore long, them six or seven men were going from one household to another asking questions, wandering over common, in and out of John Rowland's charcoal yard and Roger Wragge's mill and Randolph Swann's smithy, and then going back to gentleman and talking to him. Olly Smith and Will Dawson told us later: gentleman had got off his horse, and he'd took a pot of ink and a quill out of his saddlebag, and every time one of them men told him owt he wrote summat.

'Then he went in bailiff's house,' said Olly. 'He were there a while.'

'Half an hour, I reckon,' said Will. 'Then he come out again.'

'Didn't look happy, neither. Back on his horse and off up Doctor Talbot's road.' Olly supped more ale. 'Back to Sheffield, happen.'

'Happen not, Olly,' said Will. He turned to Black Harry and me. 'Martha Smith as does for bailiff said gentleman were Mr Henry Cavendish. That were what bailiff called him, anyroad. So he wouldn't be going to Sheffield, would he?'

'Wouldn't he? Why not?' I asked.

'Cavendish,' said Harry. 'One of Lady Shrewbury's sons. She were married to Sir William Cavendish at one time. So Will's right: when Mr Cavendish left Glossop he'd most likely go back to his mother's house; Chatsworth, not Sheffield.'

Harry were grinning. It were a while since he'd looked that happy.

'What's funny, Harry?'

'Think about it, Spiderlegs. What were Mr Cavendish's men doing, poking around and asking questions, him writing stuff down?'

'Taking a survey,' said Will.

'Right, Will. And why do surveys get took?'

'To set rates on tenancies. Decide fines, tithes, rents…' Olly's voice tailed off.

'Scargill's job, isn't it?' Harry laughed out loud. 'Happen her ladyship and Mr Henry Cavendish are reckoning to put Scargill out of work and make themselves landlords of Glossopdale. They say his lordship and her ladyship have had a falling out.'

I said if gentlefolk fell out it were nowt to do with us. I couldn't see what Harry were driving at. Olly and Will couldn't, neither. But we had another pot of ale and Harry told us: his lordship were reckoning he'd put our rents up, like he'd done in Peak Forest, but now it looked like her ladyship wanted Glossopdale rents for her own purse, or else her son's.

'What's it matter who landlord is?' I said. 'We still have to pay.'

'Right, Spiderlegs. But suppose we say we won't pay rents to nobody only his lordship's bailiff and agent,' said Harry, 'because he's landlord and her ladyship isn't. Suppose we tell Mr Cavendish he's getting nowt out of us. Then his lordship will reckon we're his faithful tenants, for all we can cause bother, because we won't let nobody take owt from Glossopdale as is rightfully his. Then he won't push rents up here like he did in Peak Forest, will he? If he's arguing with her ladyship and her son, he'll want us on his side.'

I weren't sure it would work out that road but I didn't say owt.

'Happen you're right, Harry.' Will shook his head. 'Only if we don't pay Mr Cavendish what he reckons because we'll only pay his lordship, it'll happen cause more bother between his lordship and her ladyship.'

'Going to cry over that, Will?' said Harry. 'Let's make sure bailiff knows where we stand: we pay our rents through him to Lord Shrewsbury's agent. We won't pay nowt to Mr Cavendish. You go and tell him, Spiderlegs. He's your uncle. And he doesn't like me.'

*

114

Mr Cavendish come back a fortnight afore Michelmas, demanding rents. Every Glossopdale household were in market square saying 'No' because Harry had talked to them. It were a bad day, wind and rain blowing in over Mottram and Arnfield. Everybody were soaked. Mr Cavendish wore a cloak and hat but you could tell Glossopdale rain were getting through it. His men rattled their blades, so we lifted our scythes and pitchforks and walked round them. Mr Cavendish's horse smelled bother; it were near throwing him. His men saw there were a lot more of us nor them so they put their blades away and horse calmed down.

'We pay our rents to bailiff for our landlord,' said Harry, 'not nobody else. Our landlord's Lord Shrewsbury, not you, Mr Cavendish.' He wiped rain off his face. His hair were streaming wet. His voice were stronger nor wind, though. He sounded like one of them heralds on battlefields. Mr Cavendish looked for a minute like he were bound to set his men on him like a pack of dogs, but then he looked round all of us and smiled.

'Spoken like a faithful servant.' He slid down off his saddle and beckoned with his finger. 'Step aside, fellow. We'll speak privately.'

Harry didn't shift.

'We've nowt to say to one another as all my friends can't hear.'

'Come now.' Mr Cavendish had to shout against wind. 'There need be no enmity. His lordship has raised rents in other manors because he's been ill-served and ill-advised by his agents and bailiffs. Next year your rents too will rise if he remains your landlord; rise by more than I shall ask. I'll take no more than you can afford. I won't starve you of grain. Corn prices are five or six times what your grandfathers paid, but I shall be a good lord to you.' He looked around us again, still smiling. 'To all of you.'

Harry shook his head. Rain flew off his hair same as off a dog's ears.

'If Lord Shrewsbury puts our rents up more nor we've a mind to pay, sir, it'll be our problem. We'll go and argue our case with him.'

Mr Cavendish laughed. 'You'll argue your case with the earl martial of England? One of the nation's greatest nobles?'

For a few breaths, Harry said nowt. We all looked at one another, soaked to skin, dripping cold. Happen we *would* be better off if bailiff give our rents to Mr Cavendish. It'd get rid of Scargill for a start. Then Harry spoke again.

'Right's right, sir, and law's law. We'd go to Sheffield Castle and talk face to face to Lord Shrewsbury if he set rents too high. If that didn't do no good we'd happen go to London like Peak Forest lads did. Only we wouldn't give up as easy as them.'

Mr Cavendish's men give their blades another rattle and two of them stepped forward. Harry still didn't shift. Mr Cavendish waved them back and looked at his fingernails. Telled us he didn't work soil, them fingernails. You couldn't make much of his face out under yon hat, but bit as I saw, I reckoned it looked cunning. Happen he'd be good at nine men's morris.

'If you did so,' he said, 'if – let us say – you petitioned the Queen's chief minister, you'd need help. Someone of noble rank to speak for you. Preferably someone related to his lordship… Should matters develop as you suggest, fellow, perhaps I could persuade such a person to provide support.' He looked up again and widened his smile. 'We shall adjourn this discussion.'

He got on his horse again, turned, and rode away east like he'd done afore. His men followed.

'He give up a bit easy,' I said. 'What for?'

Harry grinned. His forehead were wet. It weren't all rain.

'If we got our case in front of top nobles in London, Spiderlegs, it'd stir things up that much his lordship would want to be rid of Glossopdale. And then her ladyship and Mr Cavendish could be landlords instead of him. That's why he said he'd find help for us in London. If we went. If we needed it.'

*

Scargill come Michaelmas week with that youngster Roberts as follows him around. We paid rents and tithes to bailiff same as always, and Scargill moaned about subletting and underbush and said rents would go up, so you'd reckon nowt had changed. But two day after Michaelmas a new star shone, and when sky were clear after dark you could see it had a tail on it. Bob Rowbottom said it were called a comet and comets meant bad news. Harry grinned at Scargill.

'Happen we won't be paying you nowt. We're Lord Shrewsbury's servants while he's landlord, but we're not his servants if somebody else is landlord.'

'What are you talking about, Botham?'

'Haven't your betters telled you, Scargill? Fancy them telling you nowt! Best ask them.'

Everybody cheered and young Roberts looked like he were bound to be sick, and Scargill blustered. Harry grinned again and said nowt else. Next day, Scargill and Roberts went home. Happen my uncle had telled them what were what by then.

'Hear Scargill saying justices of peace have wrote to Lord Shrewsbury about his — what did he call us? — uncivil and riotous tenants of Glossopdale?' Bob Wolstenholme shook his head.

'That's nowt fresh,' said old Tom Jackson. 'When there's trouble with tenants in Peak, Glossopdale gets blamed, and yon Scargill's good at blaming.'

'It usually *is* us,' said Henry Warhurst. 'Scargill's all right, Tom. Been good with me and Josh. Hear what Harry did today?'

We were busy getting ewes to tup so we'd no time for worrying. Like Dad always said, get lambs born near Candlemas and they're fat for selling for a pound each come St Helenmas. We saw nowt more of Scargill that year. We didn't see Mr Cavendish's men again neither, not 'til after twelve days of Christmas, when we went other side Buxton for our lads' race against Staffordshire Moorlands. There were heavy snow on tops, but wind had cleared ground round village enough for lads to run track. Hard going; it were frozen. There were three lads of theirs and three of ours; Olly Smith were one, Harry's brother-in-law. Best runner in three parishes, Olly, nigh on six foot tall, legs long as a gossip's tongue, quicker nor ever since Agnes give him wormwood for his bowel pain.

We were wrapped up against wind, cheering runners, when a horse come up and a voice said, 'In the name of Heaven! Those youths are running without a scrap of clothing! Naked as the day they were born! How have they not died of mortal cold?'

We turned round and saw it were one of them as had come to Glossop with Mr Cavendish that wet day in October. Harry give him that sideways grin of his.

'They'll be right enough. When they've done – *Go on, Olly lad!* – they'll get mulled ale in village alehouse, hot as they can drink, and a good rub down with sacking, and then they'll be right as rain – *Yes, Olly! Yes!*'

We were all cheering, and them as had come with Staffordshire lot were hooting and cat-calling. Olly had won three mile run like he usually does.

'When they're dressed again,' somebody else told this fellow on horse, 'they'll get fed oatcake and honey and good Derbyshire cheese, and then a bit of bull beef as were salted down at back end.'

'Lads race this road every year,' I said. 'Should come and watch it again.'

Cavendish man chuckled.

'I think we'd all rather watch naked maidens racing than naked youths, eh?'

'Not up here, friend,' said Harry. 'Only get lasses' races down Derby way. Weather's kinder there. Folk are softer.'

Sheffield, August 1578

Eyre shook his head. Other justices of the peace had complained, yet again, about the rude and riotous residents of Glossopdale. How did that benighted valley poison the minds of its tenants?

'Mr Cavendish surveyed Glossopdale last year and advised the tenants to withhold their rents,' said Dickenson. 'They've misbehaved ever since. I've exchanged letters with Mr Booth on his honour's behalf. The tenants remain restless.'

'Mr Booth is Glossopdale's bailiff? I see. When Mr Cavendish advised the tenants to withhold rents, did he do so at her ladyship's behest?'

Dickenson cleared his throat.

'On St Mark's Day, his honour bade me write to Mr Booth commending his sense of duty and promising to deal with the matter "From within my own household". He said, "I know the tenants were set on by others". So yes, perhaps he thought her ladyship might be implicated.'

Will his honour learn I was obliged to obey the countess in this matter?

From a pile of documents on his table, the epitome of order, he selected one item.

'The situation's worsening, Nathaniel. His honour has just received this from Nicholas Booth: "Received your honourable letter… whereby I perceive controversy between your honour and my lady… is likely to come to an end, which I pray God may be to the content of your lordship. I understand Mr Cavendish has given orders to his men to enter into all the land and leases of Glossopdale and to use them to their best commodity, and utterly to expel us from the doing thereof. But until such time as I know your honourable pleasure I will not yield to them".' Dickenson grimaced. 'If her ladyship instigated this, perhaps she intended only to relieve his honour of one of his many burdens.'

'No, William. She meant to make Glossopdale part of her jointure. Or her eldest son's jointure. One of her sons, anyway.'

It was rumoured that the Queen had received the countess kindly at Court. Katherine surmised that London's nobility sought her ladyship's company so they might bask in first-hand accounts of the mysterious Queen of Scots. Perhaps so; but her sojourn in London meant she was not on hand to explain her intrusion into Glossopdale. *Perhaps Nathaniel is right: she's taking advantage of his honour's declining abilities.*

'She has no legal claim on Glossopdale, Nathaniel, and will have none unless his honour transfers the manor to her control or Mr Cavendish's.'

'If that was her plan it's gone awry. His honour's enraged.'

Dickenson recounted Scargill's confrontation with Botham the previous Michelmas.

'Perhaps his honour will now implement my suggestion: increase the Glossopdale rents. George will support me.'

But Lord Shrewsbury now commanded Dickenson to go in person to Glossopdale to remind the tenants who their landlord was and what their duties were. While he was there he must address the matter of the unrenewed leases.

*

'So this is Glossopdale.'

Dickenson and Scargill were riding the final three furlongs of Dr Talbot's road from Sheffield to Glossop; a miserable, boggy journey. The track was treacherous with loose stones, criss-crossed with rainwater channels. During the hundred years since it was laid it had deteriorated. Here, it ran westwards between a stinking brook on one side and a hillside of coarse grass and scrub capped by wastes on the other. Half a mile earlier they'd passed an inn with crumbling walls and roof, oozing refuse into a clough that passed its door in a miasma of stench.

Dickenson was accustomed to visiting poor hamlets with thin beasts, scraggy corn and tenants scratching livings from unforgiving soil, forced to live on peas and beans and oats. Little wonder the common people feared terrible visions if they slept in a bean field. But he believed he'd seen nowhere more wretched than Glossop.

'Aye, William. By-our-lady Glossopdale.' Scargill spat.

'No Papist curses, George! We'll go to Mr Booth's house, beg refreshment in the name of God and his honour, and ask that the tenants be summoned to the market square. We'll address them there.'

'You do the addressing. There are impertinent scum among them. They deserve a whipping or a day in the stocks to teach them manners, and I'd be glad to visit both those corrections on them. A few are honest poor people. I tell Mr Booth to take less from the poorest than they're due, but to say nothing of the matter to the others.'

Dickenson's mouth twitched.

'You say the worst of the riotous persons have farmholds in a hamlet called Simmondley. Where is it?'

Scargill pointed forwards and left, to where Coombes Edge closed the valley.

'Over there, William. Those Simmondley villains will cause trouble. The whole of Glossopdale breeds trouble.'

'We have his honour's instructions.'

*

'Almost every household is here, Mr Dickenson,' said Nicholas Booth.

The sun was past its zenith. Dickenson ran his eyes over the market square: fifty or more tenants encircling the cross, stinking, scratching, muttering. Around them, the bailiff's house, the parish church, the hovels of Glossop. An alehouse lounged a hundred yards up the hill, glowering at him. Roads undulated towards the other hamlets of the manor. George Scargill was at his side and a dozen armed servants stood with them, but his throat was dry. He held up his hand for silence and rose upright on his stirrups.

'I am William Dickenson, Bailiff of Hallamshire, servant and secretary to your liege lord, Lord Shrewsbury. Your landlord.'

121

There was a crescendo of murmuring like an approaching swarm of stings. Dickenson raised his voice.

'Mr Cavendish is not your landlord. Lady Shrewsbury is not your landlord. Glossopdale belongs to Lord Shrewsbury. Glossopdale will continue to belong to Lord Shrewsbury and to his heirs.'

'Somebody best put Mr Cavendish straight about that, then!' called a voice.

'At least Mr Cavendish come here himself,' yelled another. 'Didn't send no servants to do job for him. When's Lord Shrewsbury coming to Glossopdale?'

The murmurs blossomed into laughter. There were shouts of, 'Aye! Answer that, then!' Scargill started forwards but Dickenson stayed him. He shouted over the din:

'Your leases fall due for renewal at Michelmas. Those whose leases were not renewed twenty-five years ago will receive new ones. The fines will accord with the value of each tenancy. Rents will be set according to rates. They will be paid to Mr Booth before Lady Day. Mr Scargill will collect them as usual. Tithes and heriot payments will also be reviewed. Regulations concerning subletting, tree felling and other matters will be enforced. All those concerns –'

'How much will rents go up?' called a voice. The crowd echoed the question.

'We await his lordship's decision. He is considering a mark for every threepence or groat of present rent.'

The noise subsided. Dickenson heard the news being digested. Then one voice, loud and clear, rose to the sky. Crows scattered protesting from the trees.

'About yon subletting and felling and stuff of that sort, long usage has give us rights same as ancient rights. It's *custom* now.' The crowd began to cheer. The speaker continued: 'And folk around here won't pay no rents like you claim his lordship's reckoning on charging. Have you and that lying bastard at side of you telled his lordship we've been paying nobbut two shilling an acre?'

'That's him,' murmured Scargill. 'Botham. And those beside him are rogues of the same stamp: lame Booth; old Jackson; that loud-mouth Mellor. Damned trouble-makers, all four.'

Dickenson noted the names.

'Custom must be respected,' he declared, 'but so must a tenant's duties. During these past years, Glossopdale has neglected those duties. As for rents, I promise this, before these witnesses including your bailiff: all tenants who behave in accordance with Lord Shrewsbury's commands will keep their farmholds.' He looked around, satisfied with the silence. 'That is all. We shall return at Michelmas.'

*

Dickenson and Scargill knew Lord Shrewsbury would resent Henry Cavendish's intrusion into Glossopdale, but neither man had anticipated the magnitude of his fury. When Dickenson reported the tenants' response to the proposed new rents and mentioned "Botham", he feared his lordship would succumb to apoplexy.

'His honour,' he told Eyre, 'declared that disorder and sedition spring from Glossopdale as maggots spring from rotting meat. He's ordered us to impose huge rent increases on Glossopdale at Michaelmas. I shall take responsibility for the changes so the tenants' complaints will be directed at me, not at his honour. Complaints from commoners carry no weight. They will irritate me no more than gnat bites.'

'Many gentry said the same in '49, William. Nevertheless, the commotion time brought an end to Lord Somerset's protectorship. And gnat bites can make a man ill.'

Glossopdale, 1578

It were a bad year. Oats rotted on lands. Onions rotted in ground, for all they'd been planted while moon were waning. Stock died. There weren't much fruit because April winds had blown blossom to kingdom come and bees had gone hungry. We'd stock to mind so there weren't no time for games. God sends what He will; we couldn't do nowt about it only pray for better.

Maggie and Agnes tried to help poorly folk but it were too much for them. Maggie weren't getting no younger. I were busy with thatches; wind ripped them like rotten cloth. Agnes and me limped from house to house at same time, me mending roof, her mending them as lived under it. She give me house leeks to put in thatches to keep lightning off, and she told me house leek flowers were good for stopping fluxes and curing swellings. We built up credit, us two did. Folk would pay us when they could, cash or kind: me for thatching, Agnes for cures.

We reckoned not many would starve in Glossopdale because women would take in spinning work from towns. Town guilds didn't want spinning work going beyond reach of their fingerless mittens, but if they didn't like it they could lump it. Spinning didn't stop it being a bad year, mind, and it didn't stop hunger and sickness. Agnes skriked more nor once when she come out of a house where somebody were sick or dying.

'It's nippers, Tom,' she sobbed. 'Why does God send pain to children? I wish I could do more, that I do.'

I wished I could and all. It went right through me, pulled my heart out and wrung it like a wet rag, hearing little voices crying out that pain were like being stung with bees and pierced with swords. I put my arms round Agnes so she could cry on my jerkin. I'd never got that close to a woman in my life, only Ma when I were a nipper, and Joanna and Elena. It made me want to swyve Agnes, and that were a bad thought; worse nor bad, I reckoned, because she were proper sad. She must have felt it but she didn't pull away; so I didn't know what to think, only my face were hot. I wondered for a minute whether what Joanna had said on road back from Chapel last Lammas Fair were happen true. I started shaking and my throat weren't for letting me say owt, but I give a cough and managed a few words.

'I don't understand God, Agnes, but then there's none of us does. We can't do nowt only pray for His mercy.'

She'd stopped skriking but her face were still against my jerkin. She were like pressed against me and it were making me sweat. I swallowed. 'You and me, we're doing a lot for folks, side by side. Happen we should get wedded.'

I thought she were bound to run off when I said that, or laugh at me and tell me not to be so daft, or else shout and call me names same as Alice did. But she didn't. She said she'd ask her brother and her Ma, and I'd better talk to my brother and all and then see what vicar thought. If family and parish were happy, she'd wed me. Then she lifted her face and she were smiling. For a minute I forgot about foul weather and hunger and pain. I forgot about work.

I'd never thought much about marrying, getting a wife and looking after her, having babbies if God sent any; not even years back when I courted Alice for a week or two, or when I were away in service with young lasses I might have tupped if I hadn't been too scared to try. I reckoned I'd better have a word with Harry when he weren't off wandering.

*

Harry weren't off wandering. St Matthew's Day, he got most households in manor together. Even them Newtons come to Glossop market square to see what he were up to. Weather were bad for rich and poor alike, but bad times hit poor worst like they always do. They were begging door to door for bread. Newtons had been giving to them as were starving. They weren't all bad, Newtons weren't. I hadn't forgotten yon Christmas feast we'd had three or four year back, more fruit nor we'd ever seen in winter, and nutmeg and cinnamon and all.

Somebody said, 'Rents haven't changed in many a year, Harry, and prices go up, so happen rents do need to go up.'

Harry had said his lordship would go easy on us if we refused to pay owt to Mr Cavendish, but it weren't working out that road, not if what yon Dickenson had said were true. There were a few folk thought we should have gone with what Mr Cavendish had offered.

William Newton said, 'Aye, you can see his lordship's point. If we charge more for our goods at market we can pay higher rents. Everybody in England will do same.'

'Prices will be high this year anyroad,' somebody else said. 'Harvests'll be bad all over.'

That were true. You couldn't leave stooks of corn standing a week because they'd rot, even if you turned them regular with six foot rakes with four inch teeth; even if you cleared six acre a day; even if you made your women bind a sheaf in every field for luck.

Then Nick Mellor said: 'Aye, but how *much* will rents go up? Like Harry says, what if they go up more nor we can pay?'

'That's just it, Nick,' said Harry. 'Yon Dickenson were talking about a mark for threepence or a groat.'

Bob Wolstenholme said, 'Well, if that's what we have to pay, it's what we have to pay.'

A few heads nodded, but other folk said, 'Can't be right'; 'Dickenson can't have meant it'.

'He meant it all right,' said Harry. 'Did Nick Booth say he were wrong? Did Scargill say owt different? Did they hell as like!' He stared at Bob. 'When you sell your eggs, Bob, what do you charge? Cash?'

'What's that got to do with rents?' said Bob.

'Just tell us.'

'Depends. When chickens are laying well, happen three farthing a dozen.'

'Three farthing a dozen. Fair enough,' said Harry. 'Anybody here not happy about paying Bob three farthing a dozen for eggs? Nobody mind

126

going up Hargate Hill today and handing Bob three farthing and saying, "Give us a dozen eggs, Bob, quick, so we can get them indoors afore sunset"? Right, John. *You* wouldn't mind. Well, suppose you went again tomorrow for another dozen – I know, but just suppose – and Bob said, "Sorry, John, eggs is two shilling and sixpence a dozen today, not three farthing". Would you mind *then*? Paying half a crown for a dozen eggs?'

Everybody laughed and John told Harry he were talking daft, and Bob said nobody would be that soft in head. Harry let them go on for a bit and then told them what he meant.

'If Bob charged forty times more for eggs, half a crown instead of three farthing, you'd tell him to go to hell. But if rents go up forty times you'll pay? That's what Dickenson said: three or four mark for a shilling, forty or fifty times what we're paying now. Same as paying half a crown for a dozen eggs instead of three farthing. Are Dickenson and Scargill trying to starve us all, make beggars of us, put us out of our holdings, turn our families into wandering beggars? Because if rents go up forty, fifty, sixty times, that's what'll happen. They'll make a better job of ruining us nor this damned weather can do!'

Everybody understood that. There were an uproar like when water comes down brook after a storm up on wastes and drowns pinfold below Glossop and floods market square and houses. Nick Mellor and Tom Jackson and me were making more noise nor any. Folk were shouting about what they'd do to Scargill and Dickenson if they come back at Michaelmas with talk about rents going up forty times: there'd be knives, pitchforks and sickles, bill-hooks on poles. Harry's face looked like he'd just drunk a pot of good ale. But as crowd quietened down again, I started feeling cold inside: Newton and his cousin had sneaked off uphill to bailiff's house. It wouldn't be long afore Scargill and Dickenson knew Harry had stirred Glossopdale up. And then, when them bastards come back at Michelmas and learned nobody would pay such daft rents, they'd know it were Harry's doing. I reckoned they'd blame Nick and old Tom and me and all for backing him up.

Then Bob Rowbottom went up to Harry with a bit of parchment in his hand and said summat. I heard Harry say, 'You sure, Bob?' and Bob nodded: 'Aye, look, it's here. Copy'. Same as rest of us, Harry doesn't know his letters like Bob does, but he looked anyroad. He said, 'Right, Bob, don't tell nobody. Let Scargill and Dickenson and bailiff do whatever they've a mind.' Bob muttered summat else and Harry waved him down. 'Say nowt, Bob. Give them bastards enough rope to hang theirselves.'

I thought he might tell me what were on yon bit of parchment and what were going on, only he didn't. Followed yon old proverb, did Harry: *Tell not abroad what you pretend to do, for if you don't speed, your enemies will laugh you to scorn.*

*

'About time, Spiderlegs.' Harry grinned. 'This calls for a drink!'

'Well, nowt's settled, Harry. It's all right with Agnes's Ma and her brother Will, and it's all right with Willie, and Ma says I can do whatever I've a mind even if it's by-our-lady daft, but vicar has to –'

'Don't worry about vicar. He'll wed you and Agnes no bother. Where will you live?'

Will Dawson and me reckoned we'd build a house next to theirs at Pyegrove. Him and his Ma would sublet it under Will's leasehold, seeing it were just Agnes and me. Agnes were happy about it; and like I told Harry, that were all as mattered to me. Then I muttered question I needed to ask. My face went hot and I wanted to hide. Harry laughed.

'She's been greensick a few year, your Agnes. If women don't get pleasured they get poorly and twisted and then you can't do nowt with them. They need a lot of it, mind; a man needs to tame his wife's lust or he gets laughed at. Pump plenty of seed into her, Spiderlegs, and she'll be right enough.'

I thought about Willie and Alice but I said nowt. Harry leaned close and spoke quiet-like.

'A man swyves 'til he pumps his passion out. But woman pumps her passion *in*. Seed won't take if she doesn't. They're same as us, Spiderlegs, only wrong way about. That's why they're weaker and need bossing. See, our tackle's *outside*. Theirs is *inside*. That's why women can't do no heavy work. If they lift summat heavy their private parts turn right side out, and then they're not women no more.'

128

I heard my Dad say summat of sort when I were a nipper but I'd made nowt of it. It were stuff I needed to know now. Happen it were summat like they say about fowl: when a cock gets to seven year old it starts laying eggs. I were late on in life for learning new things; a lot were dead at thirty-four. But like they say, better late nor never.

*

Maggie spent a lot of her time dozing. She still mixed cures but it were Agnes as took them where they were needed and went to women in childbed. Happen Maggie had done her last St Mark's Eve vigil, and it weren't nowt to do with vicar reckoning to stop her. Agnes couldn't do St Mark's Eve, she told me. 'I don't have Sight, Tom, not like Ma.'

Will Dawson reckoned he were glad to have me for a brother, for all I telled him I were no use with plough. He said I were good with sheep and beasts and could get a crop of oats in any sort of weather, and anyroad I'd be worth having next door as a thatcher. So him and me set about building new house. He were shorter nor me but his shoulders were big. Strong lad. Hair as fair as Agnes's. Got on well, Will and me.

One evening when we were tired and rain were pummelling thatch I telled Maggie I reckoned Black Harry and his sisters still missed their mother. 'When Harry goes wandering, I reckon he's off looking for her.'

'Happen, Tom. I don't know. Sight won't show me nowt outside Glossopdale.'

I'd wanted Maggie to say I were right so I could tell Joanna. But you don't always get what you want.

*

When Scargill and Dickenson come back at Michaelmas they were ready for trouble; Bailiff Booth had telled them about Harry stirring folk up, same as I said he would. But we were ready for trouble and all. There were a good three dozen of us and they'd brought nobbut six or seven from Sheffield. They went straight to Storth so they could tackle Harry first.

'They reckon if they can make Black Harry pay their daft new rent then everybody in Glossopdale will do same,' said Agnes.

We all followed Scargill and Dickenson and Bailiff Booth to Storth. Most of us were carrying bill-hooks on poles, or pitchforks, or fivepenny sickles, or knives. Dickenson ran his eyes over us like we were nowt.

'Mr Booth has told you what your new rents are. They are to be paid for one quarter at Lady Day, or else to depart your holdings. Subtenancies and illegal felling will cease. The bailiff will pay your rents to Mr Scargill for his lordship. They will not be paid to Mr Cavendish.'

We started laughing. Scargill looked murder at us. Harry come out, arms folded, and stared Dickenson in face. Dickenson stood tall.

'We've no commandment to deal with you, Botham. You're evicted from your holding for preaching riot and sedition.'

He nodded to Scargill, and Scargill up with a spade and went to dig clod of earth out of Harry's field to claim farmhold back for his lordship. Yon spade never touched ground. Harry twisted it out of Scargill's hands and threw it over his shoulder. Everybody laughed louder.

'You said if I behaved like rest of Glossopdale I'd keep my tenement. Go back on your word a lot, do you, Mr Dickenson?' He spat and stared at Scargill. 'I'm saying nowt to yon rat. Devil wouldn't trust *his* word, and I reckon they've had dealings enough.'

Scargill bunched his fists but six or seven of us moved in so he didn't do nowt.

'You have stirred unrest among the people of this manor, Botham.' Dickenson were shouting over our laughter and cheering, still reckoning he could boss us. 'You've encouraged illegal subletting and felling and further abuses. You've persuaded other tenants to refuse the rents required of you. You will go!'

'Your rents are daft work and you know it. And usage has given us rights to land same as ancient rights. *Custom!*' Harry raised his fists and everybody cheered again.

'You will leave, Botham! You will go! A tenant loyal to his lordship will be placed in this farmhold! It is yours no longer!'

Harry unfolded his arms and stepped forward. If Dickenson and Scargill had looked murder at him it were nowt to what they were getting back. Harry's face were like a mad bull's, fit to make a man shit himself.

'This is my land. There's been Bothams in Simmondley for two hundred year and more, and there'll be Bothams here for two hundred yet. I won't leave it but by law, and you don't bring no law; you bring nobbut threats. My house is my castle. I've summat prepared for anybody as dares come into it, any as his lordship sends. Either I or yon as comes will die!'

Every Glossopdale man, woman and child cheered and roared. Then Dickenson said they were evicting Willie and me and all, happen for being Harry's brothers-in-law, or happen because I'd a twisted leg so they reckoned I'd a twisted soul. And old Tom Jackson were supposed to go. He hadn't stirred folk up like Harry did, but like Bob Wolstenhome said, he'd once thrown Scargill into ditch. And they were evicting Nick Mellor, but that weren't no surprise; there weren't nobody had more jaw nor Nick. Next news we were all guarding houses and lands with blades. Randoph Swann had put them to grindstone so they were sharp. It took a while, but Dickenson and Scargill backed off at finish, on their horses again and off east, their men following them, riding into wind and rain with a crowd of Glossopdale folk behind them clapping and cheering.

'This isn't finished,' said Harry. 'It's just start. But I know summat as they don't.'

Bailiff come up to me and whispered: 'I warned you, Tom: have nothing to do with Botham. Now see what's happened to you and Willie.'

'Nowt's happened only threats,' I told him, 'and threats don't break no bones.'

He went home.

*

It were a funny time of year to get wed. Most folk married on unlousing Monday if they could; after Lent and Easter were done, anyroad. But Agnes and me didn't care. We were wedded on a Wednesday, as is best day for it, and there were a hawk in sky over church while we were in porch so we knew we'd be happy. Whatever folk said about yon vicar he could talk sense, though it were in words I wouldn't have said. 'Give

131

yourself time to hear the Holy Scriptures and good doctrine, and make sure you know the laws of the realm,' he told me. 'Be merry at home amongst your household and use them gently, and always respect good husbandry. Be sure you always have provisions and necessities ready for your house and maintenance.' Like I said, all good sense. Well, I'd do my best.

He'd more to say, stuff everybody knew only them as were as daft as Hugh Platt: 'The best way to keep your wife quiet and honest is to be honest yourself, live carefully and in good order with her, and beware of jealousy. A wife is like a piece of wax, which will receive what you impose if you make it supple enough. Don't give her too much of her own will and liberty or flatter her with too much pride. Let her love her house and learn to govern the things committed to her charge.'

Fancy talk; same as I said, words I wouldn't use. But I weren't worried about last bit. Wore a cross of wiggin wood under her bodice, did Agnes, and like any good woman her besoms had wiggin handles; and I drove a horseshoe into ground outside our door so we wouldn't have no trouble with witches. And with Agnes keeping place clean, fairies might come and leave us good things. Mind, you couldn't always tell fairies from witches; same red cloaks, same hoods. Like any man with sense as gets a new lease of land, I dug a spadeful and threw it up and caught it on back of spade so crops would thrive.

Anyroad, we were wedded. I weren't used to secret bits of women, but I reckoned it couldn't be that hard to get her ready for tupping, and after a bit of pawing and fumbling and scrabbling that night we managed. What mattered were, we were together in our new house, next to where she'd lived all her life. Willie and Ma reckoned they'd miss me. Alice wouldn't; she said nowt but I reckoned she were glad I were gone. Agnes said *she* were glad I were away from Alice. I told her Alice were a scold but there weren't no real harm in her.

It weren't long afore I'd as good a household as Willie. It'd been a bad year but we could still buy from markets; bacon flitches, sacks of oats and meal. We'd cheese and butter as Agnes got out of milk, apples and pears off our trees, honey off bees. She'd gathered her herbs by waxing moon and hung them off rafters: meadow-sweet, mountain flax, sanctuary, betony, hyssop, rosemary, hoarhound, feverfew; all plucked in flower. They smelled grand. She'd dried a cat skin and all, for folk to hold against their faces when they'd toothache. We'd no riches but God blessed us with contentment, glory be His name.

Then Coney died, and Malachi were all over Glossopdale wailing and skriking. Agnes and Joanna and Alice made three-cornered cakes, and we give them to Coney's bees with a pot of burnt drink so they wouldn't all die and follow her soul. I were worried about Coney's nipper because Malachi weren't no good for her, so Agnes said, 'Let's fetch her down here and bring her up as ours, Tom. That road she'll have a proper home and a good father, and she won't need money off poor box to keep her no more.'

So we went and fetched little mite from Herod. Whether Malachi were happy about it I never knew because he died that winter and all. Agnes said he'd died of grief for Coney. We did what we could: left his door open to let his spirit out, kept a candle burning overnight for him, put a plate of salt on his chest to keep witches off him, and we got him buried with his feet pointing to Jerusalem. It were a sorry time. Never rains but it pours. Mind, it *did* rain while he were being buried. Heaven wept for him because not a lot of his neighbours did. There weren't enough of us to share burnt drink.

We called Coney's nipper *Margaret* after Agnes's mother, and we give her my family name. That were good because Agnes hadn't got a babby in her belly for all I kept tupping her and for all she kept asking for it. Harry were right when he said women were full of lust and men needed to tame them. Couldn't get enough swyving, my wife couldn't. Every man likes swyving, but it's hard work.

We were holding one another one night after passion were spent and Agnes said, 'We're not doing like vicar says, Tom. We're only supposed to do it to make babbies, and we haven't made a babby, so happen we shouldn't do it at all.'

That were a funny road of thinking, I reckoned. More like we should be doing more of it. I'd asked Maggie whether she reckoned there were owt wrong. It were like with Willie and Alice; didn't matter how much he tupped her, God never sent a babby. Maggie said it were early days

133

for Agnes and me and we'd best wait and see, but if God didn't send a babby there might be two reasons, same as why oats wouldn't grow in some places: either soil were no good or seed were bad.

'Aye, well, love,' I said to Agnes, 'you know what Joanna said last Lammas Fair, when I asked her what vicar would say about her watching yon young wrestlers in Chapel.'

'What did she say?'

'To hell with vicar.'

Agnes laughed.

'Aye. Right, Tom. To hell with vicar.'

'Aye. And if God never does give us a babby, love, let's thank Him for our little Margaret.'

Sheffield, January 1578/9

'Custom! Always the cry of these miscreants! What is this *custom* but common law perverted, artifice conjured from shadow, nothing written, no account kept, "resting only in the memory of man", wearing this mantle or that as the wind changes, law become a whore!'

Dickenson's voice smote the walls. The restored tapestries cowered before the echoes.

'William –'

'A device to cheat their lord of his due, Nathaniel, this *custom*, this descent from "a time when the memory of man does not run to the contrary" –'

'William, peace! You're frustrated because you couldn't execute his honour's commands in Glossopdale. But you're sounding like George Scargill. Let reason calm you.'

Dickenson sagged on to the bench, head in hands.

'I've more than enough to do with the accounts for his honour's estates, Nathaniel, and the lead trade, and the cutlers. Why can't Glossopdale's tenants accept *parochial* custom and acknowledge everyone who has rights to tithes? Why can't they bend to *manorial* custom and bear their duties like honest men? Their *custom* can change between dawn and dusk of a single day at the behest of knaves who glory in discord and discontent!'

Eyre squeezed his friend's shoulder and poured wine.

'Custom defines property, William. Underwrites the way people relate to one another. Defines their everyday behaviour. The duties of man to man. It's sired by common law out of local needs and the protection of

135

village livelihoods. Yes, it changes with time and place. It has to; custom is the sum of each community's negotiations and resolutions over generations; it's a process, not a fixed body of rules. But it has to be acknowledged as reasonable by all sides, "according to common right", to the profit of everyone at a given time and place. And it must be based on the laws of God, nature and man. If it meets those criteria, then "resting only in the memory of man" is a fiction that every court in England accepts.'

'You acknowledge its authority, Nathaniel?' Dickenson swallowed his wine. 'As a Manor Court judge, you don't treat this so-called "custom" with the scorn it merits? What kind of law has parts that vanish without warning and parts that appear without foundation? "Time out of memory of man" is a blatant falsehood. New threads of custom are woven by magic out of thin air whenever it suits villains who're bent on sedition. How can it justify anything?'

Eyre shook his head.

'Hard words, William. Sedition merits questioning under torture. Hanging. A local dispute in a far-away manor isn't "sedition".'

Dickenson struggled to control his exasperation.

'A rebellion of tenants against their liege lord is sedition, Nathaniel. What else can it be? Why shouldn't those scoundrels hang?'

'All mortal laws change. Only God's Law is eternal. Common law adapts to new monarchs, religious rules, sources of money, pressures on land... England now isn't the England of our childhood. Her laws aren't the laws of our childhood. So common law changes quickly; but custom can change even faster. It must; it's about settling particular differences in local settings, not broad disputes affecting the whole realm. Nevertheless, when it defines the relationship between landlord and tenant, it's binding on both. Courts enforce it as they enforce the common law. So insistence on it isn't sedition, William. Judgements based on custom can be overturned in a common law court, but only if the court hears compelling arguments and is persuaded by them.'

Dickenson gestured impatience.

'So those villains in Glossopdale have a right in law to determine whether their relationship with his honour is fair or unfair? Whether it's reasonable or exploitative? Is that what their custom means?' He paced the hall and glared at one of returned tapestries: a hunting scene picked out in reds and blues and greens and fawns, marred now by Tutbury's damp and mildew. 'Four knaves in Glossopdale are to be evicted at his honour's command. So to judge from what you say about custom, they'd no right to stop us digging a clod from Botham's tenancy, because he's no longer part of a landlord-tenant relationship.' He ventured a smile. 'We'll return in greater numbers and plough a furrow on his lands. Then his holding will be reclaimed and by law he will go. We'll do the same to the other three miscreants who stand with him. I can readily conceive that as "custom".'

Glossopdale, January 1578/9

Black Harry and Nick Mellor and old Tom Jackson said they'd die afore they'd let Scargill and Dickenson put them out of their holdings. Mr Eyre had telled all four of us to come to Sheffield and see him, but Harry said it would be a waste of time because it wouldn't change nowt. Last Michelmas he'd said we'd go there to see his lordship if we weren't happy with rents, and some folk like John Stedman reckoned we still should. John and Rose had a new babby, a boy. They were happy, only I reckoned John still missed Tilly. His brother Jim got Herod leasehold after God had took Malachi and Coney, but neither Jim nor his wife had Coney's way with stock. Happen they'd manage bees.

'If you go to Sheffield, Harry, steward might sort it out,' said John. 'If he doesn't, and Manor Court doesn't, we've Duchy Court. Worth a try, isn't it?'

'Me and my Dad tried them courts about different lots of leases in Glossopdale, John, and about some folk getting a bad deal when we shifted to closed farms. That were a few year back, afore I went for a servant in Castleton. Going to them courts didn't do nowt only kick up a stink. And see them lads in Peak Forest, going to Manor and Duchy Courts about rent rises? That weren't so long ago, and they got nowhere neither. We've same landlord as them. He's earl marshal of England so there isn't nobody above him only Queen and God. So there's only God and Queen can help us with these rent rises and breaches of custom. We can pray to God for help, and so we should; but to get Queen's help we'll need to go and see her Privy Council, and pray to *them*.'

John and a few others started muttering. Sounded like October wind in woods. Harry raised his voice.

'It won't come to that if Scargill and Dickenson show sense. But if they don't show sense, then it will. Them as are with us can come to London. Them as aren't can stay at home. We'll try Duchy Court again first so we can say we've done it, but I reckon it won't get us nowhere.'

A dozen said they were with Harry and Nick and old Tom and me. But there were lands to plough and crops to plant and beasts to care for, and there'd be lambs born if God sent us any, and later on there'd be sheep to wash and shear and all. Joanna said if ploughing were done, women would do rest of work, and men as didn't go to London would help them. Harry said most of what needed doing weren't women's work, but Joanna told him she reckoned there were nowt in Bible nor law of England as said women couldn't do men's work on land. Harry bruised her for answering back, but Joanna kept on saying it so he give up. If a woman doesn't shut up when she's had a good smack, she won't shut up at all. Best let her keep talking and just stop listening to her.

Agnes said, 'Tom, if you and Harry and rest go to London, you'd best carry a sprig of mugwort while you're walking and then you won't get as tired, you with your bad hip. Jo's right; we'll manage'.

I told her I'd be all right so she could stop fussing. If Tom Jackson could walk to London at his age, I could do same. She said she were giving me mugwort to carry anyroad, and that were that. My wife could answer back as well as any when she'd a mind, but I weren't going to beat her for it, God bless her. I always said Bob Wolstenholme were too soft with his Martha because he never beat her only when he were drunk, so happen I were too soft with Agnes, and there'd be more ivy nor holly round our house come Christmastide. But I didn't care. I weren't happy about women doing heavy lifting, mind, not after what Harry had told me. I didn't want Agnes's private parts turning inside out, nor Joanna's neither. I reckon Harry thought same. But work had to be done, and if enough of us men went to London, who else could do it only womenfolk?

It weren't no use going to London in January, mind. Sun weren't up while we'd finished breakfast and it were dark middle of afternoon, and ways were fouled with frost and snow. Anyroad, happen Dickenson and Scargill had forgot them daft rent rises and eviction threats. Agnes and me reckoned them two were doing what *they* wanted, not what his lordship wanted, so they could line their own purses. Harry and Nick reckoned they were trying to get rid of us so they could put some of his lordship's arse-licking servants in our farmholds. 'Save having to pay them wages,' Harry said. We argued about it, but we all agreed we'd do nowt unless them bastards come back again with their daft demands. If they did, then we'd need to see about London. A few men said they wouldn't go to London but they'd get a bit of money together to help them as would. Harry shook their hands.

Then that drunken ha'peth Ottewell Higginbottom shot his mouth off in a Marple alehouse saying he'd got two hundred stout lads ready to join Harry's fight against Lord Shrewsbury. No more sense nor a heather besom, Higginbottom. For a start, we weren't reckoning to fight Lord Shrewsbury, only his agents. No use stirring up trouble when there weren't no need. And neither Harry nor none of rest of us would ever ask Higginbottom for owt. Look on Harry's face when he heard, I reckoned Higginbottom were lucky he weren't nowhere near. Others just laughed at him. Damned fool.

Mr Yeaveley told us in his next sermon if we all went and submitted to Lord Shrewsbury he'd be a good lord to us, so them Newtons went and submitted and a couple of others went with them. Folk sneered at them.

'Good lord to us?' said Harry. 'Aye, if he gets rid of Scargill and Dickenson and their mad rent rises and evictions. I'll keep on praying for his lordship every day, but I'm not doing no submitting 'til Scargill and Dickenson go.'

*

'Harry means a lot to you, doesn't he, Tom?' We were in front of fire. Agnes had wrapped sheepskin round us. It were dark outside.

'Aye,' I said.

When we were nippers, and lads threw stones at me shouting *Run, cripple, run* and *Dance, cripple, go on, dance*, Harry had got stuck into them with his fists and boots, and after that they left me alone. They never reckoned much to me, but I were Black Harry's friend. One of them might pick a fight, giving me three punches on shoulder – scarding blow, fighting blow, everlasting blow – and I'd have to scrap with him. Mostly I come off worse, but none of them could spit over my head and say, 'Cock o'er midden'.

'You saved his life from a mad tup when you were seven year old,' said Agnes.

'Happen I saved tup from Harry.'

'Harry says you saved him. Tells folk about it when you're not there.'

Made me swell up warm inside, that did. There were nowt I wouldn't do for Black Harry.

Sheffield, 10th-14th April 1579

'Glossopdale. Riotous, unworthy tenants.' Dickenson leaned his elbows on the table and invited Katherine to sit opposite. She placed a mug of ale beside his hand. 'The four knaves I told you about have fomented sedition among the rest, so they're to be evicted. George chose a dozen men to plough furrows to reclaim their tenements, but four-fifths of Glossopdale's householders came to make rescue. Jackson and Mellor led them. They patrolled the farms bearing poles capped with blades. Botham has prevailed on them to pay no rent until the eviction orders are rescinded.'

'Have they a case in law? Could the eviction orders be –?'

'The Glossopdale bailiff wrote to his honour saying Mr Cavendish had advised the tenants to go to London to exclaim against him. The villains took their complaint to Duchy Court; and there, Sir John de Zouche's lawyer gave them the same advice. So Sir John and Mr Cavendish have both encouraged the tenants to rebel against his honour. To *rebel*, Kath. Rebellion, a day's walk from where the Scottish Queen is held!'

Dickenson quaffed ale. Katherine tilted her head.

'Four-fifths of Glossopdale's householders. In numbers, how many?'

'Forty at least.'

'Forty against your dozen? Did your dozen carry firearms?'

'No, Kath. Would we carry pikes or arquebuses or pistolets against a rabble of commoners?'

'Then how could your dozen have done what you set out to do? His lordship can't blame you for events beyond your control. Will he rescind –?'

Dickenson laughed a short, bitter laugh.

'He won't.' He finished his ale and banged his mug on the table. 'As we left the valley, Botham declared he'd lead men to London to complain to the Privy Council about the new rents and the evictions.'

'As they've been advised by Sir John and Mr Cavendish.'

'The *Privy Council*, Kath! Of course, the fools will achieve nothing even if they reach London, and even if the Council grants them an audience, which I don't foresee. Nonetheless they're a nuisance. We *must* enforce the evictions and impose the new rents; but if we move against the tenants while they're absent from their holdings, we'll be wrong in law.'

'They're stubborn. What can you do?'

The earl had issued orders, Dickenson explained; accordingly, the letter from the Derbyshire Justices of the Peace that condemned the "riotous behaviour of divers of your lordship's rude and uncivil tenants" had been forwarded to the Privy Council. He smiled at the phrasing; Nathaniel Eyre had advised his fellow-justices to describe the tenants as "rude and uncivil", and they'd followed his guidance. However, the letter also recommended that all the tenants save the ringleaders should be pitied not punished. That was regrettable. Nevertheless, the lords and gentlemen of the Council were forewarned of the threatened deputation.

'The Glossopdale bailiff is also too lenient, begging his honour not to deal hardly with the tenants since it was her ladyship and her son who set them on. I've therefore written separately to Tom Baldwin, and to his honour's son Gilbert, asking them to stop the Glossopdale knaves before they reach London and send them home before there can be any risk of them troubling the Council; or else to have them imprisoned pending trial for sedition.'

'What is the tenants' principal complaint, William? Rents or evictions?'

'The evictions. His honour told the Council so. The villains confessed as much. They refused Nathaniel's order to go to him in Sheffield for mediation. They refused to submit themselves to his honour when he promised to be a good lord to them.'

Katherine smiled.

'*Very* stubborn. But have tenants in England never rebelled about rents and evictions before, William?'

'Many times. There were rent strikes in Worcestershire before we were born. When I was nine years old, commoners rioted about enclosures and rents through most of England. Tenants occupied disputed land in Buckinghamshire during the Northern Rising in '69, though that was fomented by Papist noblemen, not by commoners. While her majesty's father was king, tenants protested in thirty townships in the West Riding; one township in twenty. But Glossopdale's incivility and impertinence are of a different order.'

'You think they'll dare do as they've threatened? If they go to London, who'll work their lands and discharge their responsibilities? Their wives, I suppose; as women must when men go to war.'

*

As secretary to the earl, Dickenson had many concerns. Gilbert Talbot's wife Mary, daughter of the countess, had been ill. Gilbert assured his father that Mary would make a full recovery because her physician, Mr Julio, had said so. When Dickenson wrote to him about the Glossopdale tenants he remembered to include wishes for Mary's better health.

His eyes smarted. The chimney in his chamber at the castle smoked. He should let the fire out; the weather ought to be warm enough by this time of year.

Now he must reply to Richard Topcliffe about the roof repairs on Coldharbour House; Shrewsbury House, as they'd begun to call it. And he must convey his honour's opinion of the appointment of Sir Thomas Bromley as Lord Keeper to succeed Sir Nicholas Bacon. Thomas Pullyson had sent good news: sixty fothers of lead at nine pounds the fother had reached London from John Walley in Hull. Gilbert Talbot had written to tell his father that Thomas Baldwin had delivered ten of those fothers to the Lord Treasurer, Lord Burghley, at the agent's cost, so an equal division of profits meant Pullyson owed his honour two hundred and seventy pounds. However, the market for lead in London had weakened, so Pullyson had dispatched several fothers to Rouen and asked that Walley's next shipment be delayed until midsummer. The earl ordered Dickenson and Baldwin to provide no more lead to Pullyson until his debts were paid. Dickenson wrote accordingly to Pullyson.

The Shrewsbury finances were worsening. A trading vessel had disappeared; no news. Gilbert Talbot's debts mounted; his honour was hard pressed to meet them. Baldwin said he was charged with more payments than his receipts could cover. His honour had commanded him to pay a debt to a glazier before he met the countess's demands; a brave decision by a desperate man, said Baldwin.

Dickenson had also written to the Secretary of State, Sir Francis Walsingham, begging for desperately-needed diet money for the Scottish Queen. During 1577, custody of Mary had cost his honour nine thousand one hundred and twenty-three pounds seven shillings and fivepence more than the Crown had provided. Sir Francis had explained: the Irish campaign was costing her majesty about ten thousand pounds per year, and she was obliged to pay debts totalling some twenty thousand pounds to the young King of Scots. Therefore, there could be no additional payments for care of the Scottish King's mother.

Dickenson grimaced. The Secretary of State was deemed shrewd, intelligent and loyal to her majesty, so why was he content with round-figure approximations? Dickenson distrusted estimates. Only detailed accounts could satisfy him. But he was in no position to demand full details of the Crown's finances from Sir Francis Walsingham.

George More said he'd resolved the dispute between the earl and the free tenants of Sheffield. The tenants claimed they'd been awarded the right to build on waste ground during Lord Furnival's time. Mr More had sworn in church that the tenants had no such right in law. The matter was now before the court in York. It was certain that More's resolution would be upheld on behalf of the earl. Dickenson would then be obliged to explain the court's ruling to the tenants.

The duke of Alençon's prospective marriage to the Queen was once again consuming the Privy Council's attention; it was priority for the earl marshal. Most of their lordships favoured the marriage despite

Alençon's religion and his involvement in the St Bartholomew's Day massacre: accept the French as a bulwark against the Spanish.

Tom Baldwin says the Privy Council is so preoccupied with her majesty's marriage, meeting daily from eight in the morning until dinnertime, that their lordships are unlikely to find time to accommodate the Glossopdale villains. No Englishman would wish his Queen to marry a suspect Frenchman; but while those in high places debate the prospect, our rude and uncivil tenants will have no opportunity to present a Bill against his honour.

The chimney continued to smoke.

Derby, Newmarket, Barnet: March 30th – April 14th, 1579

Harry killed first adder of spring with his ash staff; good sign. Him and me set off five day after Feast of Annunciation with old Tom and Nick Mellor, speedwell flowers on our jerkins, me with yon sprig of mugwort as Agnes had made me carry. Eight more went with us: Harry's brother-in-law Olly Smith, our runner; my brother-in-law Will Dawson, as mimicked folk; Tom Blood as sang while we walked, *Oh, no John, no John, no John, no*; Harry's other brother-in-law Ottie Wood, as knew what weather we'd have; Bob Rowbottom, as knew his letters better nor rest of us; big Edmund Bower as had nigh killed yon pedlar on May Day six year back and went out taking pigeons a-nights; poor Henry Warhurst from Crow Car, as played fiddle; and Phil Woolley, as could have been a preacher only his voice were bad. Phil wore a fox's tongue to make him bold.

Day on day we started when sun rose and walked while it were dark, buying a crust of bread here, an onion there, a bit of cheese somewhere else, a pot of ale where we could. We slept in woods or under walls when Ottie said it wouldn't rain, in alehouses or churches when it did. When it rained our clothes got wet and weighed on our shoulders like burden of sin; then sun shone like light of God's mercy and we were dry again. Sometimes a driver let us up on a cart coming back from spreading dung or summat so we could save our legs a few mile. But mostly we walked, and every evening I steeped lady's bedstraw in spring water to bathe our feet like Agnes had told me. I hadn't walked that much since I come back from being in service up Yorkshire way nine year back, only when

147

we went to Derby that time when poor Coney were had up in church court. My hip made me see stars all colours every step I took, and I were missing Agnes. But I watched old Tom: not giving up, not grumbling neither. We worried about how many days it were to London, and whether women would shear our sheep like they'd said and do other jobs like Joanna reckoned, and whether men as had stayed behind would help them. But none of us were for turning back.

Birds singing, flowers in fields, trees blossoming, leaves budding, clouds and sunshine, all kept us minded of God's goodness and lovely world He'd made for us. There were beggars and vagabonds at roadside, children crying with pain, and folk in villages sick and dying, to keep us minded of Devil's work and wicked landlords' agents as did that work for him.

We were in Matlock that Sunday and then we went on south. Just other side Derby we met three farmers as said, 'Our landlord is Sir John de Zouche', and Harry said, 'We're off to London to see Privy Council so we can get rent rises stopped, and Sir John is our landlord's enemy'. They asked, 'Who is your landlord?' and when we told them it were Lord Shrewsbury, they said, 'We'll tell Sir John where you're going and why, and perhaps he'll send you help'. Happen they'd do nowt of sort, I thought, but they took us to their houses and give us floors with clean rushes to sleep on. Harry played his bagpipe so they could dance, and Phil tried telling them Bill Goddard's tale about Elijah Sheldon finding yon magic fife and opening gates of fairyland with it. Then Nick told them another of Bill's: about Harold, as were a swineherd at Castleton, going to find his farrowing sow as had gone missing, and getting to yon Other Country behind caves, and pig and her piglets helping him solve Lord of Wind's three riddles. Everybody likes them tales, only Bill tells them best. Old Tom told about fighting Papist rebels in Yorkshire back in '36, under his lordship's father and grandfather, but said what we were doing now, going to London, were more like riots up and down England as common folk had stirred in '49. Dad used to talk about '36 and '49 and all.

Sir John's tenants give us ale and a hot stew with bacon in it, and after we'd prayed with them next morning they took us to a bridge where we could cross a wide river. Then we went on walking, rising sun to our left, setting sun to our right.

'We're not going quickest road to London,' said Ottie. 'You're taking us wrong, Harry.'

'No I'm not.' Harry pointed east. 'I know it's not quickest, Ottie, but there's places yonder where folk know me and will give us food and shelter.'

Flat country were good for walking but it didn't feel right not having no hills round us. It makes you dizzy when you can see too far, like you can from top of Coombes Edge. We had to watch there weren't no fairy rings where we slept; it weren't May Eve or Midsummer Eve or All Hallows, but fairy folk can still make away with you if you sleep on their dancing floor.

After another two day we come to a village they called Hallaton and we slept in their church. Next morning were Sunday so we went to service, and there were organ music with hymns, not just psalms chanted. After service were done, vicar asked where we'd come from and where we were going, and Harry said, 'We're from Glossopdale in Derbyshire and we're off to London to see Privy Council to get our landlord's rent rises stopped'. He asked, 'Who's your landlord?' and when we told him it were Lord Shrewsbury he said, 'To bring complaint against so great a nobleman is wicked, and if the Privy Council learn of your evil intent they will put you in prison so you may be tried in court for your wrongdoing'. So we told him it weren't Lord Shrewsbury as were making daft rent rises, it were his agents, only Lord Shrewsbury wouldn't hear nowt against them so we had to go higher. Vicar weren't having none of it, but a few folk in village heard us and they cheered, and they took us to their homes and fed us and asked us about rents, and they said, 'You're right, that's evil,' and we got floors with fresh rushes to sleep on again that night. Harry said he couldn't play his pipes and get folk dancing because it were Sabbath, so instead we told tales about what happened to folk as didn't respect Sabbath: old woman as baked oatcakes on a Sunday and her dress caught fire and burned her to death; folk as gather hay on a Sunday and their stack catches fire. Henry Warhurst told Bill's story about robber as chewed a bag of nuts in church porch while his friend were stealing a sheep in next field, and sexton and vicar thought noise of nut-chewing were Devil chewing lost souls. One Hallaton farmer said he knew that story and he told it his road, a bit different nor Bill's. Will told them what their vicar had said: 'To bring complaint against so great a nobleman is a wicked thing, and if the Privy Council learn of your evil intent they will put you in prison so you may be tried in court for your wrongdoing'. He made his voice sound just like yon vicar, Will did, and it made Hallaton folk laugh 'til they pissed themselves. We'd a comfortable night on them floors. After prayers next morning we set off same as afore.

Farms there were run different nor ours. A lot were still open field with farmed strips. There were different flowers side of road and all, some I couldn't put a name to, and birds I'd never seen. Land were flat but sometimes it were hard to see where road went; it wound around marshes and ponds as weren't fit to drink and give birth to midges. Stink from them marshes could give a man fevers. Roads in villages weren't bad because Manor Courts made folk look after them; but same as at home, nobody cared for roads from one village to another. Travellers had to make do.

We come to a place called Newmarket, only houses weren't new and there weren't no market. It were like Harry said, though; men there knew him, and they called to him and shook his hand and asked where we were going. Harry told them, 'We're off to London to see Privy Council to get our landlord's rent rises stopped', and they said, 'If you're fighting rent rises, come and fight ours when you're done', and promised they'd give us food and ale come noontide, and good floors for us to sleep on at night.

Some folk there were trying to mend a thatch. Making a right pig's breakfast of it and all. They'd good wheat straw in Newmarket, summat as won't grow in Glossopdale, but they'd no idea how to bottle it, so they were trying to lay thatch with no kick. Weren't doing much of a job fastening it, neither. Wheat straw could be fastened straight to timber; they didn't use turf in those parts. I showed them how it were done proper, and after we'd had food and ale as were promised us I ended up doing job myself, womenfolk bottling like I told them and passing mud up to me. I couldn't tell much they were saying because they talked different nor us, and I had to speak slow and loud so they'd understand me, but with good will we'd finished thatch afore bats come out. Then we went to where Harry's friends lived and had some more ale. Tom Blood sang two of his songs and then sang them again so Newmarket folk could join in.

Over the mountains
And over the waves,
Under the fountains
And under the graves,
Under floods that are deepest,
Which Neptune obey
Over rocks which are the steepest,
Love will find out the way.

Next morning they give us food to carry, bread and cheese and onions, and cheered us off. Harry were right: it were worth taking longer road to London to find good folk like them in Newmarket as would share what they had.

Two night after we'd left Newmarket we were sleeping in a field outside a village with no name as we could make out, and while it were dark, with not much moon, six beggars come on us with knives and clubs. Big Edmund were watching so he shouted and then we were all up. None of us took much harm; there were more of us nor them. Edmund roared. Four of beggars run off with their hurts and two were dead. Harry went after four as were running, but they knew road through marshes and he didn't, so he come back, teeth shining in what bit of moonlight there were, chest swelled. Beggars had reckoned to rob us because they had nowt. We put them two dead ones in a pond, said a prayer over them and pocketed their knives. Then we lay down to sleep again.

I woke after a bit; there were loveliest birdsong I'd ever heard coming from a wood. I went and had a look. Woods aren't safe at night, even without marshes where you can drown, because there's fairy folk as make you lose your path, and then you find a youth sleeping on a bed of leaves; nobody you know, so you'd best not waken him. There's night

151

creatures and all, foxes and badgers and owls, and them birds as sang yon lovely song. I got down on my knees and thanked God again for giving us such beauty.

'Nightingales,' said Harry. 'Right noisy birds. Wish damned things would shut up.'

Day after that we come to a village called Barnet. Harry said it weren't far from London. Two gentlemen on horseback were waiting for us with their servants and three men on foot wearing armour and swords. One gentleman said he were Lord Shrewsbury's son, Mr Gilbert Talbot; other were Mr Richard Topcliffe.

'We were told of your coming,' said Mr Talbot. 'You shall go no further. Turn round and go back home. Knaves, all of you.'

'Saving your presence, sir,' said Harry, 'it's been too long a road for us to give up now. We'll turn round and go home when we've finished with Privy Council, not afore.'

Mr Talbot and Mr Topcliffe tried to block our way, yon men in armour with them, but we faced them and stepped forward. Everybody started shouting. Then Harry said if they didn't let us through we'd write to her majesty about it, and he reckoned she wouldn't be happy if her subjects were denied justice; because if they were denied justice, happen some would go back to Papistry. *He* wouldn't, but some might. Both gentlemen stared at him and then they muttered to one another, and then Mr Topcliffe told us to stay where we were and he rode off south. We sat and ate what food we still had from Newmarket.

Sun were going down afore Mr Topcliffe come back. There were a very fine gentleman with him, and more servants. Mr Talbot doffed his hat to this very fine gentleman and called him Sir Francis. Sir Francis looked at us, one by one, taking his time. Eyes like January frost. He said nowt for a while but he put wind up us just looking. When he spoke, his voice were a scythe slicing through air afore it cuts your hay.

'Let them proceed, Mr Talbot. Your men will accompany them. They may sleep where they will beside the road. Tomorrow they will go to their *lodgings*. In the Marshalsea.' He looked at us again and smiled. I'd never seen lips that thin. 'You will celebrate the Sabbath in your *lodgings*. You will keep to your *lodgings* until you are summoned.'

Mr Talbot and Mr Topcliffe and yon three armed men reckoned he must have made a joke so they tried to laugh. Sir Francis turned towards them and helped them. I were scared, but Edmund Bower give me a nudge. Nigh on broke my ribs with his elbow.

'He's good luck, yon Sir Francis. See, Spiderlegs? Bay horse with one white stocking.'

Southwark, April 14th, 1579

I'd never been in a boat afore but I knew what it were. It rocked on river like a babby held in arms as didn't love it. River were wider nor yon we'd crossed after Derby. It were grey like sky, grey like an iron blade honed by north wind, grey like Ottie's face. It grumbled and sploshed and hissed like bad bowels. Harry said he could smell sea. Happen that were what I could smell and all: fish, rotting stuff, shit, and summat else I couldn't put a name to.

Them three with armour and swords as had been at Barnet with Mr Talbot and Mr Topcliffe come and shoved us into boat. Boatman grinned like a horse with no teeth. His mate looked like a tup sizing us up and dipping its horns. He were only a lad, mind. Way yon boatman moved oars I reckoned he'd be good at plough. Happen he'd farmed afore he took to ploughing rivers. Then we were out on water and boatman and mate and them three armed men were talking and laughing. I couldn't make out a lot of what they were saying. Water slapping boat, and lumps of I don't know what banging at sides, put a lid on their voices. Anyroad, they talked funny in London like they'd done in Newmarket. There were summat about 'sedition' and 'Marshalsea' and 'Privy Council'. I said I didn't reckon much to London talk.

'Not London, Spiderlegs. London's where we've been.' Harry jerked his thumb over his shoulder and then pointed forward. 'We're off to Southwark.'

There were other boats, some little like ours, some that big you'd need a ladder to get in them. Looked like they were off to here, there and everywhere, some going this road, some that. Folk shouted from one to another, and from boats to sides of river and back, and a lot of what were being shouted didn't sound like English. Dogs were barking and all.

Southwark were nowt special. It rocked up and down in front of me and looked like twenty Simmondleys huddled together. Nowt only tottering shacks and brothels, not a rood of common as I could see, nor land for corn or beast. There were one big crumbling house of stone, a good two chain long and three rod or more wide. Looked like it had stood there time out of memory of man, same as a church.

Boat got to bank and scraped on pebbles and animal bones and them three with armour pushed us out into water and up bank and towards stone house. Marshalsea Prison, they said. In front of it there were a big hut with little towers. We got shoved in there next.

We were all scared, not knowing what were happening, but Harry nodded at folk arguing at front of hut. 'Sir John's men,' he said, 'telling governor what's what.' He pointed at a fat drunkard and said, 'That's governor'.

One of them three armed men clanked up to Sir John's lot to throw his weight about, but they turned on him and he slunk back like a daft lapdog as has yapped at a boarhound. There were gentlemen among Sir John's lot, and him with armour weren't no gentleman. I could make out some of their talk now we weren't in boat. Harry were right; governor were getting telled what were what. Sir John's chief man, him as were like boarhound, said summat about a commission and Bishop of London and Dean of St. Paul's, and governor looked sick. Boarhound went on: seemed we were getting money for renting our room and for food and drink, and if governor took it off us and didn't give us proper food and ale, Knight Marshall would know. I'd never heard of no Knight Marshall but governor had. He kept trying to look cocky but he licked his lips like they were too dry for talking. Then boarhound said governor would be in worse trouble if he used skullcap or thumbscrews or bull's pizzle on any of us, and if he put us in strong room Sir John would see him hanged. I've seen men look less sick nor yon governor after they've had their balls crushed in a wrestling match. Way he stared at us I could

155

tell he weren't our friend, but he looked more scared nor what we were. When he saw Sir John's men give us money his eyes were hungry, but he said nowt and did less.

Next news Sir John's men had gone, taking them three with armour and swords with them, and governor and his crew had shoved us into a big dark room. There were other men in there afore us; no women.

'Women are separate,' one of them told us. 'Blue-ruffs go in the Clink, not Marshalsea.'

'Blue-ruffs?' I said.

'Winchester geese, mate. Whores. Could use a couple of them in here, eh?'

We soon found out who we were with. Felons, most of them, but some were in for a few shilling of debt, and there were two conjurers, and a priest, and three they called recusants (Papists, they meant); and one of other sort, a Puritan. Puritan were having a right go at priest and recusants:

'All the bishops such as John of Canterbury, Thomas of Winchester and my lord of Litchfield are petty Antichrists, like the rest of your swinish rabble. Petty popes, proud prelates,' (he spit at start of every word) 'enemies of the Gospel, foes of reformation, and covetous priests…'

Phil Woolley could have out-preached him if he'd a mind, only he hadn't. Nobody took no notice of yon Puritan talk only Harry, who telled him to shut his gob.

'They reckon John Bradford were in here thirty year back, spouting like you, and they burned him at Smithfield. Her majesty and her bishops don't like your rabble no more nor they like Papists. And somebody here might barter his way out by telling on you, and then you'll hang. If you're lucky.'

Puritan said he cared nowt for bishops or government when they turned from true reformed faith and Word of God, and if he were hanged or worse he'd be in Heaven, away from this sinful world. He started ranting again, so Harry bunched his fist and punched rants out of him, and that shut him up.

Reformed faith didn't need to be like that. I reckoned same as Phil did: if a man said his Lord's Prayer and his Ten Commandments, and kept to them, he'd be saved without running to sermons and prattling Scripture like them Puritans. I'd no learning, but I did what I could to serve God, put my faith and trust in Him, said my prayers morning and evening, meant well in what I did and made sure Agnes did same; not as she wouldn't have done it anyroad. So I reckoned I took enough care of my soul's health and Agnes's, and I didn't reckon Our Lord would ask more of me.

Old Tom Jackson asked about them things Sir John's men had said to governor, skullcap and thumbscrews and irons, and two of felons telled him what they were. We hoped governor believed them threats Sir John's men had made.

'Strong room?'

One of debtors said his father had died in it. 'Shed with no window, next to where the shit's piled and bodies lie waiting for burial. Folk die in there and rats eat their faces, so there's less of them to bury.'

'Be glad it's not summer,' another said. 'Men die like flies when they're cooped up here in summer.'

A big fellow sleeping next to priest woke up and said if we'd charity money, like Bishop of London and Dean of St Paul's said we should have, he and his mates would be taking it. Harry and Edmund and Ottie said they wouldn't. Big fellow's mates stood up. They'd all got crooked teeth, and not many of them neither.

'We've been in here a lot longer than you have.' Big fellow were all noise, like wind with no rain. 'Anybody starves for lack of food and drink it'll be you, not us.'

'Try taking off us, you fat prick,' said Harry, 'and you'll die afore you starve.'

Big fellow and two of his mates pulled knives and come at us, but we'd knives of our own so fight didn't last long, not when Edmund and Black Harry set to. Big fellow held his knife in his left hand so he were in for bad luck anyroad. There were no more talk about robbing us after that. Folk like them ought to think about yon pair as got crucified next

157

to Our Lord. Thieves get hanged instead these days, but they're just as dead at finish.

We shared what we had with everybody in that room, though. It were Christian duty, even to Puritans, and Papists, and conjurers; even to them as thought they could take what were ours. When we'd had summat to eat and drink, Harry played his bagpipes and everybody in that dark stinking hole danced, only Puritan and priest. Them two sat against walls staring at one another, each praying that God in his infinite mercy would cast other one into darkness of Hell.

Sheffield/London, April 14th-17th, 1579

The London Postmaster's man galloped into Sheffield on a sweating horse and handed two letters to Dickenson. One was from Thomas Baldwin. When Dickenson broke the seal on the second missive, hairs rose on his neck: anger, anticipation, fear. The letter was signed by Sir Francis Walsingham. Dickenson was to present himself to the Privy Council on the eighteenth, along with George Scargill and Nicholas Booth, to reply to a Bill against Lord Shrewsbury presented by the tenants of Glossopdale.

Why have the nobility of England granted those miserable tenants access to the Council? Why has the Secretary of State demanded the presence of his honour's humble secretary, plus an agent and a bailiff? And how can we contrive to reach London before the eighteenth?

He dispatched a servant to carry the summons to Scargill. There was no time to send to Nicholas Booth in Glossop. Dickenson supposed Sir Francis must have written separately to him.

Baldwin's letter thanked Dickenson for his information about Glossopdale and offered hospitality at Shrewsbury House. He confirmed that the tenants had been summoned to the Privy Council, though he suspected the nobility might not all be of one mind concerning their rights. Mr Gilbert Talbot had tried to stop the tenants' progress at Barnet, where he'd blocked the Peak Forest villagers four years earlier; but Sir Francis had intervened. Mr Talbot considered the Glossopdale disorder to be a matter only for his father, and believed the Privy Council should concern itself with matters of national importance, not local disputes. However, Sir Francis – and, it seemed, Lord Burghley

– wished to hear the tenants' complaints. Lord Shrewsbury's representatives must therefore attend to answer the Bill.

Baldwin was of Mr Talbot's mind, and Dickenson's: the Glossopdale tenants should have been turned back home; or, God willing, hanged for sedition. *If they're hanged it will save having to enforce the evictions, and the rest of Glossopdale's tenants will then be glad to come to heel and pay their new rents.*

He left a message for Eyre, hurried home, gathered food and clean clothes, bade Katherine au revoir, saddled his horse, met Scargill, and rode south from Sheffield. If they reached Derby by sunset they could find lodgings, attend the service at St Peter's in the morning, and still have more than two days to reach London; a long hard ride, but feasible.

*

'The third Sunday of Easter being past, we may let the dried fish of Lent fade from memory and rejoice anew in God's bounty.' Thomas Baldwin's mouth curled. His trim beard jutted. His table beckoned the travellers to a repast of peafowl, breast of boar, haunch of venison, apples recovered from their straw packing, plums and cherries from the south, marzipan.

'We'd have been glad to ride here just for your meats, Tom.' Dickenson patted his mouth with a napkin. 'As for this wine, never let it be said that no good comes out of France.'

'Glossopdale provides little food worth eating and none worthy of praise,' said Nicholas Booth, 'and we've nothing French there. No wine. Our riotous tenants brought us to your table, Master Baldwin. I thank them for it.'

'It's the hangman should thank them, Master Booth,' said Baldwin, 'for giving him the pleasure of dispatching them.' He looked sidelong at Dickenson. 'Why do you suppose the nobles and gentlemen of the Council have consented to see these villains, William?'

Dickenson shrugged. 'Fear of recusancy among his honour's tenants, his honour having custody of the Scottish Queen.'

'Perhaps.' Baldwin poured more wine. 'This Botham, their ringleader; clever enough to play on that fear?'

160

'Nothing clever about Botham,' growled Scargill. 'Just the more trouble he can cause, the better he likes it.'

'Do you have a view, Tom?' asked Dickenson.

Baldwin smiled.

'I wonder... As earl marshal, his honour holds greater authority than any other English noble – in principle. But because of the Scottish Queen he's seldom at Court.' Baldwin sent a servant to fetch cheese and syllabub. 'In practice, those who *are* at court hold power: my lords Burghley, Leicester and Lincoln, for example. They influence affairs of state far more than those nobles who remain in their castles and concern themselves largely or solely with their estates. Lord Leicester declares himself afraid to spend too long away from court lest his position be eroded. By entertaining the Glossopdale tenants' complaints, the Privy Council might remind his honour of this shift of power.' Baldwin poured more wine for himself. 'Also, this new rising in Munster makes them more anxious about the Papist threat. It seems likely to spread throughout Ireland, and Spain will send arms and men to support the rebels. Too close to England. The Council might favour the tenants to ensure they adhere to the reformed faith.'

The three travellers lay in comfortable beds but Dickenson slept little, visions of the Privy Council circling his mind, accusatory, menacing. Scargill's snoring didn't help; George had drunk deeply at table. In the morning, after a breakfast of beer and beef, Baldwin guided his guests to Greenwich.

'I shall pray again for a good outcome,' he said. 'Stay with me again tonight? Your company pleases me, and I'll be glad to learn what passes between the Council and his honour's tenants.'

'We accept.' Dickenson smiled. 'Despite his honour's cash crisis you seem well paid, Tom.'

'As do you, William.' Baldwin returned the smile. 'London has advantages such as the cloth trade. Without neglecting his honour's affairs, one can conduct a little business on the side.'

'I have my small land holdings and a few sheep, my percentages of rents and fines, gifts from Sheffield's cutlers... Men of our station must

161

pursue our own fortunes as best we can when opportunity affords, must we not?'

St James's, Wednesday 18th April 1579

We'd seen more nor enough of them three guards with swords and iron hats, but they come for us again anyroad, just after we'd said our prayers and had a bit of dry bread and dirty water for breakfast. Four of us as Scargill were reckoning to evict – Harry, Nick Mellor, old Tom and me – were getting took afore her majesty's most honourable Privy Council, they told us. Happen we'd be back later. Rest of lads had to stay where they were: 'keep to their lodgings'.

Southwark didn't smell sweet but it were sweeter nor Marshalea. It were good to get out of yon hole. It were raining and it weren't warm, and what with there being no wind we were locked in a pinfold of grey mist. Bit of water we had to wash our hands and face in were right cold. Then we were in yon boat again. Still stuff floating on river. Still yon stink there'd been when we come from London side a day or two back. Still shouting and barking, big and little boats going this road and that.

'Not had enough of a wash, and no Sunday best to wear for seeing them lords.' Old Tom sounded like he were bound to be sick.

'Best not wash in yon.' Harry pointed at river. 'Get dirtier.'

Me and Nick laughed, not as we'd owt much to laugh about. I asked one of guards where Privy Council were.

'St James's, Round Chamber,' he said.

I were no wiser. Then I asked him who Council were. He shrugged. One of his mates said: 'Lords and gentlemen. Fifteen or twenty of them. A lot less than there were in the old queen's time.'

'They'll all say same, lords or not.' Nick shook his head. 'They won't listen to us, Harry.'

'Bet you two groats you're wrong, Nick.'

We all knew Harry had summat up his sleeve but he still weren't saying what it were. Even Harry were quiet, though, when boat stopped and guards marched us where we were going. Never seen owt like yon St James's place. Wood panels of good oak. Coloured pictures taller nor me, made of best quality wool dyed all colours: Bible stories like Moses getting Ten Commandments; gentry hunting with horses and hounds; fairytale palaces with ladies in finery, gardens full of fruit trees. Then we were in Round Chamber with yon noble folk frowning at us, sat on chairs and benches either side a long table with broadcloth over it: fine holland shirts, capes with gold and silver thread over their doublets, fur linings, big white ruffs. We didn't know none of them only Mr Talbot, as were sitting on his own stool at side of room because he weren't one of Council; and Sir Francis, as had met us at Barnet and ordered us to "our lodgings". Couldn't read his face, that Sir Francis. Eyes like stone chisels. I were shaking.

Round Chamber weren't proper round. More shape of an egg. We took our hats off and stood like we were up in Manor Court facing steward, only steward weren't nobody at side of this lot. We were all four of us sweating. Then I thought, 'See them lords? If their fleas jump on us and bite us, will we get noble blood off them? And what'll happen when our fleas bite them? Will they turn common?'

Nick give me a nudge and pointed. There on other side of room were my uncle Nick, Glossopdale bailiff, and that Hallamshire bailiff Dickenson, and yon poxy whore's whelp Scargill. They were all dressed up and they looked like they'd slept better nor we had. Mind, they were sweating and all.

A big lord as were sat in middle of yon bench looked us up and down, sneered and started talking. Fair beard and moustache, he had, black hat with a jewel on front same as on his cape and doublet. I reckoned he looked like God will look on Judgement Day. My knees felt like they were bound to fold up and land me on floor.

'The honourable Mr Talbot and Mr Secretary' (he pointed at Master Gilbert and Sir Francis) 'advise us that you riotous villains are to be examined before this Council concerning a Bill you present against your liege lord, George Talbot, sixth earl of Shrewsbury, earl marshal of England, complaining about the increased rents on your tenancies. How do you speak to this impertinence?'

Harry were twisting his hat in his hands, but he lifted his eyes and stared yon big lord in face. His voice were a bit hushed but he answered.

'It's not against his lordship, your honour. It's against them lot' (he jerked his thumb at Dickenson and Scargill) 'reckoning to raise our rents by four mark for every twelve pence of rent we've paid since his lordship's father's time.'

All them lords looked at one another and started muttering, and Scargill's face said he wanted to kill Harry. Then one lord – big beard, chain of jewels round his neck, looked like he thought a lot of himself – said, 'You wicked and unworthy knaves! You're lying! What lord would raise a tenant's rent fortyfold or more?' Another of them said 'Go to your homes, submit to your liege lord, or it will be prison and the gallows for all of you'. A third said, 'You, Black Harry Botham, shall be dragged to the pillory. We know you're the ringleader'. But yon lord as had spoke first, him like God on Judgement Day, held his hand up and said to Dickenson, 'Four marks for every twelve pence? Four marks? Tell us the truth of this, Master Bailiff.'

Dickenson started gabbling about how rents were steady income and entry fines were only a shot of money at one time and our rents were as low as they'd been in Abbey times and he were only his lordship's humble obedient servant. Aye, I thought, and yon poxy dried neat's-tongue at side of you reckons he can rake more out us nor his lordship asks. Anyroad, God on Judgement Day didn't believe Dickenson.

'You mean to tell us, sirrah, that my lord Shrewsbury has ordered such a rent increase? Fortyfold or more?'

'Tenants all agreed it, your honour.' Scargill looked like a vicar giving a sermon, only vicars' souls aren't that ugly. Well, happen some are. He pointed at us. 'Except those four knaves from the hamlet of Simmondley, and they're being evicted.'

'There's no tenant in Glossopdale agreed it,' said Harry, 'not when they knew we'd be evicted, and we'd all be paying forty times more nor —'

'Answer my question, sirrah!' God on Judgement Day were spearing Dickenson with his eyes. Dickenson licked his lips and coughed.

'Your honour, his lordship's loyal servants can do no other than carry out his lordship's orders.'

It were like being hit with a cudgel, that were. We'd all thought this daft rent demand were down to Scargill, and happen Dickenson and Bailiff Booth and all; not to his lordship. But it weren't only us as looked cudgelled; Council did and all. I thought Mr Talbot were bound to be sick. But they got their dignity back fast enough.

Then I noticed their teeth. How come all them lords and gentlemen with their fine holland shirts and ornaments and jewels had black teeth and foul breath? We'd a few teeth missing, most of us, but them as we still had were white and sound. And they'd better food nor us, them lords and gentry, and a lot more of it. I couldn't make it out. Even yon big lord with jewelled cap on his head were that road. Would God turn up on Judgement Day with black teeth and bad breath?

'This new rent has killed our hearts and made us all half or more desperate, your honours,' said Old Tom, 'so we neither care nor scarce know what we do no more'.

'It'll make beggars of us,' said Nick. 'We'll every one of us have to give up his farmhold, for there isn't none of us can pay such a rent.'

'Thing is, your honours,' said Harry, 'some folk might feel that hard done by, having to pay a new rent like yon lot are asking, they'll not only want their old rent back, they'll start wanting their old religion back and all.'

You could see them lords didn't like that. I put in my pennyworth, saying there'd be nobody left to tend flocks and plough fields so our lands would be wasted. Happen a couple of them lords thought I were right. Yon Dickenson looked like a pig seeing its throat were bound to be cut, but he opened his mouth again.

'I believe, your honours, that my lord will moderate the rents once those four villains are expelled from their holdings. Their leases expired Michelmas past, as did all the Glossopdale leases that had been renewed in due time.' He pointed at Harry. 'Botham's long-time reputation as a troublemaker stands against him and against the three beside him.'

166

The big lord said in that case there were nowt to stop these evictions, but he'd write to Lord Shrewsbury to get to bottom of this rent business. It looked like that were that, but then at last we found out what Harry had up his sleeve; what Bob Rowbottom had found in his copy of what were on manor roll. Seemingly some of us had leasehold for life and some for passing on to our children; but there were summat else and all.

'Your honour,' said Harry, 'Mr Dickenson's mistook. Our landlord's father, fifth earl, give some of us new twenty-year leases in Year of Our Lord 1558, but them leases weren't proved while '59. So they don't expire while Michelmas coming, not Michelmas gone.'

That were an even harder cudgel blow on Council. You could see it in their faces. Everybody stared at Harry, only he kept his eyes on God on Judgement Day and didn't move a muscle. He were still sweating, mind. Nicholas Booth's face looked like a drizzly Ash Wednesday. He put his hands over it to hide it. Scargill went colour of a ripe plum. Dickenson went white.

'You have proof of this, fellow?' said one of lords.

'Oh, aye, your honour,' said Harry. 'Leaseholds. It's all wrote down.'

He pulled yon writing as Bob Rowbottom had give him from under his jerkin and held it above his head, and then he grinned at Scargill and Dickenson. Lords whispered to one another again. I heard one of them mutter summat about Lord High Treasurer – that were God on Judgement Day – writing to Lord Shrewsbury, like he'd said he would; and smug one as had called us "wicked and unworthy" said Queen wouldn't like any of this so he'd write to Lord Shrewsbury and all. Next news they'd called guards. Guards come and marched us out.

'Good one, Harry.' Nick gripped Harry's hands; and old Tom slapped his back.

'Aye, we've won a battle,' Harry said, 'but there's more nor one battle in a war.'

Next news we were on yon boat again, across river and back in Marshalsea with rest of our lads. It didn't smell no better nor when we left, and company weren't no better neither. But we were with our friends once more. And we'd seen Privy Council.

St James's, Wednesday 18ᵗʰ April 1579

Gilbert Talbot accosted the three travellers outside St James's. Dickenson bowed and inquired after Mr Talbot's wife, and after his elder brother Francis, Lord Talbot, who had also been ill.

'God be thanked, both recovered.' Mr Talbot pursed his lips. 'My brother Edward is also well, but he is still at odds with our father. I fear it was Edward who encouraged Sir Francis Walsingham to allow these Glossopdale tenants to present their Bill.'

Dickenson knew the third son was estranged from Lord Shrewsbury; but involved in the Glossopdale trouble? *Neither Edward Talbot's encouragement nor anyone else's would have moved Sir Francis to a decision he hadn't already taken,* he thought.

Servants guided them to the Round Room. The lords and others of her majesty's most honourable Privy Council took their places at the long table. *These men hold all the power in England; advise the Queen, guide parliament.* Mr Talbot whispered their names to Dickenson; Scargill and Booth crowded close to listen.

'Lord Burghley, chief minister and Lord High Treasurer, with the jewelled cap; the earl of Leicester, with the large beard and necklace of jewels; Sir Christopher Hatton; Sir Francis Walsingham, Principal Secretary to her majesty; the old earl of Lincoln, Lord High Admiral; the earl of Bedford; Lord Hunsdon…'

Then Mr Talbot crossed to the far side of the room and sat alone on a stool. Dickenson, Scargill and Booth stood five paces from the table. Dickenson tried to note such details as he could see of their lordships' clothing and jewels so he could regale Katherine with them, but his mind was too turbulent for such purposes. He couldn't even have described the tapestries.

Lord Burghley cleared his throat and stared at the visitors. Everyone fell silent.

'Which of you is William Dickenson?'

'I am, your honour.'

'When you visited Glossopdale last year, together with my lord Shrewsbury's agent George Scargill... Are you Scargill? Your intention was to regularise the behaviour of the tenants and arrange new rent and tithe payments to the bailiff.... Are you Booth? The tenants protested; Derbyshire's justices of the peace complained about them to this Council. Under my lord Shrewsbury's instructions, you and Master Scargill returned to Glossopdale in October, and again on the first day of this present month, to evict four tenants whom my lord Shrewsbury blamed for inciting the uncivil behaviour of the rest. Your legitimate attempts were resisted, and many householders of the manor came to make rescue. Is this correct?'

'Yes, your honour.'

How did he know all that? How did he contrive to summarise it so clearly? God made him a commander of men; he has knowledge, he has intellect, he has presence. As an enemy he'd be implacable.

'Have you anything to add?'

'No, your honour, thank you.'

'As Sir Francis Walsingham's letter informed you, Glossopdale's tenants have come here to present a Bill against my lord Shrewsbury concerning their rents. They are housed in the Marshalsea. The four you are ordered to evict will shortly present their Bill in this chamber. You will answer their complaint as we instruct.'

Dickenson executed a stiff bow. His two companions copied him. The Council members conversed in undertones, chuckling. Minutes passed. Then came a clinking of armour and a tramping of unworthy boots. The four miscreant tenants entered under guard. They shifted to and fro and then stood to the right of the long table, hats in hands, eyes downcast, feet shuffling.

169

Dickenson watched Lord Bughley run contemptuous eyes over them and then speak.

'The honourable Mr Talbot and Mr Secretary advise us that you riotous villains are to be examined before this Council concerning a Bill you present against your liege lord, George Talbot, sixth earl of Shrewsbury, earl marshal of England, complaining about the increased rents on your tenancies. How do you speak to this impertinence?'

The presence of so many powerful men will tie the villains' tongues, thought Dickenson. *The knaves will be dispatched with ignominy and recriminations, ordered to submit to their liege lord and make no further complaint in an English court*. Indeed, Lord Leicester called them wicked and unworthy. Old Lord Lincoln demanded prison, trial and hanging for those who wouldn't return home and submit. Lord Hunsdon said Botham was the ringleader and should go to the pillory. Another noble – the earl of Bedford, Dickenson thought – said such tenants would anger any landlord in England. But Botham raised his eyes to Lord Burghley and answered: Lord Shrewsbury wasn't to blame for the rent increases, he said; it was his servants, who'd demanded four marks for every shilling of current rent. He pointed at Dickenson, Scargill and Booth.

Dickenson received the full force of Lord Burghley's interrogation. *God help anyone who crosses this man. How would a Papist survive his questioning?* He told the Council the rent increase was his idea, not Lord Shrewsbury's. *In truth, it is my idea. I've been trying for years to persuade his honour to increase rents*. But his sleight of tongue was to no avail; he was soon compelled to admit that the fortyfold or fiftyfold increase was his honour's decision, and that as his honour's servants, he and Booth and Scargill were obliged to impose it.

The Council deliberated. They'd write to Lord Shrewsbury to seek clarification. Dickenson suspected that although he'd been forced to recant his assumption of responsibility for the new rents, Lord Burghley was still inclined to accept it. On the other hand, some of the Council, Lords Leicester and Lancaster among them, were convinced that the rent increase was the earl's idea.

Then Botham revealed that the Glossopdale leases would not fall due for renewal until Michaelmas 1579. Dickenson had been told it was

170

Michaelmas 1578. He couldn't have anticipated such an error. However, he ought to have checked the records. Why had he not done so?

Mortified by his failure, but relieved at his dismissal from the Round Chamber, Dickenson wiped his brow and sought ale. He calmed his tremors and reflected that despite his embarrassment he'd achieved a personal triumph: this morning he'd met and conversed with England's Privy Councillors, a distinction Nathaniel Eyre had never attained. However, he had no desire to repeat the experience.

What had been done could not be undone. The four evictions could not be enforced until the Glossopdale leases truly fell due for renewal.

He and his fellow travellers would stay with Baldwin one more night, and then he must return with all speed to Sheffield to assist his honour in answering the Council's promised, or threatened, letters.

Marshalsea, 19th-28th April 1579

Everybody in Marshalsea, priest and Papists and conjurers and felons, even yon Puritan, wanted to know what Privy Council were like and what had happened. Harry weren't for answering, and Tom Jackson and me weren't good at tales, so Nick told them how Harry had made Scargill and Dickenson look sick and how them lords and gentlemen were thinking twice about punishing us; and then I telled them what yon great lord with jewelled cap and smug one with big beard and jewelled necklace had said. Folk in prison are same as folk everywhere; love any story as makes great men look small. So they cheered us, and when Nick and me were done, Harry were a hero to everyone only Puritan, who reckoned all our souls were damned. I reckoned yon Puritan's soul had been dry that long it had withered, so even Devil wouldn't bother harvesting it.

A day or two after, Harry played his pipes again and nigh on everybody danced, even priest this time; only yon Puritan didn't dance. Still had a face like a sore arse.

You get used to worst stinks if you breathe them long enough. You get used to darkness all day long, and folk you don't like crowded in with you, each with his own smell. But you don't get used to homesickness. Agnes hadn't got a babby in her belly for all I'd kept tupping her, and bowing nine times to new moon, and turning my money over and wishing. She never said she were sad about not getting a babby: 'We've got our Margaret, and she's happy and doesn't have her Ma's cleft lip. Happen she'll be good with bees'. I shut my eyes in that dark stinking place and saw Agnes's smile, missing teeth and all, and her half-withered leg. I just wanted to lie beside her, and feel little Margaret climb on my lap, laughing and crowing, wanting a kiss. I wouldn't skrike, not in Marshalsea with felons and Papists and Puritans and conjurers watching, Glossopdale lads and all; but it were hard holding it back. Happen we all felt summat of sort in yon hole.

Harry got them two conjurers on one side and asked if they knew John Birtles. Happen he wanted to see his uncle again, but I reckoned he were trying another road to find his mother. Anyroad, conjurers weren't admitting owt. For all they knew, Harry were a spy; and conjurers as could talk about Master Birtles would be tortured into telling what they knew about him afore they were hanged, or happen half-hanged and then all rest as happens to them as gets charged with treason. Harry were a hero in Marshalsea for what he'd done with Privy Council, but folk weren't bound to trust him with their lives.

We kept a hold on Sir John's money so we could buy food and ale every day and we kept sharing it, even with yon Papists and priest. There were arguments about what prayers we should say and how many times a day, and who should lead them, so we all prayed road we wanted, only two of them felons as didn't say no prayers at all. And they needed to pray, them two. I told three of Bill's stories: yon small-toothed dog as rescued a merchant from thieves and then turned into a young man and got wedded to merchant's daughter; blacksmith putting a heavy shoe on Devil's hoof so he couldn't fly straight; wizard they called Doctor as turned dragon into rock and then outraced Devil to win his soul back. I couldn't tell them like Bill did, but everybody liked them, only yon Puritan. He were one as would stop May Day and Midsummer Ales if he could, and Christmas and all.

I were wondering what were worse, day after weary footsore day of walking or day after miserable day sitting in a stinking crowded prison, when I saw Nick and Harry shaking big Edmund Bower. Weren't waking up, Edmund weren't; muttered he could see ghosts of birds and hares as he'd poached. And then he died. He were strongest among us. We told guards when they come with food and water and asked if we could bury him, but they just picked his body up and threw it in strong room with all yon shit and bones and left it. We went in after it and prayed for his soul, but stench there were even worse, and Tom Blood and Will and me were sick while we were praying.

Then yon three in armour come to take same four of us as last time to see Privy Council again. Priest said, 'Tomorrow, the Sabbath, is the feast of St Catherine of Sienna. I shall pray that she may guide you.' I'd never heard of no St Catherine of Sienna but I thanked priest anyroad, and we went to boat and crossed river.

Sheffield, 23rd April 1579

'All day replying to the Council's letters.' Dickenson massaged his temples. Little Gilbert and the infant John climbed on to his lap and clung to him. 'His honour wrote all he could in his own hand, but the gout –'

'Must you return to London, William?'

Katherine's voice was as pale as her face. He didn't notice; echoes of the Glossopdale dispute filled his head. The Council wanted to limit enclosures throughout England, cap grain prices and discourage conversions of arable to pasture; they deemed those the root causes of growing landlessness and worsening scarcity. *They take too little account of bad harvests, rising demands, depressed trade...*

'Unlikely. Tom Baldwin can manage affairs in London. Though he must hope the Privy Council won't summon him. It's a foretaste of the Last Judgement.'

'In which you choose to place yourself on the Almighty's left hand.' Katherine steadied her breathing. 'You still blame yourself for the Glossopdale rent rises?'

Dickenson had watched the Privy Council members scrutinise one another, some on one side of the table, some on the other. Behind their comradeship, behind their unanimous commitment to England's security and service to the Queen, behind their chattering and chuckles, he'd perceived dogs vying for their owner's favour. *Like Nathaniel and me, but on a higher plane.* Everyone knew that Burghley and Walsingham spun webs of spies throughout England and abroad. Dickenson feared

175

entanglement in those webs. Perhaps some of the great lords feared the same, even as they foregathered in a simulacrum of harmony.

'I thought I'd persuaded the Council of my guilt, but Lord Burghley compelled me to admit I was obeying his honour's commands, and some believed it.'

The letters to Lord Shrewsbury revealed conflicting attitudes towards the Glossopdale tenants among the Council. Lord Lancaster had written: *Truly, my lord, if it be true that your officers have so extremely grated upon your tenants, it is pity they respect your honour's good name in the world so little that they seek to make such hard improvements.* A letter from Mr Wilson, the Council's secretary, divulged the Queen's personal interest in the dispute. Did this indicate that Botham's pretended fear of recusancy been reported? It seemed Lord Burghley had told her majesty that the officers had acted *too much for their lord's profit*, implying the question: why couldn't Lord Shrewsbury control his own servants? Lord Leicester, notwithstanding his vituperation against the four commoners in the Round Chamber, hoped that Lord Shrewsbury *Did not mean to make beggars of his tenants for lack of reasonable food for them and their wretched children,* and found it hard to believe that simple farmers could profit much from *A poor land of long cold winters and short wet summers.*

In his response, his honour had said he considered himself *hardly dealt with that so many wilful people had been suffered to exclaim against him for so long, and had not been remitted to him to be used as seemed best to himself.* He lamented that the nobles of the Council, even her majesty, had embroiled themselves in a private matter between landlord and tenants.

'Some of the Council blamed his honour,' said Dickenson, 'but today we have answered each of their letters in ways that should put an end to the matter. Tom Baldwin's right: the tenants' ringleaders should hang. Sedition can best be quelled by eliminating those who foment and instigate it.' He sighed again. 'However, the dispute is no longer in his honour's hands, or even in the hands of Derbyshire's justices of the peace; the Council has chosen to become involved and the Queen herself is concerned. The nobles rebuked the tenants, but said the ringleaders represented the whole manor and should not be singled out for harder dealing.'

Katherine gave a slight nod. Her eyes were shut.

'The Queen has seen enough discontent among her subjects, William. Perhaps she regrets her harshness to Yorkshire villagers ten years ago, and fears support for the Scottish Queen...'

Dickenson kissed his sons and put them aside, rose, and strode around the room. Katherine was half asleep. Despite himself he felt a sliver of admiration for the Glossopdale tenants, poor unlettered men never before in London, confronting the greatest in the land, weathering that storm of noble hostility. *I was scared, standing beside Nick Booth and George. If I'd been in the tenants' place my tongue would have deserted me. Perhaps they felt they'd nothing to lose...* However, there was no merit in sympathy for wrongdoers.

'And now,' he said, 'a scoundrel called Ottewell Higginbottom, who served the Stanleys of Marple until they dismissed him for drunken idleness, claims he can raise two hundred men to support Botham. I doubt there are two hundred men in his parish, let alone two hundred foolish enough to follow him. But his folly necessitated yet another letter to the Council. My quills are exhausted. My writing arm aches.' He stopped pacing and stared. The boys stood beside Katherine, stroking her hands. She was asleep.

'Kath, what is the matter? Are you ill again?'

St James's, 28ᵗʰ April 1579

Seemingly them Privy Council lords had wrote to his lordship like they'd said, and his lordship had wrote summat back to yon smug one with big beard and jewel necklace, and to rest of Council and all. Big lord, God on Judgement Day, telled smug lord to read out what Lord Shrewbury had wrote and then they'd hear what we had to say to it. Smug lord stared at us like we were worms and then he started reading.

'My lord Shrewsbury says your lands have so many rights, and there is so much common to share, they are worth greater rents. Also, there being many fertile pastures, your severalties may be put to tillage one year and the next year mown for hay, so you can make much profit. Furthermore, he has servants who will be glad to take your tenancies at the higher rent. What do you say to this?'

I reckon if you'd looked at Harry from a few yard off, like them lords were doing, you'd have thought he stood firm as a church tower. Standing next to him I could feel him shaking. But he answered right enough.

'Aye, your honour, happen he has got servants willing to take our farmholds, and happen this new rent's nobbut a way of getting our tenancies back into his own hands so he can give them out. And happen them servants *could* pay yon daft rent, if he paid *them* enough to start with. But they couldn't if he didn't. Them profits as his lordship says we can make, I wish he were right, only we can't. And any of them servants as didn't belong to Glossopdale, as didn't have Glossopdale's earth and water in his blood, he'd make less nor we do, so he'd starve.'

God on Judgement Day muttered, 'And after two years, such an incomer would doubtless leave, if he still lived. Continue, please, my lord Leicester.'

'Also…' smug lord held letter up. 'Also, you have no leases but have been tenants-at-will for sixteen years; you are not leaseholders as you claim.'

Harry looked him in eyes, though he had to lick his lips afore he could speak again.

'Half our households weren't given new leases like rest of us were in '63, your honour, but they had leasehold then and can prove it, and it hasn't been took away. Rest of us, them as got new leases, we've leasehold all right. There isn't none of us is tenants-at-will.'

His smug lordship's face went red. It made his beard and necklace stand out and I swear his ruff got bigger. I wondered how much all yon finery cost.

'You dare to call your liege lord a liar, sirrah? Do you? Do you?'

'No, sir,' said Harry. 'Lord Shrewbury's not lying. He's mistook, that's all.'

'Lord Shrewbury's a son of Devil!' shouted Nick. 'A good lord wouldn't –'

'Shut up, Nick!' said Harry. 'We're Lord Shrewbury's servants. We pray for him every day. We only ask him for fair rents.' He turned back to smug lord. 'Your honour, Nick here, he's suffered in Marshalsea, and that's what you've just heard off him. He doesn't talk bad about his lordship at home.'

I thought, 'He does, Harry. You know he does'. Some lords started chuckling. But him with letter held his hand up so they went quiet again. His face were still red.

'We will ignore your wild speech, Mellor, but my lord Shrewsbury shall learn of it. Better men than you have been indicted for spreading false reports or speaking seditious words.' He looked at letter again. 'His lordship states that you have divided tenements, leased them without licence, despoiled them, stocked them up, and ploughed up woods and underwoods, failing in payment of heriot; all contrary to the terms of your tenancies. What have you to say to those matters, Botham? Or any of you?'

Harry looked at me and Tom and Nick. You could see him trying to think. He were still shaking. Sweating and all. So were rest of us. It were hot in yon Round Chamber, but we'd have sweated if it had been cold as Devil's prick.

'All them doings started years back, your honour,' Harry said at last. 'Bailiff knows about them, so they've become custom and give us rights of custom. Anyroad, they make our farmholds do better, so his lordship and vicar get bigger tithes on owt as gives yearly increase. I don't see owt wrong with making our lives better, and making more money for his lordship and vicar while we're about it.' He stopped and took a breath. Then he spoke louder. 'God and his lordship give us land for our use as long as we respect them both. Vicar told us parable of talents. I reckon we've only done what yon parable teaches us.'

The lords looked at one another and went quiet. I reckon they hadn't expected answers like Harry give. But there were more to come in Lord Shrewsbury's letter.

'You have, his lordship says, entered into illegal combinations against him and outraged disorderly as the most wilful persons…' Smug lord stopped and read that bit again. I reckoned he couldn't make no more sense of it nor I could. 'And you have refused to discuss the matter with the bailiff, Nicholas Booth.'

Harry wiped his hand across his forehead. His hair and beard hung like he'd been ploughing in steady rain.

'We've talked plenty to Mr Booth, your honour. He doesn't want to try collecting rents he knows we can none of us pay. And there's nowt wrong with us getting together so his lordship's agent and Mr Booth can deal with us all in one instead of one at a time. Easier for them, better for us and all.'

Yon lords were near laughing. Happen they'd stopped thinking Harry were "wicked and unworthy". Or happen they were laughing at Lord Shrewsbury.

'I see,' said smug lord. 'So what do you say to my lord Shrewsbury's offer to moderate the rents on all Glossopdale households *except* for you four ringleaders, whom he will then expel for non-payment?'

Harry were quick on that one. Happen he'd expected it.

'I don't reckon your lordships would think that were according to law,' he said. 'Not proper justice, like. Not treating everybody same road like common law says. Anyroad, our rents can't be changed afore Michaelmas –'

'We know that, Botham; but his lordship may set what rents he chooses thereafter, and you four will be evicted.'

'Aye,' said Harry, 'it looks like that's what he wants. More likely what his agents want. Well, happen they'll try making us pay them silly rents and all other households pay rents as aren't as silly. But there's no household in Glossopdale will pay owt at all until we're every one of us back in our farmholds, all with same rent in shilling per acre.' He looked around yon table. I don't know how he did it, staring them great lords in face one after another. 'Happen you'll write to his lordship again, sirs, and kindly tell him what we've said, for we've give honest answers to all you've asked.'

Then God on Judgement Day spoke.

'What do you men know of...' he looked at a paper on table in front of him, 'Ottewell Higginbottom of Marple?'

Nick said, 'Oh, *him*,' like he were spitting. Tom nigh laughed. Harry shut his eyes; he'd answered enough questions. I give a bit of a cough.

'Saving your presence, your honour...' I reckon I sounded like a frog with a sore throat, but one of us had to say summat. 'Higginbottom's a drunken fool as talks tripe. We heard he'd talked about raising two hundred men for Harry. Well, sir, it's daft. There isn't *two* men would follow Higginbottom, never mind two hundred.'

Harry opened his eyes and nodded.

'Aye, your honour, Tom's right. Higginbottom's stupid. Nobody takes no notice of him.'

Then Sir Francis spoke, voice like a scythe. Made my legs feel like grass. Them cold eyes had watched Harry all morning.

'Then you do not intend to lead an army of two hundred against my lord Shrewsbury, Botham?'

Harry blinked.

'Against Lord Shrewbury? An army?' He give a bit of a laugh. 'He's our liege lord, your honour. God set him over us. All we ask of him is fair rents and none of these evictions. Higginbottom's nowt to do with it. He's nowt to do with Glossopdale.'

Sir Francis stared for happen half a minute. Harry stared back. It were a lot more nor I could have done. Then Sir Francis nodded.

'I believe, my lords, no more can be gained from this session. Shall we agree that these men will now return home, assured that their rents and the evictions will be considered further?'

I reckon they must have agreed, because next news we were out of yon chamber and rest of Glossopdale lads had been brought across river from Marshalsea, telling us they'd got poor Edmund Bower buried proper. We were told to go home. So we went.

Next day, St Catherine of Sienna's Day, we were all at church service in Barnet.

Newmarket/Hallaton/Derby/ Glossopdale, 30th April – 15th May 1579

Foul air in Marshalsea had made us poorly, or happen it were bad breath off them lords with black teeth. Some of us couldn't walk as far in a day as we'd done on road down to London, or as quick neither, so we couldn't get home to families and farmholds as fast as we wanted. Old Tom and me weren't slowest this time; sickest were slower. When we passed yon woods where nightingales sang, six had fevers and their wits wandered. Harry, Nick, Olly and Will half carried them as far as Newmarket. Them folk as I'd helped with thatching come out to meet us.

'What happened in London? Did you see the Privy Council? Twelve of you passed this way three weeks ago and now you're eleven. Some are sick. If it's plague you must move on.'

'It's not plague,' I said. 'It's bad air from yon prison as they shut us in.'

I wondered, mind. Had there been plague in Marshalsea? Did them vagabonds at roadside have plague, or them beggars as had tried to rob us near marshes? I'd bet a lot of them had pox, anyroad. Agnes or Maggie would have known what to do for them as were sick. I'd seen Agnes boil meadowsweet in ale for folk with fevers, and give them feverfew and all, so I went looking for them flowers and did my best. A Newmarket woman called Beth boiled verbana leaves in water and we give them that as well as meadowsweet and feverfew. Harry and Nick telled folk what had happened in London, and Will reckoned to copy yon great lords' voices, and Newmarket cheered us and said again, 'Come back and help us with *our* rent rises.' We didn't say we wouldn't.

Ottie and Bob and Henry were a bit better next morning. They had summat to eat and reckoned they could walk. But Phil Woolley and Tom Blood were still bad, so Newmarket folk give us poles and cloth to make litters. We wanted to get past them stinking marshes as fast as we could because we'd breathed enough bad air. But it weren't easy. We had to keep stopping. Bob were struggling, and rest of us weren't doing that well, and Phil and Tom lay on their litters half sleeping and still with wits wandering, muttering like poor Malachi as had died last winter.

We got to Hallaton sixth of May, day after Sabbath, so we didn't see yon vicar to start with. We got same questions off folk as we'd got in Newmarket: 'What passed in London? Did you see the Privy Council? Twelve of you passed through here three weeks ago and now you're eleven. And some of you are sick. If it's plague you must move on.' Well, happen they weren't same words, but they might as well have been. We said it weren't plague, and Otty Wood and Henry Warhurst told them they'd been as sick as any but were mending, and if it had been plague they'd have been in Heaven not Hallaton. I found more feverfew and we managed to feed it to Tom and Phil, and Tom started getting better. He carried a hare's foot in his pouch; happen that helped. But Phil died that night. God had took him to his bosom, happen so He could hear him preaching in Heaven; but in His great mercy he'd left us our singer.

We had to go and find yon vicar and get Phil buried. Vicar did what were needed, but then he started on about Phil's death being God's punishment on us for not submitting to our liege lord, so Harry turned his back and walked off and rest of us followed.

Tom said he could manage without being carried. He tried and all, but he couldn't get far without stopping again. Not to start with, anyroad. Mind, he were walking better by time we got to yon farms we'd stayed at near Derby, and folk as met us there didn't ask whether we'd plague among us. That night we thanked God for bringing ten of us back to Derbyshire, and we prayed for Phil's soul, and Edmund's.

We slept Saturday night in church at Matlock so we could hear mass there next morning, and then we were off again. It were evening of St

Matthias's Day when we got to shoulder of Nab, and Glossopdale opened its arms to welcome us. We could all of us have skriked, seeing our own valley in front of us again, and our own farmsteads inside it; but we said nowt and went one by one to our different homes. I found Pyegrove like I'd left it: fowl, bit of garden, apple tree, horseshoe in path, thatch standing guard over my wife and nipper. Agnes give me ale and pottage and let me talk. Not as I wanted to say much.

'There were twelve of us went and ten come back, love. Three or four sick. Happen you can do summat for them. But we saw them great lords in Privy Council and they listened to us. Harry told them what were what. Happen rents won't be as bad as Scargill and Dickenson want, and happen there won't be no evictions. We'll see.'

'Aye, Tom love. We'll see.'

That were about it. I needed to get to bed. It were grand being back with Agnes, but I were too tired for swyving.

Sheffield, June 1579

'Fine holland shirts, red and purple doublets and hose, gold and silver thread, jewels, bright buttons, huge white ruffs, velvet cloaks, ermine ...' Dickenson paused. 'Picture his honour dressed at his finest, Nathaniel; then imagine a dozen so attired, all together in one small room. One like his honour commands respect; three together inspire awe; twelve assembled in conclave induce terror. Weighed against all the power in the realm concentrated in that little space, any man must find himself wanting.'

'Did the twelve therefore compel courtesy from George Scargill?' asked Eyre.

'George spoke less than usual and more quietly.' Dickenson chuckled. 'Last month, he wrote to his honour at London to say the Scottish Queen was content and the household peaceful; but so tranquil a message is alien to him. He was compelled to add that Glossopdale men had caused trouble in Sheffield during the night.'

'Glossopdale men? In Sheffield? Sheffield breeds troublemakers enough.'

'Wherever George sees trouble he sees Glossopdale. Yet he's kind to the poorest even there, and every man in Sheffield prays blessings on his generosity.'

'Hmph. How *did* he perform before the Council?'

'Courteously enough; but when the error in dating of the leases was revealed he almost fell through the floor. Nick Booth had known nothing of it. Nor, to my shame, had I.'

'More to the late Thomas Sutton's shame.' Eyre frowned. 'You know Botham stirred the Ashford tenants into following Glossopdale's example, but they drew back from the brink of insurrection?'

'I believe the countess yielded to their threat and offered a generous settlement of rents and tithes. Tenants dictating to landlords! Where will it end? It must be stopped, Nathaniel.' Dickenson drew a letter bearing the Council secretary's seal from beneath his doublet. 'This strikes a lighter note.'

The Council had ordered the Sheriff of Chester to arrest Ottewell Higginbottom and bring him to the Marshalsea, and then to the Round Chamber for questioning. Eyre snorted.

'So the Council received and read your report of Higginbottom, yet they believed the Glossopdale tenants when they denied having dealings with him! I see Tom Baldwin and the Glossopdale bailiff's brother were ordered to accompany the loud-mouthed scoundrel.'

'Robert Booth,' said Dickenson. 'It seems he crumbled before the Council, despite Tom's guidance. I didn't hear what the Glossopdale tenants said of Higginbottom.'

'According to this Robert Booth, Higginbottom had said two hundred would assist the Glossopdale mob, *not* that he had two hundred in readiness.' Eyre roared with laughter. 'And then Booth called him an "honest poor man living quietly in the country"! Ha! So: insufficient proof.'

Dickenson grinned.

'They sent Higginbottom back without punishment to submit to his honour's favour. His honour will scarcely be satisfied; though facing the Council must have been punishment enough for such a timorous fool.'

'No matter. One nuisance is dealt with. However, the matter of Glossopdale hangs in the balance. No more ploughing furrows to reclaim tenancies, I fear. Not until the Council's deliberations are resolved.'

*

Was there implicit threat in Lord Burghley's latest letter, or had the memory of their encounter in the Round Chamber tainted Dickenson's judgement? The Lord High Treasurer's phrasing was courteous but his message seemed like a reprimand: Lord Shrewsbury had known and approved of the new rents, so he had strayed from the traditional norms of landlords; to wit, restraint and mercy. God would be displeased; more seriously, so would her majesty. Indeed, another letter in the Queen's own hand declared she would be loath for her good Shrewsbury to lose his honour in order to gain a little money. Dickenson had penned the earl's reply, and according to Master Gilbert the Queen had liked it well; but her majesty's potential displeasure was evident.

If your majesty paid his honour enough for custody of the Scottish Queen, he'd have no need to impose such high rents on any of his tenants. A less expensive countess and less costly sons would help him, too; but to dissolve a marriage and divide a family is beyond even your majesty's power. I would tell you all this and more if I dared.

Lord Lincoln had also written, fearing depopulation of the land and a shortfall in food production if such drastic rent rises forced men to relinquish their farmholds. However, the Council had helped the earl to devise a subtle plan. In order to undermine support for Botham, his honour decided he would take his chaplain, John Holland, to preach in Glossop parish church. Lord Shrewsbury's personal appearance in that benighted valley would impress any rebel who vacillated, and Mr Holland's sermon would confirm that his honour would be a good lord to all Glossopdale tenants who submitted to him. Then Mr Holland would return to London and testify to the Council that the assurance had been given.

*

Dickenson was obliged to deal with a contention surrounding the tithes of Mayfield. He had more than enough work without legal wrangling, the outcome still pending. Francis Lord Talbot, the earl's son and heir, had asked his father to purchase a lease from the widow of his servant Thomas Leaton; the land was convenient for him. Meanwhile, he thanked his honour for the gift of one hundred sheep. The Bishop of Carlisle had written from Rose Castle reporting the earl of Atholl's funeral and requesting a loan of one hundred pounds. Richard Topcliffe had seen the work set out for the roof of the earl's chamber at

Shrewbury House in London. His letter didn't specify the cost; Dickenson had to ask. It was a relief to find correspondence that included no fresh demands for payment: news of Duke Casimir's departure from England; a recommendation from the Archbishop of York that the benefice of Whiston be given to the Reverend John Holland's brother, Robert Holland, vicar of Sheffield. But such letters were few.

Dickenson returned to updating his records: income from Hallamshire rents and tithes, from the lead trade, the Sheffield cutlers, the settlement of wills and inheritances; collectively, it was still too little to counterbalance the expenses. Far too little.

Later, he might find time for conversation with his wife and time for educating his elder son; even, if God willed, time for sleep.

Glossopdale, June 1579

Some folk wondered whether it were worth it. Them as had gone to London weren't far behind with farm work because women had done what Joanna said, and men as had stayed had helped them. But we'd spent more nor we'd wanted, for all Sir John de Zouche's help, for all Derby and Hallaton and Newmarket had been kind to us, for all yon shilling we'd got off them as had stayed in Glossopdale. Two of our good men had died and all; their families must have blamed us, though they said nowt. And what had we gained? Happen we'd stopped daft rent rises for most folk, but four of us were still getting evicted come Michaelmas. Nick reckoned we'd stopped that and all, but we hadn't.

Agnes told me we'd done good, going to London. I'd been right to follow Harry because happen he wouldn't have gone without me at side of him. 'There were bother coming, Tom. Doing summat were better nor doing nowt. It were bad losing Edmund and Phil, but men die, and them two were doing right when God took them so their souls are in Heaven. And I'm proper proud of you, using meadowsweet and feverfew like you've seen me do. I didn't know about verbana, mind.'

It were time of year when days are longest. Sheep are sheared and marked, first cuts of hay are took, and womenfolk wash clothes and put them to dry in sun, and then happen dye them if they can get hold of madder or summat of sort. We were all busy. But there were a surprise waiting: Mr Yeaverley were getting a Sunday off because Lord Shrewsbury's chaplain were coming from Sheffield to preach, and his lordship were coming with him! In fields, on roads, in alehouses, at side of wells, folk couldn't talk about nowt else. We'd most of us never seen Lord Shrewsbury. Why were he coming? Harry snorted.

'Give you three guesses, Spiderlegs.'

'To get us all to pay yon daft rents?'

'This preacher he's fetching will tell us it's God's will we obey our lord and pay what he tells us. Half Glossopdale will believe him.'

'Happen it won't be like that,' I said; but I reckoned Harry were right like he usually were. 'Them great lords said they'd write to him again, so happen he's coming to tell us he won't want daft-like rents after all.'

'Aye. Happen pigs can fly.'

Lord Shrewsbury come and sat at front of church, staring at preacher he'd brought; Mr Holland, he were called. None of us reckoned much to him. His lordship could have been one of them nobles in Round Chamber at Greenwich. He'd have belonged, only his teeth weren't as black as most of theirs. He'd lost some of his hair and there were grey in his beard, but it were road he held himself as made you take your hat off and bow, and road he were dressed and all: fine white linen, heavy jewel on a black ribbon round his neck, purple velvet cloak as looked too heavy for hot weather. He nodded at church walls where pictures had been whitewashed over. Happen he were a Puritan.

Agnes said when we got home he'd looked worn out, like he'd been mowing hay all day long and not rested when goatsbeard told him it were noon. I told her not to be so daft; who'd ever heard of a great lord mowing hay? She said his face were lined and his cheeks sunk and his eyes looked like he'd seen himself dead and buried. I'd noticed nowt of sort, but I hadn't looked at his lordship's eyes. Harry hadn't looked at him at all. He'd sat with his arms folded, staring Mr Holland in face and putting him off his preaching.

Anyroad, Harry were right. Mr Holland told us Lord Shrewsbury would be a good lord to all Glossopdale tenants as submitted to his favour and set aside them as brewed unrest and disobedience, meaning Harry and Nick and me and Tom Jackson. If all farmholders in Glossop manor would deliver up their possessions for one night only, his lordship would deal fairly with us all. Then Mr Holland and his lordship were gone, riding back to Sheffield with their servants, and it were last we saw of either of them for a few year.

More nor half of Glossopdale folk believed yon preacher: said they'd save money up so they could pay bigger rents and then we'd all get treated right. Harry lost his rag. He scared folk when he were angry, only it didn't usually last. Joanna would keep herself and Edmund and babby out of his road 'til he quietened down and then she'd give him a pot of ale and summat to eat. But it weren't over as quick this time. She come down to see us, holding Edmund's hand and carrying babby.

'He's all over parish, Agnes: Chisworth, Charlesworth, Dinting, Hadfield and Padfield, Glossop, Whitfield, Chunal… He's yelling at everybody he meets, saying they've gone soft in head listening to shit talk from preacher and letting themselves be made beggars. "Give up our possessions for one night only?" He's right, my Harry; I never heard nowt so daft!'

Will and me had come down from meadow for a drink. Joanna said, 'You know what Harry's like, Tom. Them as says they'll submit to his lordship, he's calling them mares' arses, sons of whores, pigs' snouts, beggars' mongrels, grandsons of Serpent, lowlives, kinks in cock… Folk can turn against him as much as they've a mind, he'll go on fighting rents for everybody's sake anyroad. Will you still be with him?'

I laughed.

'Do you need to ask, Jo?'

Agnes put her arms round me.

'Tom needs to be with him anyroad, Joanna. They still reckon to evict all four of them.'

'Nick Mellor wants to mind his mouth,' said Joanna. 'He makes it worse. It isn't just men gets thrown out of farmholds on to road.'

'Aye,' said Agnes. 'It's wives and nippers and all.'

She picked little Margaret up and hugged her. I hugged them both.

'We'll not be out on no road,' I said. 'Scargill won't make us vagabonds. None of them bastards will.'

I'd seen more nor enough vagabonds on road to London, and a few between here and Chapel and all. I weren't having my wife and nipper out there, nor my sister neither, nor my friends. Custom were on our side.

You had to wonder, mind: were custom enough to stop Scargill?

Sheffield, September 1579

Dickenson ground his teeth. His honour had spent almost a thousand pounds since the previous Michaelmas on fuel, wine and spices for the Scottish Queen; a thousand more to replace the plate and the pewter vessels her retainers had destroyed, and household stuff that had been spoiled and wasted. The Crown had reimbursed him nothing. He was allocated just sixpence per day for each of twenty-four guards to secure the royal captive. Mary's recurrent schemes for escaping obliged his honour to employ twice as many. He was paying the guards four hundred pounds a year above their wages to secure their loyalty against Mary's wiles.

Dickenson had seen spoiling and wastage with his own eyes, and Eyre had described more, but he wanted exact figures. The approximate costs reported to him, "almost a thousand… a thousand more" infected the body of precise accounting. No wonder the Lord Chamberlain's man, John Huls, had been sent to search the earl's records; and, lacking keys to them, had written to Dickenson to request instructions. Huls's intrusion implied diminution of the earl's status in the eyes of the Council.

'I worry, William,' said Eyre. 'His honour is angry, bitter about his life, convinced the world's turned against him. Including the countess.'

The earl now lived separately from the lady who five years earlier had been his "beloved Bess".

'Pain, Nathaniel, in hands, legs, joints... The Buxton waters palliated it but couldn't cure it.'

The Queen had declared that taxes from the Sheffield cutlers, profits from the lead trade and rents and tithes from the vast Shrewsbury estates were more than enough to pay for the Scottish Queen's household. *They aren't*, thought Dickenson, *and her majesty ignores the ravages of an expensive countess and spendthrift children.* The cost of the new house at Worksop weakened Lord Shrewsbury's case, but an hour with the account books sufficed to prove how real his hardship was. The Glossopdale dispute had added to the hurt. *If only we'd succeeded in ousting the troublemakers. If only the Privy Council had seen them hanged.* Her ladyship's intervention in Glossopdale, using at least one of her sons as proxy, had estranged her further from her husband. The earl now accused her family and servants of persuading the Glossopdale men to withhold their rents and seek justice in London. Dickenson would never have contradicted his lordship, but he knew Glossopdale needed no persuasion from Lady Shrewsbury or anyone else to foment trouble.

'And the trouble is spreading,' said Eyre. 'Commoners in Northraw have also rioted against enclosures and rents. That's where the commontion of '49 began, William: Northraw in Hertfordshire. Sir William Cavendish held the estate then; Sir Christopher Hatton holds it now. The Privy Council crushed the Northraw trouble a few weeks ago: two of the ringleaders hanged, two more burned through the hand, others committed to prison. Yet the Council will take no such action against the Glossopdale miscreants. It is a mystery.'

'Sir Christopher is one of the Privy Council; Sir William wasn't, I believe. That could explain why the recent action was so swift.'

'Perhaps,' said Eyre. 'But Northraw proves that the Glossopdale dispute could shortly disinter the communal memory of commotion time. It's more dangerous than the feeble stirrings of the common folk in '51, which few now recall.'

He and Dickenson were now penning almost daily replies to the Privy Council's letters about Glossopdale, replies that grew ever less persuasive. His honour promised local mediation for the tenants, but when the Council pressed for details he provided none. Then he undertook to deal reasonably with the tenants if they'd give up their possessions to his agents for one night only. No one from the lowliest tenant to the highest nobleman could give credence to the assurance. Then, when he could no longer defend the huge rent rises, he commanded Dickenson to explain that the sums demanded were merely a device to force out the troublemakers and replace them with deserving servants. It was never intended that other tenants should pay such impossible rents; Scargill's surveys were only undertaken to establish the value of each property and the whole manor. This was surprising news to Dickenson, Eyre and Scargill. It failed to persuade the Council.

'Glossopdale has a vast extent of rough grazing,' they wrote, 'where one cannot conveniently distinguish among arable, meadow and pasture, and all used for ploughing, mowing and pasturage as occasion and necessity urge the occupiers, and mere subsistence rivals stockbreeding as the object of husbandry.'

That was undeniable. His honour was compelled at every turn to explain, to temporise, to retreat, and Dickenson and Eyre were hard pressed to make the succession of explanations, temporisings and retreats seem plausible. The Council urged the earl to deal honourably with the poor men; they seemed to doubt that his dealings with them had been honourable so far.

'We'd find better employment if Glossopdale were destroyed by the hand of God or invaded by Turks,' snapped Dickenson. 'This dispute consumes hours I could spend with Katherine and the boys.' He sighed. 'She's unwell, my Katherine. The fever that seized her two years ago has lingered. She strives for her former spirits but sinks deeper into lethargy.'

'Poor gratitude for the house you built for her,' said Eyre. 'Most men would beat their wives to drive out such lethargy. His honour's doctor would –'

'Doctors visit the sick and make them worse, Nathaniel.'

'Ha! Then bring Glossopdale to her aid! Wise women there are reputed to cure ills. Master Yeaverley would have had them brought before the assize as witches, save for the tenants' testimonies. He reasoned from Holy Scripture that curing ills was the Devil's work. But one tenant declared in Manor Court that Our Lord gave comfort to the sick when He was here on Earth, so it couldn't have been Devil's work then; so why was it Devil's work now?'

196

'All those tenants are servants of the Devil, Nathaniel, wise women included. And I will not expose my Katherine to the concoctions of ignorant poisoners.'

Glossopdale, November 1579

Folk still weren't paying no rent. Happen they weren't sure how much it were no more, or happen Harry had scared them into not paying owt. Newtons were different, mind; give bailiff all their new rent for quarter. Harry called them arse-licking dribble-mouths as wanted to turn their private parts inside out and sell themselves for whores. There were plenty as thought same only they wouldn't say it because Newtons were rich and they were pals with Scargill. If it hadn't been for Newtons there wouldn't have been a farthing of rent paid in Glossopdale on Lady Day. There wouldn't be none next Lady Day neither, nor any quarter day in between.

Scargill and young Roberts had come at Michelmas and tried ploughing furrows in Harry's land and mine and Nick's, but they hadn't managed it. Folk wouldn't let Scargill reclaim no farmholds whether they thought Harry were right or wrong. I said Scargill didn't have law on his side anyhow because Privy Council lords had questioned rents. Everybody shouted, 'Aye, Spiderlegs is right, he were in London when Council said it'. Scargill went home telling us he'd be back. Most of Glossopdale were jeering at him.

He rode in again on Feast of St Francis, when days were getting shorter and rain fell cold on cap and thatch, and rooks fed where we'd grown oats. Roberts were with him again, 'Like a flea on a dog', Harry said, and there were a score of Sheffield men with dirty boots following. Scargill must have thought he'd enough with him this time, because him and Roberts had another try at digging a furrow in Harry's land, and they said they'd dig mine and Tom Jackson's and Nick's and all. We telled them they wouldn't, and stood in front of them with staves and bill-hooks. Women come out carrying sticks and stones and their threepenny sickles. Fallen leaves blew past us. Next news, Tom Dewsnap and Humphrey Andrew were stood next to Scargill's horse. Now he'd got constables at side of him, Scargill started talking.

'All Glossopdale has agreed the new rents save you four ringleaders. All the other forty-eight tenants. We've told you, Botham, we've no commandment to deal with you. Begone!'

Harry strode up to Scargill's horse like he were bound to kill it, which he weren't. Harry wouldn't hurt a horse even if Devil were on it, which were near enough what Scargill were. Horse jerked its head and backed off, mind. Scargill had a job holding it.

'Aye. Drive us from our holdings, would you?' Harry said. 'Mr Dickenson told us we'd keep our tenements if we agreed a fair rent. And we will. A *fair* rent. But we won't agree to what you're trying.'

'You're not worthy of your holdings,' said Roberts. 'Take your cattle from his lordship's ground and go!'

Harry laughed in his face and hefted his bill-hook.

'Not I nor any of us will leave but by law,' he said, 'neither land nor house. We hold our tenements according to custom!'

Women cheered. We all cheered.

'The house is Lord Shrewsbury's,' said Scargill, 'not yours.'

'It's mine by right of custom. Bothams have lived in Simmondley time out of memory of man, and we hold Storth for his lordship. God willing, Bothams will hold Storth 'til Day of Judgement. I've telled you afore, Scargill: whoever comes to take my house from me shall die, or else I'll die holding it.'

Men and women alike cried, 'Aye!' Tom and Humphrey, our constables, telled Scargill he'd bet not dig furrow 'til we'd quietened down or there'd be bloodshed. Scargill telled them, and half a dozen of yon Sheffield folk, to grab hold of Harry and take bill-hook off him and hold rest of us back while they marched him over to Glossop and put him in stocks. 'You'll stay in the stocks until you submit to his lordship,' he telled him. We followed them, men carrying staves and bill-hooks, women with sticks and stones and sickles, shouting murder. Rooks flew above us; black cloud promising storms. Harry kept saying law were law and greater nor Lord Shrewsbury, and if Privy Council couldn't find no law to drive him from his holding, likes of Scargill and Roberts couldn't find none neither.

Tom Dewsnap thought he'd show his importance, for all him and Humphrey Andrew were only constables by our consent.

'You're Lord Shrewbury's tenant-at-will, Harry Botham,' he said. 'While you're sat in stocks you can pray for him.'

'Oh aye,' said Harry, 'I'll pray for him. But we're none of us tenants-at-will, Tom Dewsnap, and you know it.'

'Leaseholders, our men!' womenfolk shouted. 'Leaseholders by inheritance!'

Tom and Humphrey and that runt Roberts took no notice. Mind, they looked like they'd shit themselves when we closed in on them, waving bill-hooks and staves. Scared or not, they set Harry in stocks outside parish church, and Nicholas Booth come down from bailiff house to see what were happening. We were all ready for trouble. Then Scargill said:

'Do as Mr Dewsnap the constable said, Botham. Pray for his lordship.'

Harry spat at villain's feet and then started. Must have practised them words like he practised bagpipe.

'We heartily pray You, Lord God, to send Your Holy Spirit into heart of Lord Shrewsbury and them like him as through Your grace own all grounds, pastures and dwelling places of earth. Let them remember themselves to be Your tenants, so they won't rack and stretch out rents of their houses and lands, or take fines and tithes as are more nor poor folk can pay, like them do as forget Your Tenth Commandment, lest You cast them from *their* holdings. Move their lordships to let their tenancies so them as hold them can pay their rents and live honestly, and nourish their families and relieve poor folk. We ask this in name of our Lord and Saviour Jesus Christ, that Lord Shrewsbury's soul might yet be saved. Amen.'

Fair brought a lump to my throat, yon prayer. We were laughing, all lot of us, only Scargill and Roberts. Even them Sheffield folk with dirty boots and weary legs laughed, and Bailiff Booth and all. Scargill and Roberts looked fit to kill Harry. Only Harry weren't done.

'Right, Scargill, you've heard me pray for his lordship. Your turn now. Here's one for you: "Let me be good and gentle to tenants and love them and always have their good will and report. Let me treat them with reason, justice and good conscience and burden them with no more fines, rents nor service nor they can pay without starving. I pray God will not let me displace an honest friendly tenant for a scrap of money, but be happy to see all tenants prospering. God grant me grace to use mercy and pity, in hope He'll prosper me and mine in turn." Good prayer for a landlord's agent, yon. You want to learn it.'

There were a lot more laughing and cheering. I got hold of Tom and Humphrey.

'You'd best let Harry out of them stocks, lads, or there'll be bad bother.'

'We're constables,' said Humphrey. 'You're not.'

Then Ottie Wood and my brother-in-law Will said, 'Aye, and if you don't let Harry out we'll need two more constables because you won't neither of you be fit for duty. And happen you'll not be above ground.'

We crowded tight on constables, and on Scargill and Roberts and yon Sheffield lot, 'til they were feared we'd press them to death. Then they let Harry loose. He'd been in them stocks nobbut half an hour, dead leaves falling around him, afore he were on his feet again and chasing Tom and Humphrey back to their houses. Scargill and Roberts saw they'd get nowhere with us so they turned east, up over wastes to Sheffield, and all them dirty boots followed. Scargill should have learned he'd never get nowhere with Glossopdale. Afore we took womenfolk back home, Harry in midst of us, Tom Blood sang Ballad of Nowadays and we all joined in:

> *Great men maketh nowadays*
> *A sheepcote in the Church*
> *Commons to close and keep*
> *Poor folk for bread to cry and weep*
> *Towns pulled down to pasture sheep*
> *This is the new guise.*

201

Scargill were never bound to rest, though. Start of Advent him and his mob were back again, wanting to plough furrows on our holdings. They reckoned they'd do it while Harry were busy with his sheep so he wouldn't know they were coming, but John Rowland saw them from his charcoal hearth and told us. We threw them off lands and back into road, and Nick put plough where it belonged.

'We'll walk our grounds every day,' I said, picking my bill-hook up, 'so you'll get nowhere with your daft games. Now get your arses back to Sheffield and tell his lordship we're staying.'

It weren't like me, telling his lordship's agents where to go, but what with Harry standing up to them, and Privy Council listening to us for all they'd called us bad names, and Agnes telling me I were doing right, I reckoned I'd speak my mind. Scargill started on about how we'd no rights, but Harry heard him and come outside, wiping sheep shit on his smock.

'We'll come to Sheffield, Scargill,' he said, 'and we'll talk to Mr Eyre or Mr Dickenson. If they give us a good answer from his lordship we'll agree a fair rent and come home in peace. If there's no fair answer we'll be back to London and all men shall know why.'

Mr Eyre had sent for us in January, same as I said, but we hadn't gone. Back then, Harry had said Mr Eyre knew same as his lordship knew about rents, so there weren't nowt to talk about. Now it seemed best way of doing. It'd stop Scargill bothering us. Scargill didn't like it.

'You threaten your betters, Botham? You think yourself the lord and Lord Shrewbury your tenant? Some day you'll hang.'

'Aye, happen. But I know my place better nor you do, Scargill. Get home and tell Mr Eyre two or three of us will call on him. Send any here to plough our land or dig clods, and either they'll change their minds and shift somewhere else, or they'll die.'

Scargill mouthed summat else and then he were off back to Sheffield and his servants with him. Harry could scare anybody when he'd a mind, like his father used to do when we were nippers. Next news he were sitting with little Edmund showing him how to make a bagpipe.

'See this sheepskin bag, son? How I've stitched it to close it? Bagpipe won't play if we don't stop air leaking through them stitches. So we take a bit more sheepskin, like this, and stitch it over stitching –'

'What's it stiched with, Dad?'

Nobbut eight year old, Edmund, but he'd a good head on his shoulders. Learned quick, like his father always had. Harry never needed to thrash him above once a week.

'Linen thread, Edmund. Linen's better nor wool for this job.'

I sat five yard off and watched. Hadn't seen Harry make a bagpipe afore. He left holes in bag where sheep's legs had been and put stocks in there: hollow cane for pipe, finger holes cut with knife; two more lengths of reed mace for drones, one longer nor other; reed in end of pipe.

'Always keep two or three spare reeds, son. They don't last.'

Harry finished pipe and showed Edmund how to play it and then give it him. Lad got a noise out of it and ran off to show his mother. Harry watched him and his mouth did its sideways shift. Road he'd switched from angry leaseholder ripe for murdering Scargill to kind and loving father, it were like yon raging Old Testament God turning into Our Gentle Lord in New. I wiped my eyes and went home to Pyegrove and Agnes.

Sheffield, December 1579

I'd never seen owt like Sheffield Castle. It were all stone same as Marshalsea, only bigger. I'd seen a castle or two up in Yorkshire while I were in service, but nowt like Sheffield. It stood at top of a bit of hill where two rivers met, and there were a frozen moat with a bridge. Harry blew his cheeks out.

'How much ground between moat and yon rivers do you reckon, Spiderlegs?'

I had a look and scratched my head.

'Four acre and a rood, happen. And frost all over it. Can folk get up to top of yon walls? Looks like they can. Higher nor a lot of birds fly, Harry.'

'Grey. Dark grey.' Nick shook his head. He were quieter nor usual.

Being near a building as big as yon castle makes you feel worth less nor a gnat, and it weren't only winter air as chilled me to bone. I reckon that's why great nobles built castles, apart from keeping them and their families safe: make folk under them feel small and scared. Mind, putting up a building that size and then having to keep mending it might cost more nor it were worth.

Other side of them rivers were orchards, and what looked like a cockpit yard, and summat as were happen a brew-house. Far side of them were a space bigger nor Sheffield town, with trees taller nor I'd ever seen, all in lines, deer grazing among them. There were another building in middle of yon space. It were square and looked as big as castle, happen bigger, like a house made for giants. Same sort of gateway as castle and all, towers either side of it.

204

We walked across bridge over moat to castle. Gateway were higher nor any house in Glossopdale and there were a round arch at top of it. Two great wooden gates hung either side. I wouldn't have wanted to lift one of them hinges. Inside curved arch there were iron teeth as could drop on you and pin you to ground. I weren't happy about walking under it, but it were only road into castle.

There were two guards at sides of gateway, dressed in finery with a picture on it like a shield with sixteen quarters, all coloured shapes: lions on their back legs, patterns like a barber-surgeon's pole, crown at top. Guards weren't for letting us in 'til Harry said we were from Glossopdale and Mr Eyre wanted to see us so we'd come. Then they sent a lad into castle, and lad come back out and said aye, it were right, we could go in. There were a smell of fish cooking.

Yon castle walls were thick. Nigh on six foot, I reckoned. We got took into an open space with a well at side of it and buildings all round, some with horses in, smiths working in one. Randolph Swann would have liked it in there. There were a big grain store, and there were little houses, happen for guards and servants and suchlike. Then there were bigger houses with fancy-looking windows with glass in them and carvings all round, happen where some of his lordship's top folk like Mr Dickenson and Mr Eyre lived. They had chimneys with smoke coming out. I'd never seen chimneys only in London.

I asked guard as were taking us to see Mr Eyre about yon big square house far side of rivers and orchards, and he said it were manor house. His lordship lived there, he told me, not in castle. Scottish Queen lived in it and all, in a different bit nor his lordship, so they didn't need to see nowt of one another unless they wanted.

We got took to one of them stone houses with fancy windows and into a big room where there were a fire in a hole in end wall. A lot of smoke went up chimney. Rest come out into room and stung my eyes. Nick started coughing. It were dark in yon room and smoke didn't make it no lighter. When I could see proper, there were Steward Eyre, sat on summat. I looked again: aye, it were a *chair* he were sat on, not a stool or a bench. There were a bench and all, mind. Scargill were sat on that.

Mr Eyre started: 'You were summoned here in January to consider your rents. His lordship's order. You refused to attend upon me. Instead, you went to London. You had the impudence to present a Bill against his lordship to her majesty's Privy Council. *Now* you choose to obey your liege lord's command. Finally. Explain yourselves.'

What with staring at Scargill I'd nobbut half-listened. Harry said there hadn't been no sense coming in January because a higher court were needed to change his lordship's mind about daft rents. Scargill's, anyroad. It were a different story now Privy Council had written to his lordship about rent rises and evictions, so summat could be sorted out if Master Steward were willing. Happen we'd have got a fair answer to that, only Scargill opened his mouth afore Mr Eyre had chance to say owt.

'None of you vile knaves has the right to discuss rents with Mr Eyre or anyone. You don't speak for Glossopdale's tenants because you're not Glossopdale tenants. You're evicted. Out of your farmholds. You're low-born scum that cause riot and discord and –'

Nick's face went red as a winter sunset and he were up, fists clenched, shouting Scargill down afore Harry could say owt. I thought he were bound to pull his knife.

'I'll discord and riot you, you privy-mouthed spawn of Satan! I'll rip your by-our-lady guts out, you filthy bastard! Send you to Hell where you –!'

Mr Eyre were on his feet.

'You will not speak thus to his lordship's agent!'

'I'll speak anyroad I please to yon piece of shit, and his lordship and all if he stands –'

'Nick!' roared Harry. 'Go and stick your head in a bucket of water! As for you, Scargill, we're not evicted and we won't be. Have you forgot what Privy Council said, or are you that addle-brained you can't remember owt? Need me to tell you again what'll happen if you try evicting us? Because I –'

Mr Eyre banged his fist on table. A cup of ale spilled on some papers. Cup hit floor and broke.

'Silence, all of you, or I'll have you set in the stocks!' He stared at Harry. 'For more than half an hour, Botham!'

I said it weren't fair, telling me to be silent when I hadn't said nowt. Nick laughed. Mr Eyre and Scargill didn't. Harry stared straight at Mr Eyre.

'When Mr Dickenson first come to Glossopdale, sir, he said we'd be treated same as every other tenant. Then he come again with Scargill and went back on his word. No, sir, let me finish. Happen he didn't mean to tell lies, but that's how it were. We went to Privy Council because we know his lordship's highest in land only her majesty, and Privy Council speaks for her majesty, so where else could we go when we weren't getting justice from his lordship's agents, which were same as not getting justice from his lordship? Happen rents have to go up. If they go up like they have in some other manors we'll pay them. But we're not paying rents as have gone up forty times and more because we can't, not without starving and becoming beggars and vagabonds, and our wives and children with us.'

Mr Eyre had telled everybody to stop shouting and name-calling but he'd got proper worked up himself, what with Scargill on one side and Nick on other, so *he* were shouting and not giving Harry a proper hearing.

'Is that your answer? The way you explain your impertinence?'

Harry didn't like that, not one bit he didn't.

'Aye, it damned well is, Mr Eyre, and you won't get no more of an answer neither. I were trying to speak fair. If you don't want fair speaking there's nowt else to say.'

Scargill were on his feet again cursing, and steward were more angry nor I'd ever seen him in Manor Court; but Harry weren't done.

'Tom, get back home and tell other folk to follow Nick and me to London. Yon Privy Council will learn how their orders are getting treated. That's it. We're off.'

Sheffield, January-February 1579/80

Cold house, winter dark, weeping servants: 'Oh, Mr Dickenson, where have you been? Where were you?'

Three hours haranguing the cutlers' jury had left him ill-humoured. Where he'd been was no business of servants.

'Why are you weeping? What's toward?'

No one answered; but young Eleanor Britton scuttled from the parlour and put her arms around him. Lord Shrewsbury had brought Mistress Britton from Norfolk eighteen months earlier to be his housekeeper. Dickenson wondered at her presence in his house, her uninvited familiarity; but her explanation was quick and clear, her voice soft. Her accent was strange to his ears. Her news was stranger, too strange for his mind to assimilate. She had to say it again and again.

The house he'd built for Katherine melted around him and swam. He floated, his feet no longer sensing the ground. He closed his eyes and prayed. His lips moved but he was silent. Around him the weeping was unabated: ground bass of grief, tenor of empathy, shimmering descant of fear.

The servants had cleaned Katherine, bound her jaw and lit candles beside the bed. They'd summoned her family; Jane, her sister, had come at once. Their weeping had infected the children. Only Mistress Britton seemed calm. Beneath her warmth, her assurance, her comeliness, Dickenson sensed a hard self-seeking core; or had the sudden dagger of anguish made wormwood of his judgement? He turned to his sister-in-law.

'Jane, take care of the inn. Keep records, as – as –'

He gestured towards his wife's body. He went to her bedside. The rage within him clamoured for release. He bit his tongue lest it rail against God. Images of their wedding day swirled: her long gown, her uncertain smile, her tremulous fingers, so adept at the spinning wheel; the exchange of vows, the catch in her voice as they stood before the altar. To be desired is flattering, she'd told him; to be valued is joy.

That morning her lips had been warm. His body trembled at the memory. Now they were cold. She had begun to stiffen.

Tears could have flowed but he had no time for them. He must assert authority over his body, over his tongue, over the cauldron of disbelief, anger, grief and self-castigation boiling within him: *I knew she was ill. Why did I do nothing?* He sent for his brother John, then called his sons and made them kneel before her beloved body, one at each side of him. They would pray together.

'Gilbert, take care of your little brother. You will stay a while with Uncle John and Aunt Beth. You will continue your work at the inn. Aunt Jane will be there.'

'Father, I want to be with you.'

'You shall, my boy, but not yet. I wish you to show Uncle John how you've mastered your letters, how quickly you can reckon a page of income and expenditure, so I may be proud of you. You must make sure your brother says his prayers night and morning and that he behaves as he ought with your uncle and aunt.'

Young John looked from father to brother and back again, and then at Katherine's body.

'Will Mother wake up and play with me again soon?'

*

Thomas Baldwin had written to Lord Shrewsbury and sent a separate letter to Dickenson, unaware of his loss. Although the Glossopdale tenants had promised in November to submit to his honour, he wrote, their leaders had approached the Privy Council again before Christmas, claiming tenant right. They were condemned for their stubbornness and ordered to depart. They'd refused.

If the old religion still remained I'd pay for masses for her soul. But surely she's in Heaven.

'I told the Council the Glossopdale lands were worth the first demands,' wrote Baldwin, 'but his lordship was nevertheless content to take the third penny. Yet the knaves said their rents would still be fifteen or twenty times what they had been. I had good conversations with many of their lordships: the Lord Chancellor, Lord Lincoln, Lord Leicester, the Lord Chamberlain and Mr Secretary Wilson. They agreed the Glossopdale rebels should be confined to prison and tried for sedition, yet they declined to maintain that resolve when the Council met to chastise the villains; I have no idea why. At my instruction the rogues had been confined to the Marshalsea again, under the Knight Marshal's custody…'

Might I plead before the Council of Heaven for my wife to be restored alive to me?

'I told the Council that all other Glossopdale tenants would decline to accept these evil-minded persons as neighbours if they refused the judgement of a Commission, which their obstinate and lewd behaviour showed they would indeed refuse…'

She's there, a shadow in the shadows, seen from the corner of my eye, vanishing as I turn to embrace her; a mockery sent to taunt me for failing to care when she needed me most.

'Then the Lord Chamberlain asked whether the tenants had held their farms by lease or by copy in the time of the abbots, and I said they'd held them as the abbot pleased, either for their lives or for an allotted number of years. But they said I'd misunderstood them: did his honour have copies of leases, or court rules showing how the lands had been held in Abbey time? I said I doubted whether his honour had such writings, since his grandfather had been gifted those lands, in exchange for lands in Ireland, when they were taken from the Abbey in Wales; and his honour would not have gone to Wales to take possession of such documents because he'd have deemed them of little value. William, was I right?'

People will expect me to take another wife, but there could never be another Kath. I need servants who'll care for our sons, care for the house. The house I made for her.

The house in which her shadow lives and moves without substance, without breath, without warmth of body, without gracing me with the touch of her lips.

'I told the Council again that although the Glossopdale lands were worth the new rating, his honour had raised the rents forty times or more only in order to expel the four who stirred trouble, Botham above all. His honour would take the third penny from all the other tenants. But their lordships said those rents would still be too high for poor men to pay in a land of harsh soil where no corn but oats would grow, and they feared beggary and depopulation of the country, which God forfend. It seems the scoundrels had persuaded them, William.'

Her spinning wheel sits silent. When summer comes, spiders will spin webs upon it, unless some good servant uses it as she did; a servant such as Mistress Britton, if his honour will spare her again.

*

The pox scars on Scargill's face seemed to have deepened. Dickenson sent for ale.

'God save you, George. Your countenance isn't Mistress Britton's, but it's welcome. That stool should seat you in comfort.'

Scargill sat, drank and grunted.

'Mr Eyre seeks news of you, William. His honour heard about Katherine and said… what was it? That you are to receive all such comfort as he can provide.'

'His honour said that?'

'He values you.' Scargill cleared his throat. 'Sent Eleanor Britton to help you until you can find a servant to meet your needs.'

Dickenson stared at a shadow beyond Scargill's shoulder.

'His honour sent her? His own housekeeper?'

Scargill's laugh was short and uneasy.

'Housekeeper. Aye.'

Dickenson sipped ale, stared again at the shadow, and swallowed.

'Does her ladyship know about Mistress Britton?'

Another short laugh. Scargill shifted on his stool.

'I think her ladyship would rather his honour swyved the Scottish Queen than a Norfolk farmer's daughter. But knowing that custody of

Mary keeps her husband confined to Sheffield, she nevertheless chooses to stay at Chatsworth. What can she expect?'

Her ladyship and Mr Cavendish had meddled in the Glossopdale dispute. Dickenson was conscious of his own part in the meddling. But Glossopdale was not the only wedge driving earl and countess apart.

'You don't like Eleanor Britton, George.'

Scargill shrugged.

'No doubt a good housekeeper. No doubt a comfort in his honour's bed. But there are costs outside the reach of your account books, William. Mistress Britton has a nephew, Thomas Britton. She sends him regular parcels. He's building one of the best houses in Norfolk: rich furnishings and hangings, proper garden. No one knows where he finds the money.'

Dickenson shut his eyes.

'I'll write to thank his honour for sending her. She helped me through the worst trouble. But your words don't surprise me; in Mistress Britton I perceived a velvet façade over an iron core. I shall look into my own money chest.'

Scargill's laugh was less uncertain.

'You've good eyes, William.' He straightened his shoulders, finished the ale and laid his mug on the floor among the rushes. The dog licked it. 'As I said, there are matters... The many demands on you as bailiff, as his honour's secretary... and the cutlers' juries... Glossopdale atop it all... his honour wonders if it's too great a burden for you to carry without help. I've little patience with figures, but I'm forever reckoning tithes and fines and rents and I write things down as I do them. I make Richard do likewise. I can keep your accounts until you're able to keep pace with them again, if that will help you.'

Again, tears could have come. Compassion sat on George Scargill like a drunkard on an untamed horse, notwithstanding his kindness to the poor; yet determination can keep the worst of riders in the saddle. And who could have expected his honour to consider a humble bailiff's needs while he was beset by multiple demands, struggling to pay for custody of the Queen of Scots, his marriage disintegrating?

'Thank you, George. A little help could be welcome, but I'll meet my obligations as far as I can. Kath would expect no less of me. If I fail to do everything that his honour requires of me, I fail in my duty to my liege lord and to God.'

Scargill rose, remarking that the Glossopdale bastards had been to London again, refusing his honour's offer to reduce the intended rent rises by two thirds. Lord Shrewsbury would make no further concessions. He was seeking redress under common law.

'Yes, George, Tom Baldwin told me of their latest complaint to the Council. And Mr Eyre said his honour had spoken about his case in law. I believe hard words were spoken before the miscreants returned to London.'

'If Mr Eyre hadn't stopped me I'd have knocked Mellor to the ground for what he said about his honour. Even Botham's speech wasn't as vile. Stubborn as ever, though. Glossopdale will never be at peace until Botham's gone. If I'm not much mistaken he'll be back in London again before long, still complaining.'

Glossopdale, January 1579/80-April 1580

Old Maggie died day after Plough Monday. Bailiff witnessed her will: soul commended to keeping of Our Lord and Saviour Jesus Christ, twelve pence to poor box, forty-two shilling and fourpence to Will, twenty-three and ninepence to Agnes and me. On St Mark's Eve past she'd seen Glossopdale's deaths coming like she always had, Edmund's and Phil's among them, but she'd said nowt about her own. Happen she'd seen it, happen she hadn't.

My brother-in-law Will's face were like wastes above Peak Naze. He'd seen death coming whether his Ma had or not, so he hadn't gone to London with Harry this time. I hadn't gone neither, because him and Agnes had wanted me home. Agnes couldn't stop skriking when her Ma's soul were called, and Will couldn't think one foot in front of another, so it were me as went and saw vicar and got Maggie buried proper. I tried to do ploughing and all, yoking a couple of cows while John Stedman had ox. Then Harry and rest of lads come home from London with tales of snowdrifts and deathly cold, and more knife fights with beggars, and he took plough off me and did our lands for us, God bless and keep him.

When snowdrops were done and daffodils shone through wind and sleet like woodland creatures wanting a home, Will started on fields again: Long Sutt, Padfield Heap, Shirrelside, Meane Hill, Sprey Field, Kinnock Ley, Howgate Dole. But he were still quiet. Hadn't got his spirit back since God had took his Ma. We minded him copying Mr Holland's

214

voice after his lordship had brought yon preacher to Glossop. Got some laughs with that. But he weren't making us laugh no more.

Still and all, things were getting better. But I were bothered about Agnes. She carried on taking cures to sick folk, attending women in childbirth like young Rose Stedman having her second, but lengthening days weren't taking darkness off her soul. She were right enough with me, doing what a wife ought; but same as her brother, it were like spirit had left her when Maggie died. I sat with her at side of fire afore we went to bed and talked to her, but she said nowt only yes and no and happen, and she'd always been a talker. Made me feel like I weren't no use. I could do nowt for her only pray.

Daffodils were still in flower, and there were wood anemones and dog's mercury, and you could put your foot on twelve daisies, and robins and great-tits telled us it were spring; only weather thought different. Harry said there were unfinished business in London and we had to sort out this third-penny offer his lordship had made.

'What does it mean?' Joanna asked.

'It means if he'd wanted to put your rent up from two shilling an acre to ninety shilling, like we were getting telled, he'll only put it up to thirty shilling instead. So if you've twenty acre you'll pay thirty pound a year when you used to pay two.' Harry spat. 'And we're supposed to say, "Thank you for such kindness, your lordship, we'll all be happy to pay such a gnat-sized rent".'

Joanna stood and worked it out.

'There's not many as *can* pay thirty shilling an acre. Only them Newtons. But they've a lot more nor twenty acre, so happen they'll not manage neither.'

Harry wanted me to go to London again because I hadn't gone in December while Maggie were bad, but I reckoned Agnes still needed me at home. Olly Smith said he'd go because he hadn't been in December neither. Will said it might shift some of gloom off him if he went, even if it meant another two week in Marshalsea. I went up to Cloud to see Willie, and he said he'd go instead of me so there'd still be a Booth in front of Council, and anyroad he wanted to see London and Privy Council for himself after tales we'd telled about them.

215

That were good, but I still felt like I were letting Harry down. I told Agnes I weren't going because summat had telled me I ought to stay with her, and she skriked like she'd done when her Ma were buried. I said if she reckoned I were bad for not following Harry, I'd go anyroad so Will could stop at home; but she sobbed some more and said what a good man I were. Same as I've said afore, I couldn't make no sense of women.

At finish, Harry and Will and Willie and Olly went. Come April they still weren't back so we reckoned summat were up. Joanna and Alice and Kathy – Harry's sister Kathy, as were Olly's wife – they were all proper worried. Agnes were wondering and all. Then old Tom Jackson come down to Pyegrove.

'We'd best get to London, Tom,' he said. 'See if we can sort this out.'

I looked at Agnes and she nodded.

'Happen best, Tom. We'll manage same as we did afore, us women, and there's men will help if we need, and they'll give you money again so you won't starve.'

She hugged me and pinned some dried mugwort on my jerkin and told me to take care of myself and bring everybody home safe, and when Tom and me set off she were back to skriking. I didn't like Agnes skriking, but she'd started saying more nor 'yes – no – happen', which were a comfort. And Mr Yeaverley had blessed our sheep on Good Shepherd Sunday, like a vicar should, so we'd have fat lambs and good fleeces.

*

It took us nigh on three week going same road as we'd done afore, through Derby and Hallaton and Newmarket and Barnet. We could neither of us walk fast, and with days getting longer we couldn't go from sunrise to sunset. Look and sound and smell of wayside flowers and birdsong, sheep and beasts crying to their babbies, corn sprouting, hay meadows with poppies and cornflowers; it all filled us with praise for Our Lord and kept us going. But when we got to London it were across to Southwark and into Marshalsea again, and there were Harry and Willie and Will and Olly saying Council weren't letting them go until they made a submission. Old Tom scratched his head, which weren't good for it because he hadn't a lot of hair, and asked what it meant.

'We must submit to his lordship and say we'll pay what he wants,' said Olly.

'Aye, Olly, only Sir Francis and Lord Burghley promised we'll get summat back,' said Harry.

'What, like?' I asked. 'We still can't pay yon daft rents, Harry.'

'That we can't,' said old Tom.

'We'll need to talk about it,' said Harry. 'Anyroad, if we send a message agreeing, they'll see us again, write what we've agreed and keep it in Council chest. That's what they're saying.'

My brother Willie looked like he didn't know his head from his arse, Marshalsea being nowt like home. Will looked poorly and all. Old Tom didn't look happy.

'We should find out what them lords say they'll give us back and *then* send message,' he said.

*

We were across river to Greenwich and into Round Chamber again, great lords sitting both sides of yon long table, big dyed wool pictures on wall, us standing caps in hands. Mr Talbot were there and all, and another man dressed fine; Harry said this man were Mr Baldwin, his lordship's agent in London. We got telled all yon stuff about being wicked and unworthy knaves again; but same as they say, sticks and stones might break my bones but words'll never hurt me. Then them lords said we must seek his lordship's favour and they wouldn't be writing no more letters to him. Guards took us outside so we could talk about it. Sir Francis followed us, beckoned Harry a few yard off and started whispering, and Harry whispered summat back. I couldn't hear what they said. Then Sir Francis went back in Round Chamber and Harry come to us and said, 'We're getting a proper deal. They're writing it down. We go in and say all right, we'll seek Lord Shrewsbury's favour, and then Council will tell him to get mediation.'

Will asked what "mediation" were. Harry said some gentlemen as weren't his lordship's friends would survey Glossopdale and reckon what were fair rents. Council would choose the gentlemen.

Willie said, 'What about evictions?' and Harry said we'd deal with them ourselves; but we'd have muscle behind us because Council weren't happy about us getting evicted, reckoning we'd cause more trouble if we went nor if we stayed.

After a bit, Mr Baldwin come and called us back into Round Chamber. We had to swear we'd seek his lordship's favour, and Lord Burghley – God on Judgement Day – showed us a piece of writing and said it were our submission. Then two more lords said we weren't to come to London in a party no more; any of us as had summat to say about rents and suchlike would need to do it on his own. Then Lord Burghley put submission paper in a big chest and locked it, and that were that. We were off.

Well, we thought we were. Only when we got out of yon Chamber there were a woman glaring at us. Finest clothes and brightest jewels you could dream about, only you wouldn't dream nowt like them unless you'd ate bad mushrooms. It were like she'd come out of nowhere, and when she spoke it were like a knife: '*Get you gone, you villains, and obey your liege lord!*' One look at her face, never mind clothes and jewels, and we knew who she were. So we stood aside and bowed and said nowt. Then Lord Burghley and Sir Francis come out of Round Chamber, and they bowed and all and started whispering to her, and she waved a fan while she listened. Covered with bright little pictures, yon fan, all colours, only I couldn't make out what they were. Then she nodded and said, 'That is good,' and off she went, four or five serving women chasing after her.

My jaw felt like it were on floor. For a minute I couldn't neither move nor speak. Harry told me to shut my mouth or flies would get in it. Then Sir Francis turned his head, and him and Harry looked at one another. He give a quick nod and his thin lips did summat as might have been a smile, and him and Lord Burghley went back in Round Chamber and we set off home.

'What were that about, Harry?' I asked.

'They won't tell Lord Shrewsbury he's right, and they won't say we should give third penny, and they'll ask him for mediation. That's what we've got for submitting. It's all wrote down and in yon chest.' He grinned. 'Mind, they can forget yon stuff about each of us arguing on his own if we've complaints. Glossopdale men stand together.'

We give him a cheer, but we were none of us sure what were what.

'Aye, Harry, but what if his lordship won't do mediation?' said Will.

'Then we'll be back in London again,' said Harry. 'All of us.'

That seemed right enough, but I knew there were more to it. Harry were keeping summat up his sleeve again. Had he asked Sir Francis where his mother were? Looked like he knew where to find everybody in England, yon Sir Francis, like he were watching from sky; same as when you stand over an anthill watching ants. Happen it were summat else, mind. Harry would tell us when he wanted. If he wanted.

We were nigh half way home when he come up beside me and muttered, 'Here, Spiderlegs; if your Ma still has them Papist pictures she took out of church or yon Mary Magdalene chapel, tell her to get shot of them'.

There were lapwings in fields, crying 'beware'. Poor souls as can't find their way to Heaven and are stuck here as birds.

Sheffield, April 1580

Katherine's soul had fled to Heaven. Dickenson dreamed that if God hadn't taken her from him, Lord Shrewsbury's marriage wouldn't have collapsed. Eyes accused him from the unseen borders of awareness, her majesty's eyes foremost. Entries in his account books blurred, swam over the page and faded. Even under the thrall of Morpheus he was disorientated. He felt anger surge again within him.

His reason returned shred by shred, but concentration eluded him. Eyre recounted news: Edmund Campion and Robert Parsons had returned to England to build a Jesuit mission. They were to be executed for treason. Scargill approved: 'Teach the Papist swine a lesson.' Richard Topcliffe had apprised his honour that the bad tenants of Glossopdale desired coal for their irons. The French marriage proposal for her majesty had been resurrected: Lord Leicester had accompanied the duke of Alençon to Antwerp; Monsieur Simier was due at Court. His honour had declined Tom Baldwin's offer to deal for Sir Thomas Gresham's house in London because of Sir Thomas's debts. Dorothy Browne had been tried for witchcraft before the retiring High Sheriff of Derbyshire, Sir Thomas Cockayne; case dismissed for lack of evidence. Her majesty had refused his honour's request to remove the Scottish Queen to Chatsworth or Buxton so that her part of the Sheffield manor house could be sweetened; Elizabeth wanted no Papists close to his honour's daughter-in-law Talbot when she gave birth. Tom Baldwin reported that the Queen had become ill through taking a bath; the bill for the Scottish Queen's diet money, a year overdue, had not been signed. Most of the information passed Dickenson by. One duty dominated his thoughts:

the need to ask Lord Shrewsbury's creditors to accept only the interest on their loans for the coming year since his honour could pay none of the capital.

'So much to do, Nathaniel,' he said. 'Always so much.'

'George promised help. Let him carry some of the burden.'

I must write to William Every, too, concerning his offer of four hundred pounds for wool at eleven shillings the stone. The offer is of long standing. I should have replied before now.

'Sir Francis Walsingham has written again, Nathaniel. You saw the letter?'

'The Glossopdale tenants have agreed to submit, the Council having ordered that their rents be moderated by disinterested mediators, justices of the peace. I shan't be among them; I can scarcely be thought disinterested.'

'His honour orders me to write again to Lord Leicester asking that sharp punishment be visited on the Glossopdale troublemakers, which they well deserve. He promises to make one of the villains called Nicholas Mellor smart for his wild speeches against him. He's enraged by the Council's leniency, their request for medition.'

Eyre laughed.

'Mellor! Wild speeches indeed! George so angered Mellor at Christmas that I had to prevent a fight. Two gunpowder tempers.' He grew solemn. 'His honour might agree to mediation if the countess didn't unsettle him. He deems her less obedient and dutiful than his first wife.'

'Whose name I have forgotten.'

'Gertrude. Sister of John Manners of Haddon.'

'Ah yes. His honour accuses the countess of devoting herself to her children and her Chatsworth estate instead of to him. No doubt that's why he considers her disobedient and undutiful. He says he doesn't want half a wife. He complains about her extravagance, too; perhaps with justification.'

'While his great new house in Worksop is being built. At greater cost than he can afford, William.'

'The Crown still gives him far too little, and the rents –'

'Also, the countess still seeks control of the Glossopdale farmholds. As I said, she'll demand them as jointure for her sons. And his honour won't yield them. Glossopdale has done more to sever them than her ladyship's jealousy of the Scottish Queen.'

Kath believed Mary sought to manipulate his honour by deploying her charm, her skill in cajoling; so that whenever her ladyship was absent from Sheffield, she had more opportunities to correspond with her supporters. In Kath's opinion, Mary herself had spread rumours that she'd bedded his honour, presuming the Shrewsburys' mutual hostility to be always to her advantage.

'The rumours about his honour and the Scottish Queen are wild,' said Dickenson, 'but her ladyship declares she knows things that would harm him if she made them public.'

'What passes in privacy between man and wife is known to no other. But his honour's letters to Lord Leicester slander her ladyship and her children. And have you seen his letters to the Queen? "My wicked and malicious wife, my professed enemy, shrew with a wicked tongue …" His mind's deteriorating, William. Glossopdale must bear much of the blame.' Eyre shouted at a servant and drank wine. 'Bishop Bentham took him to task for those words. Did you read the Bishop's letter? "If shrewdness or sharpness may be a just cause for separation between a man and wife, I think very few men in England would keep their wives long… it is a common jest that there is but one shrew in all the world and every man has her".'

Dickenson could have answered the bishop: not every man considered his wife a shrew. Instead, he wrote to the earl concerning the fine buck that had been killed at Tankersley, leaving no offspring in the park. Uncharacteristically, his honour vouchsafed no reply. Eyre was right: the earl's mind was failing under the stresses of chronic pain, financial worry, broken marriage, custody of the Scottish Queen, demands upon him as earl martial, and continuing trouble with Glossopdale.

There was still so much to do. Always so much.

Glossopdale, August 1580

Agnes had made half a rood of garden on south side of our house: onion, mallow, mugwort, parsley and borage, same as Joanna's garden, but stuff she needed for cures and all, each in its own patch. I knew some: comfrey for bruises, tansy for worms, dandelion for stoppage of water; but she'd lavender, marjoram, dog rose, elder, and some she called allium and dianthus, and summat else as started *eryn* but I couldn't remember rest of name. She said most were for helping folk sleep because there were nowt like sleep for mending sick bodies, and sick souls and all. Little Margaret pottered round on her tiny bare feet, reckoning to help. My insides went like curds when Agnes told nipper what herb were good for what, and nipper listened and looked up at her and called her Ma.

One wet Friday, St Bartholomew's Day, Scargill come again with half a dozen following him. John Rowland saw them first like he usually does and he come and told us. We reckoned there'd be fun if Scargill started owt with Harry, so we went up Simmondley. I were slow; they were already at it when I got there.

'Wrong, Scargill. When have you heard me say owt bad about his lordship?'

'You made mockery of prayer, Botham, when I put you into the stocks last –'

'Put me in stocks? Aye, and I were soon out again, or you wouldn't have left Glossopdale in one piece.'

'You mocked Lord Shrewsbury in prayer!'

'You want to get a pair of ears as works right.'

Three quarters of Glossopdale were round them, giving Scargill a proper welcome. He said summat else as I didn't hear and there were a right howl from crowd. Harry put his hand up and they went quiet again.

'Lord Shrewsbury's in my prayers every day. He won't treat me nor Nick Mellor nor Tom there any different nor rest of us, not when it comes down to it.'

'His lordship has ordered you, Booth, Mellor and Jackson evicted. Evicted you'll be.'

There were another howl. Crowd closed in. I never reckoned much to Scargill, but give him his due, he had guts. Stood his ground. Harry shook his head.

'That's not what her majesty's Privy Council says, Scargill. Try that and you'll be on wrong side of law, if you live long enough.'

Then half a dozen men pushed forward at Scargill: Roger Capper and Henry Waterhouse from Whitfield, Reg Cartledge from Chunal, John Beard and Tom Partridge from Charlesworth, Will Bramwell from Dinting. They'd none of them been to London with us but they knew what Harry had done for Glossopdale.

'Tell his lordship this much,' Reg Cartledge said: 'if any of our four friends gets shoved out of his farmhold, we'll take no offer from you. There's none of us will pay no rent.'

'Right, everybody,' Roger Capper shouted, 'let's take our oath and pledge our word to what Reg says! All of us together in name of custom! Harry, Tom, Nick and Tom keep their tenencies, or there's no rents paid in Glossopdale!'

Four dozen throats cheered. I couldn't help joining in and grinning.

'Aye,' said Will Bramwell, 'that means us in Dinting and all. Happen Newtons will think different, mind.'

'Happen there's more of their sort and all, Will,' said John Beard, 'but they're not our friends!'

It were good to hear. I hadn't reckoned on Henry Waterhouse being on Harry's side; he were Richard Shuttleworth's brother-in-law, another as didn't like Bothams. Anyroad, there it were: all together in name of custom. Scargill didn't like it one bit but there weren't nowt he could do. Harry looked like he'd burst with joy, and Joanna at side of him had her arm round him and tears on her face. Young Edmund come out of house and stood side of his Dad waving a stick, a little Harry with a little ash staff.

Scargill and his men went off again with their tails between their legs. All Glossopdale cheered 'til they scared rooks off fields. Folk threw their hats in air. Then Will preached a mock sermon, sounding that much like Mr Yeaverley you had to look twice; got his spirit back, had Will, since he'd been to London. And then half a dozen young lads made an effigy of his lordship out of old rags and hanged it off an oak branch.

*

I were on my way home when I heard Ottie Wood had dropped dead. We'd need to pray for Mary and see she were all right. Poor woman had never had a babby as had lived more nor three week, and now God had took her husband. It would hit Harry bad, losing his brother-in-law and happen having to take his sister back under his roof.

Sheffield, November 1580

'Can you tolerate good news, William?' Eyre bit his lip.

'In preference to bad.'

'George was enthusiastic. Very enthusiastic.' Eyre chuckled. 'His honour's pursued his suit against the Glossopdale tenants in the Court of Common Pleas.'

'I knew he'd planned such action. Also, he asked permission to go to London to press her majesty for the Scottish Queen's diet money. To no avail; her majesty upbraided him for his three-day absence from Sheffield while he had business in Bolsover.'

'And in Worksop.'

'And in Worksop. So was he permitted –?'

'For those few days I was his deputy. A castle steward and Manor Court judge, custodian of a queen! Infernal woman! You were right, William: a viper.'

'What befell his honour's suit at Common Pleas? And why there? Surely the matter should have been taken –'

'The Privy Council referred the case down to Westminster Hall, either to Common Pleas or Queen's Bench, whichever had the shorter backlog.'

'I'd have thought Chancery –'

'No. In fine: you recall the Council's ruling that the Glossopdale rents are to be mediated by three Derbyshire justices of the peace?'

'Has his honour accepted this ruling?'

'It was part of the Court's decision. George liked the other part.'

'The eviction orders are upheld?'

'Mellor and Jackson are to leave their farmholds at Christmas. Botham and Booth will be gone by next Lady Day.'

Dickenson shook his head.

'Good news indeed, but it won't end the matter, Nathaniel. Botham will defy the court's ruling. Or he'll find a way to challenge it. The others will follow him.' He sighed. 'Nevertheless, it's reassuring that a court of law champions reason over sedition.'

*

It was a cold night in Attercliffe. Dickenson finished witnessing John Bowman's last will and testament and rode through the darkness to Sheffield and his empty home. Ill-nourished, and with little appetite, he was weary.

His horse's hooves snapped sparks from the frozen track. The sky overflowed with stars, among them the new comet of which there had been much talk. What did it foretell? Men feared such signs. Perhaps women feared them, too. How would he know?

His honour would soon order him to make his yearly Advent gifts to undeserving commoners. He could not afford such gifts. Expenditure on the Scottish Queen, the countess, the Talbot sons and the house at Worksop totalled more than twice the earl's gross yearly income from lead sales, cutlers' taxes, rents on tenancies, and the Crown's meagre provision for Mary. Tom Baldwin reported that he would be unable to pay off Lord Francis Talbot's debts unless Alderman Pullyson handed over the money due for his lead purchases, Lord Burghley persuaded the Queen to pay Mary's diet money, and Roger Manners would lend two hundred pounds. Pending those payments his honour would be unable to buy the two parks he desired from the earl of Warwick. In other letters, Lord Shrewsbury complained that the Queen must consider him unworthy of a proper allowance for Mary, protesting nevertheless that his desire to serve his sovereign made pain and peril a pleasure to him. *Such pleasure*, thought Dickenson, *swiftly exhausts the capacity for enjoyment.*

His honour's bedroom in the manor house must hold chests of gold and silver coins. How secure were they? How depleted by Eleanor Britton?

When that woman was stifling me with kindness, Kath spoke in my mind, counselling caution. Why did his honour's housekeeper and mistress prepare food for me, bring me fresh linen, and fetch sweet herbs into my house to expel the foul air? She was putting me in her debt so I'd be loath to investigate the connection between his honour's store of money and the house her nephew is building in Norfolk. Indeed, I can't find it in my heart to voice suspicion. And I can't report it to Lord Talbot or Master Gilbert because I've no proof. In any case, what could they do? His honour will dispose of his money as he pleases. If his weakening mind is seduced to ruin by a predatory mistress, even his sons can't intervene. I certainly cannot.

Despite Katherine's warning voice, Dickenson had been slow to suspect. Not until Scargill had complained about Mistress Britton had he checked his own money chest. It hadn't been touched. Therefore, his only reasons for doubting Eleanor's honesty were Scargill's insinuations, the whispers from Katherine's shadow, and his own intuition about the housekeeper's self-seeking core. None of that constituted evidence.

The Scottish Queen, the countess, Eleanor Britton: his honour was beset on all sides by rapacious women. *Or*, wondered Dickenson, *is my opinion of womankind too jaundiced?*

All the Michaelmas valuations of tenancies had to be updated: Wadley and Owlerton, Walkley and Crookes, Broomhall, Eccleshall, Pitsmoor and Heeley, Attercliffe and Darnall, Norton, Nortonlees, Eccleshall, Beauchief, Greenhill… George Scargill had managed half of them but his records were untidy. Dickenson needed sleep before he could disentangle the chaos. As for Glossopdale, despite Nathaniel Eyre's advice to wait until the Privy Council had clarified its position, and the outcomes of his honour's petitions to Queen's Bench and Common Pleas were known, George had taken a paltry half dozen to evict the four whom his honour had ordered to leave. He'd succeeded only in uniting the manor once again behind the troublemakers. *George Scargill. Ever the subtle negotiator.*

Dickenson had ridden past the cottages of Oakes Green and was approaching Washford Bridge when he was alerted by movement

228

among the branches above the road. Before the robber's body landed behind him, startling the horse, he'd drawn his sword; and as the horse reared he grasped the reins with one hand and smashed the pommel into the assailant's face with the other. The robber fell to the road, gasping blasphemies, dagger bouncing and clattering, blade sparkling in the starlight. By the time Dickenson had controlled the horse and dismounted, the villain was crawling into the undergrowth that fringed the river. Dickenson made short work of him. *Cheaper and quicker than sending him to the hangman,* he reflected, sheathing his sword and remounting.

His heart raced and blood ran warm and vital to his hands and feet. It was deemed foolish to ride alone at night through lands where hobs and sprites lurked, and creatures with bulls' bodies and dragons' heads; lands where robbers were rife. But he'd done it often; he'd survived more than one attack, and this fresh incident had lifted the leaden cloak of lethargy from his shoulders. *Had there been two of them, I'd have been in Heaven with Kath by now.*

He reached home more alert than he'd been since his wife's death. Now he could take Scargill's scattered figures and thrash them into order, impose upon them the ineffable beauty of precision.

First, though, he must sleep.

Glossopdale, February 1580/81

In a way, it were same as every year afore Shrove Tuesday: ewes in lamb led to best pasture, bull put to beasts and folk cheering him on, us getting ready for forty day of fasting while we think of Our Lord fasting in yon desert and arguing with Devil. But in another way it were different. Harry and Joanna were struggling with Mary now God had took Ottie. Agnes and me and rest of us helped where we could, but it were a bad do for Mary. Then moon got ate up with shadow on St Wufstan's Night and that should have telled us there were bother coming. We'd our own devil to argue with in Glossopdale: Scargill were after his tithes and he wanted them in kind not money. We weren't having none of that.

'Tithes in kind? It would be to overthrow of every plough in Glossopdale,' said Harry. 'Five hundred folk would be undone and starving.'

We knew Scargill wanted more nor his fair share of our oats and hay and wool and chickens in a bad year, so he could sell it all at top prices while everybody were short. He wouldn't care about Glossopdale starving if his pockets were lined. Harry and me and a dozen others telled him he could stop asking for tithes in kind or he'd get nowt, so he shouted about his right and duty to collect both tithes and rent for his lordship. Harry tied a noose on a rope and threw it over an oak branch and said, 'Come on and dance in air, Scargill, and then take your tithes'. Scargill said he'd take tithes in kind because that were what his lordship ordered. Then off he went afore yon noose got put round his neck for real.

That weren't worst of it. Seemingly, his lordship had been to some court in London and this court had said four evictions were right and we all had to go. Mind, same court said Council were right about mediation. That were good for forty-eight households as kept their tenancies. Weren't a lot of use for Tom Jackson and Nick Mellor, or for Harry and me.

We weren't putting up with it, court or no court. We reckoned Privy Council had said summat different about evictions. Where were we if one lot of lords said evictions weren't bound to happen and another lot said they were? Harry told us: we were staying, except we'd need to go and see Privy Council again to sort it out once and for all.

Anyroad, Scargill and his servants shifted Tom and Nick out of their farmholds and said two of his lordship's loyal servants would be put there instead. Aye, we said, just wait and see what happens to yon loyal servants if they think they can run a Glossopdale farm and rest of us will let them. John Stedman took Nick and his wife in. They worked both farms between them, John's and Nick's, because there weren't none of them loyal servants as were willing or able to take Nick's place; and John's brother Jim took old Tom in at Herod. It were hard work farming up at Herod because it were on edge of wastes, so Jim were glad to have Tom with him. Court had bothered more about Harry and me; said we'd to be out on Lady Day, not afore. They'd made a right pig's breakfast of it where I were concerned because they reckoned they were kicking me out of Cloud. Agnes and me weren't at Cloud, and I'd never held leasehold anyroad. When Scargill's men went to Cloud, Ma and Alice chased them off with brooms and sickles saying there weren't no Thomas Booth there, it were William Booth's farmhold and they could take their ugly by-our-lady faces back to Pit where they belonged.

It weren't same for Harry, though, with Joanna and Edmund and little Samuel, as were still nobbut a babby, and Mary and all. There'd be a right load of bother if they come to shift him and his family on Lady Day.

There were summat else and all, a dark shadow in dark days of February. It were like wearing a jerkin of cold air while sun tries to creep above Nab for two or three hour and snow lays its shroud over bones of January. Bishop of Lichfield and Coventry, Bishop Bentham, sent some of his clergy to Glossopdale and they sniffed round folks' houses, and then they took Bob Wolstenholme, Will Garlick and John Beely to Church Court in Derby. We knew them three were Papists at heart, for all they went to church regular like rest of us and joined in prayers and psalms, but they didn't do nobody no harm. Harry went round alehouses saying it were Mr Yeaverley had told Bishop about them three, so everybody were down on vicar again, even more nor they'd been when Coney were punished for fornication. Stones and shit got thrown at his door.

I minded Harry saying vicar had made an enemy of him after Coney were up in Manor Court. And I minded how he'd looked at Bob one day in Jacob's alehouse after Bob had talked like a Papist. Then there were St James's and Round Chamber: deal to stop daft rent rises, and Sir Francis and Harry whispering to one another. Sir Francis were ridding England of Papists; that weren't no secret. So putting two and two together give me an answer I didn't want. I knew what Harry were like, but I didn't like what I were thinking.

Agnes reckoned I were right: somebody had told Mr Yeaverley about Bob, Will and John, and vicar had told Bishop. If Church Court found them guilty of being Papists they'd happen be sent to quarter session. Will's brother Nick were an ordained Catholic priest as did services down at Padley Hall, so it wouldn't be good news for him neither.

'Agnes, if I'd been a Papist on quiet, do you reckon Harry would have give vicar my name?'

She thought about it and shook her head.

'No, Tom, I don't. Them three as has been took to Church Court, they were never close to Harry. Not like you are.'

Happen you're right, love, I thought. Happen. But I were glad Ma had got shot of them pictures she'd took out of ruin of St Mary Magdalene Chapel. At least Harry had put me wise about that, and Ma had done what I told her for once.

Sheffield, February 1580/81

Scargill was shaking. Dickenson handed him a mug of ale.

'Glossopdale's tenants will be pacified once Botham's gone, George. Sedition withers and dies once its root is cut.'

'Glossopdale's lawless. They threatened –'

'They wouldn't dare. The Council asked his honour to place Jackson in a new holding because they deemed him old and feeble. He's promised to do so. No matter. Once the valley is pacified the tenants will pay their tithes. In kind, as demanded. *And* their mediated rents.' Dickenson smiled. 'Let us hope the mediators will set the rents high enough to teach the knaves their place.'

The need for increased rents was greater than ever. Far from providing fifty pounds per week for custody of the Scottish Queen, her majesty had reduced it to thirty-two pounds, insisting once again that the rents and tithes from the Shrewsbury estates, the taxes on the cutlers and the profits from lead provided his honour with abundant cash. She ordered Mary's household to be halved. How could that order be enforced? Eyre deemed it impossible. In any case, there was no way of reducing the earl's required payments to the countess or his Talbot offspring. Also, the Queen knew nothing of Eleanor Britton's rapacity.

Dickenson had dispatched a letter to Sir Francis Walsingham begging the Queen to reconsider the custody allowance. Sir Francis said the Queen's mind couldn't be changed. He advised his honour to tell the Privy Council he could no longer manage custody of Mary. However, the earl preferred his ever-mounting debt to the humiliation of confessing his incapacity.

233

'I overhear hard words,' said Eyre. 'The Scottish Queen mistrusts the countess. Even when her ladyship is in Sheffield they avoid each other. Lately, Mary's household dined in the great hall with the Shrewsburys and their staff. Their antipathy to each other could have set the manor house ablaze.'

'Perhaps it's fortunate that the countess is seldom in Sheffield,' said Dickenson.

'She still demands her allowance. Part of the marriage agreement. But —'

'His honour is barely able to pay it.'

'She says he uses cruel and bitter speeches against her, though she never utters undutiful words.'

'Accusing her husband of adultery with the Scottish Queen isn't dutiful.'

'He speaks gently to the Scottish Queen, William, which makes gossiping mouths take rumour for fact. Poison tongues everywhere. Some fools even say Mary's borne him a son. And when his honour ordered the child Arbella to be taken from Master Gilbert and returned to Chatsworth, Gilbert's wife pursued her. His honour ordered Master Gilbert not to follow on pain of losing his allowance. Gilbert sympathises more with his stepmother than his father. Father and son have become estranged.'

'Lord Leicester still seeks to reconcile earl with countess.'

'In vain. But her majesty fears for the security of the Scottish Queen if the Shrewsburys aren't reunited. The younger Talbot sons remain at Court. They have her majesty's favour. But they can do nothing to bring father and stepmother back together.'

Dickenson's back ached. His hair was thinning, his joints stiffening. Neither prayer nor the remedies he'd learned from his late mother and his late wife had proved efficacious. He thought his bodily ills might be alleviated if his honour's coffers were healthier. God be thanked, though, his eyes remained keen and his writing hand never faltered. Always there were accounts awaiting his notice, begging to be reviewed and updated. But even Dickenson's unrelenting efforts couldn't conjure up sufficient income to meet his honour's burgeoning expenses.

Glossopdale, April-July 1581

Lady Day come and went and Harry still hadn't been shifted out of Storth. Nigh on all Glossopdale were behind him, even more because they'd seen road he cared for Mary after she were widowed. But Joanna knew they'd get evicted; his lordship had won his court case. Willie said they could live at Cloud but Alice weren't having that. Right enough, it wouldn't have suited; Alice and Joanna were cat and dog. But nobody wanted to see Harry and Joanna and their nippers homeless only Scargill, and happen his lordship.

'What do you reckon, Will?' I said. 'Could we give them a home at Pyegrove, them and Mary and all?'

'Houses would be like tight jerkins, Tom. All right if we don't all breathe in at same time.'

Agnes said it were Christian duty to give Harry's family a home, and Alice were a sour bitch and Willie wanted to slap her around more. She'd brewed foxglove for Ma's dropsy, my Agnes had. Ma said it were more like fox's piss nor a glove.

Bailff Booth still wanted rents fifteen time what we'd been paying. He reckoned his lordship were being kind to take third penny because Mr Scargill said so. We told him Privy Council reckoned different so he could chase himself; we'd see what mediators said. Next news, Harry were off to London again. Took Henry Warhurst like he'd done afore, though Henry kept saying him and Josh got kind treatment off Scargill over rent at Crow Car. Tom Blood, Bill Goddard and Bob Rowbottom went with Harry and all. Bob would be handy if summat needed reading, or happen writing. Tom Jackson weren't going; busy helping Jim up at

235

Herod. I weren't going neither: spring oats to plant, lambs and calves to geld, lambs' tails to dock so maggots wouldn't breed on them, willow to cut for folding, ewes to get up to tops.

That's what I telled Harry, anyroad; but truth were, I weren't happy about Bob Wolstenholme and Will Garlick and John Beeley. Bob and John had come back from Church Court, fined twenty shilling each and telled to rid their houses of Papist stuff, but Will were in Derby for assize because he'd talked to his brother as were a priest. I could still hear Harry's voice: "If your Ma still has any of them Papist pictures, tell her to get shot of them".' They'd all had some of them pictures, Bob and Will and John; only Will hadn't made no secret of them.

We give money to Harry, Tom, Bill, Henry and Bob and wished God's blessings on them afore they went. We'd look after their farms while they were away.

*

When they come back they met us in alehouse. Bill made a story about what had happened. Seemingly, yon smug lord with big beard and necklace of jewels (Lord Leicester, Bill said) had wrote to his lordship asking for "forbearance". That meant Council wanted his lordship to show mercy and patience. Well, happen his lordship *would* show mercy and patience, being as how Lord Leicester asked him, but Scargill wouldn't know forbearance if it bit his bollocks.

'Best news is,' said Bill, 'his lordship won't give Tom Jackson his old farmhold back, but he'll give him another just as good.'

'Oh aye?' I said. 'Where? And what does Tom say?'

'Biding his time. Reckons there'll be vacant tenements afore long.'

Happen there would. Happen Will Garlick wouldn't come home. And happen Scargill would try and put old Tom in Storth if he got Harry shifted.

'Did they say owt about Nick Mellor?' John Stedman asked.

'No, John. You know how Nick talks. His lordship will be hard on him.' Bill swigged his ale. 'Harry doesn't shoot his mouth off same road. Mind, Harry won't shift when he's set. Stood in front of them lords and telled them there wouldn't be no mediation while Lord Shrewsbury were still wanting third penny.' He shook his head. 'Wonder they didn't lock him up and have him hanged.'

Middle of May, day after St Matthias, they come for Black Harry.

*

John Rowland were busy with his charcoal and didn't see them. Will did. He were docking lambs' tails while I were mending our thatch.

'Forty of them,' he shouted, 'coming down Doctor Talbot's road, carrying bows. Guns and all!'

That weren't good.

'Scargill?' I said.

'Aye, at front. And there's two or three at side of him looks like gentry, road they're dressed.' Will looked again. 'Can't see yon Dickenson.'

Afore they were past pinfold, all Glossopdale knew they'd come. I took my bow and a few arrows, and John Stedman and others did same, and Randolph left his forge and come with his hammer and a scythe, and there were men with daggers he'd sharpened for them, and one or two swords. But bows and knives and even swords don't answer guns. And Will were right, they'd as many as we had. It had took Scargill a while to work out he'd never shift Harry unless he fetched half an army.

My uncle Bailiff Booth were with them. Newtons were there and all. Asking for knives in their guts and happen one of my arrows, Newtons were, walking up to Storth at side of Scargill looking like they owned valley. But Will were right again: there were two gentry with yon lot from Sheffield. When Harry and Joanna and Mary and young Edmund and little Samuel come out to face them, one of them gentry spoke.

'I am Sir Godfrey Foljambe, justice of the peace, High Sheriff of Derbyshire three years past. I speak for Lord Shrewsbury and her majesty's most honourable Privy Council.'

'Aye, right,' said Harry. 'I'm Harry Botham. I speak for Glossopdale.'

We gathered in a half circle with our bows and knives and Randolph's scythe and hammer. It went quiet. Sir Godfrey looked around us and licked his lips.

'The tenants of Glossopdale have submitted to Lord Shrewsbury and will pay the rents agreed after mediation,' he said.

Harry nodded.

'Right enough. Only nobody won't pay nowt if these evictions happen.'

Sir Godfrey got off his horse and stepped forward. John and me nocked an arrow each. Half a dozen of yon Sheffield servants hoisted their arquebuses.

'Jackson and Mellor are evicted, Master Botham. Booth, it seems, never had leasehold, but he must be expelled from the parish. Today, you too will go.'

Harry stared at him, and then at rest of them, and then at Scargill. His mouth did that sideways shift.

'Aye, three dozen of you to one of me. Might be enough.' He grinned at Scargill and bailiff. 'But then you won't get no rents, will you?'

'You think not?' said Scargill. 'Your father's agreed to pay.'

Harry sort of shrunk. He were quiet for a minute and then said, 'Edmund, go up Bank and fetch your granddad'.

Turned out Scargill were right. Old Harry said he'd pay whatever rent were decided after mediation.

'It's yon Privy Council, son,' he said. 'They listened to you. They're sending folk as will see we get a fair deal. I reckoned if we all said "Aye", yon dog's turd' (he pointed his thumb at Scargill) 'would stop his daft talk about four pound for every shilling.'

He weren't well, Old Harry. Agnes were giving him St John's Wort oil for his ulcers. He'd never have give road to Scargill's lot that easy when he were younger.

'Happen he will and all, Dad, only them of us as won with Privy Council are getting thrown out. You reckon Storth will ever be worked right without a Botham in it?'

'It'll be worked all right, you young shit,' said Scargill. 'This loyal servant of his lordship will be working it from today. Storth Farm's his leasehold now.'

He pointed at a lad none of us hadn't seen afore: lanky with thin fair hair and a soft grin. My uncle nodded and said it were true: lanky with soft grin had proved his right in Manor Court and paid his due.

'Harry.' Joanna put her hand on his arm. Happen she thought he were bound to kill Scargill then and there in front of two justices of peace and four score witnesses. 'Best go. Follow path as God and our good friends has opened for us. It'll come right.'

'Happen.' Harry looked at his Dad and shook his head. Then he faced Scargill again. 'If you reckon this is last you'll see or hear of me, Scargill, you can think again.'

One of Scargill's men, Roger Andrew they called him, went and grabbed hold of Joanna to shift her. Some folk are born stupid. Next news he were on his back, blood pouring out of his nose and mouth, and Harry were stood at top of him, shouting if bastard touched his wife again he'd gralloch him. He got a five shilling fine next Manor Court but he said it were worth it.

Will, John, me and half a dozen others were like a guard of honour around Mary, Harry and Joanna and their nippers while we took them to Pyegrove. Old Harry were nigh skriking. Rest of Glossopdale stayed where they were. Their anger hung in air like thunder, growing and darkening. Scargill and justices of peace and them with guns and bows went off home. They knew there were bound to be trouble.

It were as well they went or there'd have been folk dead on both sides. Roaring and cheering echoed across whole of Glossopdale. Sounded like men going into battle. Scargill and my uncle and Sir Godfrey had shifted Harry out of Storth, but they'd stirred a cartload of bother doing it.

*

Getting Joanna and Mary and nippers settled meant we missed some of it, but Harry and Will and me followed noise to Dinting soon as we could. Afore long we were ripping Newton's enclosure walls down and telling him common land as he'd robbed off poor folk were common again, and if he said owt about it we'd shut him up good and proper so he wouldn't ever say nowt else. He barred his house and we heard his wife and nippers skriking. Happen they thought we'd fire their thatch.

Some lads would have and all, only Harry said no, pulling Newton's enclosure down were enough.

'Reckon you can join us now we've bested his lordship, Newton? Too late. We'll take neither cow nor corn from you. You won't trade in Glossopdale again.'

Next news we were pulling enclosure walls down at Newton's cousin's. Everybody were cheering and throwing their hats in air. Hugh Platt said, 'Enemies of commonwealth, folk as enclose commons.' Hugh were nobbut elevenpence in shilling but he were right.

We were fit to drink alehouse dry, and when day got old we come out singing and off to Storth, Henry Warhurst at front of us. He dragged yon lanky fool with thin hair and soft grin out of house by his jerkin and Harry pointed east.

'Back to whatever hole you come from, you streak of piss, and don't show your ugly face in Glossopdale again!'

'But his lordship's bailiff gave me leasehold, and I paid my fine, and agreed heriot, and Sir Godfrey said –'

'Do what Harry tells you!' shouted Will. 'Back where you belong! Now!'

I were still carrying my bow. I nocked an arrow and pointed it at daftie.

'If you're still in Glossopdale when sun rises in morning, you won't live to see it set,' I said.

I never talked that road but I were half-drunk and I were angry. Anyroad, yon lanky fool shat himself and ran. Folk cheered, and Harry laughed and give me a slap on back as nigh knocked me into middle of next week.

Old Harry went back into Storth for a while. There'd always be a Botham in Storth.

*

That weren't end of it. After sheep had been sheared and marked, while haymaking were doing, while we were watching oats grow as we'd be reaping in a couple of month, we sang songs as Tom Blood made up, songs about how no rents would get paid while our friends got their

240

farmholds back. We sang them that loud I reckon they could hear us in Sheffield. Scared crows out of trees.

Newton and his cousin tried bargaining but it weren't no use. Nobody would trade with them. Randolph wouldn't sharpen their shears or sickles. Roger wouldn't grind corn for them and wouldn't sell them flour. Nobody wouldn't help with their sheep or their oats neither. They shouted back at us, saying mediators as Privy Council were sending wouldn't do nowt for miscreants as had been rightly evicted (I reckon they'd heard yon word "miscreants" off Scargill or happen Dickenson), and we laughed. But Harry said happen it were true, because Council hadn't promised nowt about that. So him and Tom Blood and Bob Rowbottom and Bill Goddard and old Tom Jackson went to Sheffield to see his lordship about it, and when Mr Eyre saw them he set constables on them. They got brought back to Glossopdale and put in lockup on Ashes Hill.

Tom Dewsnap had retired and Ted Wagstaff had been made constable with Humphrey Andrew. They reckoned they'd keep all six of our friends in lockup while mediators come, only we heard mediators weren't bound to come while November and we weren't having that, so we broke lockup open and let all six out. Humfrey and Ted went running to bailiff, but there weren't nowt he could do only give us orders and we weren't taking no notice of orders, not from him or nobody else neither. Harry, Tom, Bob, Bill and Old Tom were loose again, and constables had enough sense not to try locking them back up.

Sheffield, September 1581

Thomas Baldwin's letter revealed that on Wednesday, the seventeenth of the month, the Privy Council had allowed four Glossopdale tenants to address them: Harry Botham, Oliver Smith, William Dawson and John Booth. In spite of the ruling that only one or two might come to London to voice grievances, many from Glossopdale had walked there, the men threatening to parade their miserable wives and children before the Council. The four had been chosen to speak for all.

'John Booth could be Thomas Booth,' said Dickenson, 'one of the miscreants who's been evicted. Do you know the others, George?'

Scargill shrugged.

'Dawson was one who went to London last March or April. Smith's married to one of Botham's sisters. John Booth? No, he's not Thomas Booth. He's the bailiff's nephew. Bangs a tabor at Glossopdale ales.'

'Did he bang it before the Council?' Eyre laughed.

Baldwin declared himself gratified: the Council had ruled that his lordship might by law dispose of their tenements as he pleased. The four were ordered to tell the rest they must go home peacefully, with no evil speeches or reports against Lord Shrewsbury. Once again they were reminded that if they were dissatisfied after mediation, just one or two of their number might come to London. They must not come again in a body.

'The Council's ordered mediation of their rents,' said Eyre. 'What more can the villains want?'

'Tithes in money, not kind,' said Scargill, 'against his honour's orders.'

'And they want those who've been evicted to be restored to their farmholds,' said Dickenson. 'The other tenants submitted to his honour but beseeched the Council to "set our poor neighbours at liberty".'

'And refused any offers until the four were back in their farms,' growled Scargill.

According to Baldwin's letter, the Council had promised to write earnestly to his honour once more in the tenants' favour. They would also write to three justices of the peace, each a former High Sheriff of Derbyshire, instructing them to make a full inquiry and decision. If his honour would not assent to their mediation they were to inform the Council.

'Did the tenants argue about the Council's terms?'

'They accepted them.' Scargill scowled. 'They've been set at liberty.'

*

Dickenson returned to the correspondence. Sir Francis Walsingham asked that letters intended for him be redirected to the Lord Treasurer; he was back in France, once again discussing the Queen's proposed marriage to the duke of Alençon. Master Gilbert declared that the country people were preparing a great welcome for the earl when he returned to Sheffield. *A welcome no doubt, Master Gilbert, but I think more modest than great.* The Privy Council complained that the Scottish Queen had had 'So few dishes, and so bad meat in them, as it was too bad to see it'. His honour retorted that the cut-off of his allowance meant he could yield her no better. This had elicited a warning that her majesty would 'Much mislike it'.

In these dark days I thank God I'm not a nobleman. I thank Him twice that I'm not a nobleman constrained to dwell on his estates, forbidden to make his way at Court. I thank Him thrice that the Devil isn't committed to my custody.

The Council had also written further concerning Glossopdale. Lord Leicester assured his honour that, 'Your tenants were discharged from us with a good lesson only to seek your lordship, and not to trust to any further exclamation or complaints here except that they have just matter to show they have been injured contrary to the law of the realm; they are gone from us, without any comfort and encouragement, but only

243

that they trust to yourself hereafter; so your goodness must now be the greater to them'.

A warning to a friend? Will my son Gilbert learn to read what a nobleman intends in his letters but doesn't write in words? It's a skill he must learn if he's to follow in my footsteps.

In another letter, Lord Leicester advised his honour that he 'Needed to stop the tenants' mouths because they give matter for your lordship's enemies to work on, to your great harm and disadvantage'. According to Baldwin, the Lord Chancellor had told Master Gilbert that they 'respected Lord Shrewsbury, but respected above all the common quiet of her majesty's people and her realm'. The Queen had written in person, fearing that if the Council merely sent the Glossopdale men home, or transferred them to Star Chamber or the Court of Requests (which would simply dismiss them), 'peril might issue thereby'. And Sir Francis had told his honour, 'settlement with your tenants is more important than your lordship realises. The Queen is disposed to have all causes of grief among her subjects removed'.

The warnings from his honour's friends are clear, yet God be thanked he retains the Queen's favour. All the nobility live in fear of unrest, sedition, vagrancy, desolation of fields; recusancy above all. Must his honour therefore yield to the clamours of commoners? Do the highest in the land demand this? The lord who stays with his estates and seldom attends Court must now maintain peace among his tenants; must he yield to their exactions in order to do so?

The barrage of correspondence continued. Lord Shrewsbury was asked 'of mere compassion' to settle with the tenants and restore the ringleaders to their houses, and 'to deal favourably to the poor men's contentment as a matter greatly importing to you in honour and security, on which the Queen's favour or displeasure hangs'. He was begged to accept tithes in money not kind.

Their lordships pay too much heed to the demands of common villains. But if their lordships so decide, those of us who are beneath them must accept and accommodate.

'If any have cause for complaint it is I,' replied the earl, 'for the tenants are two years rents behind with me... My enmity is towards the tenants who are the chief and continual kindlers of these coals of contention between me and my tenants of the simpler sort. They would all have settled, but feared murder in their beds if they did. If they will only pay the same yearly rents they have paid for the past sixteen years they may keep their tenancies, except the four who must leave.'

In penning this letter, Dickenson reflected, *I struggled to find words that would urge the Council to reinforce his honour's authority instead of undermining it. Riotous tenants threaten the social order that God ordained. I pray the moderators will restore it.*

Dickenson noted that the three justices chosen by the Council were commanded to observe Lord Shrewsbury's negotiations with the tenants, question his officers about leases and rentals, and lay down a rate of rentals as a guide. *They may examine my accounts as they please. They'll find no fault.* His honour said the land could not be valued rightly by anyone unfamiliar with it, and if the tenants were assured they should only pay as they were able, it would encourage idleness, drunkenness and disorder. His pleas fell on deaf ears. Only his promise of 'the same yearly rents they have paid for the past sixteen years' elicited a response. The Council declared this assurance a voluntary act of good lordship and Christian fellowship, 'requiting good for evil and preferring pity and charity before revenge'.

Tears pricked Dickenson's eyelids. To the shadows beyond the circle of candlelight he whispered his bewilderment, his fear for England, his rage on his honour's behalf. Why were the rest of England's nobility unwilling to support one of their own, the earl martial no less, against seditious commoners who could bring nothing but harm to the realm by their rude and riotous behaviour?

Katherine's shade offered no comfort.

Glossopdale, November 1581

Mediation were getting started, and not afore time. We'd slaughtered stock as we couldn't keep 'til spring, winter oats were planted, and some had started mending their walls and thatch, when three gentry come riding into Glossopdale with a score of clerks. Folk asked why they wanted another survey, seeing as how Mr Cavendish and by-our-lady Scargill had done enough by-our-lady surveying already. But seemingly Privy Council wanted these gentlemen to do it because none of three of them wanted to own Glossopdale himself, or to squeeze more out of poor folk nor they could afford.

Sir Godfrey Foljambe were one of three, him as had come in May when they drove Harry out of Storth. Seemingly he were a big landlord round Aldwark, between Grangemill and Brassington. It were funny, a Derbyshire place called Aldwark; there were an Aldwark in Yorkshire and all, a day's walk out of York. I'd been there. Other two gentry had never been in Glossopdale afore. One were Sir Thomas Cockayne, come from Ashbourne. Other were Sir John Manners from Haddon, another fair ride. Rich noble family, them Mannerses. Harry weren't happy about Sir John coming.

'His sister were Lord Shrewsbury's first wife. She give him four sons and a few daughters afore God called her. I reckon Sir John and his lordship are pals, so he won't help us.'

'Where do you learn such a lot about higher-ups, Harry?'

'Kept my eyes and ears open, Spiderlegs.'

'Aren't Mannerses Papists? His lordship isn't, so I reckon they can't be that pally.'

Harry's mouth did its sideways shift.

'You've been keeping your ears open and all! Aye, they're Papists, but they're well in with Privy Council for all that. I'll have summat to say to Sir John when they come to Pyegrove.'

Harry didn't have leasehold no more, so them as were taking survey wouldn't want to ask him owt. But Harry had summat to say to Sir John so he said it. I didn't hear what it were, mind. I were showing Sir Thomas Cockayne how to use reeds for thatching when your corn stalks aren't big enough.

*

Sunday after them three gentry had been and gone, Bailiff Booth stood up after vicar had finished service and telled us they'd reckoned our farmholds at five shilling an acre in rent. It were two and a half times what we'd been paying for as long as I could mind. Folk weren't happy about it, but we mostly said it were fair. It were two and a half times, not forty or fifty times. We could manage it, most of us.

'Lord Shrewsbury must agree the proposed rent before the matter is settled,' said bailiff, 'but her majesty's Privy Council will follow the mediators' guidance, so agreement is likely.'

It were end of rent fight for most of us. Only Harry and Nick said they weren't stopping 'til they got their farmholds back. I knew then what Harry had said to Sir John Manners.

'Happen you're right, Tom,' Agnes said. 'But whether Sir John listened to him, that's summat else.'

*

Nowt come of it for a while because a fever started in Glossopdale a week or two after. Sickness gets sent to us no matter how you guard against it, and for all my Agnes did, it were all over Glossopdale in three days. At one time folk were feared of plague and smallpox. I'd never seen a lot of plague, and we didn't get smallpox like they did in towns, but fevers still come and folk died. Old Harry reckoned this one had started when two of Josh Warhurst's ewes got loping ill; you could see them trying to run while their front legs looked like they were tied together, and their back legs and all. Said he'd seen fevers spread through farms afore when sheep got that road. Josh and Henry slaughtered sick ewes but fever still spread. Some folk said it were nowt to do with sheep as had got loping ill, it were God's punishment for rebelling against his lordship.

It couldn't have been punishment just for rebels, mind, because Lizzie Newton went first, for all her pewter pots and red-dyed skirts and buttons on her sleeves. Two of her children followed her. Agnes did what she could, but when God calls you, you go. Willie Newton looked like a ghost after he lost his wife. Folk were that sorry for him they started helping with his sheep and oats and trading with him again.

Agnes went to one house after another where sickness had landed. Sometimes them as she treated lived. Then it were her turn; she got sick. I prayed my heart out for her, but she just lay mumbling and soaked with sweat. I were nigh tearing my hair when little Margaret took my hand and pointed at verbana hanging off rafter. Happen God had answered my prayers through nipper. I brewed verbana best I could and give it Agnes and she got a bit better; but she weren't fit for going round houses again for another week, for all she were needed. Every day, somebody died in one hamlet and somebody else died in another. And then it were Joanna.

God in His wisdom knows what's right for us all, but watching Joanna's soul go to Heaven weren't right for me. I'd nearly lost my wife. Now I'd lost my sister. Will got cart and old horse and took Edmund and little Samuel up to Cloud so Ma and Alice could look after them 'til Harry found some road of managing. Ma would make them two lads work so they didn't grieve too much, and she'd make sure they got fed proper, for all there weren't a lot of food for none of us.

Harry said nowt. It were like when we come home from Chinley back in '74; not a word. Just kept staring at wastes. Then he walked up to Simmondley, drank pot after pot of Jacob's dagger ale, and then started smashing pots and breaking stools. Jacob tackled him, and pair of them were yelling and swearing, and they punched and threw and kicked shit out of one another. Reggie Harrop reckoned they were at it best part of an hour. At finish, both of them were battered and bruised and bleeding

248

and struggling to stay on their feet. Then they hugged one another and they were friends again.

It loosened Harry's tongue, anyroad, yon fight with Jacob. When he got back to Pyegrove he could talk like he usually did. Went to see vicar about getting his wife buried proper, and then said he were sending his sister Mary to fetch Edmund and Samuel back from Cloud. She'd help him look after them.

'You all right, Harry?' said Will.

'Aye, Will. Nowt like a punch-up with somebody as can fight as well as you.'

I wondered whether he missed Jo like I did. Agnes, on her feet again, said, 'Aye, he does, Tom. Jo were sun and moon to him. He won't get over losing her in a hurry.'

Happen she were right, but Harry were more himself after he'd fought Jacob and Mary had fetched his two lads back to Pyegrove. Quiet woman, Mary. Kept her grief to herself. But she were grand with Edmund and little Samuel.

Sheffield, 1582

Katherine's death had ripped a ragged tear through the fabric of Dickenson's life and no stitching could mend it. His sons were healthy and obedient; they learned their letters and numbers and catechism; his brother was well; Jane managed the inn; he prospered. Yet he felt his prospects were bleak, his descent into misery inexorable. The fortunes of the earl and his family impinged on his own, but he felt less and less able to fulfil his many duties. He wrote to Thomas Baldwin:

'His honour speaks and writes with growing ire and diminishing calm. The smallest setback unmans him. Since the death of my beloved wife I'm no longer equal to accomplishing all the tasks that now fall upon me. I beg your help, first and foremost in denying that his honour permitted the Scottish Queen to walk in Sherwood Forest while she was with him at Worksop. Where or how that rumour began I have no idea, but it will much displease her majesty should it come to her ears.'

It seemed Lord Shrewsbury had failed to pay the countess her contractual monthly allowance in respect of the lands she'd brought to their marriage. His honour's indecipherable complaints to his noble friends, not copied and dispatched by Dickenson or Eyre, cited her claims for money; he said the profits from her sheep, and her capacity to buy more land for her sons, made all her demands on his purse unwarranted. Work on his house in Worksop had ceased for lack of funds. However, building at Chatsworth continued.

Her ladyship complained to those selfsame friends about her husband's treatment; unlike him, she could write legibly. She told Lord Burghley she wanted to buy Hardwick Hall back from the Crown, to which it had fallen forfeit, but couldn't do so because the earl refused to pay what he owed her. Meetings between the couple grew ever less frequent, ever less joyful. Lord Leicester still strove to reconcile them, but still in vain.

During the previous winter the Scottish Queen's health had again alarmed the earl and countess and their doctors. The clerk of the Privy Council had travelled to Sheffield to assess her condition. True to form, Mary had exaggerated her indisposition and deceived the clerk. *If there's one matter about which his honour and her ladyship can still agree*, thought Dickenson, *it's Mary's deviousness*. Thanks to the clerk's report, Mary's supplication to the Crown had borne fruit. She would now be allowed to travel two or three miles outside Sheffield Great Park, to have a coach and six horses for such exercise, to replace some of her old and exhausted servants, and to enjoy plays or masques. Her majesty, Dickenson noted, had acceded to all the Scottish Queen's demands except one: the request that Lord Shrewsbury be paid his long-overdue expenses for her maintenance. Now Mary had written directly to Thomas Baldwin, begging him to approach Sir Francis Walsingham for money, her need being desperate.

His honour had ordered Dickenson and Baldwin to pursue his many debtors; his riches, he said, were in other men's purses; he was surrounded by spies; and Baldwin must also borrow money against the supply of lead.

'And now his honour must recommend two new foresters for the Peak Forest,' Dickenson told Eyre. 'He's barely capable of –'

'I'll deal with that, William. But we must ask Tom to double-check those letters from Lord Burghley and Lord Leicester, and from Blanche Perry. His honour suspects they're forged.'

'He believes he's encircled by enemies, mostly in the countess's employ.' *And his suspicions aren't wholly unfounded.*

The countess's daughter Elizabeth, mother of little Arbella, had died. Her ladyship was inconsolable. His honour deemed her grief self-indulgent, yet he instructed Baldwin and Lord Talbot to provide her with a handsome horse-litter. Her majesty would not permit him to visit Court or take the Scottish Queen to Buxton again. After a further altercation with his wife he'd moved from the manor house to the castle, declaring he was most at peace when he had the fewest women about him. Dickenson empathised.

Sir Francis Walsingham had located his honour's former secretary Thomas Morgan in France, acting as the Scottish Queen's agent. Letters had been intercepted. A French diplomat who'd been permitted to visit Mary had carried letters to her supporters in France and Spain. The earl was reprimanded for allowing another escape plot to be hatched. Dickenson sighed.

More family deaths followed: Margaret, wife of her ladyship's son Sir Charles, died after giving birth; and then the earl's heir and eldest son, Francis, died of plague. Francis's brother-in-law, the earl of Pembroke, demanded the widow's jointure for himself. Dickenson despaired; his honour's coffers could not support such payments. Rumours of an affair between his honour and the Scottish Queen were renewed at Court. Hearing of it, Mary blamed the slander on the poisonous tongues of the countess and two of her sons.

Master Gilbert was now Lord Talbot.

A doctor dispatched by the Queen to attend Lord Shrewsbury for his gout promised to send biscuit bread and serecloth against future attacks. His honour asked Baldwin to reward the doctor as best he could. The biscuit bread and serecloth failed to alleviate the earl's pains. Dickenson and Eyre were obliged to write ever more of his letters.

It seemed the Glossopdale dispute was settled at last, but then Sir John Manners wrote to his honour begging that new farmholds be given to the evicted rabble-rousers lest they cause even greater trouble as vagrants. His honour had dictated the reply to Sir John: 'In what I should do for young Botham, you shall rule me'.

Those villains must not receive new tenancies, thought Dickenson, *Botham and Mellor especially. Incalculable harm will follow if the world comes to believe that commoners can overturn the rule of lord over tenant. And are local gentry, justices of the peace, gaining too much power? The realm of England is falling into confusion. I am falling with it.*

Glossopdale 1582

Same as I've always said, it never rains but it pours; but then summat happens and sun comes out again. It were a right mixed-up year.

Yon fever kept taking folk. Ma died. She were swearing when her soul rose to Heaven, but I reckoned our good Lord would turn a deaf ear to it and let her in anyroad. She'd had a lot of pain, for all Agnes give her willow bark and valerian. Knocked me down, losing Ma that soon after Joanna. I couldn't think straight for a while and it were hard work not skriking. Ma would have called me every name under sun if I had. Willie said it were a relief she'd gone, she'd been that bad. Alice weren't happy; apart from a bit for poor box, Ma left her money half each to Willie and me instead of it all going to Willie.

A week after, God took Old Harry to his bosom. I weren't there because we were reaping oats, but Agnes were with him. She telled me he thought she were Morag come back. She didn't tell him she weren't. His three children got equal shares of money, he give a bit to poor box same as folk do, and he left rest for Harry to give his mother if he ever found her. Church Court didn't have no problem with that. But Harry were in a right state. He'd lost his brother-in-law, wife and Dad one after other. I reckoned he might go and fight Jacob again, only he didn't. Just drank more nor he usually did and kept quiet.

Little Margaret had telled us Ma were bound to pass on to a better world a few day afore she went. She did same afore Old Harry were took. Agnes said Sight can go from mother to granddaughter when daughter doesn't have it, and that's what had happened, even though she hadn't carried Margaret in her belly. It give me a funny turn, nipper

253

telling us folk were bound to die when she were nobbut four year old, then seeing their souls leave them. She were frightened of spiders, mind, our little Margaret. I told her she must never hurt spiders because they bring you luck, same as toads do.

There were talk about Spaniards wanting to make war on England, and stuff about America as sounded like one of Bill's fairy tales, but there's always talk. Folk pick it up at markets and fairs, or listen to pedlars, and then they add summat of their own to make story sound better, and at finish you don't know what's true and what's fit for a laystall. There's some as likes stories as frighten them – ghosts in woods, Spain invading England, stuff of that sort – because that's what makes them happy. I like a good story but I'm happier not listening to rubbish. There were one bit of gossip as made us all sit up and take notice, mind, and it must have been true because everybody were saying it: Lord and Lady Shrewsbury had parted.

'If that's right I don't reckon much to it,' I said. 'I know noble folk are different, but if God's joined man and woman in marriage, noble or common, that's that. If you fall out with one another you just need to put up with it.'

'Not falling out with me, are you, Tom?' said Agnes.

'No, love, but if I did I'd put up with you anyroad, like I said.'

Bob and Bill and John and Will said it weren't nowt to do with us, his lordship and her ladyship parting, but Harry said they were wrong.

'If they get divorced, her ladyship will want Glossopdale again, happen for her sons. Mind, I don't reckon his lordship will give it her.'

'Her ladyship's agent would happen be worse nor what we have now,' said Will.

'Worse nor Scargill?' Harry laughed.

Whatever were happening between him and his wife, his lordship had been good as his word. Tom Jackson were settled in Storth Bank, where Old Harry had flitted after Harry and Joanna were wedded. Then Nick Mellor got given Storth. Bailiff told Nick it were take it or leave it; either have Storth or go homeless. I could see what his lordship were up to: Privy Council, or happen yon three gentry as had mediated, had told Lord Shrewsbury he shouldn't make Nick homeless and turn him into a vagrant, he should give him a different tenancy instead; so his lordship had said 'all right', and give orders to put Nick in Harry's place so Harry would fall out with him. I telled Harry what I thought and he did that sideways shift of his mouth and said, 'Only just worked that out, Spiderlegs?' And then I went and saw Nick, and he said, 'Aye, Spiderlegs, I'm keeping it warm for Harry. Storth's his. It'll always be Botham land. When things settle down I'll flit somewhere and he'll come back here.'

He weren't far off mark, Nick weren't, though he hadn't hit bull's eye.

Sheffield, 1584

'Some mornings I awake feeling Katherine beside me,' said Dickenson. 'I doze over my accounts and hear her voice. I hear her spinning-wheel.'

He never spoke of what he saw from the tail of his eye, present for no longer than a gasp. He never admitted that his prayers for her soul were prayers for peace in his own.

'It'll pass,' said his sister-in-law. 'Takes time.'

The spinning-wheel stood beside the wall, its recriminations silent.

'People say I should marry again,' he said.

'Do you want to?' asked Jane.

'No.'

Would he wish to father another child at forty-four? His sons were healthy and growing. They seldom needed chastisement. He was satisfied with their learning. He prayed for them still as he and Katherine had prayed together: 'I commit you to God's tuition and I pray God to give you grace and wisdom so you will spend your time well in this wretched world, and so earn the love of all your neighbours, family and tenants. I pray you will see all your children placed and able to live well and honestly by themselves, so that after this life is ended we may enjoy the life everlasting.'

'Neither do I,' said Jane, 'so that's that.'

Jane managed the inn with all her sister's assiduousness and competence. Dickenson felt comfortable with her. He wished the earl and countess could enjoy such comfort and companionship together, but the rift between them was now a chasm. His honour retired more and more to his little manor at Hansworth. During the summer he had ordered the bailiffs on her ladyship's St Loe estates in southwest England to pay the rents to his agents, not to hers. The countess had countermanded the order. Now the bailiffs had no idea whom they should pay.

For reprisal, Lady Shrewsbury had sent her servants to survey Glossopdale again. His honour had ordered his own servants to stop them. Then Charles Cavendish visited Glossop and called upon the bailiff, who gave him short shrift and reported the intrusion to the earl. Mr Cavendish proceeded next to harass the Peak Forest tenants, spreading false rumours; they begged his honour for relief. Dickenson wrote to Tom Baldwin on the earl's behalf complaining about the countess and her sons, but what could Baldwin do except ask Gilbert, Lord Talbot, to raise the matter with her majesty?

Glossopdale and Peak Forest again. If you want to wreak havoc, summon Glossopdale.

'Havoc?' Eyre barked. 'Mr Booth led a party of armed Glossopdale men to confront Charles Cavendish. At Stoke Hall. On his honour's orders, of course. Confiscated the tenants' cattle in lieu of rent and sent them here to Sheffield. Beasts are in the Great Park now, awaiting his honour's pleasure. Then his honour joined Booth and his men and they attacked Chatsworth. *Chatsworth*, William! Brought cartloads of valuables from there to the castle. His honour said they were owed to him.'

'I believe his honour had battlefield experience in his youth, back in '49, when Protector Somerset –'

'Sir William Cavendish attacked us here three days later with his own little army. Took the Chatsworth valuables back.'

'*Sir* William?'

'Lately made knight of the shire, along with his honour's son Henry. Said the valuables were his property and his mother's. Law was on his side. The bad blood between his honour and her ladyship has blossomed into war.' Eyre shook his head. 'Pray God will yet grant a happy resolution.'

How could a marriage between great nobles come to this? No doubt Mistress Britton gives his honour comfort. But Glossopdale will always breed sedition and riot.

'I hazard the guess that Mr Booth's Glossopdale army included names we know.'

Another bark of laughter. Then Eyre looked puzzled.

'Yes. But Botham told his honour he'd seen Bailiff Booth pocketing spoils from Chatsworth for himself. His honour made Booth return them. Then he fined him. Threatened dismissal.'

'Did his honour reward Botham for informing on the bailiff?'

Eyre snorted.

'Why would he?'

Why indeed? Yet his honour had made concessions elsewhere. The Peak Forest tenants had had their customs confirmed by the Duchy Court. The tenants and miners of Ashford had reached a settlement: under a Chancery agreement, they recognised his honour's authority as lord and accepted his power to impose a manorial pre-emption on lead ore sales; however, the price was set at nine shillings per load, as the Wirksworth Wappentake had decided. Moreover, the earl had confirmed the right of free mining within his lordship, which he'd previously opposed.

'Worthwhile,' said Eyre. 'Ensures the Ashford tenants support him against her ladyship and the Cavendishes, and income from sales of lead will continue.'

'Tom Baldwin says his honour's dispute with the countess could still be settled by arbitration.'

'Pfah! Meanwhile, the Scottish Queen costs more and more. Master Stringer recorded the outlay at Wingfield while his honour was at Court: sixteen dishes at Mary's first and second courses, all her officers and their servants to feed, and a score of her women, and a hundred gentlemen and yeomen to guard her, and fifty soldiers... His honour must beg to be relieved of this burden.'

'He might still deem it humiliation, Nathaniel, though Heaven knows he can no longer support it. The people of Tutbury also demand relief from the pressures imposed on their purses for the Scottish Queen's sake. As you say, there are more and more costs. Always more and more.'

'The Tutbury coachman, Sharp, dances attendance on Mary, just as Thomas Morgan did years ago. Another Papist plot in the offing, perhaps.'

Dickenson ached with the need to talk to Katherine about the earl's mounting troubles. But such aches could never be eased now. They could only worsen.

Stoke Hall, Chatsworth, Sheffield, August 1584

What we did that St Augustine's Day were like bother we'd kicked up in Chinley a few year afore, only this time my uncle were leading us instead of running out of Harry's road. And it weren't nowt to do with enclosures, it were about this argy-bargy between Lord and Lady Shrewsbury. I didn't understand what were at back of it; summat about taking rents in kind as hadn't been paid. Anyroad, his lordship had ordered Bailiff Booth to raise forty armed men for a set-to with yon Cavendish gentry. So he did. Forty Glossopdale men.

'A right beggar of a do, Glossopdale lads sorting other folk out for not paying rent,' I said.

'There's more to it nor that, Spiderlegs,' said Harry. 'This is his lordship warning her ladyship off Glossopdale.'

'I thought they'd settled all that six or seven year back, after Mr Cavendish –'

'I reckon yon countess thinks same road as I do: if you want summat, keep at it, don't ever give in.' Harry give that sideways grin of his. It were good to see it. He hadn't grinned much since God had took Joanna and his Dad. 'Mind, you're right, Spiderlegs; it's a funny do, me and you fighting on his lordship's side over other folks' rents.'

I'd never been to Stoke Hall. It's between Grindleford and Hathersage, down near Derwent, and it were where Mr Charles Cavendish lived. While forty of us were on our way there, Harry walked at side of William Newton like they were pals. That were worth seeing. Happen they felt closer since they'd both lost their wives to yon fever, or happen they were remembering that Christmas as Newton had paid for back in '74, and forgetting all bother they'd had between them since. But it were a funny do; old enemies turning into friends, and us making other folk pay rents. Next news, England will be pals with Spain.

Bailiff went up to Hall and shouted summat about seizing Mr Cavendish's tenants' cattle because rent hadn't been paid to Lord Shrewsbury's agent, and Mr Cavendish come out door carrying an arquebus and said his tenants had paid full rents in cash to his lady mother's agents, so that were that. Seemingly it weren't good enough. Mr Booth give orders, a dozen of our lads started rounding up beasts, and Mr Cavendish shot his arquebus. He didn't hurt nobody, but it set us off. Next news we were breaking walls down and smashing glass windows, and afore long Mr Cavendish had run off and hid in church, and when his tenants come out of their houses to stop us taking their beasts there were a fist-fight. Folk as fought Glossopdale men come out losers, especially when Harry were there. It weren't long afore Stoke Hall tenants were running off bleeding, leaving a few teeth among summer flowers, and six of our lads had been telled to drive their beasts to Sheffield Castle and give them to Mr Eyre. Bailiff telled rest of us to go on to Chatsworth.

Stoke Hall were big; white stone walls with timber frame and a roof of tiles instead of thatch. But Chatsworth were that big it scared me. I wouldn't have gone near it if bailiff hadn't ordered us to. Harry and Nick and a few others were having a right good time.

'Who needs a place that big, even if they've servants and a score of nippers?' I asked.

'Her ladyship and Sir William Cavendish,' bailiff said. 'His lordship will join us here soon.'

He were right. Lord Shrewsbury rode up on a grand horse, leading a pack of Sheffield servants with three big carts. He looked an old man now, worse nor he'd been when he come to Glossop; white beard, wrinkled face, trembling hands. I'd seen one or two of them Sheffield servants afore when they'd been fetched to Glossopdale, but we were on same side this time. Bailiff bowed and rest of us stood waiting, but everybody's blood were up. We wanted another fight. I heard his

261

lordship say summat about his wife running away to Hardwick Hall taking valuables from Chatsworth, so he'd take what remained as payment of his dues.

'It's a bad do when man and wife come to this,' said Willie Newton.

It weren't often I liked owt Newton said, but he were right about that. I wondered what Agnes and me would do if we fell out like earl and countess had. There weren't much we could pinch off one another. Not a lot of valuables. She'd laugh when I told her that. Hearing her laugh inside my head made me smile. Two year back I thought I'd lost her to yon fever. Thanks be to God she were still with me.

Sir William Cavendish wouldn't let us in. He started putting barricades up. Then he sent his servants out with bows and guns.

'They'll be for it if they shoot his lordship,' I said.

'They won't shoot nobody, Tom,' said John Stedman. 'Won't dare while his lordship's here.'

John were wrong. Well, nobody got shot, but they fired their guns to scare us and that were a mistake. You don't want to rile Glossopdale men when their blood's up. We knocked Sir William's barriers down, smashed windows – there were plenty of windows to smash at Chatsworth – and forced our way inside.

What a place! I'd never seen owt like it, even yon Round Chamber in Greenwich. His lordship started giving orders. Bailiff did what he were telled, same as rest of us did. We lifted candlesticks, pictures, coloured carpets hanging on walls, plate out of dressers, chests full of coins; you name it, we lifted it. It all went on them three carts as they'd brought from Sheffield. Sir William's men tried to stop us, but there were more of us nor them. Sir William were afire with anger, and he didn't get no happier when his lordship ordered servants down to cellar to fetch ale, meat and bread. We cheered when ale barrels were rolled out. We ate bread and meat and drank his lordship's health.

Then Harry went up to his lordship and took his hat off and bowed and said summat. Just whispered, same as he'd done with Sir Francis outside yon Round Chamber. His lordship said summat back. Talked for a couple of minutes, and Harry listened and bowed again. We were all shouting and laughing and drinking so none of us took much notice and we hadn't heard what were said, but next news his lordship collared my uncle and he weren't happy.

Harry told me about it later. Harry had seen my uncle pocketing stuff and told his lordship, so my uncle were lucky he were still bailiff and not hanged for thieving. There were summat else, too: one of them mediators, Sir John Manners, had seemingly got orders about Harry off Privy Council, and his lordship had promised he'd do some of what Sir John told him. Harry weren't getting Storth back, but when Edmund come of age he'd get given leasehold. So it were like Nick said: Storth were still Botham land. Nick would only stop there 'til Edmund were old enough to manage it.

'What about you?' I asked. Harry and his boys and poor Mary were still with us at Pyegrove. They needed a farmhold of their own.

'Getting a place other side Stoney Middleton, Wardlow way.' Harry give that sideways shift of his mouth. 'Made a deal with Sir Francis when we were in London.'

Aye, I thought, you did and all. Stuck Bob Wolstenholme and Will Garlick and John Beely in for being Papists, and Bob and John got fined heavy and Will got hanged, so I hope it were a good deal for you, Harry. I didn't say any of that, mind. I just said other side Stoney Middleton were a fair way from Simmondley.

'Walk it easy in a day, Spiderlegs.'

Couple of days later, my uncle sent constable Humfrey Andrew to Pyegrove, and next news Harry were in lockup again. Seemingly he hadn't liked what Harry had told his lordship at Chatsworth, but he'd never liked Harry anyroad. We soon got him out again.

Longstone Moor, April 1587

There'd been a shower, but sun were out when I started walking up hill out of Stoney Middleton. Slow going with my hip. 'St Alphege's Day,' I thought. 'Weren't it St Alphege's Day when Harry come home from being in service in Castleton, and wherever else he'd been? How long back were that? Sixteen year? Seventeen?' Happen more. I weren't sure. Time doesn't half shift when you get older.

Harry had come back to Glossopdale to see us a time or two with Mary and boys, but I'd not been up to Longstone Moor since they'd flitted. Will and me were always busy at Pyegrove. At end of a working day I'd a job walking as far as alehouse. Not many year back I'd walked to London and home again, twice. Walking nigh as far as Wardlow were a beggar of a job for me now.

Last time Harry had been in Glossopdale, not long back, he'd had a set-to with bailiff again, my uncle Nicholas, and with Scargill and all. They'd argued about him sharing Storth rent with Nick Mellor, seeing as how young Edmund were bound to get leasehold when he were old enough. Harry and Nick had agreed, but Scargill had wanted more nor his share, like he always did. So Harry knocked two of his teeth out, and then he were in lockup again. Same as I said, my uncle had never liked him. I paid to get him out.

Their house on Longstone Moor looked all right. Thatch were sound. It felt good, sitting on a stool at side of their table and sharing ale and bread and cheese with them, and two of last year's apples. Harry and Mary were well enough. Mary looked older nor she had three year back when they'd left Glossopdale. Well, she *were* older, same as we all were, but she looked it more nor most. Harry's hair and beard were still thick but there were white in them now. Edmund were nigh on sixteen year old: looked like his father only a bit taller, or happen Harry had shrunk; and he'd more filling out to do, but you'd expect that in a lad. He were coming to Pyegrove as a servant this year. That would build him up. Him and young Samuel were outside, scrapping with one another like brothers do. You could tell they were strong healthy lads.

'Both play bagpipe,' said Harry, 'but Sam's going to be good at it.'

'Not as good as his Dad,' said Mary.

'I reckon he'll be better,' said Harry.

We talked like you'd expect: how were Agnes, and young Margaret, and Will, and my brother Willie, and Alice, and rest of Glossopdale folk? I told them Agnes were treating folks for ailments and helping babbies into world, like she always had, and little Margaret had got Sight same as old Maggie, and she were right good with animals like her poor mother had been. God had taken old Tom Jackson, and Willie Newton had followed his wife to grave and all. There were always more under sod nor wick ones. After we'd spent an hour or two eating and drinking and talking, an old woman with white hair and bowed legs come in from kitchen. She were carrying an iron griddle, and what were on it smelled good. Harry's mouth did its sideways shift.

'Remember my Ma, Spiderlegs? She's made welshcakes.'

I stared at yon old woman. Mistress Botham? Were it really Morag Botham? I wouldn't have known her. Last time I'd seen her I were a nipper, and she'd been tall and upright with black hair. Were this what Harry had meant three year back, saying Sir Francis had give him what he wanted most? Were it trade-off they'd agreed outside Round Chamber? Harry would report Glossopdale Papists, Privy Council would sort rents out for us, and Sir Francis would find his mother? Happen. But it weren't no use asking. Anyroad, what were past were past.

'I remember you, Thomas Booth,' old woman said. 'My Harry and your sister drove away the boys who tormented you, and you saved my Harry from the ram, and every day since that day you have been in my prayers, and may God for ever reward your goodness.'

265

Same as I said, Harry would happen have killed yon ram if I hadn't kicked its balls so it turned on me, and I weren't sure I were good enough for God to give me that much of a reward. But I liked old woman's voice. It weren't a Glossopdale voice, or a London voice, or a Yorkshire voice, or a voice anywhere I'd been. It were more like singing nor talking.

'Aye,' said Mary, 'a rider come from London and told us where Ma were, and Harry went and fetched her.' She give me a smile. She'd lost three teeth but her smile had sunshine in it. 'It were yon Sir Francis as sent rider.'

'That were good of him,' I said.

'Aye,' said Harry, 'but it weren't no trouble for him. He were more bothered about finding my Uncle John Birtles. Seemingly Uncle John had got into a plot against her majesty with a few higher-ups – Lord Paget, Sir Geoffrey Hastings, a few others – and a couple of sorcerers and witches. Ma were living with Uncle John. He hadn't telled me she were there.'

'My brother was clever but foolish,' old woman said. 'I told him many's the time he should leave off his reading of the stars, and his spells and incantations, and his plots and devices, but look you, listen he would not.' She shook her head. 'What befell him, it was God's will, but...'

'You're safe here with us, Ma,' said Mary, 'and I promised you Tom would come to see us, and here he is.'

'You did great things, I am told,' Morag Botham went on, 'you and Harry, making Lord Shrewsbury and his servants give up their wicked scheme to make you pay rents that none could pay. Now farmers all over England are doing as you did, and God and His angels and her majesty's Council smile upon them, so not as many are starving or cast out from their homes and made vagabonds.'

I said it were Harry as had won our fight about rents, but I reckoned yon Privy Council must have had their own reasons for helping us. Happen a few of them nobles didn't like his lordship, or happen it were just trade-off of some sort, like Sir Francis had done with Harry. Anyroad, it didn't matter why, because we'd ended up with rents as we could pay; and if what we'd done helped other folk in England get fair rents and all, well, happen we'd done God's work while we were doing our own.

Later on, Edmund and Samuel played pipes as Harry had made for them. Harry were right; young Samuel had music in his soul and in his fingers. Music makes you happy when it's played well. Yon lad could play.

I stopped at Black Harry's Farm that night. We didn't see no boggarts or headless women on Longstone Moor like we'd done up on wastes in times long past. Next morning I walked back to Glossopdale, and larks sprinkled me with their songs from Heaven as I crossed shoulder of Nab, and curlews were mourning up on wastes, and archangel and forget-me-not were smiling around my feet. Same as I've said afore, God puts souls in men and He put a soul in Glossopdale, and our valley opened its arms when it saw me coming back, same as it always does. I reckon its soul is partly made from souls of folk as live here and partly from its streams and woods and fields, its birds and flowers, smell of its earth, song of its breezes.

It were good to be with Agnes and little Margaret again, and Will and his wife, and Pyegrove, but I left part of myself on Longstone Moor with my dearest and oldest friend. Glossopdale would never be what it were without Black Harry Botham. But his spirit were still there, part of Glossopdale's soul now and forever, and we'd none of us forget him. I could still hear sound of his bagpipe when wind stirred trees up side of Shirrell.

Night I got back from Longstone Moor, me and Agnes prayed together:

The Lord our omnipotent God be always praised and to Him let us give most humble and hearty thanks, for it's pleased Him of His great mercy and goodness to preserve and keep us and He did our fathers. Let's pray that He will of His grace help us all to remember and consider our duties towards Him and to confess that all we ever have comes only from Him and His goodness and not from ourselves or our own deserving. And most merciful God, grant that we and our children will care for whatever You shall give us so it will be to Your honour, will and pleasure. So let us run our course here in this wretched world, so that after this life is ended we may enjoy everlasting Kingdom of God, to whom be all honour and praise both now and for evermore. Amen.

Afterword

The Glossopdale dispute was a local affair that gained national notoriety. In order to write this novel I had to try to understand both its local roots and the tangle of politics, economic concerns and religious conflicts within which it grew. On the face of it, it's a David and Goliath story. However, it would have been crass to decorate the David with wings and harp, or the Goliath with horns and tail; each side in the dispute had its reasons and virtues, its passions and vices. I've used two historical figures to personify those two sides: Harry Botham of Glossopdale, known in Privy Council records and the Talbot Papers as "Black Harry"; and William Dickenson of Sheffield, who represented Lord Shrewsbury's interests.

My interest in Harry was piqued when I read *The Book of Glossop* by Jack Hanmer and Dennis Winterbottom (limited edition local publication, 1991; now out of print), but further information proved elusive. A few specialist historians had written about the Glossopdale dispute of the 1570s and '80s, but their sources didn't reveal Harry's dates of birth and death, his marital status, his family connections, his physical appearance, or any other detail. He must have married and had children because Storth Farm in Simmondley, Glossopdale, remained in the Botham family until the mid-twentieth century. Also, some of his characteristics can be inferred. He was presumably a typical northern English tenant farmer, unlearned, illiterate and with a limited grasp of national politics, and he appears to have been strong, charismatic, stubborn and quarrelsome. Nothing else is known, except that he elicited arguments among the highest in the realm.

It's hard to exaggerate the courage and determination that men of Harry's rank would have required to confront Elizabeth's Privy Council. Apart from their long and perilous walk to London and the very real prospect of imprisonment or even death at the end of it, they willingly confronted the full power of the realm and voiced their complaints in the face of naked hostility and threats. A modern equivalent might be a party of tradesmen with limited education facing an enraged gathering of inner cabinet members, senior Supreme Court judges and leaders of MI5 and MI6. To have repeated this ordeal three times was extraordinary. To have achieved a final victory, however Pyrrhic, was even more extraordinary.

Perhaps Harry's mostly peaceful insurrection had a wider impact than careful historians dare speculate, as I've surmised. Bess of Hardwick's generous settlement with her Ashford tenants suggests they'd been prepared to follow in Harry's footsteps (again, as I've conjectured). No one is sure what finally triggered the marital breakdown between Bess and the earl of Shrewsbury following years of ostensible love and happiness, though speculations abound, mainly involving an alleged though implausible relationship with Mary Queen of Scots. However, there's indisputable evidence that Bess involved herself in the simmering Glossopdale dispute in 1577-8 via one or more of her Cavendish sons. Her motives could have been partly laudable (as I've guessed, *contra* Hanmer and Winterbottom), but to say the least her involvement displeased her husband.

Much more information is available about William Dickenson than about Harry Botham. In the Sheffield City archives I was able to read *The Diary and Accounts of William Dickenson, 1574* and its successor, a collection of his accounts from 1584 onwards. I found passing references to Dickenson in other sources, too. He was born in 1540 and died in 1606 and we know he was married, though I've had to invent his wife's name and character. He might not have become Lord Shrewsbury's Receiver immediately after Thomas Sutton's death, and my decision to make him effectively Bailiff of Hallamshire (albeit not officially) as early as 1570, while Bailiff Turner was still alive, isn't justified by any historical record; it was a literary device for which I beg indulgence. Dickenson appears to have been intelligent, meticulous, honest, a devoted and dedicated servant of Lord Shrewsbury, probably fussy, possibly proud, undoubtedly God-fearing; but despite his regular contacts with tenant farmers on the Shrewsbury estates he seems to have had scant empathy with them.

Lord Shrewsbury's correpondence was prolific, not least during the Glossopdale dispute, but such were the demands on his time and so debilitating was the pain in his hands (he called it "gout"; it was probably arthritis, though whether rheumatoid or osteoarthritis it's impossible to say) that he required secretarial help. It isn't clear who replaced Thomas Morgan in this role after he was dismissed for excessive closeness to Mary Queen of Scots and Catholic leanings. I've assumed that William Dickenson took on most of the burden, probably helped by the Sheffield Castle steward, Nathaniel Eyre, with whom he must have been closely acquainted. I've imagined a friendship between Eyre and Dickenson despite their contrasting ancestries. Dickenson was the son of a minor burgess, a brewer. Eyre's family had been Derbyshire gentry for centuries, along with the Foljambes, Archers, Bagshawes, Needhams, Wadschefes and Kirkes; foresters of fee in the Royal Forest of Peak, and often Masters Foresters.

Dickenson was required to undertake other tasks in addition to his roles as Receiver for the Shrewsbury estates and Bailiff of Hallamshire, mostly to help allay the earl's burgeoning cash flow crisis. At one point he was obliged to ask his lordship's stepdaughter, Mrs Pierrepont, to defer half her annuity. He once wrote to Lord Burghley on the earl's behalf, asking him to further his suit to the Queen for a grant of lands in fee farm to compensate for non-payment of the diet money for the Queen of Scots. Similar demands fell on Lord Shrewsbury's London agent, Thomas Baldwin. At one point, Baldwin reported that his lordship had asked about the going price for silver in London since he'd have to sell plate to appease his creditors. The Shrewsbury cash crisis was chronic but it evidently had acute episodes.

Dickenson's diary and account books give meticulous details of his regular work, which often involved dealing with recalcitrant tenant farmers. For example: John Reynolds, who held one tenement of James

271

Rowson on which he got hay, declined to pay for it; Richard Frith refused to pay more than one penny per year for hay. Dickenson had to bring such defaulters to heel. On another occasion he was obliged to resolve a contention surrounding the tithes of Mayfield: Francis Ralston claimed they were his by right, not Lord Shrewsbury's; the balance of evidence favoured Mr Ralston, but Dickenson wrote to Lord Chancellor Sir Thomas Bromley arguing otherwise. Clearly, despite his humble origins, he'd acquired a fair grasp of the law.

His legal knowledge, his unswerving loyalty to Lord Shrewsbury and his well-earned suspicion of tenant farmers seem to have combined to generate an intemperate attitude towards Glossopdale's rebels; an attitude he shared with Thomas Baldwin, and with the agent George Scargill.

*

The population of England seems to have grown by about fifty percent during the sixteenth century, perhaps in part because some recurring diseases had become less virulent. As a result, prices rose and there was a need for increased food production. Together with the sharp decline in broadcloth exports after around 1550, which had made sheep less profitable, this helped to initiate the slow transition from the mediaeval three-field system (strip farming with wide commons) to closed centralised farms, which yielded more crops per acre. I've assumed – though the evidence isn't compelling – that the transition was underway in Glossopdale by 1570. This sort of "enclosure", the formation of closed farms, was a mixed blessing. It benefited those who received the better land but impoverished those who were left with the marshy and stony parts; under the open field system the tenants had moved to different strips year on year, alternating good soil with bad, ensuring equal fortunes over time. I've speculated that the reported clash between the Bothams (Old Harry) and Lord Shrewsbury and his agents during the 1550s was driven by such differences in land quality among closed farms, as well as by local inconsistencies in rents.

George Talbot, the sixth Lord Shrewsbury, owned huge amounts of land, so why did he have a cash flow problem? In 1558 he married his second wife, Bess of Hardwick. She was very expensive; so were her sons; so were his lordship's sons, all of whom seemed to have been spendthrifts. Custody of Mary Queen of Scots, foisted on the Shrewsburys in 1569 and lasting into the 1580s, was extremely costly and ill-recompensed by the Crown. Also, the Talbots had invested heavily in sheep, so the failure of broadcloth exports hit their income-expenditure balance hard. The rise of the steel industry in Sheffield had eclipsed the cutlers of Ashbourne, Salisbury and Thaxted by the early 1570s and provided some tax income for Lord Shrewsbury, but this was never enough to alleviate his cash problems. One powerful motive for marrying Bess was that it gave him control over the rich Derbyshire lead fields, which provided much-needed revenue thanks to technological improvements: the Humfrey smelting furnace and German sieve had boosted the efficiency of lead smelting dramatically.

Shrewsbury's agents prevented Humfrey from profiting from those innovations despite his patents. He'd been Assay Master at the Mint, but he'd abused the position and stolen money. He'd probably have been hanged if Lord Shrewsbury's friend William Cecil hadn't extended patronage to him. The brilliant and devious Cecil no doubt saw that Humfrey's patents had economic potential, which because of the inventor's crimes could be exploited without compensation.

*

Most readers are probably familiar with the religious conflicts of later sixteenth century England, at least in broad terms. After her brother's extreme Protestant ("reformed faith") government and her sister's extreme Catholic administration, Elizabeth began her reign in 1558 seeking balance, tolerance and relative freedom of worship. Indeed, the church of which she became head epitomised the English spirit of compromise, blending traditional Catholic with reformed "Protestant" elements. Her archbishop of Canterbury, Matthew Parker, was the principal designer of that compromise. The revolt of the Catholic northern earls in 1569, the brutal reprisals visited on the northern counties in its aftermath, and the Pope's subsequent excommunication of Elizabeth put an end to the period of tolerance. Thereafter, the

273

Catholic faith was outlawed in England. To celebrate a Catholic mass became a capital offence. Concomitantly, the Puritan movement gathered momentum, seeking to expunge all Catholic elements, real or alleged, from church services. Matthew Parker was replaced as archbishop of Canterbury by Edmund Grindal in 1576. Grindal was sympathetic to the Puritans and fell foul of Elizabeth as a result. Elizabeth's antipathy deterred Puritan sympathisers among the nobility from expressing their views too loudly.

Closer inspection reveals a more tangled picture. For example, Lord Shrewsbury's cousin Lady Bray, who was a long-term guest in Sheffield Castle after her husband Lord Wharton died, almost certainly had Catholic leanings. Moreover, shortly before the rising of 1569, the Catholic northern earls had been welcomed in Sheffield as Lord Shrewsbury's guests. His lordship was also a close friend of the Catholic Thomas Howard, fourth duke of Norfolk, who plotted at least twice against Elizabeth and was finally executed, Lord Shrewsbury himself being obliged to preside at the trial. Yet Shrewsbury was a stalwart Protestant and seemed to favour the Puritans, appointing Richard Robinson as tutor to his younger sons, Edward and Henry. Richardson had written the snappily-titled *The Reward of Wickedness, discoursing the sundry monstrous abuses of wicked and ungodly worldlings: in such sort set down and written as the same have been diversely practised in the persons of popes, harlots, proud princes, tyrants, Romish bishops and others.* It appears that religious affiliations among the nobility were neither absolute nor exclusive.

It isn't certain whether Elizabeth's spymasters, Cecil (Lord Burghley) and Walsingham, were covert Puritans, but they were fanatically anti-Catholic and unrelentingly suspicious of Mary Queen of Scots, who throughout her confinement under the Shrewsburys' custody served as focus, inspiration and talisman for Catholic plotters. Mary is widely regarded as a sympathetic and indeed romantic character; misguided, perhaps, but more sinned against than sinning. In fact, she was devious and dangerous. She was almost certainly complicit in the murder of her second husband, Lord Darnley, and in the assassination of her enemy Lord Murray by James Hamilton. Under a mask of friendship she spread poisonous rumours about Bess of Hardwick, as I've reported in the novel. She tried to ally herself with the duke of Norfolk to usurp the English throne and have her marriage to her third husband Bothwell annulled so she could marry Norfolk. The pope would have granted the annulment, and Bothwell, imprisoned in Denmark, couldn't have opposed it. Catholics in England and Scotland, and more importantly in Spain and France, would have championed her cause. Long years as custodian of this loose (and loaded) cannon put enormous strain on Lord Shrewsbury's mental health as well as his finances.

If the Scottish Regency hadn't blocked the transfer of funds to Mary, such custody might have been less fraught. Elizabeth was blind, perhaps wilfully, to his lordship's financial distress, notwithstanding his repeated pleas for 'diet money' for his royal captive. But even if the financial burden had been lightened, the tacit fomenting of Catholic unrest would have persisted; and in that regard, too, Lord Shrewsbury received less support from his peers than he might reasonably have expected. The Catholic chaplains on his estates who spread evil rumours were apprehended, as I've reported in the novel, but when the Lords of the Council examined Thomas Corker they judged him innocent. To Lord Shrewsbury, that must have seemed like betrayal. In a sense, it presaged his back-to-the-wall experience of Privy Council censure when the Glossopdale dispute reached its height.

*

Despite all his problems, and despite being effectively excluded from Court by his role as Mary's jailor-come-host, Lord Shrewsbury was expected to fulfil his obligations as a senior peer and particularly as earl marshal. It seems certain that Elizabeth never intended to marry anyone because it would have entailed relinquishing much of her power as monarch to a husband. It is equally certain that members of the Privy Council were determined to find her a husband they could control, or at least influence and manipulate. François Valois, duke of Alençon, seemed a promising choice despite his involvement in the St Bartholomew's Day massacre; marriage of Elizabeth to a relative of the French royal family would have undermined Spanish pretentions. Lord Shrewsbury would have been obliged to oversee the marriage arrangements. Fortunately for him, Elizabeth's shrewd pretence of capriciousness precluded the finalisation of a contract with Alençon, or anyone else.

Spain had a legitimate claim to the English throne through the marriage of Philip II to Elizabeth's sister Mary, which had made him the royal consort. Spain was the richest and most powerful kingdom in Europe and had designs on England, with papal backing. Small wonder that England feared Spain, and feared that the Queen of Scots would encourage Spanish pretentions; small wonder, too, that the famous Armada was launched a couple of years after the end of my story.

In 1579-81 there was a major uprising against English rule in Ireland, initally in Munster but later spreading to Leinster, which received Spanish and papal support. This so-called Geraldine or Desmond rebellion (it was led by Gerald earl of Desmond) was a serious concern for the government and enjoyed considerable military success, but it was finally suppressed with such brutality, swathes of land being laid waste, that the consequences for the Irish people could be compared only to the potato famine of the nineteenth century. This rebellion, with its menacing political and religious connotations, coincided exactly with the Glossopdale dispute; and Glossopdale was just a long day's walk from where Mary Queen of Scots was housed.

It was against this background that I imagined Harry Botham feigning concern that some Glossopdale residents would revert to Catholicism if their demands were ignored. There's no evidence that he did so, but he was probably smart enough – and it would have disquieted the Privy Council. I also invented his "deal" with Walsingham. It's plausible that Sir Francis could have added Harry to his national network of anti-Catholic spies, but extremely unlikely that he'd have taken the time to trace Harry's mother. However, he could well have been involved in apprehending the (historical) John Birtles, who had indeed plotted against Elizabeth, and in the process he could have located the (fictional) Morag. The idea that Harry and his family finally moved to a farm between Wardlow and Stoney Middleton, there to be joined by his mother, is yet another invention on my part. However, it's a matter of historical fact that during the late seventeenth or early eighteenth century a highwayman who haunted the Longstone Moor area took the name "Black Harry" and was associated with "Black Harry Farm", which has now disappeared. One can only wonder at the coincidence of soubriquets.

The example set by Harry's stubborn determination remained influential after the death of the sixth earl of Shrewsbury in 1590 and, probably, his own demise. The Glossopdale tenants continued to be rebellious well into the seventeenth century. Harry's example might even have inspired similar unrest among tenant farmers in other parts of England. Could the topic of Jennifer S. Holt's *The financial rewards of winning the battle for secure customary tenure*, chapter 8 (pp. 133-149) in Jane Whittle's *Landlords and Tenants in Britain, 1440-1660*, be one illustration? Could the case of the Kent clothiers during the 1590s be another? The Privy Council noted in 1589 that it had become so 'troubled and pestered' by private suitors it could 'scarce attend' to the business of state. No doubt such slow changes in the order of English government would have happened anyway, but I speculate that Black Harry Botham's resolute and courageous persistence hastened them and to an extent shaped them.

Acknowledgments and sources

Professor Jane Whittle of Exeter University was kind enough not only to exchange correspondence with me about my plan for this novel and recommend some background reading, including Amanda Jones's PhD thesis about the 'commotion time' of 1549, but also to read the draft manuscript and point out my most egregious historical errors and implausible conjectures, which I was then able to correct. Anna Carvanova of Plymouth University read the amended manuscript and made invaluable stylistic suggestions, which enabled me to submit a substantially improved version to Stairwell Books. I'm also grateful to Mark Franklin (http://www.markfranklinarts.co.uk) for the sketch map of sixteenth century Glossopdale; I recommend this service to anyone in need of quality illustrations. I thank Mike Brown of the Glossopdale Heritage Trust for lending me HMSO's abstracts of the *Talbot Papers* and for directing me to the five somewhat randomly-ordered volumes of the *Chambers Papers*, an unpublished collection housed in Glossop Library. I gleaned details from those sources that I hadn't found elsewhere. My friend and colleague Tim Knebel and his colleagues in the Sheffield City archives helped me to find more otherwise unobtainable sources, which also proved invaluable.

Needless to say, none of the aforementioned advisors is responsible for my interpretations of events. I haven't tinkered with indisputably-established facts, incidents or utterances save for one or two minor alterations of chronology, as indicated above, but these weren't enough to build even the skeleton of a novel. (The encounter between the Glossopdale men and the Queen at Greenwich is probably legend, not history.) To invent the rest I've perforce resorted to inference and guesswork, guided by the following sources:

Andy Wood's *The Politics of Social Conflict: The Peak Country, 1520–1770* (Cambridge University Press, 1999), *Riot, Rebellion and Popular Politics in Early Modern England* (Palgrave Macmillan, 2001), and *The Memory of the People: Custom and Popular Senses of the Past in Early Modern England* (Cambridge University Press, 2013); Keith Wrightson's *Earthly Necessities: Economic Lives in Early Modern Britain* (Yale University Press, 2000) and *A Social History of England 1500-1750* (Cambridge University Press, 2017); Robert Furse's *A Devon Family Memoir of 1593*, edited by Anita Travers (Devon and Cornwall Record Society, 2010); *Robert Loder's Farm Accounts 1610-1620*, edited by G. Fussell (Royal Historical Society, 1936); *The Farming and Memorandum Books of Henry Best of Elmswell, 1642*, edited by Donald Woodward (British Academy, 1984); and Jane Whittle's *Landlords and Tenants in Britain, 1440-1660* (Boydell, 2014). In Sheffield City Archives I studied Joseph Hunter's *History of Hallamshire* (1819), J.D. Leader's *Sheffield Castle and Mary, Queen of Scots* (Leader and Sons, Sheffield, 1880), Mary Walton's article 'Sheffield Castle Manuscripts' in *Transactions of the Hunter Archaeological Society* vol. 5 (1940), the informative little pamphlet by David Bostwick, *Sheffield in Tudor and Stuart Times* (Sheffield Galleries and Museums Trust, 2004), and of course William Dickenson's diary and account books. My rendering of the story was much influenced by Stephen Kershaw's *Power and duty in the Elizabethan aristocracy: George, earl of Shrewsbury, the Glossopdale dispute and the Council* in G. W. Bernard's *The Tudor Nobility* (Manchester University Press, 1992); Joan Thirsk's now somewhat outdated *The Agrarian History of England and Wales: 1500-1640*, Chapter 5, 'Landlords in England' (Cambridge University Press, 1967, pp. 256-356); Margaret Yates's 'Between fact and fiction: Henry Brinklow's *complaynt* against rapacious landlords,' *Agricultural Historical Review* 54(1), 2006, pp. 24-44; and Mary Lovell's biography *Bess of Hardwick* (Abacus, 2006).

In addition, I've made considerable use of my personal knowledge of Peak District folklore, superstitions and traditional remedies.

Other novels, novellas and short story collections available from
Stairwell Books

Eboracvm: Carved in Stone	Graham Clews
Down to Earth	Andrew Crowther
The Iron Brooch	Yvonne Hendrie
Pandemonium of Parrots	Dawn Treacher
The Electric	Tim Murgatroyd
The Pirate Queen	Charlie Hill
Djoser and the Gods	Michael J. Lowis
The Tally Man	Rita Jerram
Needleham	Terry Simpson
The Keepers	Pauline Kirk
A Business of Ferrets	Alwyn Bathan
Shadow Cat Summer	Rebecca Smith
Shadows of Fathers	Simon Cullerton
Blackbird's Song	Katy Turton
Eboracvm the Fortress	Graham Clews
The Warder	Susie Williamson
The Great Billy Butlin Race	Robin Richards
Mistress	Lorraine White
Life Lessons by Libby	Libby and Laura Engel-Sahr
Waters of Time	Pauline Kirk
The Tao of Revolution	Chris Taylor
The Water Bailiff's Daughter	Yvonne Hendrie
O Man of Clay	Eliza Mood
Eboracvm: the Village	Graham Clews
Sammy Blue Eyes	Frank Beill
Serpent Child	Pat Riley
Rocket Boy	John Wheatcroft
Virginia	Alan Smith
Looking for Githa	Patricia Riley
Poetic Justice	P J Quinn
Return of the Mantra	Susie Williamson
The Go-To Guy	Neal Hardin
Abernathy	Claire Patel-Campbell
Tyrants Rex	Clint Wastling
A Shadow in My Life	Rita Jerram
Thinking of You Always	Lewis Hill
How to be a Man	Alan Smith
Tales from a Prairie Journal	Rita Jerram

For further information please contact rose@stairwellbooks.com

www.stairwellbooks.co.uk
@stairwellbooks